CW00468489

Voyage of the Damned

Frances White is a creative writing and English literature graduate from Royal Holloway University of London. Originally from Leicester and now based in Nottingham, she has a soft spot for writing unlikely, flawed, messy heroes and loves mixing humour and heartbreak. Frances is also passionate about bringing more LGBTQIA+ representation and fat positivity into fantasy. When not writing, she can be found sewing nerdy costumes for comic conventions or researching obscure historical facts.

Voyage of the Damned

FRANCES WHITE

MICHAEL  JOSEPH

PENGUIN MICHAEL JOSEPH

UK | USA | Canada | Ireland | Australia
India | New Zealand | South Africa

Penguin Michael Joseph is part of the Penguin Random House group of companies
whose addresses can be found at global.penguinrandomhouse.com

First published 2024
001

Copyright © Frances White, 2024

The moral right of the author has been asserted

Set in 13.5/16pt Garamond MT Std
Typeset by Jouve (UK), Milton Keynes
Printed and bound in Great Britain by Clays Ltd, Elcograf S.p.A.

The authorized representative in the EEA is Penguin Random House Ireland,
Morrison Chambers, 32 Nassau Street, Dublin D02 YH68

A CIP catalogue record for this book is available from the British Library

HARDBACK ISBN: 978–0–241–64007–4
TRADE PAPERBACK ISBN: 978–0–241–64008–1

www.greenpenguin.co.uk

MIX
Paper | Supporting
responsible forestry
FSC
www.fsc.org   FSC® C018179

Penguin Random House is committed to a
sustainable future for our business, our readers
and our planet. This book is made from Forest
Stewardship Council® certified paper.

For everyone who has ever entered a room and
felt they did not belong.

① Greenhouse
② Shrine
③ Ballroom
④ Cabins
⑤ Deck

⑥ Kitchen
⑦ Dining Room
⑧ Lounge

THE DRA

⑤

⑨　⑩　⑪

⑬　⑭

⑯

N'S DAWN

⑨ Games Room
⑩ Art Gallery
⑪ Library

⑫ Changing Room
⑬ Bathhouse
⑭ Gymnasium
⑮ Brig
⑯ Engine Room

The United Empire
of Concordia

DRAGON PROVINCE *Seat of the Dragon*
Imperial Heir: Eudora Draco (Her Divine
Majesty, All-Mother, Goddess Incarnate)

TIGER PROVINCE *Shield of the Dragon*
Blessed: Leofric Tigris

SPIDER PROVINCE
Blessed: Nergüi Aranea

TORTOISE PROVINCE
Blessed: Cordelia Testudo

ELEPHANT PROVINCE
aka 'the Funnel'
Blessed: Tendai Elephas

BUNNERFLY PROVINCE
Voice of the Goddess
Blessed: Shinjiro Lepus

OX PROVINCE
aka 'the Bandage'
Blessed: Jasper Bos

CROW PROVINCE
Blessed: Ravinder Corvus

BEAR PROVINCE
Blessed: Wyatt Ursus

ERMINE PROVINCE
Blessed: Eska Mustela

GRASSHOPPER PROVINCE
Blessed: Yewande Locusta

FISH PROVINCE
Blessed: Ganymedes Piscero

Chapter One

Day One – Feast of the Dragon

Early evening

My father always says: 'You can't run from your responsibilities,' but he lacks imagination. Besides, I'm not *running*. I'm sidestepping. Crossing the road so me and my responsibilities don't make eye contact and aren't forced into awkward small talk both of us know isn't going anywhere.

Those cute twins by the toffee apple stall, however, are worth a second look. I throw the boy a wink and he returns a heart-wrenchingly shy smile. Blessed hells, he has *flowers* in his hair. His sister looks as though she wants to beat the crap out of me. When I shoot her the finger guns, she clutches her hotdog so hard the sausage shoots out of the bun.

Resistance. Strength, Dee. You do not need that hotdog-wielding temptress, or her petal-soft brother. Not tonight. You're here for a *higher purpose.*

That purpose is everywhere. It's beneath my feet, in the chalk animals dancing across cobblestones. It's overhead, in the red waves of paper kites rising into the black night. And when a man slams into me, upending his drink, it's down my shirt, and a little in my mouth.

The Festival of the Blessing.

The twelve-day celebration marking the end of one era, and the beginning of a new one. Twelve days for the twelve provinces of the Empire of Concordia. Twelve days to celebrate the many things which make us different, and the few things which unite us.

The perfect opportunity to make headway on a simple ambition: consume every food in Concordia before I expire from presumed heart failure.

Merchants from all over Concordia have travelled to Dragon Province to sell every conceivable export. Gilded masks inlaid with Spider Province jewels sit alongside luminescent flowers plucked from Crow Province. Winged Grasshopper Province costumes flutter alongside Fish Province toy windmills. The stalls weave through the streets like a parade from a drug-induced fever dream.

Of course the festival is held in Dragon Province – Concordia's crowning jewel and seat of Emperor Eugenios. The capital is a haven of possibilities, an eclectic hybrid of every province. The blood of the twelve is so mixed here that Dragon citizens (Dragons, for short) no longer possess the traditional green hair of their province. Their skin is a ruddy brown, and their hair a greyish-brown mix of every hue in existence. The great melting pot of the empire.

Dragons live in this dreamlike world where unity isn't a word said in legends, but reality.

Dragons are really fucking naive.

Today the hecticness of the capital is to my advantage. It's the only place I can slip silently out of view. Where I can dash down a narrow street into the city's eager arms and vanish forever.

Those pesky responsibilities have my scent – Dragon Province guards in their mint-green uniforms weave through the crowd, searching the thousands of heads for the one who does not belong. Me.

I just need to evade them for a little longer: meld into the crowd and stuff myself with food for a couple of hours; then they can drag me back if they really must. But by then it will be too late. My ship will have sailed. Quite literally.

I duck behind a stall. They're easy to track. Green is the Goddess's colour, to be wielded by the emperor and his forces alone.

'Dumplings! Dumplings!'

I spy the plump delicacies, huddled together in their reed baskets. While the vendor is distracted by the crowd, I swipe a handful.

I chew the soft squishy dough, pushing through the damp heat of bodies.

Ten different bands are playing, attacking all my senses at once. A banjo mated with a drum mated with a marimba. The 'music' sounds like how a firework would taste, fired directly into your mouth.

Cute girls kneel before goldfish stalls, fishing for coloured balls. I slip behind them and snatch a candied pumpkin. It melts in my mouth like sticky sweet nectar.

Crap. More guards, blocking my path to the culinary delights beyond.

I split off from the food hub and slide against a wall, hidden from sight.

Two hours until the ship leaves without me. I just need to be quiet and unremarkable for two hours. Easy peasy.

'I don't want to be the pissfish!'

A skinny Dragon boy stands before a stall; a ring of children around him chant: 'Pissfish! Pissfish!'

3

I push away from the wall. 'Who's a pissfish?'

Twelve sets of eyes swing to me.

'How comes you got white hair, mister?' a hawk-faced girl asks. 'Are you old?'

Cheeky little bugger. 'I'm twenty-two. My hair used to be black, but then I started being an annoying prick calling kids "Pissfish" and all the colour drained.'

'That's a lie.' The girl seems unsure, confirming that Dragon kids don't have a clue about the other provinces and their respective hair colours. 'B-Besides, Dado is the pissfish.'

Dado recoils as if she's stabbed him. 'I'm not! You take it!' He thrusts a plush toy of a white fish at me. It looks as though it was sewn by a blind man with places to be – uneven stuffing, messy stitches, eyes bulging, mouth gaping.

Piscero are the most populous fish in all of Concordia. They're the staple diet of the working class and can survive in any environment. Even sewers. Yes, these fish literally eat human shit. And piss, presumably. Hence – pissfish.

'We're playing province animals.' The fish's dull head bobs up and down. 'I get to be the Dragon if I win one . . . but I keep getting this stupid pissfish!' He throws the unfortunate creature. It gapes up from a muddy puddle, yellow eyes screaming *put me out of my misery.*

I'm aware my green-clad responsibilities may well find me in a matter of minutes. But the kid is staring, bottom lip trembling.

There's one thing I know: nobody should be forced to be a pissfish.

I observe the stall. Mounted on its roof is an elaborate sculpture of the twelve province animals, encircling a glacier-like mountain.

Inside, mounds of soft toys sit atop shelves, snaking up

into the rafters. At the bottom: identical brainless piscero. At the top: a green dragon with two antler-like horns.

'Knock down twelve – win the grand prize!' the vendor hollers. She wears a garish hat. Cork tokens of the twelve animals dangle from the rim.

A man swaps some coins for a handful of balls. He chucks them at a pyramid of stacked tins. Every ball hits it square in the centre. The structure wobbles but does not fall.

'Better luck next time!' She hands a misshapen piscero to the disappointed recipient. Nobody is ever pleased to see that fish.

I check a board nailed to the wall. The more cans knocked down, the better the prize. Two for Grasshopper, three for Ermine, four for Bear, five for Crow, six for Ox, seven for Bunnerfly, eight for Elephant, nine for Tortoise, ten for Spider, eleven for Tiger and for knocking down all twelve cans you get the symbol of the emperor himself – the Dragon. And for one or zero – pissfish.

'Kid.' I snatch Dado's collar. 'Give me some money.'

'You smell funny.'

'You must like your new nickname, Pissfish.'

With a scowl, Dado hands over a fistful of coins, dragon heads embossed on one side, the glacier mountain on the other.

The sound of change summons the stall-owner like a dog to steak. 'Prize every time!'

'That's not a prize.' Dado gestures to the sad fish.

The stallholder swaps my change for three balls as the children gather, jostling to watch.

I stretch my arm. This kid is gonna be a fucking dragon by the time I'm done.

My first throw misses the pyramid entirely. It slams into the shelf with the soft toys on.

The children screech with laughter.

I throw another. I hit the shelf once more.

'Perhaps you can pay and try again?' I can practically see the dragon dollars in the vendor's eyes.

I swing my arm back. Dado has lost hope already, looking miserably to the puddle fish.

My final ball soars over the pyramid. The stall-owner is already celebrating, cork animals dancing on her hat. The ball slams into the shelf.

'Better luck next—' An awful creaking drowns her words.

'Step back, kids.' I push the children behind me. 'You're about to witness something real special.'

They're barely out of crushing distance by the time the shelf collapses. The piscero fall first, drowning the cans in a flurry of gaping mouths and bulging eyes. The grasshoppers follow, then the ermines. One by one the shelves collapse in a torrent of adorable rain. Exactly as intended.

What I didn't plan for was the shelves to be supporting the entire stall. The kids and I stare as the mountain on the roof sinks with a goddessawful crunch.

'Don't worry,' I say to the terrified children. 'It won't collapse.'

It collapses. The roof folds inwards and then the mountain crashes to the ground with an almighty blast, drowning us in a wave of dust.

The smartarse girl wipes her eyes. 'You still didn't win.'

Lying at our feet is the pyramid of cans. Still in one complete piece.

I dash around the smouldering remains, kick the cans over, and rescue the dragon from the devastation. I throw it to Dado. 'Don't let anyone call you Pissfish. You're a dragon.'

He's covered with soot and trembling. But I think he's happy. He'll be happy once the aftershock wears off.

A roar behind me. A hand emerges from the mound of plushies and splintered wood. The vendor claws her way out, twitching eyes fixed on me.

'You've still got your hat on,' I say. 'Incredible. Did you use the same glue on the tins?'

'What have you done?'

As she storms towards me, I grab the nearest thing, which happens to be Dado. 'Now, calm down.'

'Face the consequences, you little git!' Spit sprays from her mouth. 'You're using a child as a shield!'

'Not quite.' I dart behind Dado. 'I'm *trying* to use a child as a shield.'

She flings him aside and then snatches my collar, dragging me so close I can see every bead of sweat. 'You destroyed my stall.'

'Do I win a prize for that?' I rasp.

Rage peels her lips from her teeth. As she raises a fist, a ribbon of red light cracks the sky in two. The thunder strikes like a whip. Then a single voice: 'Unhand him.'

He stands alone, silhouetted against the distant lights of the festival. He has my golden eyes, my mass of curly white hair. He's me, but stretched out on a rack – nothing soft about him, and all that intimidating height. If I'm a dumpling, my father is a breadstick.

When the lightning cracks again, the vendor drops me.

'Ganymedes,' he says.

'Father.' I shake the dust from my shoulders. 'How'd you find me?'

His gaze passes over the scene – the ruined stall, the trembling children. 'I simply followed the path of destruction.'

'Smart.'

Dado dashes forward, clutching the dragon. 'That light – was that a Blessing? Are you Blessed?'

The Blessed. The duces of each province, chosen by the Goddess herself to lead. Blessed because they have been 'blessed' with a slice of her gift to the world. Magic.

My father levels his eyes at me. 'Tell them the truth, Ganymedes. Tell them who it was.'

The children's heads snap to me.

The food in my gut makes a bid for freedom. My father has that effect. He's a regular old swig of prune juice. Still, I know this dance well. 'Me,' I lie. 'I'm a Blessed. I'm to be dux once the festival is over.'

Dado's mouth falls open, gaping like the fish he hates so much. 'Which province?'

My father's gaze burns into me. Overhead, the lightning strikes again. My responsibilities have found me, even if the guards haven't.

I raise my head and the smile comes easily. 'Just call me Mr Pissfish.'

*

'I suppose you think this is awfully funny?' My father, Dux of Fish Province, keeps his grip firmly around my arm.

'No.' I'm not lying. My father saps all humour out of every moment in his vicinity.

He's dragged me far from the hub of the festival, to the harbour. White marble effigies of emperors and empresses past stand fifteen feet tall along the water, facing the black sea. The waters are so still and silent, for a moment I think they've frozen over.

In Fish Province, the sound of the sea is a constant rhythm. We live atop the ocean, in stilted houses and on floating islands connected by rope bridges. The relentless back and forth of waves greeted my birth and lulled me to sleep every night.

8

This silence feels *wrong*, as if something essential has been drained from this place.

Distant lights are twisted and dull in the black water. After tonight, the festival will continue for eleven more nights. But for me, the party is over.

'I had to meet the emperor alone. *Alone*, Ganymedes. All the other duces were with their Blessed to wish them well for the voyage. As if our situation is not precarious enough, you cast further suspicion upon us with your frivolous jaunt into the city. They sent the guards out after you, afraid you'd been kidnapped or worse.' He eyes me. 'What in Concordia were you doing?'

'Eating.'

His face darkens. 'I think you've done quite enough of that.'

I'm going to eat an extra portion tonight just to spite him. He and I both know a fat son is not the worst thing he could be saddled with.

He clicks his tongue. 'You're not a commoner. You're a scion. The true-born heir of Fish Province. Unless you start behaving like a Blessed, nobody will believe you are one.'

My stomach knots painfully. And I can't blame the dumplings. 'I can't behave like a Blessed. Because . . .' *I'm not one.* The words lodge in my throat.

And it's all his fault. For all his civilities and worship of the emperor, my father is the root cause of the lie called Ganymedes.

Blessings, to put it frankly, are kinda weird.

They're hereditary but can only exist in one person. Only twelve people across the whole of Concordia can possess a Blessing at any one time – one Blessed per province. Concordia is *big* on unity like that. Problem is there's no rhyme or reason for which offspring will inherit a Blessing. Bear Province can

9

tell you all about that. Five strapping musclebound heirs, and their Blessing emerges in the one brother so plagued with illness he'll likely drop dead before he can pass it on.

Once a kid shows their Blessing, it vanishes from their parent. And most show their Blessing young, around eight or nine. So when I, lone heir of the Fish Dux, reached the grand age of thirteen without showing a Blessing, people began to talk.

Then my father talked to me.

Most people have fond memories of their childhood. My strongest memory, pushing out all the little joys like learning how to fish and my first lick of ice cream, is the day my dear old pa sat me down and had the most awkward conversation any teenager has likely had to endure since the dawn of civilization:

'All right, there, sonny-boy? Just thought I'd clue you in – I've been screwing any woman who isn't your mother. And seeing as the closest thing to a Blessing you have is your impressive swagger, I'd wager one of my dozens of illegitimate spawn is set to inherit my Blessing. Also, don't tell anyone, or our entire province is royally fucked.'

Because Concordia doesn't *do* bastard heirs. We did once, and it ended in a big war and lots of people dying. So now, any dux daring to spread their seed to commoners is akin to taking a massive shit in the emperor's porridge. Which generally doesn't go down well.

So, from the age of thirteen, I lied to the emperor, my mother and everyone in Concordia to save my province. I told them I possessed a Blessing that I didn't. That is what Ganymedes is. A sheet to toss over the ugly truth.

'The emperor suspects nothing,' my father says. 'The effort of maintaining the Bandage is draining his sanity. As long as you don't do anything *stupid* on the pilgrimage, then nobody will discover you're not a Blessed.'

The words slip easily from his lips, as if the lie is a mere inconvenience – a spot of rain or a fishbone stuck in his teeth.

'Stupid – like you using a Blessing you're not supposed to have in front of people?'

He bats my words away. 'A gaggle of street rats. It is not them we have to worry about.'

He's probably right, but you'd think he'd at least attempt to exercise the caution he berates me for not possessing.

'Well, I can't make any promises about the stupid thing. Like father, like son.'

'This is not a joke.' He grips my shoulders. 'If the other Blessed discover the truth, everyone in Fish Province will pay. I have worked tirelessly to build us up out of the mud, and your dalliances threaten all of that.'

'Out of the mud and into the piss.' I watch my words land upon him, how they deepen the creases in his forehead. I want him to hurt, the same way his lie has ruined me.

He is not dissimilar to all Fish Province residents; they are unduly proud of their contributions to the empire, when in reality all we have done is fish the same waters for a thousand years while everyone else calls us Pissfish.

My father's grasp tightens. 'Do *not* pull anything like that again. All I ask of you is to pretend, for the sake of our people.'

'Were you thinking of our people when you cast out your seed like a net?'

He strikes me.

I stagger, tasting blood.

'For the next twelve nights, I am still your superior. You will do well to remember that.'

Because once the festival is over, the leadership of the twelve provinces will pass to the new generation of Blessed.

Ganymedes, Lord of the Fish. While my father retires to (presumably) sleep with as many women as possible who find pale, unfunny stick insects sexy, I'll have to maintain the lie he has given me. A lifetime of Blessed gatherings. A lifetime of sitting in rooms where I do not belong. A lifetime of people looking for me to lead when all I want to do is run.

Because I'm not and never will be Blessed. The Goddess did not deem me worthy to bear an ounce of her power. I'm not amongst that dazzling elite of humanity. I'm just a piss-fish, pretending to be a shark.

We stop before the *Dragon's Dawn*. Even in my sombre mood, it's difficult not to be dazzled by the emperor's ship. Back home we only have small, rusted fishing vessels, built to travel no more than a mile or so. But the *Dragon's Dawn* was designed to carry Blessed on the most important journey of their lives.

It's shaped like its namesake, with a great roaring head at the bow, and a spiked tail at the stern. Its hull is adorned in gold, jade and silver, with three levels of decks above the water. Instead of white sails, the wings of the beast have been imbued by the emperor's Blessing – displaying a moving, snarling image of a green dragon. Like a painting brought to life and trapped within canvas.

It's the most beautiful and terrifying thing I've ever seen. A wonder and a horror.

Home for the next twelve nights.

As impressive as the ship is, its cargo is far less appealing. Eleven Blessed scions. Gifted and brilliant and the most likely people to see what I am lacking beneath the smiles and swagger.

'Why can't I stay in the city?'

'Because you *are* Blessed,' he says loudly, as if volume will make it true. 'And this is tradition. The journey to the

Goddess's mountain will take just twelve nights. You will never see all the other duces for a longer period than that again.'

Because the duces are primarily concerned with the running of their own provinces, they only interact with the individual duces they have business with, usually from the neighbouring regions. Gatherings of all twelve Blessed are rare, reserved for empire-wide affairs, and last only a day or so. But that's still a day or so for almost every year of the rest of my life.

My father grips my chin, forcing my gaze to lock with his. 'For once, keep your head down. Be unremarkable. They think so little of us they will not pay you any mind if you do not give them reason to. For the Goddess's sake, do *not* draw attention to yourself, Ganymedes. Once we get through the pilgrimage, you will be Dux of Fish Province. And the rest will be simple.'

Simple. Easy for a Blessed to say.

I will have to bear the lie alone, then inflict the same wretched fate upon my unblessed child. A legacy of deception.

Or perhaps he expects me to hunt down my illegitimate Blessed sibling and take their offspring as my own. Swap my worthless child for one with value.

Either way, there's no end to it. Not the way he wants to play it.

'You will do as I say?'

'Of course, Father.'

Perhaps we're more alike than I give us credit for because the lie slips through my teeth as easily as breathing.

I don't want to do this. It's the main reason I tried to miss the ship's departure in the first place. But now he's left me no choice.

I'm going to create a scene so explosive it'll be enough to sink this magnificent vessel.

Chapter Two

Day One – Feast of the Dragon

Night

There are two things which are undeniably cool: walking away from explosions without looking back, and turning up late to parties. I was already late, thanks to my escape bid, and the time it takes preparing my costume makes me even later. The ship has set sail and Dragon Province is a cluster of rapidly vanishing lights. Achingly, as I enter the ballroom, nobody notices my fashionably late arrival. I'm truly wasted on these people.

The ballroom could fit twenty Fish Province houses inside. Great circular windows frame the night beyond, and the floor is polished black with specks of silver, so the whole room feels as though it's suspended amongst the stars. A long table sits in the centre, and a sweeping staircase leads to an upper level of jutting balconies.

The space is *glowing*, with incandescent flowers wrapped around stone columns. A birdcage chandelier hangs from the ceiling. Disturbingly, it appears to be tweeting. I hope they're not real birds.

I tug my collar. Someone, probably some eccentric emperor, decided long ago that the best way to kick off a pilgrimage is a costume party, with all scions dressed as their province animals. As my proud province is too poor to shell out for a new outfit, I'm draped in what could only be described as a kelp fishing net, complete with seaweed arms and droopy piscero heads. I can empathize – I too feel like a captured fish, flailing against the ropes to return to the sea.

Still, this awful costume is essential to my plan. I scan the room, repressing the urge to vomit. It's been years since I've seen most of these Blessed. So whenever I'm around them I feel like that awkward thirteen-year-old boy, convinced they will see through my deception.

I'm lucky they already thought so little of Fish Province before I showed up. They blame my meagre province for my ineptitude. After all, who expects a Fish to contribute intelligently to the running of an empire? Who even wants one to? It blinds them to the truth – that I lack the very thing uniting them, a Blessing.

But tonight, I need them all to see me.

I'm going to make them *hate* me.

Maybe I can't tell them the truth. But I *can* disgrace myself enough, offend them enough, that they ostracize me. That they deem me to be what I am – unworthy.

It's happened before. Not frequently, but enough for me to form this plan. Blessed who have been judged unfit to rule for various reasons. Their position is filled by a suitable regent who leads and attends the summits in their stead. The whole province won't be punished just for having an incompetent Blessed.

And then I'll retreat, run for the hills, and Fish Province will be better for it.

Once the time comes, I'll find someone willing to pose as

my legitimate heir. Someone who doesn't mind lying every day of their life. Someone not like me.

I take a deep breath and ready myself.

Bye bye, responsibilities. Hello, food quest.

I spot my first prey. He leans against the staircase, observing the chattering partygoers like a man surveying a battlefield, his grim expression too old for his young face.

I slide up beside him. 'Ox.'

I duck as the wooden horns mounted on his head swing in my direction. He's otherwise dressed as he always is: black military uniform with red trim, polished knee-high boots, and twin rows of perfectly shined buttons. His red hair is cropped short, an Ox Province-mandated haircut.

'Bugger off, Pissfish.'

'You've not seen me for a year.' I reach for his skinny shoulder, but he flinches away. 'You should be nicer to your elders, Jasper.'

'Please, no. Don't wind me up.' His red eyes dart. 'Not now. Not *tonight.*'

I smirk, placing one hand on the bannister above his head. That's one thing (perhaps the only thing) I love about Jasper – he's shorter than me. He's also fourteen, but I'm still counting the win. 'How's life at the Bandage?'

'Like you give one solitary shit.' He's just as I remember – all snarled retorts and spiky hormones.

'I do give a shit! A whole heap of shit.'

He claws his hands down his face. 'I need to get the upper provinces' support on this trip. I need more divinium, weapons, supplies. I can't have a pissfish messing it up. *Again.*'

'I would never! It's very admirable what you do – all the brave soldiers of the Bandage, defending our lands from the goblins and oogley-boogies beyond.'

I swerve as his horns jab at me. 'It's not goblins. Not that you would know, because my soldiers are sacrificing themselves to defend your cesspit of a province, despite you contributing absolutely fuck all.'

Jasper is so *easy*. It almost feels like cheating.

Jasper's the Ox Blessed. His province's entire purpose revolves around the Bandage – a luminous green wall that runs along Concordia's southern border through Fish, Ermine, Bear and Grasshopper Provinces. Because Concordia is a peninsula shaped like an arrowhead (or, as I prefer, slice of pie) jutting into the sea, that border is the only thing connecting us to the world outside the empire.

The Bandage was created by an emperor a thousand years ago, and the duty of maintaining it is passed down from ruler to ruler. Emperor Eugenios has been pouring most of his Blessing into that wall to keep it standing since he inherited it, but as he ages, the Bandage has begun to crack, along with his sanity.

Ox Province is a military encampment running alongside the Bandage, with battlements positioned at the weakest points, where the wall is crumbling. Jasper and his band of merry men ensure the border isn't breached by the nasties beyond. A duty that, in my opinion, Jasper takes far too seriously. Mind you, he is fourteen. Everything feels uber-important when you're fourteen.

I lean over him. 'Calm down, Jasps. The Bandage will still be there when you get back.'

A muscle in his cheek twitches. 'My people are dying. And the only way I can help them is to go on a *cruise* to fairy mountain with some useless cunts I have to play nice with just to get some resources they should already be giving us.' He runs his hands down his face. 'They keep refusing my requests to meet with them. Apparently, they have more important issues than the defence of our empire. But they can't escape here. I'm gonna get the uppers alone, get them to see how dire the situation is, then they'll help. They gotta. Or we're all fucked.'

'Chill out. The Bandage has never fallen in Concordia's history.'

'The Bandage *is* falling,' he snarls. 'The emperor ain't got enough Blessing to maintain it. And fuck knows when I last saw a shipment of divinium. It's gonna keep falling apart until the Crabs overrun us.'

Ah yes, the Crabs. The reason I'm stuck here pretending to be something I'm not. Concordia didn't always have twelve provinces, it once had thirteen. You know that big war I mentioned earlier? That happened when a Crab dux had a bastard Blessed who went off his rocker and tried to take down the emperor. As a result, the Crabs were kicked out, and the Bandage slathered over the wound. Now they're trapped on the other side, and aren't keen on dying in the arid wasteland, so keep trying to get back in. That is until Ox soldiers throw flaming boulders at them.

To be fair, Concordia hasn't had a war since. Instead, we've been maintaining a thousand-year siege.

Jasper crosses his arms at his chest. This close, I can see the smattering of freckles across his brown skin, the boyish upturn of his nose. 'Are you gonna piss off now? If they see you talking to me, they won't take me seriously.'

Jasper already hates me. I just need to . . . rip the bandage off.

I take a few steps back. Six feet. That'll do.

'Aye aye . . . *bastard.*'

The moment happens in slow motion. First his face contorts. Then his arms tense at his sides. Finally, his mouth opens, and red flames spew forth.

'You're dead to me, Pissfish! Dead! You can go live with

the Crabs for all I care. You crawled out of the same stinking ocean!'

Everyone is staring. I raise my voice: 'He doesn't like to be called "bastard", apparently. So don't call him "bastard". Despite it being completely accurate, due to his illegitimate birth by sordid affair.'

The next blast singes my eyebrows. Worth it.

I slink away to plan my next move.

Normal Blessings manifest in one ability per province, unlike the emperor's super special shiny Blessing, which can do pretty much anything. My father, for example, can control the weather. But asking a Blessed what form their Blessing takes is like asking someone's bra size. You just don't do it. But with Jasper, it was hard to ignore a recruit breathing fire.

The existence of a Blessed bastard is usually enough to damn a province to exile outside the Bandage. But that's a bit difficult when the province is the Bandage itself, and the citizens are hardened warriors who have spent their lives learning the best way to disembowel their enemies. Even Concordia's staunch traditions couldn't rationalize exiling its own army and turning it into an attacking force with a grudge to settle.

What also helped was the fact they needed a leader, as dear old Ox dad decided jumping over a hundred-foot wall was a great way to give the Crabs 'what for'. So, Jasper was granted command and the whole filthy ordeal swept under the rug – something he's a *tad* sensitive about. So now we're protected from the kin of an infamous bastard by a fourteen-year-old firebreather with an army and an attitude problem, who is a bastard himself. Got it?

If only I had been born at the Bandage; no other province could have an illegitimate Blessed and escape the death sentence of the barren wastes.

On my escape, I almost topple straight into the Elephant Blessed's lap. I swerve, positioning myself before her wheel-chair. It's an impressive device, the kind of beautiful but ingenious creation only Elephant Province could conceive of. It appears the entire thing was carved out of one tree. It's less of a chair, and more a throne.

'Tendai!' I plant my hands on the armrests.

The dazzling array of linens and silks Tendai wears are far from elephant grey. But her headwrap ends in a sort-of-suggestion of an elephant's trunk, and two white tusk earrings dangle from her ears. I get the feeling nobody has taken this 'costume' rule as seriously as me.

Tricky, this one. She's blanked me at every summit. I don't know much about the Elephant scion other than everyone seems to loathe her for some reason. Maybe I can get some tips.

She gazes at me from beneath gold-powdered eyelids. Purple hair spills from her headwrap, cascading against deep brown skin. It's easy to tell where people are from in Concordia – you simply look at the hair. Mine is bereft of any colour, as white as dove feathers. It's a Fish Province trait, but I can't help but think it sends a message: 'This one is lacking.'

I clear my throat. 'How's life in the Fun—'

'You did *not* just touch my chair,' her deep voice snaps.

'Sorry!' I say on instinct, then remember I'm meant to be offending her and throw in a '*you bitch*' for good measure.

One pierced eyebrow raises. Her eyes cling to me, as if searching for something. 'Is that *really* all you've got, Fish? Why don't you try a little harder?'

'Uh . . . super . . . bitch?'

She clicks her tongue, disappointed. 'Irrelevant.' She rolls away.

Not my smoothest encounter. I need to offend these

people enough that they forbid me from communicating with them again. I don't think randomly calling everyone a bitch is going to cut it.

One person stands at a distance, back to the wall, icy-blue hair as cold as her personality. She scans the room, sharpening a short blade I suspect she intends to insert into anyone who approaches – Eska, Ermine Province, and my dear neighbour. She's forgone a costume, but she's wrapped in so many layers of white furs, she resembles her province animal regardless. Her clothing isn't for show. Eska lives in endless miles of frozen tundra, the kind of place where happiness goes to die. The only thing more terrifying than her province are *her* neighbours – fifteen-foot-tall snow mammoths her people hunt for survival because Goddess knows nothing else could live in Ermine Province.

Truthfully, I'm surprised she's even here. Ermines are notorious for distancing themselves from the rest of the empire, doing Goddess knows what in their ice cities. Maybe refusing to attend the pilgrimage would be a step too far, even for them.

Her gaze swerves to me. Oval eyes narrow. Then she traces the knife through the air.

I've decided I'm OK with *not* approaching Eska. The last time I did – aged thirteen, eager to convince everyone I was a totally normal Blessed – I tried to embrace her and was rewarded with a fork through the hand.

I'm pretty sure that chunky bundle of loathing is already firmly in the we-hate-Dee camp.

A little 'ahem' comes from behind me.

I turn and my heart drops into my arse.

The Spider Blessed is dressed in all the splendours of their province. Layers of embroidered robes enswathe them in red, gold and amber. Their clothes should be heavy, as they're inlaid with hundreds of gleaming jewels, but as they stand still before me, their robes flutter about their feet, as if connected to some unknown force, unique entirely to them.

Nergüi.

My mind screams escape. But my body is frozen.

Their ashen-grey hair is swooped upwards into a golden headdress. Mounted atop it are eight of the largest, darkest jewels I've ever seen. Eight black eyes for a spider. As I look into them, my own terrified expression stares back.

'You're behaving very oddly, Fish. Even more so than usual.'

I swallow hard. My throat burns. 'You know me. Odd.' I laugh a strange, choked noise.

Nergüi flashes a smile.

Did that give something away? Mentally, I build a wall between my mind and my mouth, and another between Nergüi and me, for good measure.

They lock their gaze with mine, holding me in the storm grey of their eyes.

Amendment to the plan: I want to offend everyone *except* Nergüi.

There's something about the Spider Blessed, behind the perfect cheekbones and red-lipped smile, that has always made my skin crawl. The way they look at me. As if they see straight through my disguise, and I'm not talking about the costume.

'Could it be you're planning something, little fish?'

I take a step back. 'I'm not planning anything. Other than to have a damn good time.' I laugh again. I'm laughing an *awful* lot.

Nergüi moves closer. Even their voice is perfectly measured, with low even tones. 'These gatherings are usually awfully dull. But this night is going to be *legendary*. Don't you agree, Ganymedes?'

Not many of the northern Blessed use my name, but Nergüi wields it like a weapon.

'Not sure what you mean.' I laugh again. 'Well . . . nice seeing you! Toodles!'

'Wait—'

I wrench myself free of their gaze and find a corner to hide in.

Nergüi knows. I'm sure of it. Somehow Nergüi knows I do not belong. That I am not Blessed.

Everyone's heard the whispers about Nergüi. About the whispers *they* collect. Secrets that wind their way to them from every province. A person who turns information into threats, and threats to their advantage.

It would be easy to chalk this up to superstition or prejudice. Spider Province doesn't believe in binaries, they celebrate the unique, the individual, the rebel – a terrifying concept in a black and white place like Fish Province.

But I have felt it in Nergüi's gaze since we first met. The weight of knowledge with the power to destroy. Whenever I'm around them I feel that knowledge hovering above my head like a swinging blade. Is that what they meant when they said this night would be *'legendary'*? Do they plan to expose me?

I can't waste any time. I need to cause a colossal upset before Nergüi does it for me.

Besides the emperor's heir, there's one person I can upset and guarantee my expulsion from the league of creepy fuckers.

I scan the room for the dashing Tortoise scion. Everyone adores that golden heir with his naive idealism. If I piss him off, the others will follow. Nobody likes the guy who kicks the puppy.

Instead, my gaze falls on someone else.

My heart jumps to my throat. The music fades to a distant echo, like a noise heard underwater.

He's here.

The thread connecting us draws taut. My body has an instinctual need to close the distance. As natural as breathing.

Tortoise boy will have to wait.

Every time I see Ravi he looks better than the last. But in this room, at this moment, he's so beautiful it makes my soul ache. Obsidian-black hair hanging to his waist, like an oil sheen against the ocean. Black looks so good on Ravi that I suspect the Goddess created the shade exclusively for him. Black shirt, black leather gloves, a collar of black feathers draped across his sharp shoulders in a casual attempt at a crow costume, and *too*-tight trousers he's worn to torment me.

I'm grabbing his arm before I've thought of something to say.

He stares. Blessed hells, that jawbone could cut steel. Eyes so dark I forget I'm in a room with ten others, and it's not just us two, alone in a cave on a cliff in a storm.

He's still staring.

Say something. Anything, Dee. Speak!

'Your arse looks amazing in those trousers.'

Anything but THAT.

'I . . . err . . . thank you?'

Well, I'm in now. Might as well roll with it. 'You should charge people to look at it.'

He blinks.

I'm still holding his arm. I peel my fingers away. 'I didn't think you'd come, Ravi. It's been so long.'

Five years.

He glances behind, fiddling with his shirt cuffs. 'We all have to come. The twelve Blessed have been declared, so . . . it's tradition.'

24

His words are stilted. I don't blame him. He's the only other heir who knows this pilgrimage is a sham. The tradition is clear: Blessed only. Always Blessed only since records began. The ship itself is powered by the Emperor's Blessing, because even one non-Blessed aboard would taint everything with their unworthy presence.

But I swapped my secrets for Ravi's five years ago.

Ravi knows the truth – there're only eleven Blessed here.

He's looking at everything apart from me. Mother of mercy, does he have his *ears pierced*?

'If we're stuck here for eleven days, we should catch up.' I swing on my heels, shooting him my best let's-fuck-shit-up smirk.

'I have business to attend to. The divinium.'

The damned divinium. If I could, I'd crush every one of those stones to dust.

Ravi's home, Crow Province, used to be as irrelevant as mine. An unhabitable ragged mountain region. His people were cave-dwellers, more used to talking to the coal they mined than fellow humans. Then they discovered something deep in the heart of their mountains. That gleaming blue mineral: iridescent, priceless divinium.

Divinium is why Jasper is eyeing up Ravi like a juicy steak. Those stones are the only substance capable of mending the tears in the Bandage, where the emperor's Blessing is failing. Those stones are saving Concordia. And I hate them.

Ravi went from being an ignored, shy child of caves and coal to the heir to a fortune. Now everyone wants a piece of the only person I showed my truth to.

Before divinium, he was mine. I couldn't conceive of a world where he was not.

I still won't.

'Fuck divinium. Let's have some fun.'

He gasps, as if I was actually suggesting he romance the stones. 'T-That is . . .' He glances around. 'I need to speak to Jasper about the Bandage, and the All-Mother about—'

'Bugger that.' I grab his hand. It's cold and stiffens at my touch. 'Remember how we escaped the summit when we were fourteen? We hid up that tree all night.' *And it was so cold we had to huddle together, and I got all those confusing feelings.* 'I bet we can find some secret places on this ship.'

This isn't part of the plan. *He* isn't ever part of the plan. But fuck the plan.

Ravi leans into me. Goddess, his dark skin looks so smooth. 'To the corner.'

The corner. Nice.

By the time we're there he's so close I can smell his scent. A collision of coal dust and lavender. Smoky and floral. He still smells the same. He's still my Ravi.

I grin. 'How are we gonna bust our way out of here?'

Ravi fiddles with his blazer buttons. 'Listen, Ganymedes—'

I drop his hand. '*Gany . . . medes?*'

'That's your name.'

'I'm Dee. You call me Dee.'

My father, in his infinite dedication to Dragon Province, named his only legitimate heir using their traditions – names taken from their ancient, dead language. That name has always been a reminder of his lie. Ravi knows this. I told him.

'Once this is over, we will be duces of our provinces. Leaders. We can't go around calling each other nicknames any more.' His tongue almost speaks in his old accent. The lyrical sounds try to break through, but his white teeth keep them contained.

I reach for his hand again. 'What are you talking about? You hate all that stuff. You told me—'

'Forget what I told you.' His hand twitches away. 'Things

have changed. Do you not see that? This isn't some childish friendship where we clamber out of windows.'

'*Friendship*? You kiss your friends, do you?'

He anxiously hushes me. 'You were drowning.'

'But you enjoyed it.'

'That's irrelevant.'

'You don't deny it!'

'Ganymedes!' He grips both my arms. 'Please don't do this. I appreciate you reaching out to me when we were children. But that time is over. It *needs* to be over. Do you understand? I can't be that person any more. I need to be someone else. I have responsibilities now.'

Responsibilities. Ugh.

'And they don't involve me?'

His shoulders tense. 'All of Concordia relies on my province mining the divinium. The emperor's strength is failing. If my stones do not make it to the Bandage, then the whole nation will suffer the consequences.'

'Consequences,' I repeat, my eyes locking with his. 'Crabs, you mean.'

His gaze falters. 'Every single stone is precious. Just one could save thousands of lives. My province's livelihood relies on it.'

I can see that burden on him now, in the slope of his shoulders, as if he's already exhausted from carrying the weight of all those lives.

'Let me help you,' I whisper.

'I can't risk upsetting the uppers.'

By '*uppers*' he means the northern provinces – Dragon, Tiger, Spider, Tortoise, Elephant and, despite its central position, Bunnerfly. The same ones who ignored Ravi's existence for most of his life.

Officially, every province in Concordia is equal. Unofficially, that's a crock of horse dung.

I lick my dry lips. 'So being near me is a risk.'

'The northern provinces' contributions are vital to the mining. We couldn't afford to manage it without their help.' His fingers drive into my shoulders. 'I cannot waste my time on people who are of no value.'

His words hit me like an anchor dropped on my chest. For a moment, I'm convinced I must not be speaking to him. Not my Ravi. Someone else must be dressed like him, saying these poisonous words.

But then our gazes meet, and I know it is him. I would know the darkness of his eyes anywhere.

'You're hurting me.'

He removes his hands. But we both know that's not what I mean.

'No value.' I am of no value.

I need to get out of here. But before I can move, a new voice speaks.

'Ravinder.' A girl is at his side. A tiny, waifish thing with long golden hair and round glasses magnifying curious blue eyes. Her skin is almost as pale as mine, as if she has never glimpsed the sun.

She wears a ruffled blouse, embroidered bodice and knee-length skirt with a flurry of petticoats. She looks like a doll. A pretty porcelain thing you would place on a shelf and let the dust settle on.

Ravi's back straightens. 'Apologies. I had matters to deal with. I'm yours now.'

She smiles shyly and adjusts something on her back. A shell. Far too unwieldy for her petite frame.

'You're wearing a tortoise shell,' I say.

She leaps so violently you'd think I'd just threatened her

life. 'Y-Yes. This costume was made for my brother. I admit it is a little . . . cumbersome.'

'Your brother.' I check the blonde hair. 'That must be Lysander. Where is he?'

That's right – back to the plan. Offend Lysander and the rest will follow. Then I can get the hell out of here forever.

The doll clasps her gloved hands then, almost theatrically, wails into her palms.

'Ganymedes!' Ravi hisses.

If he calls me that one more time, I'm going to throw myself off this ship.

She falls into his shoulder, smearing snot over all his beautiful feathers.

'What's wrong with her?' I ask.

Ravi strokes her hair. 'Lysander died six months ago.'

The shock roots me to the ground. 'How the hell was I supposed to know that?'

'Everyone knows. There was a funeral.'

'I wasn't invited!'

The girl frees herself of Ravi's arms. 'I apologize. I may have overlooked to inform the southern provinces.'

Of course you did. We're too busy catching and growing your food to be told of trivial things like a Blessed's death.

It's not unusual for the uppers to have the occasional meeting without the lower provinces, but not inviting us to a Blessed's funeral really takes that snobbery to a new level.

I've never heard of a Blessed dying before they were able to pass on their Blessing to their child. Because Blessed are chosen by the Goddess herself, protecting and keeping them alive is a source of national pride for their province. I wonder how much shit Tortoise Province is in with the Church after losing their golden heir.

'This is huge,' I say. 'Everyone loved him.'

She sways and Ravi catches her. 'Do you want to go to your cabin?'

'It's quite all right. I can do this.' She takes a deep breath. 'My name is Cordelia. I inherited Lysander's Blessing. I am the Tortoise Blessed now.' She says it as though she's announcing a flesh-eating plague. She seems about as pleased with her situation as I am with mine.

Although the knowledge that Blessings pass to siblings if the Blessed doesn't have a child is useful. I *probably* don't have it in me, but it's nice to know a bastard killing spree isn't off the table. I'm surprised my father didn't try it – hunt all my half-siblings down, one by one, until the Blessing has no choice but to jump to me.

Cordelia has her brother's eyes, his exact shade of golden hair.

Lysander. That glimmering, effervescent heir. Tortoises generally think themselves superior, with all their books and hallowed institutions. But Lysander seemed genuinely interested in everyone, even a son of fisherfolk. He was his province's love of learning and progress manifested in a positive way, instead of the usual smarter-than-thou jerks that strut out of there.

I stare at her. 'Does Leofric know?'

Ravi glares. 'Not now, Ganymedes.'

Cordelia turns to him. 'Ravinder, Nergüi wishes to speak with you.'

'He hates that name,' I say, stronger than I mean to.

'Do you?' She clasps her hands to her mouth, horrified.

Ravi tugs his shirt cuffs. 'No. *Ravinder* is my name.' Then he leaves me in his wake.

This is fine. Totally fine. That's just the ache of your heart shattering into a thousand pieces.

My body moves towards the closest thing resembling a

bar. I'm more of a eat-my-feelings kinda guy. But right now, I need a drink.

I slam my fist on the counter, slumping into a stool. 'Barkeep, two of anything with alcohol.'

'There ain't no barkeep here, moron.'

I don't check to see who has spoken. They called me 'moron' so that doesn't narrow it down.

I clamber over the bar, landing in a heap behind it. I grab the nearest bottles and pour out shots, downing them one by one. I don't drink straight from the bottle. I'm not a *monster*.

'D'ya know how much of an embarrassment you are?'

I drag myself back up to the countertop. He's barely visible beneath the bear fur engulfing his long, skinny frame. Only the mad bastards from Bear Province would skin their totem animal and wear it as a costume. It probably would have looked impressive on his bulky brothers, but he looks like he's halfway through being consumed.

'Wyatt. A pleasure.' I down another shot.

He looks as though he hates me already – glowering beneath wisps of toffee-brown hair. But it doesn't hurt to be certain.

'Still dying then?'

He flinches. 'You ain't funny.'

Wrong. I'm fucking hilarious. It's all I am.

Wyatt is the aforementioned illness-stricken Blessed who was chosen over his impressive brothers. Never say the Goddess doesn't have a sense of humour.

Wyatt rarely attends the summits. He doesn't cope well with travel. And while most of Concordia is linked by railways, Bear Province, who are so committed to their horses I suspect they may actually marry them, stubbornly resisted the change.

He's gleaming with sweat beneath the bulky costume.

Bears are nuts like that – comfort or sanity aren't a consideration. Great drinking buddies, but not someone you'd rely on for getting out of any situation with all your limbs intact.

Wyatt, however, is a bag of anxieties squirming beneath fish-pale skin.

I lean across the counter, wielding my most devious grin.

He shifts. 'Don't talk to me in front of the others.'

'You're a lower province, Wyatt. They don't give two shits about you.'

He grips his chest as if his diseased heart has finally given up. 'You're wrong! I just spoke with Nergüi for ten minutes.'

Poor Wyatt. I wonder what information they spun out of him in that time.

'They're upper. We're lower.' My voice slurs. 'They don't care about you. None of them do.' My own words burn me. I throw back another shot.

'Maybe not about *you*. But some of us actually have a chance of doing well by our provinces.' He raises an indignant chin.

'Wyatt, last time you tried to speak to Leofric you choked on your own tongue.'

He gags. 'That ain't true! They know I'm not like you.'

I down another shot. 'If that's true, why didn't they tell you Lysander's dead?'

The remaining colour drains from his pale face. Swing and a hit – he didn't get an invitation either. 'Lysander ain't dead.'

'Then where is he? And why's his sister here instead?'

Wyatt eyes the crowd. When he turns back, the bear head slips from his own, revealing a mess of unruly hair. 'R-Really?'

I nod solemnly. 'Dead.'

Wyatt looks shell-shocked. Perhaps he's never had to contemplate other people's mortality, with his own hovering so obviously. 'Lysander was always nice to me. He visited last year. Wanted to learn about the province, push past the feud.'

Blessed hells. Lysander was perfect. The provinces are supposed to be interested in each other, as we *are* part of one empire ultimately answering to the emperor. But because we're mostly self-governed by the duces, in reality there's little interaction between us. An upper showing interest in a lower province is highly unusual. 'Yeah, he was nice to everyone. Even us measly lowers.' Oh shit. The plan. Got to make him hate me. 'He probably only spoke to you because you're easier to manipulate than your brothers.'

Wyatt recoils, as if struck. 'Why don't you—' His words snap off. The room hushes. I follow his gaze, and it leads me to *her*.

Eudora. Imperial Heir. All-Mother. Goddess Incarnate.

The pale green of her hair is a declaration of her divinity, cascading down the soft brown skin of her back. Her dress hugs the curves of her body; layered jade jewels and sequins serve as dragon's scales, as if anyone would not know who she is without a costume.

The Dragon Province Blessed is the Goddess made flesh. But there's a special occurrence when that Blessed is female. The Goddess, after all, is a woman. Through the centuries, Dragon empresses have ruled over the most prosperous periods of Concordia's history.

The last Dragon empress reigned more than three hundred years ago. When Eudora was born – first child and female – the celebrations reached even Fish Province. The emperor didn't have any more children. The risk that his Blessing might not pass to her was too high.

People have been capturing Eudora's likeness in statues and paintings since her birth. She is adored the empire over, before her reign has even begun.

She stands in the centre of the room, head held high, back straight. How is it possible for one person to command so much power, and yet also be the least powerful person in the room? Eudora has not inherited her Blessing yet; that won't happen until the emperor finally pops his clogs.

At her side, as always, is the Tiger Blessed, Leofric. Bodyguard, shield and surly pain in my backside. Only a six-foot-seven man with muscles the size of his would wear blue tiger print, confident nobody will mock him for it. His arms are covered with a giant, sprawling tiger tattoo. Even his dark blue mullet has goddessdamn tiger stripes shaved into the sides. What a colossal cunt.

His gaze scans the room. When it falls upon me, he scowls.

I'm fairly sure the man has always desired my corpse displayed publicly, and now his buddy Lysander isn't around to stop him, I wouldn't put it past him to fulfil that bloody destiny.

Everyone hurries into a bow. I stand until Leofric flexes his muscles at me. He watches me descend to the floor, as if I'm bowing to him.

'There is no need for such formalities.' Eudora smiles, bejewelled lips gleaming green. 'We are here as equals. We share the Goddess's Blessing. That makes you all my siblings.'

Yeah, right. The same way a pebble is the sibling of a mountain.

Her voice fills the room without her raising it, caramel smooth. 'With the Grasshopper Blessed emerging, all provinces have now shown their Blessing. This pilgrimage is particularly special, as this year marks a thousand years of peace in Concordia.'

A thousand years since we flung the Crabs over the Bandage.

'We will undertake the same journey honoured by our forefathers and foremothers. To mark this occasion for these twelve sacred days we will celebrate the wonders of one province per day. Once we reach the Goddess's mountain, we will give thanks for her Blessing. We have even more to show gratitude for than our parents did, as she has bestowed upon us sacred divinium, a precious gift to protect our lands against the foes that plague us.'

So now divinium is from the Goddess too. Nothing to do with the Crows who drilled deep into their mountains, desperate to fulfil the coal quotas set by Dragon Province.

She smiles softly. 'Where is my Grasshopper sister?'

Nobody speaks.

'She is here? Is she not?'

'I saw her earlier, Divine Majesty,' Nergüi says, somehow raising their head without wobbling their colossal headpiece. 'I believe she was trying to escape out of a window.'

Eudora laughs lightly. 'Our sister is full of the Goddess's spirit.'

'We should find her,' Leofric says in his baritone. 'You know how wild those Grasshoppers are. Could be destroying something as we speak.'

Eudora tilts her head. 'Once our sister has been found, we will gather at the table. Today is the feast of the Dragon, and I will begin the festival by recounting the legend that has marked all our existences.'

Eudora is perfect. The perfect glimmering heir to a nation of a thousand years of peace. And if I want to escape this hellscape, I'm going to have to do something monumental to blast that disciplined smile from her face.

Wyatt stands frozen, tracking Eudora around the room as if she will disappear from existence if he breaks eye contact.

'Still in love with her then?'

He spins to me. 'Stop talking to me!'

'So cute.' I lean forward. 'I'm sure she'll be queuing up to change your diaper.'

'I don't wear diapers! If anyone does, it's you – you self-absorbed child.'

Ohh, this bear bites.

'Wyatt!' I gasp with mock shock. 'I didn't know you felt that way.'

'Of course you didn't,' he snaps. 'You've never made an effort with me. I bet you don't even know *why* I hate you, d'ya?'

So many possibilities.

'Jasper's Blessing ceremony. You and that Crow boy following you like a shadow. You two idiots thought it was funny to throw curry on me.'

'To be fair, it *was* funny.'

'Eudora *saw me*! It was the first time I spoke to her! And thanks to you I was covered in masala.' He grips his chest, gasping for breath.

'Goddess. You really think she gave a shit? She loves us all. You just heard her. Can't get enough of us.'

'I don't want her to love me like she loves you,' he says ruefully.

I do feel a little sorry for him, but I don't have time to sympathize with sad sacks. 'She needs an heir, Wyatt. Else the empire goes to shit.' All of us do, but it's especially important for Dragon Province. Goddess knows what would happen to the Bandage if the emperor didn't pass his Blessing on. A Blessing so vital it has its own name – the Primus Blessing.

'What're you trying to say?'

'Seeing as you get breathless climbing on to a chair, I'm thinking she needs someone with a bit more stamina.'

He throws down his skinny arms. 'We *will* be married, and when I'm her consort I won't be inviting—'

Before Wyatt can finish what sounds like the lamest threat ever, a new voice speaks.

'The Goddess's mercy to you both, my two favourite

Blessed.' A figure has appeared beside Wyatt – a sheet of pastel-pink hair, cloth bunny ears nestled atop his head, and white silken robes, sleeves so long I suspect he's smuggling something in there. Shinjiro. Bunnerfly Province. Because the monks couldn't have a normal old animal like everyone else. They had to have a flying bunny. 'I hope I am not interrupting, Ganymedes, but may I borrow this cuddly bear?'

'Please, for the love of the Goddess – do.' Wyatt is already dragging Shinjiro from the bar.

My gaze travels the room and rests on *him*. I'd give anything to be thirteen again, Ravi giggling as I unleashed whatever devious plan I'd devised. He never took the other provinces seriously back then, because they completely disregarded us – the fisherman and the cave-dweller. It was *them* and *us*.

Now there is no us. There is only *me*.

I sink behind the bar, nursing my throbbing head. I need it to settle before I unleash my final hand. I have to do everything right. A clean break. No loose ends.

'Where's the little gremlin?' Leofric's voice booms.

'I've looked everywhere,' Jasper says. 'She's vanished.'

'People don't just vanish. *Find her.*'

Their footsteps thunder away. I rub my hands down my face, but then freeze.

There's candy. And it's floating.

A white and red sweet rises out of a jar beneath the bar, unwraps itself, then disappears into thin air. The wrapper drifts to the floor.

Maybe I should have checked what was in that alcohol.

I reach into the empty space and snatch a handful of something very *real*. It tries to wriggle away, but I crawl beneath the bar and lower my voice.

'I've got enough shit on my plate to start believing ghosts are real. Please don't tell me ghosts are real.'

37

Silence.

Then a high-pitched *pop*.

A girl appears. A tiny thing, all elbows and knees. Dark brown skin and a round mass of curly lilac hair that takes up almost as much space beneath the bar as her body.

'Ah, little Grasshopper,' I sigh. 'Nice to meet you. I'm the fish guy. You can call me Dee.' *Somebody might as well.*

She stares, as silent as the grave. Her purple eyes are wide and curious, but her body trembles. Green is reserved for the empress, so she's dressed in a hideous brown dress that looks as much a hand-me-down as my costume.

I've met a handful of Grasshoppers, and they were all loud, unfiltered and excessively fun. The kind of people who would keep you up all night with thumping music, then make you a breakfast fit for the emperor.

But this girl looks as if she would run screaming from a party. In fact, she looks very close to doing exactly that.

'Those sweets are shit. Try these.' I shove my hand into my pocket and offer a handful of slightly crushed meringue cookies.

Her hand darts out and seizes them, like a cat swiping a bowl of cream.

'How old are you, little grasshopper? I'm twenty-two and a quarter.'

She nibbles the corner of the cookie. 'Six.'

That's young for a Blessed. In such situations, the previous dux will usually act as regent until the Blessed is old enough to lead.

A voice behind us. 'What if she fell overboard?'

'Nothing. The ship is powered by the emperor's Blessing, we can't stop for her,' Leofric says.

Nice. Leave a six-year-old to drown. Very on brand for Leoprick.

The Tiger Blessed is known as the 'shield', a bodyguard role fulfilled by every Tiger Blessed since records began, but that position is limited to guarding the empress. Nobody else. As he has made abundantly clear, I do not think my death would be of any great concern to him. Neither will Grasshopper's, evidently.

Speaking of which – she's vanished again.

'Badass Blessing. They're gone, by the way.'

With a *pop*, she returns. 'What can you do?'

'What *can't* I do?'

She fingers a pendant hanging from her neck. I don't recognize the material; it's brown and dull, whittled into the shape of a grasshopper. 'I don't want to be here.'

'I know the feeling.'

'Momma . . .' She gasps a shuddering breath. 'Momma left me here all alone. Now everyone's yelling at me. I didn't *do* anything.' She curls inwards, cradling her knees to her chest. 'I wanna go home.'

'Find the gremlin!' comes Leofric's booming voice. 'Find her and tie her to the mast if you have to.'

Grasshopper cringes. 'Why do they hate me?'

Because she's a lower province – only one above Fish. The truth is simple, but I won't break it to her.

I shuffle closer. 'Hey, look at me.'

Her face rises over her knees.

'They don't hate you. Why would they? You're cool. You can disappear!'

She sniffs.

'Besides, you're the last to show your Blessing – this trip wouldn't be happening without you. So this is *your* party. Your big Blessing bash. You deserve to have some fun.'

'Like singing?'

Grasshoppers and their singing. Considering they live in

the rainforest from hell, maybe singing is as far as fun goes there.

'I was thinking something different . . .' I poke my head over the bar and she mirrors me. 'Tell me, little Grasshopper . . .' I motion over the crowd. 'Which of these bollocks upset you the most? Who shall we get revenge on?'

Her bottom lip pouts out. 'All of them.'

'Wonderful choice.' I poke her button nose.

She looks very proud of herself. 'What are you going to do?'

I sway to my feet. 'Piss them off.'

'Piss on them?'

'We'll see how things pan out.'

I take a few steps. My head pounds and the ground sways. Shit. One foot in front of the other. *Easy does it, Dee.*

I don't need a reason to wreck this party. It's the main objective. But having another one invigorates my spirit.

You see, I'm doing it for the kids.

I don't plan to climb on to the table, but it feels right. Plates clatter to the floor, making the whole thing less elegant than I intended.

Jasper stares at me, mouthing, *Get the hell down.* But it's too late.

'Attention, everyone!' I yell.

Every pair of eyes turns to me. Grasshopper's poof of hair crowns over the top of the bar. The silence is deafening.

Eudora's hallowed gaze meets mine. The flash of green almost makes me fall to my knees and beg for divine forgiveness.

Maybe this was a terrible idea.

No. Definitely not. It's the best idea I've ever had. No regrets.

'Today is a special day. A thousand years of peace! Go us!'

40

My voice slurs. 'And all the costumes have been amazing.' I raise a glass to Nergüi. 'You really brought it.'

I ignore the knowing smile Nergüi gives me, as if somehow they're even aware of this plan.

I fiddle with the straps on my clothes. 'But I must confess I think I'm going to win the contest.'

There isn't a contest.

'I've been working on this for about . . . a year? Was not cheap, let me tell you.'

'Get down immediately,' Leofric demands. I'm not sure why he's annoyed. It's not his party I'm ruining.

'But I think you'll agree it's a showstopper.'

I release the final straps. The costume drops, and the gasp of the crowd is the only applause I need.

Every inch of me – from my ankle boots to my trousers to my hooded jacket – is dazzling with iridescent blue. I reach into my hood and tug a pair of goggles atop my head. I am a gleaming beautiful fish. Who would have guessed that divinium, when cut into discs and attached to clothes, could look like scales?

There are hundreds. A fortune of sacred stones. Enough to keep the Bandage safe for a year. Enough to keep Concordia safe for a year.

Instead, I've used them for a fish costume.

And I look fucking incredible.

Chapter Three

Day One – Feast of the Dragon

Midnight

Setting myself on fire would have caused less devastation.

The wall of faces before me displays the entire range of human emotion.

Jasper furious, flames shooting from his mouth, as Leofric holds him back, fuming enough to spit fire himself.

Cordelia sobbing. She seems to like sobbing.

Eudora, so tight-lipped she's barely lipped at all. For a whisper of a second, she looks human.

Then there's Ravi, eyes fixed upon me with an expression I have never witnessed upon his face. In that rush of a moment, I cannot place it.

My strut up and down the table probably didn't help the situation. But it felt necessary. It was definitely necessary.

As Eudora hastily summons the Blessed to the table, Grasshopper bounds over and sits beside me. She squirms gleefully, rapturous eyes fixed upon me as if *I'm* the empress.

Everyone else has moved their chairs to occupy the top

half of the table. Even Eska, my stabby neighbour, seems to possess capacity to hate me more than she already did.

'Guys,' I say. 'There's plenty of room here.'

'A little in poor taste, Ganymedes,' Shinjiro says, leaning as far over as he can without entering the outcast half. 'Divinium is essential for our survival. And rather rare. I fear you may have inadvertently upset some people.'

'I will burn every limb from your body,' Jasper snarls.

'It's just a costume.' I stand and wiggle my butt at them. 'See? I have a fish tail.'

'Tail!' Grasshopper tugs it.

'You ain't got a single ounce of shame.' Wyatt has made a valiant effort to reach the head of the table beside Eudora, but Leofric is blocking his access with well-practised positioning of his bulk.

Tendai stares with the kind of disbelief a parent reserves for a child who has done something remarkably stupid. It's the longest she's ever looked at me.

'Sit *down*, Fish,' Leofric spits.

I shrug and do so.

I try to prevent the relief reading on my face.

They're convinced. Which is just as well, because – small confession – I'm not *actually* wearing divinium. Shinjiro's right, the stuff's impossible to get, and besides, the whole endangering-hundreds-of-lives thing sat uneasily in my gut. It's a similar gemstone replacement, painstakingly painted by yours truly. Fakinium, if you will.

Using divinium was never the point. I just needed them to believe I had.

And they do. Mission success. They all loathe me.

If I'm lucky, I'll be banned from all summits. If I'm extra lucky, they'll strip me of the dux title too.

'We should string him up from his ankles,' Jasper growls.

'I will do the beating,' Eska volunteers.

I wring my hands. Perhaps this worked a little too well. 'Steady on, no need for bodily harm.'

Eudora watches as they squabble over who gets to injure which of my limbs, then clears her throat.

The table falls silent.

'This is an offence against the empire, and so it falls upon me to deal with it. And I will once we return to the capital,' she says calmly. 'But I will not allow it to sow discord on this hallowed pilgrimage. Our traditions must be upheld. Nobody is to harm Ganymedes without my instruction.'

I don't like the second part of that sentence. But I'll take it.

'And so we will continue as planned.' She rises. 'I will begin our journey by recounting the legend upon which the Empire of Concordia is built – that which has led us twelve here today.'

Shinjiro clasps his hands. 'Wonderful. This is my favourite.'

As Eudora's dulcet tones fill the room, the lights dim until she's encased in an orb of silver:

'Long ago, Concordia was a place of beasts, divided by land and culture. For a thousand years, these beasts fought one another. Tiger fought dragon, tortoise fought bear and crow fought spider. As their kin fell, others rose and continued the fight. The cycle of discord was eternal.

'Then the great flood came.

'The beasts were so concerned with fighting one another they did not notice the tides swallowing their lands. On and on they fought, climbing higher as the waters rose around them, engulfing the plains and fields and forests that were once their homes.

'By the time the beasts noticed the flood, the only sanctuary

44

was the highest point of Concordia – the sacred mountain. Desperate, the beasts climbed the mountain. At the summit, they saw a woman.

'Her hair was the colour of fresh spring roots, her skin the brown of the earth. When she spoke, it was the noise of a babbling brook. "I am the Goddess of all that is and all that was and all that will be."

'The dragon, the largest and bravest of the beasts, came forth. "O wise and gentle Goddess, our lands are drowning. Bestow upon me the power to push back the tide."

'But the Goddess shook her head. "To do this will require all my power. You are not strong enough, Dragon. My power will destroy you."

'But the dragon was reckless and proud. "Do you not see my long body? My glimmering scales? My sharp teeth? Who but I is strong enough to bear your power?"

'The Goddess bowed her head. "So it will be." But as her power entered him, the dragon fell to the earth, writhing in agony.

'Seeing his pain, the tiger stepped forward. "I cannot let the dragon suffer. Let me help bear this burden."

'And so the Goddess split her power in two. But it was not enough. The tiger joined the dragon in pain.

'The spider descended from a web. "These two are strong. But I am strong in different ways. I will also bear this burden."

'The tortoise emerged from its shell. "I have lived longer than any other. My mind is powerful enough to bear this burden."

'And so, the power was split four ways. But still, it was not enough.

'The elephant was next. "I am a mother to hundreds. I will bear this burden as I have borne my young."

'The bunnerfly approached. "We have spoken before,

Goddess. I am one of your children. Surely I can bear this burden?"

'But even spread six ways, it still was not enough.

'Seeing their pain, the ox offered itself. "I am strong, and sturdy. Give me the pain and I will bear it."

'"And I." The crow spoke. "I have eyes that see all over the lands. I notice things others do not. I will help bear this burden."

'But even split eight ways, it was not enough.

'"Let me help," said the bear. "For I am daring and can traverse any terrain. It would be an honour to die bearing this burden."

'The ermine scurried forward. "I have braved the frozen tundra for millennia. My strength is unmatched, this burden is nothing to me."

'Finally, the grasshopper appeared. "My life is constant danger, but I still prevail. This burden is mine to bear also."

'And so, the power was split eleven ways. But still the animals were consumed by pain. As the water rose around them, all seemed lost.

'In those final moments, a small voice spoke. "I can help." A head emerged from the water. It was a fish. "I am but one in a school of thousands, and the water is my home. But I cannot bear to see your pain. I will help because I can."

'As the final piece of the Goddess's power was bestowed upon the fish, the pain left the dragon's body. It faced the tide. With the burden of power shouldered by the other beasts, it was able to summon the Goddess's Blessing and push back the ocean. The waters drained from the land and returned to the sea.

'From that day, the twelve animals agreed to never again raise their hands in violence against each other. To ensure the dragon could keep their lands protected, they vowed to forever shoulder their piece of the Goddess's Blessing.'

Shinjiro claps enthusiastically. 'Simply enchanting. It's finer every time you tell it, Divine Highness.'

The room fills with light, and the spotlight upon Eudora vanishes.

She'd told the edited version, of course. No need to mention the crab and mess up the whole 'united forever' angle.

Wyatt claps with an enthusiasm which is somewhat – scratch that – incredibly awkward. 'Great! You're just . . . great . . .'

Eudora smiles placidly. 'We twelve were chosen by the Goddess to shoulder her power, and it is our duty to keep our empire protected from outside dangers.' Her gaze flashes to my costume. 'Though much of that burden falls to me, I cannot amply express my thanks for the sacrifice you make in bearing your Blessings. Our lives may suffer, but our lands are safe.'

That's the double-edged sword of a Blessing. You get a cool power, but the strain on the body shortens your lifespan. You're 'blessed' to die young.

Almost everyone here will be dead before they reach fifty. I'll outlive every damn one of them. It doesn't feel as good as it should, especially with a six-year-old gazing up at me.

'The *Dragon's Dawn* will travel to the mountain where the Blessing was first bestowed upon our ancestors. In eleven days, we will climb to the summit and give thanks to the Goddess, united once more.'

Worst trip ever. I get to climb a cold-arse mountain to say some prayers for a Blessing I never even got. The others get to thank the Goddess for the gift of an early death. She could have pushed the flood back herself and saved us all this trauma. Cheers, you spiteful old git.

'Enjoy the celebrations. And remember, though we may have our differences, we are all brothers and sisters.' Eudora raises her glass, and the others follow. 'Let us not forget the ones we have lost. Lysander should be here, celebrating our ascension. Life is precious. We should not squander it.'

Tendai throws back her drink. 'I would have liked to have said farewell at his funeral. A shame my invitation was lost.'

Along with mine and Wyatt's.

Shinjiro clears his throat. 'It is a pertinent reminder of how sacred our lives are. You were chosen by the Goddess; you must honour her by looking after your bodies – the vessels of her Blessing.'

Cordelia's hair hangs over her face. Leofric is a statue. All unmoving, hard lines. I always suspected he had more love for Lysander than he does for even the All-Mother. But his expression betrays nothing.

'Please, All-Mother, forgive the interruption.' It's Cordelia. She's leapt to her feet, tears gleaming.

'Do you have something to add, sister?' Eudora asks.

'I . . .' She fiddles with her bodice. 'Something to . . . announce, rather.' She glances at Ravi.

He sits silent and still for what feels like an eternity, staring down at the tablecloth. Eventually, Cordelia places her hand on his shoulder. He looks up, startled, as if woken from some deep sleep.

He rises, eyes darting over the table. Briefly, they fix upon me.

'Cordelia and I . . .' He pauses, pushing his hair away from those killer cheekbones. 'We're getting married.'

Someone is saying, 'How wonderful.' Someone else is clapping. But my world sways.

I'm on the floor but don't remember falling. I try to scramble to my feet but crash into the table. A plate smashes.

Eudora gasps and looks at me. 'Are you quite all right?'

'I'M FINE.'

Did I just yell that?

They're all staring. But this time, I don't want them to see me. Not now.

My stomach squirms. Dragon's dick. I'm going to vomit.

Leofric leaps up. 'Stop making a fool of yourself, Fish, and—'

I'm away before the Tiger can snarl his command, staggering from the room with my hand to my mouth.

*

I find a bathroom with four stalls on the upper floor of the ballroom, just in time. And time is very much of the essence.

I was wrong. I don't vomit. I vomit *and* shit. Always nice to exceed your expectations.

At least I didn't do it in front of Ravi.

Ravi, who – despite years of separation – I always believed would return to me. Because I felt it instantly when I saw him – that thread which connects his heart to mine.

There are moments that cannot be minimized, forgotten or swept aside. And ours is tangible – a cloak I wrap around myself when the night is cold and dark.

I assumed secrets uttered in a cave on a cliff in a storm had woven our hearts together. Secrets that could devastate our lives. I had trusted him. Not for a moment did I hesitate to show Ravi the hollow centre of myself. I tore down all my walls for him.

But then he had left, hadn't he? I showed him what I was; then he left. And now he's replaced me with some skinny blonde who can barely whisper her own name. What did she give him that I could not? Which part of me is lacking?

'Who is she?' I mutter, then unleash another mouthful of vomit into the bog.

Just as well I've upset them enough to never be welcomed

49

back. Just as well I'll never see him again. Yeah. It's good. Great. *Fab.*

'You stupid fucking idiot.' Surprisingly, it's not my subconscious speaking, but an actual human.

There is no mercy. Couldn't even let a pissfish drown himself in the toilet.

'Everyone is going to see what a fool you are.'

That can't be about me. I never pretend to be anything but a fool.

'You're a total disappointment.'

The high voice is followed by a dull thump.

I swing the door open and miraculously stagger to my feet without vomiting.

'Idiot!'

Thump.

I round the corner and stop dead.

Standing before the sinks, slamming her head into the bathroom mirror, is the Imperial Majesty, All-Mother and Heir Apparent of Concordia.

Eudora glares groggily at her reflection, divine green hair slipping from plaits. 'They see right through you.' Then, in the mirror, her eyes fix on me.

She turns with a screech, perfect face flooded with emotion. It looks bizarre, like a piece of classic art come to life. 'This is a girl's toilet!'

'I didn't have time to che—'

She slams her palm into my chest. Once. Twice. I'm being gently battered by the Goddess Incarnate.

I grab her arms. 'I only came here to vomit. So, if you want your private time to . . . bang your head against mirrors and insult your reflection, who am I to judge?'

'I was just . . .' Her eyes travel, trying to think of any possible way to explain *that*.

'I'd go with "practising for a play".' I lower my voice. 'Are you . . . all right?'

'I'm fine.'

'But you—'

'I said I'm fine,' she says stiffly.

She clearly isn't. But I don't want to make her more uncomfortable than I already have.

I release her arms. 'Don't worry. Your secret's safe with me.'

'I do not have any secrets.' Her voice returns to that plummy measured tone. 'I am the Goddess Incarnate, my life is lived in service to—'

'You said "fuck".'

She throws her arms down. 'I did not say "fuck"!'

'And again!' I point at her. 'Would the Goddess approve of "fuck"?'

'I would . . . need to consult Shinjiro.'

'Feels good, doesn't it? How can one syllable feel so good? Fuck!' I say, then louder: 'Fuck!'

She purses her lips.

I approach the mirror. Dragon's dick. I've got vomit all over my masterpiece. I wet a towel and attempt to dab my jacket clean.

Eudora returns to the mirror, adjusting the hair she banged out of place. 'We've never spoken before, have we?'

'No.' I scrub the stones. 'Although I have said "Yes, ma'am". And one time "Thank you, ma'am".'

'Do not call me ma'am. I'm younger than you.'

I bow my head. 'Whatever you say, ma'am.'

She hits me again.

'This is an assault upon your loyal subjects.'

Her green eyes batter down my fakinium-laden form. 'I don't see a loyal subject here.'

'Fair.'

She pulls out blusher from *somewhere* and applies it to her cheeks. 'I'll be seizing that outfit the moment we return to the capital.'

Not ideal. I'll have to throw it overboard before she has the chance.

'You won't look as good in it as me.'

A twitch. Her throat trembles. She's trying not to laugh.

I *may* have misjudged this woman. I wonder how many laughs she's repressed throughout her life.

'Surprised to find you alone,' I say. 'I don't think I've ever seen you without that lumbering brute.'

'Leo isn't that bad.' She tucks a curl behind her ear. 'He has it tough. His role demands certain things. But he *is* hard to shake, especially today. I think he suspects all of you have it in your minds to slit my throat. Honestly, he's already wearing the imperial collar, did you see?'

I didn't. 'It's hard to notice jewellery on a man wearing tiger print on tiger print.'

Her throat trembles again. I've decided it's my life's ambition to make this woman laugh.

The imperial collar isn't strictly jewellery. It's a goddess-awful metal contraption the shields wear upon the heir's succession, to symbolize their loyalty and obedience. It's locked tight and the Dragon Blessed holds the only key.

'Leo is dedicated,' she says evenly. 'But I don't know why he's wearing that ridiculous thing already. It's not like I'm empress yet. I don't even have the key.'

So, it's not the *actual* collar. It's a copy. 'What a twat.'

'I must warn you: he is outside the toilet.'

'Thanks for the heads-up,' I say. 'He wants to crush my trachea, I think.'

'I believe everyone seems keen on that.'

Guess that's 'mission success'.

'I don't see you crushing it.' I gesture to her heels. 'And man alive, you could do some real damage.'

Her mirror version meets my gaze. 'Give me time.' She smirks.

Blessed hells. The Goddess Incarnate just smirked at me.

'If I had to choose one person to crush my trachea.' I click my fingers at her.

'Truly, I'm honoured.'

She was definitely crying. Her eyes are red, and her nose a little wet.

I seize a tissue box. 'Does her highness need a tissue for her blessed snot?'

She takes one. 'How is it that you speak to me like that?'

'I'm the disgraced son of the lowest province in the entire empire. I haven't got much to lose.'

She dabs at her nose. 'I could have you flogged.'

'Oooh, the suspense. First a trachea crushing then a flogging. You really are spoiling me.'

She snorts, then covers her mouth in horror.

I just stare. The All-Mother *snorts*.

Goddess, she's enchanting. Even snotty and snorty she's the most captivating thing I've ever seen. It's like sharing a mirror with a sunrise. No wonder Wyatt goes all gooey-eyed over her.

She lowers the tissue. 'Fish, why did you do that?'

'What?'

'Act like a fool? Purposely offend them?' Her emerald gaze pins me. 'Why do you push them away?'

Her questions catch me off guard, like an arrow to the knee. 'I'm not pushing anyone away. I spoke to most of them.'

'There are many ways to build walls.'

I almost gag. 'I'm not building any walls.'

'You're going to have to lie better than that if you're going to be a dux.'

'I don't think I can still be a dux, can I? Bit unsuitable, after all this.' I try to strip the pleading from my voice.

As she studies me, I sense something behind her eyes – not judgement or pity, something far more personal. 'The Goddess has chosen us. We all must do our duty.'

My body sags.

'You know the legend,' she says softly, returning to the mirror. 'We must all make our *sacrifices*.' There is a certain heaviness to that word.

I edge closer. 'Are you worried about something?'

'Aren't you? Our lives are going to change forever when we reach that mountain.'

'Yours won't. Until your father dies you won't get his Blessing.' The Primus Blessing is unique, it only passes to heirs upon the death of the previous holder.

'He's not got long.'

A chill creeps down my spine. Cutting your lifespan in half isn't ideal, but it's better than what happens to the Dragon Blessed. They get to live a normal lifespan, but maintaining the Bandage drains them not only of their lifeblood, but also their sanity, their very *selves*. The emperor is a shell now. Fuel to maintain a wall which is crumbling regardless of the magic he pours into it.

All Dragon Blessed go out the same way – soulless shadows of the men and women they were.

Eudora grips the sink. Green nails tap the porcelain.

I hover awkwardly, wondering how to comfort someone who knows they will become a husk.

But it turns out I don't need to. She breathes deeply, and then faces her reflection. 'I do not like social gatherings. They expect me to be perfect. I am not perfect.' She dabs a lingering tear. 'But bearing the Primus Blessing – using it to sustain the Bandage – it's what I was born to do. People can live and die without making a mark upon the world. I get to die to protect it. To be Concordia's shield against the Crabs and save the lives of millions. If bleeding out my soul is the price of that, it is really not that high.' She turns to me. She has always been beautiful. Always poised and elegant. But in this moment, I think Eudora is the strongest person in the empire.

'I am going to be the best damn fuel in Concordia's history.'

'Of course you will,' I say breathlessly. 'The dragon is the hero of the legend, after all.'

A crease forms between her eyebrows. 'What?'

'The legend. The dragon's the hero.'

She releases a huff of a laugh, like my tutor when I miss something obvious. 'The dragon is not the hero.'

'The dragon is the first to offer itself up. It sacrifices—'

'Its life to save its life. So do the others. They were going to die. What did they have to lose?'

'Nothing, I guess.'

A twitch of a smile. 'And that's why you're wrong. The hero isn't the dragon. The hero is the fish.'

My arms drop. 'The fish?'

'The fish did not have to share the burden. The fish could have survived without it. But it sacrificed itself because it saw the suffering of others. The world would have been doomed without the fish.' She holds my gaze, her expression utterly serious. And in that moment, I am, for once, speechless.

*

I exit the toilet at pace, but Leofric isn't around, thank fuck. I wasn't joking about the trachea crushing.

Grasshopper bounds over as I walk on to the ballroom floor. I surrender the remains of the cookies to her eager hands and scan the crowd.

Eska stands alone, fingering that blade as if she expects one of her loathed mammoths to crash through the wall.

Jasper is glaring at me, smoke drifting from his mouth. Cordelia rambles at him, so focused on what she's jabbering on about she doesn't notice he's not listening.

A dangerous part of me wants to approach her, demand she reveal how she and Ravi got together. She's not his type. She's not *me*.

'You're certainly hard to miss.'

I yelp and grip my chest.

Shinjiro is behind me. His pearlescent skin and white monk robes make him appear otherworldly, as if he's glowing from inside with the Goddess's light.

Meanwhile, Wyatt is beside him, looking like some contemptuous hobgoblin captured from beyond the Bandage.

'Having a good night, fellas?' I ask.

Wyatt grunts at Shinjiro, 'Please can we stop talking to them? You said you'd start a conversation between me and Eudora.'

We're a 'them' now? I stare at Grasshopper, her mouth smeared with sugar. Poor girl.

'Patience.' Shinjiro bats a hand at Wyatt. 'I believe I understand what your goal was with this outfit, Ganymedes. I have sensed discord amongst the Blessed in the past year. But your "stunt" has united them in – well – hate against you. Just look at Tendai and Nergüi.'

The Elephant and Spider – that terrifying combination – are speaking in low voices. But although Nergüi is wearing something resembling a smile, Tendai looks as if she's working out the ways she could dismember Nergüi without anyone noticing.

'Those two have been in discord most of their lives,' Shinjiro says. 'But your trick has worked wonders! However, to rely on such extreme emotions to achieve unity is not in accordance with the Goddess's wishes. A calm mind achieves more than an unbalanced one.'

As Shinjiro rabbits on, I look for Ravi. He's sitting alone, head in his hands, expression shadowed by his dark hair.

It reminds me of the first time I saw him. Thirteen years old, tall and lanky but wrapped in layers of wool, bundled up like a child venturing out into the snow for the first time. He sat, wringing his hands, unable to raise his gaze from his own feet. Back then, his accent was so thick, nobody could understand him. So they laughed instead. Then he stopped speaking completely.

I was tempted to join them. I needed to blend in after all, to sell the lie.

But I couldn't let that mute boy suffer. He didn't fit in. Neither did I. I felt the wall build before him, a circle of bricks around his ankles. I had to stop it, before it grew too high to break.

In Fish Province, if someone needs help, you offer it to them. No questions asked. It's what unites people in the cold winters, when we ship out every last fish to people we will never meet, and all we have left are bones.

So, I threw cake at Ravi.

He almost cried.

But then I smiled, and told him I liked his boots.

His wall shattered. All the tension left his body. And he smiled – unguarded and genuine and wonderful. As if I had done something miraculous, not just ruined his clothes.

I knew then nobody had ever treated this boy with kindness. I also knew I would never let him place another brick at his feet.

He threw the cake back. We were inseparable from that moment.

Bollocks to it. Fiancée or not, this is *Ravi*. My Ravi. Deep down, he's still that boy, hoping someone will rescue him. If I speak to him alone, he'll realize he doesn't need to change who he is to fit in with them. He doesn't need to change at all.

But as I move, a voice almost shatters my eardrums.

'What have you done with her?' It's that brute, Leofric. He's manhandling Wyatt. Shaking his shoulders so hard the boy's head rocks on his skinny neck.

Grasshopper vanishes with a *pop*.

Wyatt flails uselessly. 'I-I-I haven't. I don't know what—'

'Listen to me, freak,' he snarls. 'I see the way you look at her. Don't you understand "no"? If you've touched—'

'Calm down, pussy cat.' I place a hand on his arm. 'Bear Province won't be pleased if you shake the last wisps of life out of their heir.'

His gaze settles on me. 'You're up to something, Fish. If you don't tell me where—'

Then we're plunged into darkness.

Someone screams. Probably Cordelia. The wimp.

'Has the ship stopped moving?' Shinjiro asks, as if politely commenting on the weather. 'That would be an awful shame. It's powered by the emperor's Blessing so that probably means he's dead.'

Nobody responds.

The lights blaze with sudden colour, momentarily blinding me.

And because of that, I hear Wyatt before I see anything.

The boy wails, desperate keening noises like the cry of a

wounded animal. Then the sound snaps off. When my vision returns, he's in Shinjiro's arms, eyes rolling to the back of his head.

Leofric is utterly pale, his expression stripped and empty, tree-trunk arms limp at his sides. I follow his gaze in the silence, all the way up to the chandelier. All the way up to the body.

I didn't think anything could steal my thunder tonight. As far as they know, I'm wearing millions in life-saving divinium. Nothing could cause more uproar.

Nothing, that is, except the lifeless, hanging body of the heir apparent of Concordia.

Chapter Four

Day Two – Feast of the Tiger

Morning

I wake to Grasshopper's foot on my face.

I surrendered my bed to her last night. When I tried to leave her in her cabin, she screamed like a banshee. I don't really blame the kid; she did just encounter a corpse.

This morning, however, she seemed worryingly unscarred: 'Deedee!' she chirps. 'Deedee!'

'I'm awake.' I push myself off the floor, hair stuck to my cheeks with drool.

Instead of Grasshopper's adorable visage, I come face to face with the curious jade eyes of a dragon. A plump fluffy thing the size of a cat. It looks like a miniature version of the Dragon Province's animal – stubs of antlers and a sleek green mane. Also, it's wearing a bowtie.

It politely says, 'Master Fish.'

Dragons, for the record, don't exist in Concordia. Jasper makes wild claims about the Bandage, but there are none in the empire. And they definitely don't talk.

'I've finally cracked.'

The dragon's long ears perk up. 'Not cracked, Master Fish. You're as sane as you were when you set foot on this ship.'

I notice he doesn't directly call me sane.

'I am a server, formed by the emperor's Blessing, created to attend to your needs on this pilgrimage. Each server is assigned to one Blessed. We are responsible for preparing your meals, doing your laundry, and ensuring the ship is in a workable condition. How may I be of use, Master Fish?'

The emperor's power never ceases to amaze me. He's simultaneously maintaining the Bandage, powering this ship, and creating twelve of these adorable apparitions.

'You'll do anything?'

He levels his eyes at me in a manner not far from accusatory. 'Anything that does not disgrace me.'

I clear my throat. 'What do I call you?'

'I am Server Twelve.'

'Not very catchy.'

'We advise our masters to name us; might I suggest something that lightens your mood?' His white teeth flash. 'The atmosphere aboard is rather sombre.'

Ravi? Nah, too weird. Food, then. 'Dumpling.'

If 'Dumpling' is insulted, he does a stellar job of hiding it. 'Wonderful choice.'

'Deedee!' Grasshopper is half hugging, half smothering her own miniature dragon. Its purple, mournful eyes meet mine.

'What is it, Grasshopper?'

'No. Her name is Deedee. Something that makes me happy. Doubled!'

I'm so touched, I can't form words.

I sway to my feet. 'Dumpling, when is the ship returning to the capital?'

He adjusts his bowtie. 'The voyage to the mountain will take eleven more days. Upon arrival—'

'No. I mean, because of Eudora's—'

'Death!' Grasshopper screams with such glee I wonder if she planned it herself. When I stare at her, she says, 'She will turn to dirt and the circle is complete.' In a totally-not-at-all creepy way.

'Um . . . Dumpling?'

More bowtie shifting. 'I follow my creator's commands. The ship is not to stop for *any* reason.'

'There wasn't a caveat for his only heir dying?' My words awaken unexpected pain in my chest. A flash of memory. Her body hanging. I push it aside.

Dumpling's eyes go blank, as if checking records. 'No caveats. The journey will continue as planned. You will reach the mountain in eleven days.'

Eleven days with a royal corpse on board. That'll lighten the mood.

I crack my aching back. With daylight streaming through the circular window, I can finally examine my cabin.

The cramped space is decked out to look exactly like Fish Province. The bed, wardrobe and desk are crafted from drift-wood, held together with sailing rope. The floor resembles a sandy beach, with dotted seashells. It doesn't *feel* like sand, thankfully. I love my province, but I don't want to be washing that out of my arse crack for the next eleven days.

The walls display an illusion of the ocean. White waves break against a golden shore. The sound of the sea surrounds me. The constant rush of the waves, the creak of sails. It even *smells* like home – a fresh salty breeze.

Fisherfolk are not the smartest, most ambitious, or even most skilled, but they are good, honest people. Because our lives follow the migrations of the piscero, they have remained unchanged for generations. Fish Province has a permanency, a stability that has been lacking in every other aspect of my life. Even if I did lie to those good people for nine years of it.

'Dumpling, can you change the walls?'

'To what, Master Fish?'

'Just make them blank.'

The water vanishes and my shoulders relax.

'Breakfast is being served in the dining room.' Dumpling nods, ears flopping. 'We encourage you to attend and form lasting friendships with your fellow Blessed.'

'That'll be hard in these.' I pluck at my clothes. I haven't changed since last night. 'Bring me the clothes I packed, please.'

Dumpling's tail twitches. 'I'm afraid I cannot do that.'

'Don't tell me they weren't brought aboard?'

'They were. Your clothes arrived before you, Master Fish.'

'Where are they then?'

He smiles, all sharp teeth. 'Your clothes are being withheld from you.'

I stare. 'Why?'

'Because the command to withhold your clothes was given to a server before you commanded me to retrieve them.'

'Who gave the command?'

He clasps his paws. 'Commands between master and server are confidential.'

'How can I overrule it?'

'The command can only be overruled if the person who gave it dismisses it. Or they die, upon which their server will cease to exist.'

I run my palms over the discs of fakinium.

It isn't the strangest thing to happen in the past twelve hours, but something about it sits uneasily.

'Dee looks great in shiny blue crystals!' Grasshopper pokes at them.

'Did you tell your server to take my clothes?'

She shakes her head.

'You're not lying?'

'Back home we speak what's in our hearts,' she says – which is lovely. And then: 'Because any day a tree can fall and crush your skull.' Which is less so.

'True.' I hold out my arm. 'Shall we dine, my lady?'

*

We're as welcome at breakfast as a turd in a swimming pool.

'You are still wearing that costume,' Nergüi states, spooning cream on to a thick heel of bread. 'Impressive.'

'I'll tear it off your body,' Jasper growls.

'Jasper,' I gasp. 'You're underage!'

He puffs out a huff of smoke.

As well as the bearer of immense power, Emperor Eugenios may be the most *flamboyant* person in existence. Every room on this ship is decorated like the swan song of a dying eccentric.

The dining hall is beneath sea level, so you'd expect it to be dark. But he's placed round glowing balls inside, the size of buoys. They're not attached to anything, but instead hover ominously overhead. The room is inlaid with wood panelling adorned with jade and crystal. Paintings of emperors and empresses stare down at me with immense displeasure.

The centrepiece is a gigantic table, reflecting the orange light of those hovering balls of doom. Twelve chairs are placed around it, each crafted out of what I assume is excessively expensive rock that fifty Crow miners died extracting. Each slab is sculpted to resemble a province animal in the according colour, and while most of the chairs are impressive, my white fish with its bulging yellow eyes is somewhat less intimidating.

Ravi isn't here, and I don't see Wyatt or Leofric either. Eska is also not present, thank the Goddess. I don't fancy sitting next to her in the vicinity of cutlery.

But the biggest absence is at the head of the table, where a snarling dragon throne, jade wings outstretched, stands empty.

The seats are ordered in alternating fashion. Dragon at the head with, on its left-hand side, Spider, Elephant, Ox, Bear then Grasshopper. And, on its right, Tiger, Tortoise, Bunnerfly, Crow, Ermine and, finally, Fish.

I give Dumpling my breakfast order (rye bread topped with smoked salmon and cream cheese) and stare at the empty throne.

The silence is unsettling. Usually, these people are so engrossed in their conversations, I could probably perform a lap dance and they wouldn't notice.

Her death hangs heavy over the room. This silence is a testament to the weight of it. I feel as if we are all survivors of some terrible natural disaster, unable to contemplate the devastation, the ramifications of it. It's too big to look at. Like a sinkhole that has opened and consumed a city overnight, leaving us gazing at the gaping emptiness left behind.

Cordelia mournfully spoons a bowl of grey gruel. Thank my stars I wasn't born in Tortoise Province, where they believe food with too much flavour (or *any* bodily delights for that matter) is a distraction from the superior pursuits of the mind. As if the only barrier to solving the world's problems is a plate of poutine.

When my breakfast arrives, I shovel it down, consuming as much as possible to fill the terrible silence. Food fills a lot of holes.

Shinjiro sets down his teacup. If the rumours about what the monks put in their tea are to be believed, that would explain why he's so damn calm all the time. 'Thank you for your help last night, Ganymedes.'

'No problem.' I helped him carry an unconscious Bear to his room. Anything to get away from the ballroom and *her* body. 'How's Wyatt?'

Shinjiro's face remains placid. 'Not well. The passing has hit him hard. He cared deeply for the All-Mother. And he already has a weak constitution.'

Nice way of saying 'almost dead'.

'I was up all night with him but had to leave for sunrise prayers. Now he won't open his door.' He sips his tea.

I suppose Eudora dying has scuppered Wyatt's plan to marry her. That guy can't catch a break.

'Has anyone seen our Crow and Ermine siblings?' Shinjiro asks. 'I hoped we could all breakfast together.'

'Ravinder wasn't hungry,' Cordelia says.

'And you really expect Eska to be here?' I snort. Pretty optimistic of him to expect her to engage with us at all at any point in the voyage.

'I saw the Ermine fishing off the side of the boat,' Jasper mutters. 'She said some shite about me being weak for relying on the emperor's dragons to feed me.' Jasper forms a fist atop the table. 'Then she tried to stab me. Her whole province needs to start acting like they're actually in a *united* empire. You know how impossible it is to man the Bandage there? My soldiers go missing all the time.'

'Eska tries to stab everyone.' I take a bite of my bread. 'You're not special, Jasps.'

'What happens if the emperor dies?' It's Tendai, the Elephant Blessed who dismissed me so offhandedly at the party. She casually dips a slice of pancake into honey, as if her

66

question was less about the fate of Concordia, but rather about whether we all slept well.

'Why would you ask that, *sister*?' Nergüi comments. 'You would speak of our beloved emperor's death so indifferently?' They wear a red suit with jewelled buttons, grey hair cropped around cheekbones sharp enough to match their words.

'It's natural to be worried for Concordia's future,' Tendai says.

Nergüi steeples their fingers. '*You* are worried about Concordia's future?'

The question is so cutting, the '*you*' so loaded, I'm amazed nobody steps in. Blessed don't talk to each other like that. Not the upper ones anyway. They have to maintain the illusion that they respect each other.

Cordelia and Jasper tensed the moment Tendai spoke. What in the Goddess's name did this woman do to make them treat her like a charged explosive?

'I don't recall mumbling,' Tendai says. 'Did I mumble, Fish?'

I gag on my salmon. Last thing I want is to be dragged into *this*. 'No.'

'I didn't mumble.' Tendai's eyes never leave Nergüi.

'I just wished to ensure I understood. You're worried about the fate of our nation.' They purse their lips. 'We could all learn something from your considerate nature.'

Shinjiro wasn't wrong about those two. The tension between them is tight enough to snap. I feel like yelling *Fight!* or, preferably, *Kiss already!*

Instead, I turn to Shinjiro and ask: 'So what *would* happen if the emperor died now, without an heir to pass the Primus Blessing to?'

All eyes spin to the monk. He feels like the only stable

thing here with his mask of serenity. He takes his time sipping his tea. 'The Primus Blessing is not like the ones we bear, which pass from parent to offspring when the child is old enough to carry it. The Primus Blessing passes only upon death. So, it is currently safe. It resides inside His Majesty, praise be to the Goddess.' He bows his pink head.

'Like all provinces, the birth of an heir is a closely guarded thing. You, and any siblings, are prepared for the duties which may be bestowed upon you.' He coughs lightly into his sleeve. 'That is not the way in Bunnerfly Province. All infants are taken from their birth parents and raised collectively, including the Blessed's offspring. This means *all* children are treated as if they are to become Blessed. In my youth, nobody was aware it was I until my Blessing showed.'

Fish Province is the opposite; we follow the emperor's example and almost always have only one heir. Raising a single child in the teachings of the Goddess is seen as the most 'pure' way to pass on Blessings when you don't possess the infrastructure the monks have. But they got me this time, so results do vary.

Shinjiro clears his throat. 'I understand that putting such a structure in place is a vast undertaking to ask of you, especially the provinces with fewer resources, but—'

'Shinjiro,' I say, 'the emperor?'

He gives me a slow smile that makes me regret ever interrupting him.

'Regardless, Dragon Province has produced reliable leaders throughout millennia, ensuring our empire remains in harmony. But they're guarded so deftly by their shields that the death of a royal child prior to the leader's passing has never occurred before.' He sips his tea. 'Apart from once. But that was an unfortunate accident, and in that occurrence the emperor had another son.'

I think of Emperor Eugenios – old and bent and drooling. 'Any volunteers, ladies?'

Nergüi chuckles. The sound is horrifying. 'A Blessed breeding with an emperor? That's just not done, Ganymedes, dear.'

Ignoring the 'dear' . . . 'I-It's not?'

'The line of the Dragon must remain pure. If another province were to get mixed up in it, their descendants might start believing they are blood of the Goddess too, and get silly ideas about being *owed something*. That would be awfully messy, wouldn't it, Monk?' Nergüi smiles at Shinjiro, their teeth so gleaming white they could be mistaken for daggers.

Shinjiro presses his palms together, eyes closed. 'Indeed. Marriages between Blessed have occurred in the past, with at least two children produced to pass the Blessings to. But despite Wyatt's hopes, the Dragon Blessed only produce offspring with Dragon nobles.' He breathes out slowly. 'That is to say, *this* situation has never occurred before. As he possesses no living siblings, if the emperor were to pass now, I imagine it will be quite disastrous for all concerned.'

'For all concerned?' Cordelia squeaks.

'For all concerned with living.'

Jasper leaps from his seat. 'The Bandage will fall. The Crabs will overrun us.'

My mouth goes dry. I rub the raised scar on my right palm.

'I like living.' Grasshopper tugs the pendant around her neck.

Shinjiro taps his chin. 'The Primus Blessing is mysterious, far more powerful than anything we possess. But I believe the Bandage failing is inevitable. However, there's no need to panic. As long as this ship continues to sail, the emperor's life continues. It is, after all, powered by his Blessing.'

The fact Shinjiro isn't running around screaming speaks

volumes about whatever's in his tea. The Bunnerfly Blessed's role is to serve as head of the religion, to ensure the empire remains in balance. Surely he must know Eudora's death will hit Concordia like a sledgehammer?

'We need to tell someone.' Jasper pulls at his jagged crop of hair. 'We gotta get word to my soldiers. We've all seen the emperor – he ain't exactly the picture of health.'

To put it mildly. He looks like a corpse propped up.

'If you haven't noticed, we're stuck on this goddessforsaken cruise for the next eleven days,' Tendai mutters.

'Quite,' Shinjiro says. 'This pilgrimage is designed to isolate us and to foster harmony between the twelve provinces. There is no way to communicate with the mainland.'

Jasper paces about the room. 'The Crabs will leap as soon as they spot a weakness in the Bandage. Those ginger shits never miss a chance.'

I glance around the table. 'Don't suppose anyone's Blessing is to . . . shout very loudly? So people on land can hear?'

Everyone looks at me as if I just spat in their mouths. They're all so bloody secretive about their Blessings. If I had one, I'd scream it from the rooftops.

'Fuck that. I'm swimming to Dragon Province.' Jasper storms to the door.

'That would be unwise,' Nergüi says coolly.

'Why?'

'We're over two hundred miles from shore. And the water is very cold.' Their gaze flickers to Jasper. 'But please, do try.'

He actually considers it. But logic beats teenage bravado, and he slumps back into his seat.

'O-Once we get to the mountain, there is a monk who can send a message to the mainland,' Cordelia says, pushing up her glasses. 'We just need to last eleven more days.'

'The Crabs only need *one* day!' Jasper rages. '*One* moment!'

'Monks are trained to keep their emotions measured. Discord, not death, is the enemy of harmony.' Steam rises from Shinjiro's tea. 'I understand this is distressing. But we must remain calm.'

'*Calm?*' Jasper releases a spurt of flame. 'My people can barely guard the Bandage as it is. If it falls we won't stand a chance. There're *millions* of them.'

'We will have to pray to the Goddess that the emperor does not die before we can return. May I suggest we take time to meditate? There is a beautiful shrine aboard. Yes, that is a wonderful idea,' Shinjiro declares, as if he had not just come up with it himself. 'Of course, in true prayer, you do not need a shrine at all.'

The table looks as if they would rather watch Eudora die all over again.

But Shinjiro is already speaking in low, solemn tones: 'Goddess, in your infinite wisdom you have seen fit to take the heir of our great empire away. Please bestow your guidance upon us eleven, blessed with a fraction of your power. As harmony saved the twelve animals from the discord of the flood, please guide us to live in concord with one another for these eleven days. Please show us a path forward, in this dark world without Eudora.'

I look at that great empty chair.

And, finally, I must face it.

She's gone. She's dead. I didn't know her really. But last night in the bathroom, I felt as though I saw her. Truly saw her. Not the poised, perfect Goddess, but a woman with a terrible duty, and the strength to bear it.

A Goddess who snorted.

Eudora is a memory now. A dead name whispered in a prayer. She never got to bear the burden she was born to. A sob of sunlight that never breached the horizon.

'Where is she?' I ask.

'The shield is guarding her body inside her cabin,' Shinjiro says. 'He hasn't left her side since she passed.'

*

I deposit Grasshopper outside her room before I find Leofric. I'm not the most uptight of people, but taking a six-year-old to see a dead body feels like crossing a line.

The cabins are arranged on the lower deck in a horseshoe shape – mine at the bottom left-hand side, Grasshopper's next, then Ermine, and so on. It's easy to tell them apart – they bear a gold sigil of the province animal upon each door. While Fish to Elephant are squeezed together on the left, the right-hand corridor of the horseshoe houses only Tortoise, Spider, Tiger and Dragon, with walls and a staircase separating the two sides. Not that we're not all equal, of course.

This senseless formation means I have to walk past every room until I find Leofric, stalking outside the Dragon cabin like a feral cat.

In daylight, the awful tiger tattoo is much clearer against his white skin. The snarling beast wraps across his shoulders and down his bulging forearms. I wonder at what age he became enough of a twat to request that.

'You're a disgrace,' he says as I approach. His blue mullet is wild; there are dark bags under his eyes. 'Why are you still wearing that? It's an insult to everyone aboard.'

'I want to see her.'

'Absolutely not.'

'What do you think I'm going to do? I can hardly harm her.'

The words crash into him with the force of a hurricane. I take a few steps back. Tiger Blessed are said to possess some kind of terrifying Blessing, and although poking the kitty can be fun, I don't particularly want to discover the truth of that rumour.

'You think I would let an irresponsible, disaster-ridden lump like you anywhere near the heir apparent of Concordia?'

'I'll take over watch duty.' I adjust my goggles. 'It's your feast day, after all. You can teach the others about . . . discipline? Waving swords?'

'I don't care about the damn feast day.'

I'm used to him being uptight; it's a Tiger trait. With the province's excellent schools and hospitals, you'd think Tigers would be delighted with their sheer luck to be born there. Instead, they're all total stick-in-the-muds, so married to their rules they'd hand their own grandma to the military police if she dared let dust settle on her province-mandated portrait of the emperor.

Tigers rarely leave their province other than to send their militia to scrub out any *disturbances*. Which is just as well; I'd rather drink my own piss than have a beer with them and be told all the ways I'm a shameless sinner.

Just as Eudora said, Leofric's wearing the collar – a strip of green metal snug against his neck, with a thick padlock resting between his collarbones.

Against my better judgement, I feel a stab of pity. Losing Lysander – the one person he seemed to genuinely like – must have been hard. Now he's lost his empress too, the person he dedicated his life to protect.

'I'm sorry about what happened. It wasn't your—'

'You think I need the pity of a pissfish?'

I scuff my boot against the ground. I'm not sure why I want to visit Eudora. It just doesn't feel real. I need to look at the body and *see* her.

I might have been the last person to speak to her. There

was a gap of less than thirty minutes between our conversation and her death.

It was the first – and only – time I'd seen her alone. Not stalked by the Tiger, or her adoring public. She was raw in that moment. Perhaps I was the only one who ever saw her that way.

I turn to Leofric. 'Why weren't you guarding her last night?'

He looks up sharply. 'What?'

'At the party you lost her – you were asking Wyatt what he'd done with her.'

'In what world do *I* report to *you*?'

A wave of heat rushes up my body. I'm probably angry at myself, but it's literally Leofric's role to protect her. He didn't protect her. Neither did I. And if he's not going to take my pity, maybe something sharper will persuade him.

I tug up my jacket to cover my neck. 'You're supposed to be her shield.'

Surprisingly, my trachea remains unharmed. When he speaks, his words are hushed: 'Her condition was known.'

'Condition?'

'She was fragile. It will not be of any great surprise to those who knew her that she took her own life.'

I step closer. 'You think she did it to herself? Why would she?'

'Not that you could comprehend for even one pathetic moment of your insignificant existence, but being the heir to Concordia is a heavy burden, one she attempted to escape on multiple occasions. I just didn't think she would do so by . . . these means.'

My body goes cold. She tried to run away. Now I understand, I know what that emotion was that passed behind her eyes. The one I could not place in the bathroom. *Understanding.* She knew what it meant to want to escape.

But there's a big difference between wanting a thing and acting upon it. Eudora and I may have understood one another, but we were not the same.

Eudora was strong.

'Are you sure?' I ask. 'I spoke to her last night and—'

'What?' He whirls on me, grabbing my shoulders. 'You spoke to her? When? Where?'

I wince. 'In the bathroom.'

'What were you doing there?'

'What do you think?'

His nostrils flare. 'You were with her shortly before she died, Fish. Didn't you think to tell anyone this?'

I open and close my mouth uselessly.

'What happened? Tell me everything.'

'We just spoke! Although she did seem a little stressed.' I remember her tears, her banging her head against the mirror.

Leofric nods.

'But she didn't seem like she'd given up. She was proud, more than anything. About her future, and her "burden".'

His grip loosens. 'How does that make sense to you? Why would someone proud of themselves take their own life?'

I glance at the door. 'I'm not sure.'

He crosses his arms at his chest. 'You didn't know her. Nobody did. That's the problem.'

I felt like I did know her, for those fifteen minutes. A glimpse of the real woman behind the mask of divinity. Someone with a dry wit. Someone who hit me. And someone who wanted to die for her people. Certainly not for this. Not for nothing.

'If I could just see her,' I say. 'Did she write a note or—'

'Leave, Fish.'

'But—'

'Dee!' Grasshopper comes bounding up so fast Leofric almost crashes backwards into the door.

'What's up?'

'There's something . . .' She eyes Leofric. 'Don't like him.'

Leofric twitches. 'What did that little gremlin just say?'

'His grumpy face makes my head hurt.'

'Maybe try smiling,' I say. Then I'm off, following Grasshopper before Leofric can change his mind about my trachea.

*

The 'thing' Grasshopper wants to show me is her cabin.

Like mine, it's an echo of her province. Huge leafy plants cover almost every inch of it. Spiked flowers twine around her bamboo bed, and vines dangle from the ceiling. At our feet is fresh unearthed dirt. It even has the humid heat of it. Crickets and insects can be heard, chirping and buzzing, and, in the distance, chanting music.

There's just one problem. The room is completely ransacked.

The bed has been flipped over. The wardrobe doors flung open. Even the woven-leaf rug has been torn to shreds.

'I didn't do it!' Grasshopper says emphatically before I even have a chance to accuse her.

'Did you give your key to someone?' I ask, trying to keep my voice calm.

'Nuh-uh!'

That doesn't make sense. There's only one key for each cabin so how . . .

There's something on the floor which does not belong in this rainforest. A shiny piece of metal.

I kneel and pick it up. It's part of the door handle and the entire inward mechanism of the lock. It's been torn from the door, all bent and twisted out of shape.

My fingers tremble around the broken lock.

Grasshopper fixes me with her intense lilac gaze. 'I sleep in Dee's bed again tonight?'

I clasp her hand. 'You're sleeping in my bed every night, Grasshopper.'

'Yay!'

I don't tell her what my mind is screaming. I don't tell her that someone broke into this room, looking for something they did not find, something that should have been here. I don't tell her that my soft heart may have saved her life last night.

Chapter Five

Day Two – Feast of the Tiger

Afternoon

Ravi stands in his doorway, tugging at his shirt cuffs. He glances down the corridor at anything that isn't me.

Even now I think he's going to chuckle that achingly wonderful laugh and reveal the last five years have been one elaborate prank. That he's paid me back for all the times I played tricks on him. The long con.

Instead, he stands before me a stranger. A man I do not know wearing a face I do.

'Don't worry,' I say. 'I wasn't followed. Your reputation is intact.'

He gestures towards Grasshopper.

'We're a package deal.'

'We're a swarm!' Grasshopper leaps in place.

'I guess I have a way of picking up strays,' I say with a meaningful look.

He rubs his temples. 'What is it, Ganymedes? I'm very busy.'

There it is again – Ganymedes. Why not thrust a blade through my heart while you're at it?

When I try to peer inside his cabin, he steps outside and closes his door.

'Is she in there?' I ask.

'She?'

'Your fiancée. Love of your life.'

He runs his hands through his hair. 'She's in the library.'

'Why's she there?'

'I imagine to read.'

'Blessed hells. She's worse than I thought,' I mutter.

'Ganymedes—'

'You never told me you liked skinny girls.'

'I didn't tell you everything.'

That's a lie. I know *everything* about him. Maybe that's why he's avoiding me – thinks I'm going to blurt it out and ruin him.

I would never tell anyone. They could offer me everything, skin me alive, break me into a thousand pieces. I'd never tell. I keep his secrets as close to my heart as my own. Closer, even.

I want to ask him why he *really* stopped coming to me. Why he cast me aside the moment other people started paying him attention.

But Ravi already said the reason at the party.

'*No value.*'

'If that's all . . .' He edges to the door.

'Don't go!' *Shit. That sounded more genuinely desperate than I meant it to.*

For the briefest flicker, his face softens. 'Why are you really here, D— Ganymedes?'

He almost called me Dee.

I scan the corridor. Shinjiro is keeping his vigil outside Wyatt's room. He sits cross-legged and eyes closed, meditating probably. 'I need to talk to you privately. Please, Ravi?'

He twitches at his nickname. Maybe it still has power. 'Make it quick.'

I smile and follow him inside.

I've been to Crow Province. I've looked upon the mountains blanketed with trees and wildflowers. But Ravi's cabin has not captured that side of his homeland. The walls are black as coal. There are occasional glimmers of blue light – divinium nested in the rockface – but otherwise it is the utter darkness of a cave. Even his window is covered. A chill raises the hair on my arms and, in the distance, I hear the *tap tap* of tools against rock. It smells like half of him – the half that smells like coal dust and smoke. Not the half that smells like flowers.

Grasshopper's eyes widen. 'You have returned to the earth.'

She may like it, but the place makes my chest seize, as though I'm being buried alive. Ravi stands in the centre, slender arms limp at his sides.

Ravi grew up in caves, but he wasn't fond of them. He was terrified things would crawl out of the darkness and snatch him away, down into the pits where so many Crows vanished. When he first visited Fish Province and looked upon the sunlit ocean he sank to his knees and cried.

Ravi shouldn't be in this dark cold room. Ravi belongs in the sun.

'You can come to my room,' I whisper, fighting every urge to take his hand. 'I asked my dragon to hide the waves, but I'll put them back up for you?'

His mouth opens, but then snaps shut. His neck bobs, swallowing whatever precious words he was going to give me.

'Ganymedes.'

I stagger back as Nergüi emerges from the darkness.

'What a wonderful surprise,' they say.

80

So *that's* who Ravi was hiding in his cabin.

'Ganymedes wants to speak to me alone,' Ravi says.

'Of course. We were just finishing anyway.' They sweep past Ravi. 'It will be as discussed.'

Ravi nods stiffly. 'Understood.'

I freeze, praying lack of movement will stop Nergüi from engaging with me. They *are* a spider, after all.

Instead, a cold hand closes around my wrist. 'We should talk later, Ganymedes.'

I'd rather take a cheese grater to my dick.

'I'm a bit busy,' I say.

'You *will* find time.' They squeeze my arm, then leave, jewels clacking.

I tear back my sleeve and examine the bare skin.

'What are you doing?' Ravi stares.

'Checking for poison marks. Needles. What the hell was Nergüi doing in here?'

'It's not important.' Ravi used to be as terrified of them as me. He was thankful his border was protected from Nergüi's by lots of spiky mountains. 'What did you want to talk to me about?'

I tuck a hand in my pocket and rock in place. *Nice and casual.* 'You know the whole . . . heir to the empire committing suicide thing?'

'I'm aware of it, yes.'

'Well . . . I'm not sure she did. Actually.'

He sighs. 'Her decomposing body begs to differ.'

He never used to be so dry. That's more like a joke *I* would make. What have they done to him to turn him so bitter?

His people are known for being hard, dull, slow-witted miners. But Ravi was the sweetest person I knew, beneath the layers of wool and silence. He noticed things about myself that I'd never considered wonderful. *'You're so pale that colours beam through your cheeks,'* he told me once. *'I can watch my words light up your face.'*

'Ganymedes?'

I clear my throat. 'I spoke to her, shortly before *it* happened.'

'You did? Where?'

'Doesn't matter. Anyway, she didn't seem like she was on the verge of giving up. She seemed *honoured* to offer up her sanity for Concordia.'

'You barely knew her,' Ravi dismisses swiftly.

'Why the heck would she kill herself now? On this ship? Don't you think that's strange?'

He touches the wall, long fingers brushing over a gleam of blue. 'She had a burden. I know how that feels.'

Don't hug him. You're mad at him. Do not hug him.

Grasshopper fills the awkward silence by blurting out, 'Dee like-likes you! Shall we sing of your bonding?'

I repress the urge to strangle a literal child.

Grasshopper looks between our horrified faces, clearly delighted, and starts to sing, 'Ohhh, hearts bonded in ha—'

'Ignore her.' I press my hand over her mouth.

Ravi suddenly becomes very interested in his nails.

'T-That's not all,' I say.

His thick eyebrows narrow as my speech stumbles. Stuttering is *not* very Ganymedes Piscero.

'Fingers in ears,' I tell Grasshopper.

She obliges.

'Someone broke into Grasshopper's room.' I dig into my pocket and show him the twisted metal. 'We found this.'

'A broken lock? Was anything missing?'

'I don't know. Her room was completely trashed,' I hiss. 'First Eudora "commits suicide" just after telling me she's ready to dedicate her life to protecting Concordia. Then I find Grasshopper's cabin broken into and wrecked. Something is very *wrong* about all this.'

'Why are you here? You think I did it?'

'Goddess no, Ravi. Never.' He once cried when I stepped on a crab. We had to hold a funeral. I know this man is not hurting anyone.

'Then why?'

I wring my hands, fighting the urge to flee. I can't be rejected by him again. I just can't. Back then, Ravi was the only person who believed in me. Who saw me as more than a pissfish. I need that Ravi back. 'I need your help. I need a sleuthing partner.'

His dark gaze cuts through me in the way only Ravi's can. 'Why do you need my help?'

I unzip my jacket a little. 'Is it hot in here or . . . ?'

He stares silently.

'Because I can't do it by myself,' I state. 'Because I'm not smart, or brave, or talented. People don't like me. I just annoy them. I'm all round useless. You said it yourself – I'm of "no value". So, I need your help.'

The silence is a blade, cutting the thread between us.

He would have fought those words. Once. Now he lets them hang. Like a noose around our past.

'I'm not much good at anything,' I whisper. 'I can't work out the truth alone. I'll just mess it up. That's all I'm good at.'

There are certain fisherfolk who have a coveted ability. A hundred people can fish the same stretch of ocean and come back with empty nets, but some have the gift. They throw out their lines and reel in fish after fish, as if they have the key to the sea. That's what Ravi does to me. He drags all the hiding fish from the depths. And now I'm flopping on the deck, white belly exposed. Waiting to be gutted.

He steps back. Darkness masks his face.

'You'll help me?'

Silence. My chest feels like it's going to explode.

He grasps my arm and drags me across the room. He swings the door open, pushing me through it.

'Ravi?'

But he only says, 'I'm sorry. You'll have to do this alone.' Then he closes the door between us.

Chapter Six

Day Two – Feast of the Tiger

Night

I've never cried in front of a child. But I don't want to leave Grasshopper alone, so when I return to my room she rubs my back as I ugly-sob.

'I'll put bugs in his food,' she says. 'Skitter bugs are poisonous.'

I'd love to see that.

Except not really. Because Ravi deserves to be happy, and if he has to cut me away like some rotting limb to do that, so be it.

I'm allowed to cry about it though.

My father always cautioned me against showing emotions. I think he was worried I'd blurt out our secret in a fit of hysteria. He taught me how to tell a different story on my face than what's in my heart. He helped me build my walls, brick by brick. And I only let them fall around one person.

When I go for a second round Grasshopper tells me, 'Tears blur your eyes to tigers.' She's probably right.

Instead, I form a plan.

I don't care what Ravi or Leoprick say. Something is *off* about this 'suicide' and the only place I can start is Eudora's body. I can't take the Tiger on – the guy is double my size, not to mention his likely deadly Blessing.

So, I'll use the best tool at my disposal – an invisible girl.

*

'You know what to do, right?' I pin my body against the wall.

Grasshopper nods, hair bouncing. 'Throw things at big blue guy.'

'Remember to turn invisible.'

'Grasshopper isn't idiot.'

Not my most elegant plan, but I need Leofric away from that room long enough to examine Eudora. And if chucking things works, why overcomplicate it?

I scan the corridor. My room is opposite Eudora's, but there's a wall between us, with a staircase inside. That means we need to loop around the wall, sneaking past all the cabins. Then Grasshopper will turn invisible and do the aforementioned chucking. There are two sets of doors on to the main deck, one beside my room, and one at the top of the corridor. Grasshopper will escape out on to the deck through the centre doors, making lots of noise. Leofric will hopefully follow, then the coast will be clear for me to enter Eudora's cabin.

I crouch low, taking miniscule footsteps, Grasshopper eerily silent at my side. It's so dark I have to run my hand along the centre wall to guide me. The golden sigils upon the doors glimmer, reflecting the silver moonlight.

I breathe softly, convinced Leofric can hear even that. Tigers are trained to be killers from the age they can hold a sword. I do not doubt his instincts.

I'm halfway down the corridor when a door springs open. I grab Grasshopper, pinning us against the wall. She's already invisible. The girl's reflexes to danger are second to none. Which confirms my decision to never visit Grasshopper Province.

I press my annoyingly reflective body against the wall, heart thudding.

A bulky shape moves in the darkness. Their long strides are confident, fearless. And they're not stopping. They're going to walk right by us.

I shift. My scales clink.

They freeze, head raised like a startled deer.

I hold my breath, biting my lip.

Finally, they stride towards a cabin, then slam their fist against the door. I would recognize that ferocity anywhere.

Eska. My dear Ermine neighbour.

What is she doing out at this time? Everyone knows Eska doesn't make friends. She fills anyone who attempts to befriend her with holes. She's very committed to her province's desire to close itself off from the rest of Concordia. Their Blessed attend *just* enough summits to not be formally reprimanded, but clearly loathe every moment of them.

The door swings open. No words are exchanged before she strides inside; then it locks behind her.

Grasshopper flickers back, crouched low, like a cat before the pounce.

I shuffle forward to check the sigil on the door. A golden elephant. Tendai. Who, as far as I'm aware, everyone hates.

So why the hell is Eska visiting her?

Miss I Hate Everyone visiting Miss Everyone Hates Me.

I file that in my what-the-fuck folder for later contemplation, before returning to the wall of safety. I crouch, following it around the loop in the corridor.

A sharp snapping noise almost evacuates my bowels. I freeze, but only silence follows. I release a long breath, then glance down the other side of the wall.

One window offers muted moonlight. It's enough.

Leofric is *still* there, the wanker. Standing to attention outside Eudora's room as if he's just begun his vigil, not stood there for twenty-four fucking hours. Tiger Blessed really are something else. Though I suppose they are a double sacrifice. Once to the life-shortening Blessing, and again in surrendering their existence to servitude. They're forbidden even to have sex with anyone, apart from to pass on the Blessing. Which may explain why Leofric is so uptight.

Lysander used to humanize him. Now he's just a statue – cold, hard stone all the way through.

'Lead him out, to the right,' I whisper. Do kids know right from left? Grasshopper just stares so I point towards the centre deck doors.

She scowls. 'I know right.'

'Didn't say you didn't.'

'Pointed.'

A voice. A new one. So quiet I almost mistake it for the wind. A high, distant wailing.

Grasshopper disappears. Her trembling arms lock around my legs.

Maybe it *was* the wind. People don't wail like—

It comes again, louder. The cry snakes around the corridor.

Leofric stands still, shrouded in darkness. Maybe they really did replace him with a statue.

I grip Grasshopper. 'We'll try—'

My legs go weak. The wailing continues. It sounds almost like the cry of seagulls. But there won't be any gulls out here.

The Crows believe in legends of lost souls, trapped within the caves. Ravi said their haunted cries can be heard on dark nights when the moon is full. I suppose you go that long without seeing the sun, you start to believe all kinds of crazy shit.

But this is no spirit; it sounds distinctly human. Someone wailing on this ship after what happened with Eudora cannot be good.

Leofric will be here all night. I can come back later, after I discover the source of the creepy wailing.

I move down the corridor, trying to follow the echo, but Grasshopper digs her heels in. 'Bad noise.'

'You stay here.'

She puffs out her cheeks. 'Won't leave Dee.'

My heart skips. *That makes one person.*

I clasp her hand and we seek out the ghost together. As I creep down the corridor, the sound grows quieter. It must be coming from outside, somewhere on the deck. I lead Grasshopper towards the centre doors, and slip out into the night.

I've avoided going out on to the deck so far, and now it appears to be furious at me. The wind howls, lashings of rain pummelling the wood panelling so hard I'm amazed I couldn't hear it inside. Maybe that's the emperor's doing.

Grasshopper clings to me, nuzzling into my arm.

The night is bereft of stars thanks to the angry grey storm clouds. But then they shift and the moon peeks through, casting cold silver light upon the glistening deck. The sails glow faintly – a snarling blue tiger stalking across his canvas prison.

Despite the downpour, the wailing is louder than ever. It almost forms words, words that sound like '... back ... come back ...'

With Grasshopper tucked under one arm, I push against the storm, following the noise around the outside of the cabins.

'Please return to me!' The voice pierces through the storm like a blade.

Grasshopper vanishes with a *pop*, and slips out from under my arm.

The wind picks up, lashing ice-cold rain against my face. I tug my goggles over my eyes and struggle on.

Then I see her.

To the left of the cabins, hanging off the side of the ship and clinging to the railings, is a girl. Her white nightdress is slick with sea spray, blonde hair tousled by the wind. So petite I'm amazed she's not been tossed overboard already.

'Cordelia?' I gasp.

She's turned away from me, one pale hand gripping the slick rail, the other reaching out to the dark of the ocean. As the ship sways, she rocks forward. That thin wrist and her bare feet are the only things keeping her on board.

I could leave her. The temptation is greater than I'm comfortable confronting. Leave her or . . . give her a little push.

'Please!' The storm drowns her in sea spray.

Fuck it. Of course I have to save her. Nobody else will.

'Cordelia!' I stagger forward, arms outstretched.

She doesn't react. She doesn't even appear to hear me. Her eyes are half open, as if drugged. Her glasses sit haphazardly, smeared with water.

'Come down off the railings.' I take a step closer, running my fingers over the cool steel.

She doesn't respond. Her back arches as she reaches out, away from the ship.

'Come down, you prat!'

Her eyes flicker, and her hand leaves the railing.

I lurch forward, fingers locking around her flute-thin wrist. I'm bent over the side of the ship, kicking furiously for purchase. Cordelia dangles beneath me, the black sea stretched out below.

My chest seizes. Noises drift into muffled silence.

No. Not now.

I close my eyes and grasp Cordelia's arm with my free one. I'm not strong, but Ravi's bride is as light as a songbird. I wrench her back over the railings, and we crash on to the soaked deck in a tangle of limbs.

I tear my goggles off, breathing more heavily than her. I'm soaked through. But it's not rain, it's sweat.

She pushes herself up, blinking water from her eyes.

Goddess, her nightdress is very thin. And wet. And transparent.

Her eyes widen. 'Fish . . .'

Couldn't even be arsed to learn my name. Probably too late to throw her overboard now.

'Ganymedes.' I hold out a hand. 'Need some help?'

She shakes her head, wet hair hanging limply. 'No. I'm . . . fine.' She sways to her feet, stick-thin legs almost buckling.

She shivers, clasping her arms around her chest. She thinks she's getting my jacket. I'm charitable but not *that* charitable.

'It is i-i-illegal in Tortoise Province to sh-sh-show skin below the neck and above the a-a-ankles.' Her teeth chatter. 'It encourages sexual urges. D-Distracts from mindly pursuits.'

Interesting. Still ain't getting my jacket. At least I know Ravi isn't getting any.

'What were you doing out here?'

Her gaze skims the deck. 'I saw someone.'

'Out here?'

'I saw them inside first. I followed them on to the deck.'

'Who?'

She stares down at her bare feet. 'My brother.'

'Lysander? But he's dead!'

Her body recoils as if I'd just broken the news. 'I-I-I'm aware he's dead. But I thought I s-s-saw him.'

Great. Ravi's marrying someone off their bloody rocker. Maybe this is why they paired up; I always poked fun at his ghost stories.

She rubs her bare arms. 'No. I *did* see him. I definitely saw Lysander.'

'Uh-huh. I didn't know Lysander well, but he didn't seem the type to lure his little sister into – you know – the ocean? Certain death?'

She glances out to sea, quick breaths racking her thin body.

Blessed hells. I'm taking off my jacket. Stupid Tortoise, if she ate something that wasn't grey gruel she'd have more natural padding, like me.

I drape it over her. She stares at me like a lost doll a child has abandoned.

'Let's get you inside.' I take her arm. It's bone cold. We've barely walked two steps before her legs lock. She stares at Grasshopper, who has finally popped back into existence.

'Don't worry, she doesn't . . .'

Grasshopper is glaring at Cordelia, eyebrows knitted. The moment stretches a little too long. Then she snatches my other arm in a manner more than a little territorial.

I smirk. 'There's enough to go around, little lady.'

She makes a little 'humph' noise which means I'll probably be getting more feet in my face later.

'Sh-Sh-She rather likes you.' Cordelia trembles as I drag both girls towards the centre door into the cabins.

'All the best people do.'

She doesn't respond. Lysander would have agreed, with a knowing sparkle in his eyes.

I reach the door. Fucking finally. But when I tug the handle, it clanks and doesn't budge.

'Locked!' Grasshopper proclaims.

'But we just came out of it.'

Cordelia shudders into my shoulder. 'Maybe Lysander—'

'I don't think a ghost can lock doors. It was probably Leofric closing the door against the storm.' I try to remember if I left it open, but can't recall.

I'll have to go through the door on the other side of the deck, the one near my cabin.

There's no way I'm getting inside Eudora's room tonight. *Goddessdammit, Cordelia.*

I rub her shoulders – probably a little too roughly – as we stagger to the other side of the cabins, her bare feet slipping against the slick deck.

'How long have you known Ravi?' I ask.

'W-w-we met at Ly's funeral.'

Not even a year. Not even a bloody year.

'Has he mentioned me?'

She shifts. 'He is a very private person.'

That's a no.

'He was there for me,' she whispers.

'Huh?'

She clings to my arm. 'When Ly died, I felt like I'd lost a limb. The only person who ever understood me snatched out of the world. But Ravinder saw my suffering, even when I tried to hide it. He notices things. The little things nobody else does.'

I stagger. In my head, voices from the past push through the storm: *'Your hair curls upwards at the back. Like a duck's tuft . . . Your eyes are such deep gold. It's like gazing into a sunset.'*

'Yeah,' I say, my voice rasping. 'Yeah, he does.'

Grasshopper tugs my hand. 'She stinks.'

93

Social anxiety horror roils my stomach. 'You can't just say people stink!'

'But she does.'

She's not wrong – I can smell it too. A rusted scent. Like the metal cages fisherfolk leave out in summer.

At least I have that. At least I smell better than her.

'Like a sea breeze. Like the ocean, Dee.'

Cordelia skids. I catch her before she falls. Grasshopper's hand slips from mine.

'Take it easy,' I say. 'The deck is . . .' I stare down at it. It's wet. That makes sense; there's a storm. But this area is darker than the rest of it. The clouds shift, and a blade of silver moonlight hits my feet.

The smell isn't coming from Cordelia.

My boots are stained red. As if crimson paint has been smeared across the blue scales. And a few feet away, before the cabin door, there's a shape. A lump. A dark mass upon the bloodied deck.

My body moves on instinct. The storm is a distant echo. A memory. I'm somewhere else. A different storm. A different night.

Two boys in a cave on a cliff in a storm.

I approach the shape.

His hand in mine.

Maybe it's just a bundle of ropes.

He grasps my jaw with petal-soft fingers.

It's so dark I can barely see. The images come in flashes.

I'm afraid to look at him.

The outline of slender limbs.

Because I know what will happen.

Black hair splayed across the wood.

That surge of feeling. A vow broken.

Blood. So much blood. The scent is everywhere.

Our eyes lock.

Cordelia is screaming. Something about it not happening, it's not happening.

Dancing coloured lights in an obsidian sea.

My knees hit the floor, a distant throbbing.

The chains around my heart shatter. And then I'm his.

Vicious gashes across his body. Shredded clothes around a gaping chest cavity. Only his face is unblemished. Untouched. Eyes open and fixed upon me.

I tell him everything. Everything. In a cave on a cliff in a storm.

My mind doesn't try to pretend it's someone else. It cannot fool me.

I know those eyes.

I see them in the gloom of a storm. I see them in the blackness of the deepest parts of the ocean. I see them in the dark places of my mind, where only silence and surrender live.

I know Ravi's eyes better than my own.

Chapter Seven

Day Three – Feast of the Spider

Morning

The night lights were dancing when Ravi and I exchanged our deepest secrets in a cave on a cliff in a storm.

The rain pummelled our backs as we scaled the cliffside. I took his hand and led him towards a little cave carved into the rock, fifty feet above sea level.

The wind nipped our clothes as we huddled together. Facing out towards the purple and orange streaks across the sky, it seemed as though we were gazing upon another world. Like two travellers at sea, looking through a telescope at something ethereal.

We were both seventeen. He was so skinny I was terrified the storm would tear him away. So I clung to his arm, gripping him so hard my fingers, pink with cold, turned white.

I had shared this cave just once before. And I would not lose anyone else within it.

His face was exquisite. The curve of his nose. The bow of his lips. The rich brown tone of his skin. He wore a flower that night, a white bloom against the black of his hair.

Crows venture out of their caves four times a year to gather seasonal plants, crushing them into dye for cloth. The luminosity is lost when they do that. But Ravi adored flowers as they were. Once he wore one to a summit and was mocked mercilessly. He stopped wearing flowers around others after that.

Everyone thought Ravi was a wimp. He came to the summits, silent as the grave, unable to meet anyone's eyes, begging me to escape with him. But they were wrong – Ravi was brave. Braver than me. He went first.

He fiddled with his sleeves, colour flashing in the inky pools of his eyes. 'I-I heard a story about these lights.'

I knew the story. Lovers exchanged oaths beneath them. They were a popular choice for weddings. But also any contracts. Agreements. Deals. Vows.

'If we tell each other secrets beneath them, then we can never tell another soul.'

I released my grip on him, half terrified, half excited. 'That's what they say.'

'If I tell you something, you promise you won't tell?'

'Promise.'

Ravi laced my fingers in his. My heart thumped. It was usually me grabbing Ravi's hand, dragging him off on some adventure. It was very rare he would take mine.

I get it now – the distance was a shield. A barrier against the truth. The distance and the silence were the walls Ravi built.

'You have to swear. Nobody can know. No matter what I say.'

My skin tingled against his.

I wanted to kiss him. To close that final breath of distance. But I worried that, if I did, all the affection I'd been storing would burst out of me. That it would send him flittering away, like a terrified bird.

97

'I swear.'

His fingers left mine. He stared out into the storm, the wind playing with silken strands of his hair. 'I'm sorry. I've been lying to you. To everyone. And I just . . . I need to tell one person. And I think – I *know* that person is you, Dee.'

I didn't speak. I knew when silence was what Ravi needed – not a wall, but a blanket.

'I'm . . .' He stared down the cliff. For a moment, I feared he would cast himself off it. But then he spoke in small broken tones: 'I'm not from here.'

'I know,' I said. 'You're from Crow Province.'

He hugged his knees. 'No. I'm not from Concordia. I'm from outside the Bandage.'

'You're . . . a Crab?'

'Yes. That's why I had to tell you. I can't let you get close to me. I'm one of *them*. If you want to––'

He yelped as I snatched his hands. 'That's amazing!'

'I-It is?'

I couldn't stop smiling. I always knew Ravi was the most interesting person in the world. 'What's it like out there? Can you take me?'

His dark eyes studied me. 'How are you real?'

'What?'

A sweet smile crossed his lips. His smiles were so rare, it felt like witnessing an eclipse. A place where the sun and moon meet. 'Thank you.' He turned away. I sat, awkwardly crouched in the mud, wondering how I'd messed up this time.

It wasn't until he sniffed that I realized he was crying.

'Ravi––'

He turned back, still smiling. 'I've never been outside the Bandage. My mother sneaked out when she was younger. I don't think she liked being dux. She was curious and didn't follow rules – *like you.*' He said the last part so fondly I was momentarily struck dumb. 'Let's just say she came back with more than stories.'

'So your father . . . ?'

'Isn't my real father. Nobody else knows apart from my mother and me.'

'So you're half Crow and half Crab?' I scooted forward. 'That's the coolest thing I've ever heard. I wonder what—'

He yanked my shoulders and pressed me to his chest, skinny arms entwined against my wet back. The scent of smoke and lavender.

I had held him plenty of times, but he had only ever held me once before.

Green light flooded the cave. How rare and beautiful a thing, I thought, that this child of two worlds exists at the same time, in the same place as me.

I wanted to live in that moment forever, but my guilt sat heavy in my gut. Ravi's secret was obviously important to him. It was the reason he stayed silent, why he was so eager to escape notice, why he would agree to anything to not draw eyes. But I was also shouldering my own.

I gripped my knees. In my mind my father's voice.

'Nobody can know. Nobody.'

But I hadn't prepared for Ravi when I promised him. And that vow was not made beneath the night lights.

'We're meant to exchange secrets,' I said. 'So, I'll tell you one of mine.'

'*One* of yours?' he snickered. 'What did you do, Dee? Steal your father's cream cakes again?'

I forced a smile. Maybe this was a terrible idea. If my father knew I was even contemplating it, he would never let me see Ravi again.

'Dee?'

Ravi's hand wandered atop mine. His other was at my cheek, urging our gazes to lock. He was gentle. Never forceful, my Ravi.

And then I was his. Completely.

'I'm not Blessed.'

Ravi's hand dropped. 'What?'

'I don't have a Blessing. I just pretend. My father still has his. We lied to the emperor. To everyone.'

'But you're seventeen,' he breathed. 'You're his only child—'

'I'm not.'

'Ah.' Understanding dawned. His hand went limp.

Now he knew what I was. Worthless. Unworthy.

I had to escape. Throw myself into the ocean. As I went to stand, his hand gripped my wrist.

'I don't care if you're Blessed or not, Dee. A Blessing doesn't make you strong, or special. Not where it counts,' he said with more conviction than I thought this soft boy capable of.

'What do you mean?'

'You see the world in a way nobody else does. You're better than *all of them*.' He rested his forehead against mine, fingers knotting in my tousled hair. 'Because you don't need a Blessing to be a miracle.'

*

'Master Fish?'

Something soft against my cheek. Dumpling stares back at me.

I groan and turn over in bed.

'The Blessed have gathered in the dining room to discuss the recent departures.'

Departures. As if they rode off in a carriage or something.

'Do I look like I want to attend a meeting?' I can't see my reflection but it's likely my hair is *significant.*

'I cannot say. What do you look like when you want to attend a meeting?' He hovers, tail twitching.

'Not like this.' I press the pillow against my face.

'I have measured your vitals, and there are several problems.'

I grunt.

'Your sugar levels are very high. I believe that is due to the mountain of jam doughnuts you demanded I bring last night.'

'That'll be it.'

'I advise a brisk jog to lower the sugars to acceptable levels.'

I shudder, removing the pillow. 'Never suggest that again.'

'You also seem to be under a great degree of stress.'

No shit. My head feels like my brain is making an escape bid with a hammer and chisel. I couldn't even wake and believe it wasn't real for one blessed moment. The dread in my body clued me in immediately.

Dumpling drifts above me. 'What can I do for you then, Master Fish?'

There's only one thing I want.

'Bring Ravi back.' I sit up. 'Or turn back time to before he got stabbed. Make it so I'm back inside his cabin asking for help, and I don't take no for an answer. Make it so I don't leave him.'

Dumpling shakes his head, antlers waggling. 'I'm afraid the ability to manipulate time is not available, even to my creator. Necromancy is also forbidden.'

I fall back in bed. 'Then let me die.'

'Executing you would go against my creator's orders.'

'I didn't mean – oof!'

Something heavy slams into my chest. Fingers tug at my cheeks. 'Up!' Grasshopper yells. 'Up! Up!'

'No.'

She slaps me. 'Up now!'

'Why?'

'If you don't move, Grootslang will eat you.'

'There are no monsters here. They're all beyond the Bandage.'

'Not all monsters are beyond the Bandage,' she says, which is very astute, but then she presses her nose against mine and mutters, '*I'll* eat you.'

'You're not—'

She seizes my arm, closing her mouth around it with a try-me look.

I know what she's doing. She's more astute than a six-year-old should be. She knows if I don't move from this bed now, I'll probably never leave it. But why would I? There's nothing out there for me. Not any more.

'I know you're trying to help, Grasshopper.' My voice shakes. 'But I don't want your help. Or anyone's. I want to lie here and feel nothing.'

She drops my arm, then falls into my chest, squeezing me. 'It'll get better.'

Bruises get better. Headaches get better. This won't get better. And I don't want it to. I don't ever want to feel a single slice of happiness or joy when *he's* not here.

A knock at the door.

'Open up, Fish,' Leofric's gruff voice commands. 'Your presence is required.'

Not needed. Not wanted. 'Required'.

I remain silent. Maybe he'll think I've died too and I can stay in this cabin forever.

Sadly, Grasshopper flings open the door. Then Leofric is in my room, with his muscles and in no mood to take my shit.

His dark blue eyes pass over my prone form, half-eaten doughnuts dotted about my body, last night's sugar smeared across my mouth. '*Good Goddess.*'

'Piss off.'

He takes this better than expected and doesn't punch me in the nuts. 'Are you going to snap out of this ridiculous malaise, or must I carry you to the meeting?'

*

Tiger Province has a reputation for producing powerful Blessed. But still, I'm impressed by how strong Leofric is. By the time he sets me down in my lowly chair, he's not even broken a sweat.

I slump over the table, flicking at crumbs. I barely register who's here, just a collection of bodies, none of them relevant to me.

Leofric stands at the head of the table, where Eudora should be sitting. 'Now we're all gathered, I wish to discuss last night's . . . events. I have laid our Crow brother's body with the All-Mother's.'

Last night is a collection of flashes. Black hair across the red deck. Someone screaming. A great emptiness carved through me, as if something vital had been scooped out. Cordelia must have run for help, or perhaps Leofric heard the screaming. Was I screaming? Or was it her?

'I do not know what this will mean for the divinium trade. But I believe Ravinder has siblings so I imagine there will be only a few disruptions.'

His words settle the anxious bodies. I taste something

rancid which definitely isn't doughnuts. They never cared about him. His worth was measured in blue rocks. None of them knew him, not the real him. Now they never would.

Leofric adjusts his metal collar. 'It has become apparent that what transpired regarding Her Majesty was most likely, in fact, murder.'

'You don't say,' I mutter. 'What gave it away? Ravi's seventeen stab wounds?' It's a venomous joke, and it burns my throat on the way out. But this mirthless humour is easy. It's comforting. I lean into it.

'If you're just here to gloat then you can return to your room.'

'*You're* the one who carried me here. So you'll have to carry me back.'

Nergüi steeples their fingers. 'For two nights in a row a Blessed has died in suspicious circumstances. As much as I'd like to believe the imperial heir's death was not malicious, it would be foolish to assume that Ravinder's murder was merely a coincidence.'

Someone is sobbing. Cordelia probably. Her eyes and skin are red and blotchy. She doesn't look as if she's slept a wink. I'm the opposite – sleeping too much. My mind is always looking for an exit route.

Shinjiro places a hand on her shoulder, pushing his teacup closer. 'Take a sip. It would be a shame for you to regress; you've been doing so well since Lysander's passing.'

The monk clearly didn't see her chasing his ghost last night.

'It's not . . .' Her voice is high and tight. 'It's not right.'

Her crying makes me furious. If tears could bring him back, I'd be rubbing onions into my eyes.

The hair on my neck prickles. Nergüi's storm-cloud eyes are upon me. I should be terrified, but even Nergüi doesn't scare me any more. What do I have to lose? What can they possibly take from me now?

'What are we going to do about this?' Jasper demands, leaping from his seat. 'There's a murderer on this ship. We need to find them!'

'That's why I've called you here. To determine everyone's whereabouts,' Leofric says.

'You first, kitty cat,' I say.

'I was guarding Eudora's . . . remains.' I think he wanted to avoid saying 'body' but 'remains' is somehow worse. Like a plate of half-eaten sandwiches. Just the crusts. 'Ox?'

Jasper lowers into his chair. 'I was in my room. It was almost midnight, who the hell wasn't?'

'I certainly was,' Nergüi says.

'And I,' Tendai says.

'I . . . I . . .' Cordelia stammers. 'I was on the deck.'

'Where the body was?' Jasper asks sharply. 'What were you doing there?'

Cordelia pushes her glasses up. 'Um . . .'

Following a ghost. Not the most convincing argument of sanity.

'What were you doing there?' Jasper repeats.

Everyone is staring. Her nose is red from all the damn crying. Somewhere, in the deep hollows within me, pity swells. She's like a mouse, trapped by a league of assholes.

'I . . . I . . .'

'I asked her to meet me there,' I say.

Her head snaps towards me.

'*You?*' Jasper says incredulously. 'You don't give a shit about anyone.'

'I wanted to talk to her about Ravi.' My voice cracks on his name. 'She's marrying him, so I wanted to make sure she treated him right. Grasshopper was with me.'

Grasshopper nods enthusiastically. As always, the best wingwoman.

Cordelia's pink lips open and close, as if I'm a curious riddle she has never encountered before. Finally, she mouths, *Thank you.*

Leofric turns to the monk. 'And you, holy brother?'

Shinjiro takes a very long sip of tea. We silently watch as he dabs his mouth with his sleeve. 'I was keeping vigil outside Wyatt's room; I'm worried about him. I've not seen him since the first night.'

The Bear Blessed isn't here. I'm so used to him not being present I didn't even notice the lack of him.

Leofric stiffens. 'He wouldn't open his door for me either.'

'Isn't that a little suspicious?' Nergüi says. 'Nobody's seen him.'

Shinjiro shakes his head. 'The poor boy is heartbroken.'

'We're all heartbroken, Monk,' Leofric says.

He sips his tea. 'Indeed, but Bear Province has a unique relationship with legacy.'

That's a polite way of putting it. The mad bastards are convinced that dying in the most batshit way ensures they go down in history. My tutor told me about a guy who got torn apart by hyenas. His family celebrated for a week.

'Wyatt can't fulfil their usual "conditions". So he had his heart set on marrying Eudora,' Shinjiro says.

Leofric scoffs. 'Those Bears have always had ideas above their station. As if carting a few cattle across the desert means they have any right to such a thing.'

Shinjiro purses his lips. 'However impossible, he aspired to prove his legacy in his own unique way. Now even the hope of that has been stolen.' He fingers the rim of his cup. 'I remained outside his door from sunset prayers until the commotion, then I returned there until sunrise prayers.'

I raise my head. He's lying. I walked that corridor last night long after sunset and far before sunrise. He was not there.

'So that's everyone? That's useless!' Jasper says.

Shinjiro taps his cup. 'We also must account for our whereabouts on the night of the All-Mother's death.'

'We were all on the ballroom floor,' Jasper states. 'She was asking about the Bandage.' He points to Cordelia.

'Alas, you're right, we were together, so perhaps that does not help at all. But surely . . .' Shinjiro's eyes linger on Leofric. 'Her shield must have seen something?'

'Pardon?' It's the politest response I've heard from the Tiger, though it's snarled like a swear.

'You were guarding her all night, correct?'

Leofric's face pales. He looks *shattered*. His hair is in knotted mats, and he hasn't changed his clothes. He looks, frankly, as bad as me. 'I . . . I didn't . . .'

'You wouldn't abandon your duty, would you?' Shinjiro raises his cup to his lips. 'That is, I believe, an offence.'

'I will be justly punished.' That and more. Leofric let his empress die. He'll be lucky not to be executed by the senate.

'Please,' Cordelia says, shaking hands clasped to her chest. 'I apologize for the interruption, but this is not fair.'

'Don't—' Leofric begins.

'I was struggling at the party. It has not been easy, following my brother's footsteps. Leo noticed I was upset, and he left his position to comfort me.'

I stare at that hunk of unfeeling man meat. I can't imagine him comforting anyone. What did it consist of? A headlock? But Cordelia speaks so passionately, tears glistening, I know she's not lying.

'I was gone for a few minutes. Ten at the most,' he says. 'I returned to my position outside the bathroom. But when Her Majesty didn't come out, I began to worry.' He glances to Shinjiro. 'That's when you saw me. I thought that Bear Province freak was involved with Her Majesty's disappearance. He's always been unhealthily obsessed with her.'

'As previously stated, Wyatt was staking his legacy on Eudora. He would never have harmed her.' Shinjiro added, 'Yet you handled him rather roughly before the lights went out.'

'This doesn't help at all!' Jasper rages. 'You confirmed it yourself, Monk. You saw him on the floor when it happened. Nobody had the time to get up to the second floor and kill her in the seconds the lights went out.'

'What a pickle,' I muse, drumming my knuckles on the table. 'What a fine old mess.' One of these people probably killed him. I should hate them all. But I don't. I just feel empty.

'If you're looking for someone with a track record of brash actions, I can volunteer a suggestion,' Nergüi comments, examining Tendai over their red fingernails.

Tendai pushes herself up in her chair. 'And if you're seeking someone with a family history of wishing to dismantle authority—'

'Quiet,' Leofric says. 'Someone has *murdered* the All-Mother. I will not let your ridiculous feud interfere with determining the truth.'

'Ridiculous, is it?' Nergüi's voice rises by the slightest incline. 'You know what she's capable of, Tiger.'

Tendai snorts. 'That almost sounds like you're afraid of me.'

'And why might that be, *sister*?'

'Be still!' Leofric rages. 'This madness will derail us.'

Nergüi looks as if they wish to be anything but still. But as Leofric glares, they settle back in their chair. 'As you say, Shield.'

'Excuse me,' Shinjiro says. 'Where is Eska, our Ermine sister? She's not attended any meals.'

Cordelia scoots forward. 'I saw her this morning on my way to the library. She was pacing around the ship at quite a speed.'

Leofric tucks his hands behind his back. 'And this brings me to my conclusion. There is no need to panic or fling around baseless accusations. I've solved the mystery already.'

'Oh golly,' I say. 'If you're as good at solving murders as you are at protecting empresses this'll at least be entertaining.'

'Listen to me, Fish,' he growls, heavy-lidded eyes upon me. 'I've allowed you to speak to me like this thus far because you've lost the only person who could tolerate being in your presence for longer than ten minutes. That is, until he found a higher calibre of people. But remember this – I am still the shield of the empress. And you are a glorified king of fishermen. Disrespect me again and I'll tear out your throat.'

So many replies. So many comebacks. And none worth the effort to summon them into speech. I lower my chest flat against the table.

Grasshopper is glaring at him hard enough for the both of us. If looks could kill, Leofric would be the one swinging from the chandelier.

He leans forward, hands planted on the table. 'This murderer of our brother and sister has no respect for what this pilgrimage represents. No respect for the harmony of Concordia.'

Somewhere deep in my pit of nothingness a curl of dread snakes around my gut.

'Long have the citizens of Ermine Province distanced themselves. Long have they thought themselves above our ways and traditions. Years ago, my mother tried to bring them to heel.'

The previous Tiger Blessed was convinced the Ermines were plotting against the emperor. But the envoys sent to apprehend the Ermine dux did not return. It's not easy to return from Ermine Province.

Shinjiro rubs his chin. 'It's true. They have shown whispers of separatist thoughts. I visited myself, only to be rebuffed.'

Correction – it's not easy *unless you're Shinjiro.*

'But, brother, there is no need to jump to—'

'We warned them once,' Leofric continues in earnest. 'We told them they must work in unity with us. We were not harsh enough. Now they have enacted their plan.'

'What plan?' Cordelia asks.

Leofric clutches the table. 'Revolution.'

A united intake of breath. That word is akin to a curse in Concordia.

'Why else would the Ermine attend this pilgrimage, when she has rebuffed our invitations for years?' Leofric says. 'Suddenly she shows her face, and then two of us are slain.'

Tendai leans forward. I expect her to tell him that she was with Eska last night. But instead, she says, 'Where is she?'

'I've locked her inside her cabin. When we return to the capital, I'll have her arrested, and finally expose the truth of that rebellious province.'

Chapter Eight

Day Three – Feast of the Spider

Afternoon

Most of the Blessed followed Leofric to interrogate Eska. But I dragged my body to my room and returned to my blanket cocoon, Grasshopper nestling in beside me.

Dumpling has filled what space remains with enough sweets and chocolates to send a school of children bouncing off the walls.

Maybe Eska did do it. She certainly has a history of stabbing, and her province's contempt for the empire is a popular ranting topic for elderly fisherfolk. But it doesn't matter. It doesn't matter who killed him or why. Just that he's gone.

I lie spreadeagled on my bed, caramels, marzipan swirls and laddus piled as high as my head. I'll stay here, inside my sugar igloo, until death claims me.

Then maybe I'll see *him* again. If such an afterlife exists. My soul will follow the thread and find his.

I wonder if he'll slam doors in my face there too.

A knock. I seize the hem of Grasshopper's dress before she opens the door.

'Piss off, Leofric,' I say. 'I came to your stupid meeting. Now leave me alone to die.'

'It ain't Leofric.' A melodic drawl of a voice.

My curiosity is the only thing powering my muscles as I climb over my candy mountain and open the door.

He stands in the doorway, wind whipping toffee-brown hair against sunken cheeks. A corpse reanimated to haunt my life.

'Wyatt?'

He winces. 'You look goddessdamn terrible.'

'You're one to talk. I didn't know they made eyes that shade of red.'

'They do. Ox Province. Their eyes are literally red, moron.'

I grit my teeth. 'What do you want?'

He glances down the corridor. 'Reckon I can come in?'

He could be the murderer. Nobody can account for him last night. Nobody's seen him since the party.

I let him in. Hopefully he'll make it quick.

He surveys my sugar empire. 'This is how you live?'

I pop a toffee in my mouth without breaking eye contact. It tastes like ash. Everything does.

'You're a strange man.'

I fall back on the bed. Grasshopper sits beside me, cautious eyes upon him as she munches a cookie.

Wyatt stands stiffly in the silence. My bejewelled jacket is hitched up to my chest, my belly making an escape bid.

'Listen . . . Ganymedes. I'm here 'cause . . .'

I want to tear your head off. I want to cut you up into little pieces. I want to consume your life energy to sustain me from this mysterious illness.

'I wanna team up with you.'

My eyes flicker open. 'Why the hell would you want to do that?'

He stares at the ground, fists clenched. "Cause Eudora

treated me with kindness. She gave me hope that I could live a worthwhile life. The only person who ever did.'

Goddess. This boy must be totally unfamiliar with basic human decency. 'She's dead. You can't leverage her marriage for your legacy any more, so just leave it.'

'I don't care about that. I need to find out who killed her. I need justice. She deserves justice.'

'Do it yourself,' I garble through a mouthful of toffee.

'I can't do it alone,' he says, reminding me a little too closely of my encounter yesterday. Except now I'm in Ravi's place. Hopefully I wasn't as annoying as Wyatt.

'Why not?'

'My condition makes it difficult to achieve anything alone. Even avenge her.' His words are laced with a weary bitterness.

'Why me?' To prove my point, my trousers finally give up the fight. A button pings across the room, narrowly missing his head. 'Thought you hated me?'

He wrings his hands. 'I do. But I hate whoever killed her more.'

I shift to face him. He wilts under my gaze, scratching his neck.

'You already asked everyone else,' I say dully. 'None of them gave you the time of day, did they?'

'They ain't ever given me the time of day. A bunch of them are outside, trying to interrogate Eska through a locked door. They're convinced it's her just because they don't like Ermine Province. But I ain't sure. And I'm not willing to stake Eudora's memory on something that ain't sure.' He runs a hand through his hair. 'You're not out there with them, so I'm guessing you ain't sure either. And I wanna team up with someone who wants the truth for a *personal* reason, not someone who is gonna let empire politics decide for them. So, you gonna help me or not?'

I chew slowly. 'Not.'

Silence. He almost responds, but whatever he's fighting wins. He moves to the door.

Didn't even have the courtesy to murder me on the way out.

I swallow the rest of the toffee, closing my eyes. Finally, some fucking peace to die in.

A weight hits my chest. Hands grab my arms, yanking me upright. Wyatt is breathless before me, sweat gleaming on his brow. Perhaps he has more of his wild province in him than I gave him credit for.

'Look at you! Look at the state of you.' Wyatt's bony fingers drive into my arms. 'What are you gonna do? Lie here and eat every feeling until you can't move?'

'Good plan.'

'I've lived that life. And not through choice,' he says. 'Trust me, it ain't all that.'

'I don't intend to last long.'

'What's wrong with you? They *killed* Ravinder.'

'There's nothing I can do about that.'

'Didn't he mean something to you?' His voice cracks.

'He meant *everything* to me.' It takes me a moment to realize I've spoken the words out loud. And a moment more to realize they're true.

Wyatt's head dips. 'Then why don't—'

'Because now he's gone there's nothing left to fight for. So piss off back to your own deathbed and let me worry about mine.'

He doesn't release me.

'Wyatt—'

'Do you know how long it took me to get to your room?' His lank hair falls over his face.

I don't respond.

'Ten minutes. It's *three* doors away,' he breathes. 'My body is so goddessdamn weak I had to take a break while getting dressed.' A bead of sweat runs down his long nose. 'But I did it. Because I still have legs. I can still walk.' He raises his head and fixes me with determined hazel eyes. 'Ravinder's gone. But you still have legs. You still have arms. And something I haven't – a heart that works.'

It doesn't feel like it works. It feels like an empty shell.

How can I possibly unravel this mystery when I lack the very thing which makes all these people special? How can I hope to outsmart any of them?

He drags me from the bed. Both of us are so weak I end up half pinned, half slumped against the wall. His breaths come in wheezes and rattles.

'Wyatt,' I say, hushed. 'Don't—'

'I didn't ask *anyone* else. I came to you first.'

My breath catches. 'Why?'

'Because I know you didn't do it. Because I know you cared about him. Because I've seen the way everything about you changed when you looked at him. You'd never hurt him, just as I'd never hurt her. And I was *so sure* you'd want to fight for him.'

My heart throbs.

Then I'm not with Wyatt. I'm with Ravi. Light dancing in dark eyes. My hand laced in his, unveiling the parts of myself I'd been commanded to hide. And him calling me a miracle.

I'm not a miracle. Not even close. But he believed I was.

'I'll ask you one last time. If you tell me to piss off, I will. Are you gonna fight for them with me, Ganymedes?' Wyatt shakes me. 'Or are you just gonna lie down and die?'

I made two promises to Ravi. And I don't intend to break either.

'I'll fight.'

Wyatt smiles a crooked grin. 'You're damn right you will.'

Chapter Nine

Day Three – Feast of the Spider

Night

As far as sleuthing partners go, I didn't think through teaming up with a man who rarely has the physical stability to step outside his province, and a child who has never met another Blessed in her depressingly short life.

That means it's down to me to puzzle this out, which isn't ideal – I've dedicated most my life to conceiving of plots to escape talking to these people. Now I need to work out which is capable of murder, or better yet – why.

'Are you done yet?' Wyatt's voice echoes from my bathroom.

Grasshopper rattles the door. 'Freedom!'

I do feel *slightly* guilty for shoving them in the bathroom while I completed my masterpiece. But genius needs thinking space.

I add the final touches to what will soon become a wonder of Concordia, and then spring open the bathroom door.

Grasshopper pounces out, burying her face into my stomach. 'Don't leave again.'

Wyatt freezes, staring at my wall. 'What in the name of the Goddess is *that*?'

'*This* – my reclusive friend – is Detective Dee's Diagram of Deduction!'

I've covered the wall with a map of Concordia – the slice of pie – the curved border of the Bandage in the south, then diagonal lines meeting at the northernmost point of Dragon Province. I've sectioned it off by province (my long-suffering tutors *will* be proud) and have pinned hand-drawn portraits to each, alongside my genius workings.

Wyatt squints. 'You've put red crosses over Dragon and Crow Provinces. It sorta looks like a hit list.'

The crosses were *probably* a bit much. But I have the sinking feeling I'll need to keep track of who's dead. 'It's not a hitlist.'

He narrows his eyes.

'It's *not* a hit list.'

He sighs and lowers himself on to the bed. 'Talk me through it, O wise one.'

Grasshopper scoots next to Wyatt. 'A bear ate my uncle's arm. Now we have one in our swarm!'

I should probably be worried how taken she is by a boy who slammed me against a wall mere hours ago. But her endorsement does make me a little more trusting.

'If we're going to be solving this, we need to evaluate our potential suspects, keep track of what's occurred, put all our clues in one place. Dumpling!' The dragon appears in a puff of green glitter. 'Play something dramatic.'

The fanfare is glorious. Grasshopper does a little shuffle dance. When Dumpling has finished, I proclaim, 'Thus – Detective Dee's Diagram of Deduction!'

Wyatt raises an eyebrow. 'You called your butler Dumpling?'

'Sure. What did you name yours?'

His cheeks blaze. 'Annie . . . It was my horse's name.'

'I ate horse once,' Grasshopper says.

Wyatt looks *horrified*.

'She's joking,' I say.

'No, I'm not.'

Dumpling adjusts his bowtie. 'Am I needed, Master Fish?'

'Yes. Two questions.' I say, eager to move past *that*. 'First – is there anyone present on this ship apart from the twelve heirs and their servers?'

'No. The ship is powered by my creator's Blessing, and maintenance is handled by the servers.'

'So that rules out any stowaways,' Wyatt says.

'Second – Dumpling, would you please stab me in the throat?'

Wyatt leaps up. 'W-What?'

Dumpling blinks placidly. 'I'm afraid I cannot comply. Servers are forbidden from inflicting harm on passengers.'

I spread my hands. 'Then we know one of the servers isn't—'

'What's wrong with you?' Wyatt gapes.

'I knew it wouldn't work.'

'What if it had?'

I shrug.

He angrily blows a flick of hair from his face and settles back on the bed. Prickly one, this bear.

'That'll be all, Dumpling.'

He bows, and then vanishes in a flurry of glitter.

I take up a cane and slam it into the top of the map. The tip of the pie.

I read out what I've written:

'Province: Dragon.
Heir: Eudora Draco.
Age: 20.
Blessing: Bloody everything, but died before inheriting it.'

I add, 'If she'd had the Primus Blessing, maybe she could have stopped it.' There seems no limit to what the emperor can do, apart from the strain on his sanity.

'Details of death: Found hanging from the ballroom chandelier on the first night shortly after midnight. The lights went out for several seconds beforehand.'

'How the hell were you able to keep track of time? You were drunk.'

'I'm an attentive drunk.' I continue:

'Suspicions: Suicide?'

'She wouldn't. Not Eudora.' Wyatt's voice cracks on her name, the same way mine did on Ravi's.

I nod, skipping over the fact that Wyatt met her approximately three times so probably isn't the one to make that call. 'I don't think so either, but I have to record it for posterity. The detective must be disconnected from the crime and treat all information as relevant until proven otherwise.'

Wyatt runs his hands through his hair. 'Why would anyone kill *her*? She's our leader. Everyone adores her. She was perfect.'

I think he was more in love with the idea of her, the legacy she could give him, than the woman herself, but there's no point saying that now.

'Our empire relies on her for its harmony,' he says.

True. The provinces are rather disconnected, focused on their own economies, cultures and lifestyles. With the notable exception of Shinjiro's monks, who have temples across Concordia, few ever leave the province they were born in. Most only concern themselves with their direct neighbours.

But they all ultimately answer to the Dragon throne. The emperor is the linchpin of Concordia.

'Killing the imperial heir,' Wyatt says, hushed. 'It's like chopping off your own head.'

Grasshopper looks up. 'My uncle once—'

I cough. 'We'll come to motives later. All we know at this time is that everyone was present in the ballroom when it occurred.'

'So anyone could have done it.'

'Yes and no.' I scratch my chin with the cane. 'We were all on the ballroom floor, and she was hanging from the chandelier.'

'Someone could have gone upstairs to the balconies when it went dark,' Wyatt says. 'Put the rope around her and pushed her off it.'

'Not in the time those lights were out. It was only moments.'

I try to move my pointer down to the next victim, but my hand seizes.

Grasshopper caw-caws like a bird, snapping me out of it.

'Province: Crow.
Blessed: Ravinder Corvus.
Age: 22.
Blessing: Unknown.'

I never knew. Now I never would. I didn't care about Blessings. Neither did he.

'Details of death: Found—'

My words snap off. I can't do this. Whenever I think about it, I see him again. The ruin of his body. I don't want to remember him that way.

Wyatt takes over:

'Details of death: Found dead on the deck in front of the cabin
side doors at approximately midnight of the second night.
Seventeen stab wounds. The blood was still warm.'

That's right. He was still warm. Someone made me wash my hands.

'Ganymedes?'

I snap back to attention. 'We went out on to the deck from the centre doors. But when I tried to get back inside, they were locked. I had to go around to the cabin side doors.'

Wyatt clicks his tongue. 'You're saying the murderer locked them? Why would they?'

'Maybe to stop people going out on to the deck and discovering the body?' I sigh. 'But then why not lock the cabin side doors too?'

He knuckles his chin. 'It's damn strange.'

'I have a suspicion it happened while I was on the other side of the ship,' I say. 'It was freezing, he wouldn't have stayed warm long.'

'So Ravinder encountered someone on the deck.'

'Or someone followed him. It would have been easy to sneak up on someone in that weather.' A chill crawls down my spine. I can't – won't – think about it. Someone following Ravi, blade in hand, footsteps silenced by the storm.

'He was stabbed, right? Who would carry a knife?' Wyatt asks.

'Dumpling!'

A burst of glitter. 'Master?'

'Can you fetch me a knife, a nice sharp one perfect for stabbing?'

He obliges. It looks bizarre, grasped in his clawed paw.

Wyatt rubs his forehead. 'Point taken: anyone could get a knife.'

'That'll be all, Dumpling.'

He vanishes, taking his weapon with him.

'Why would someone want Ravinder dead?' Wyatt asks. 'Maybe he had an enemy?'

'No way,' I say instantly. 'Nobody would ever want to hurt Ravi. He wouldn't do anything to make anyone dislike him.' He was obsessed by what they all thought of him.

'I thought detectives had to be objective?'

'I am!'

Wyatt's eyebrow quirks up.

'Crow Province is where divinium was discovered,' I say bitterly, hating that Ravi died believing I had squandered precious divinium on a costume. 'It's the only substance capable of filling the cracks in the Bandage, where the emperor's Blessing is failing. If they wanted access to the divinium, killing Ravi and taking advantage of the resulting upheaval in Crow Province would be the easiest way to do it. It's worth a fortune.'

Wyatt nods. 'I heard people started streaming into Crow Province. The population tripled in a year.'

When I visited, Crow Province was beautiful, ragged and wild. But lonely. You could walk all day and never encounter another soul. As a boy who grew up surrounded by the same faces, I couldn't comprehend how secluded Ravi's life must have been, alone in those cold caves.

Wyatt's gaze digs into me. 'Any other reason someone would want Ravinder dead?'

Yes. One terrible one. A secret he only told me. Anyone who discovered that would have killed him, no questions asked. 'Yes. But I can't tell you.'

'We're supposed to be solving this together.'

'I promised him.' A vow beneath the night lights. 'I can't say.'

Wyatt crosses his arms, but drops the issue.

'Now – suspects.'

My pointer moves to the section running along Dragon Province's southern border.

'Province: Tiger.
Blessed: Leofric Tigris.'

I smirk. 'Or as I prefer – Leoprick.' I wait for a laugh. 'Did you hear me? I said—'

'I heard you.'

'You didn't laugh.'

'No.'

'Age: 26.
Blessing: Unknown.'

I pause. 'Unless "being a gigantic cock" counts.' *Having one* might.

'Your eyes are glazing,' Wyatt says.

'I'm here.' I shake my head.

'Suspicions: Has unique access to Eudora. Wasn't guarding Eudora night
one. Was present in the corridor night two.'

I scratch my chin. 'Cordelia said he was comforting her that first night.'

'Do you believe that?' Wyatt asks.

'Yes. It's *annoyingly* believable.' I stare at the sketch of a grumpy tiger. 'Considering how close he was to Lysander they probably bonded. Grief does that to people.'

Wyatt says nothing. He doesn't need to.

'Motive: None.'

I tuck the cane behind my back. My knowledge of other provinces, especially the uppers, isn't extensive. But it's better than most thanks to my father employing tutors to torture me in my youth. 'Tiger Province is the smallest province but possesses the biggest ego. Scions have served as shields since Concordia was founded. When the Crabs led their revolution, it was Tiger Province that stopped them.' A story they've been repeating for the last thousand years. 'They believe it's their sacred duty or some shit. They take it *very* seriously. Protecting the emperor is their sole purpose – you've seen that collar they wear. Only the leader has the key. Leofric's mother fucked up one time; an assassin managed to stab Emperor Eugenios.'

Wyatt's eyes bulge. 'I heard about that. The emperor was bedridden.'

'Leofric gets *super* spiky if you ever mention it. Considering Eudora's death has screwed his entire legacy, I'm not sure what his motivation would be to kill her.'

I turn back to my diagram.

'Murderer level: 2/5.'

'You're giving them a rating?' Wyatt doesn't hide the judgement in his voice.

'You wanted to team up.'

He looks like he may be regretting that.

'This is based mainly on how terrifying his Blessing probably is, if we believe the Tigers' reputation. He likely has the strength and the access but none of the motive. On the night Ravi was . . .' I still can't say 'murdered'; it jams in my throat.

'On *that* night he was guarding Eudora's room, and came running when Cordelia screamed.'

'Out of which door?' Wyatt asks.

I shrug. I only remember strong arms prising my hands from Ravi's. 'He would've had to act fast to leave his post, attack Ravi, then return to come running out again when Cordelia screamed. Unless he never went back inside.' I tap the cane against my head. 'But he would have *had* to know Ravi was on the deck. If we assume Ravi came from his room, Leofric wouldn't have seen him from his spot outside Eudora's cabin. The wall is in the way. Also, I can't imagine him leaving his post.'

'He left it when he heard Cordelia screaming.'

'True. But I can't get past his lack of motive,' I say. 'I know he manhandled you at the party, but Leofric has more to lose from Eudora's death than anyone.'

Wyatt relents and waves his hand for me to continue.

'Province: Spider "Blessed" Province.'

It's a strange nickname for what is essentially a crater. For ten out of twelve months it rains non-stop, flooding the crater. But the rain has a use – it sifts precious stones to the surface. When it finally stops and the water level drops, it's harvesting season. In Fish Province, we go fishing for – well – fish. But in Spider Province they fish for rubies, emeralds and sapphires. That's why it's known as 'Blessed Province' and why it's second only to Dragon in wealth. Cut the earth in Spider Province, and it bleeds jewels.

'Blessed: Nergüi Aranea.
Age: 24.
Blessing: Unknown.'

125

I tried to make a spider look sinister. It kind of worked.

'Creepy,' Grasshopper offers.

I nod.

My father calls Spider Province a 'lawless' place without notions of good or evil. Nothing is forbidden there. A horrifying notion for fisherfolk who pride themselves on following the emperor's laws. But it has created a province where difference is embraced and pushing the empire's stifling boundaries is applauded.

If Fish are the emperor's obedient hounds, loyally fetching dinner, then Spiders are cats, pushing ornaments from shelves to see what they can get away with.

'Suspicions: Generally suspicious.'

'You can't write that,' Wyatt says.

'Whose diagram is this?'

He throws up his hands in surrender.

'Nergüi's an enigma. I suspect they know how often I shit in a day,' I say.

'I heard they have spies all over Concordia.' Wyatt shifts. 'My brothers found Spider nests in Bear Province.'

It's believable. Bar the monks, Spider Province inhabitants are the most well travelled in the empire. I even grew up seeing them: curious figures draped in jewels who offered me sweets if I spent an hour chatting with them, then vanished without a trace.

'They said something strange at the party.' I glance aside. 'That the night was going to be "legendary". They knew something was going to happen. I'm just not sure if that was my "legendary" outfit, or Eudora's "legendary" death.'

Wyatt glares. 'You say those two things like they're equal.'

I clear my throat. 'Either way, Nergüi knowing about

something and Nergüi being the one responsible are two very different things.' I pray they're not involved. Firstly, because if they are it means I'll have to face them, and secondly, I doubt I'll be able to untangle this web if Nergüi's the one spinning it.

'Motive: Fuck knows.
Murderer level: 3/5.'

I clear my throat. 'That's purely on a shiftiness basis. They probably know *something*, even if they didn't do it themselves.' Maybe Nergüi would have been a better sleuthing partner.

Great idea, Dee. Team up with the person who likely knows your deepest secret.

My pointer moves east to a weepy tortoise.

'Province: Tortoise.
Blessed: Cordelia Testudo (RIP Lysander).
Age: 19.'

Wyatt raises a hand.
'A question from the class?'
'You've written "goddessdammit" before her name.'
'You can read then.'
'Big library!' Grasshopper offers.
I point the cane at her. 'Correct! The Tortoises' traditional role is that of chroniclers, recording events for future generations. That big library is full of every damn thing that has happened in Concordia.' With some omissions involving Crabs, I suspect. 'But in the last few centuries they've been more concerned with technological advancements. Lysander never stopped jabbering on about his "dream of a new world".'

Wyatt grips his knees. 'They think they're better than us 'cause they spend decades reading books written by dead guys. But Lysander was different. He listened to me.'

'He invited me to his province once.' I'd been tempted, I'd heard stories of their smog-covered capital, fuelled by factories and industries. But then I learned about the terrible food and the alcohol ban, and decided bugger that.

'Blessing: Determining others' greatest desires.'

Cordelia inherited Lysander's Blessing. He was never coy about hiding it. It's probably why so many adored him – he knew the key to their hearts. Perhaps that's why he treated me so gently.

'Suspicions: Was wandering around delirious on the deck when Ravi . . .'

Couldn't even write it. Coward.

'What was she doing out there?'

I eye Wyatt. I feel guilty dropping her in it, but I can't keep everything from him. 'She said she was following her brother.'

'The dead one?'

'The very same. She was convinced she followed him on to the deck. Considering her cabin is on the right-hand side, I assume she used the centre doors too.'

'Guessing you don't buy the Lysander thing?'

'No. But I think *she* did,' I say. '*Annoyingly*, I don't think she killed him. Ravi was covered with blood. She was wearing a white nightdress and it was spotless. Plus, that door can only be locked from the inside and she was with me the whole time. I don't think she stabbed him.'

'You seem irritated by that.'

'It's *fine*,' I say through gritted teeth.

'*Motive: None.*'

I sigh. 'She wasn't married to Ravi yet, and she was set to inherit a fortune, not only in money, but power. Killing him before that transpired would have been the action of a moron. And as much as I loathe to admit it, I don't think she's a moron.'

Wyatt squints. 'Why is her murderer level 5/5 then?'

'It's my diagram!' I snap. 'I can write what I want!' I swerve my pointer west to an elephant rolling its eyes.

'*Province: Elephant (aka the Funnel).*'

The nickname of Tendai's province is due to its unique position. Most northern provinces are bordered by impassable jagged mountains – the same ones that comprise the entirety of Crow Province. But Elephant occupies an arid, flat strip of land that runs straight through the centre, up to Tiger and Dragon Provinces. Because of this all of Concordia's trade is 'funnelled' through it.

'*Blessed: Tendai Elephas.*
Age: 24.
Blessing: Unknown.
Suspicions: Met with Eska the night of Ravi's . . .'

'Try . . . departure?' Wyatt suggests.

I know he's trying to help, but Dumpling already tried 'departure'. And it still sounds like Ravi just slipped off on a dinghy. Instead of rotting in Eudora's cabin.

'I saw Eska enter her room. Could've been scheming.' I screw up my face. 'It's such an odd pairing. The only thing they have in common is they both detest everyone else. Either way, she was certainly up and about when *it* happened.'

'But if Eska was in Tendai's room, maybe that's an alibi?'

'Seeing as Tendai hasn't piped up since they accused Eska, I doubt it,' I say.

'Motive: Everyone hates her. Has history of pissing people off.'

I search my memory for an incredibly boring conversation. 'My father's always moaning about her. I think she raised the prices for passing trade through the Funnel. There was a lot of "back in my day this never happened".'

Wyatt nods. 'My brothers were discussing toll increases when they returned from the cattle drive. Maybe that's why they hate her?'

I think back to the previous day's breakfast. To that thinly disguised tension from Cordelia and Jasper – half terrified, half disgusted. How Nergüi, who carefully considers every action, knew being rude to Tendai was a safe choice in a room full of Blessed: *'You know what she's capable of, Tiger.'*

'No. She did something else. I'm just not sure if it's related to the murders,' I say.

'Murderer level: 1/5.'

I shrug. 'I think I would've heard a wheelchair rolling along the decks, storm or no. Also, killing Blessed is a pretty extreme way to annoy people, I can't imagine even Tendai's that dedicated.'

I move my marker to the heart of the map.

'Province: Bunnerfly.
Blessed: Shinjiro Lepus.
Age: 30.'

I clasp my hands together in mock prayer. 'Head of the religion, voice of the Goddess and whacked off his tits 24/7.'

'Ganymedes!' Wyatt winces.

'I know what he puts in that tea.'

'It's *calming* tea,' Wyatt says. 'The monks believe everything must be in balance, including emotions.'

I suppose it's easy to be balanced when you live in a mountain paradise. Bunnerfly Province doesn't have to battle with the horrendous heat of Bear Province, or the blistering cold of Ermine. The weather is perfectly temperate, with their crystalline streams, paddies of rice and perfectly symmetrical temples.

'Blessing: Unknown.'

I look at Wyatt. 'You must know. You seemed close at the party.'

He taps his fingers together. 'It's not my place to say. If you ask, he'll probably tell.'

I write: 'To be confirmed' and roll my eyes.

'Suspicions: Falsely claimed he was at Wyatt's door night two. Location unknown.'

I point at Wyatt. 'He said he was outside your door all night when Leofric questioned us, but he wasn't there when I was in the corridor.'

Wyatt's brow furrows. 'He's an irritatingly patient man. He asked to be let in for a *long* time, barring breaks for prayers.' That's three times a day – sunrise, midday and sunset. 'Then it went quiet. I assumed he'd finally given up.'

'Do you remember when?'

131

He scratches his neck. 'I wasn't watching the clock, but I think shortly before midnight?'

I *just* missed him. If he's involved, then a few minutes sooner and I could've saved Ravi.

'Motive: None.
Murderer level: 2/5.'

I tap the cane against the map. 'The monks' loyalty to the Crown is second only to the Tigers'. They *are* the voice of the Goddess. Fuck knows enough of them go on pilgrimages to Fish Province to rabbit on about it.' I snicker at my own joke. 'Other than some mad power play from the Church, I can't see why he'd do this. The monks worship harmony. It's like crack to them.' *Which is probably also what's in their tea.*

Wyatt smirks. 'Eloquently put.'

I move the pointer south, to the biggest region on the map. A mass of sprawling deserts and canyons, bursting with beasts designed to tear humans to shreds. There's a reason Bears live every day as if it's their last, a reason they celebrate their triumphant deaths. Because when you live in a place like that, it's better to embrace death as a companion than try to fight it.

'Province: Bear.
Blessed: Wyatt Ursus.
Age: 22.
Blessing: . . .'

He fiddles with his shirt. 'Not relevant. If it was, d'ya think I'd spend most of my days trying not to die?'

'Just tell me.' I pout.

The tips of his ears turn pink. 'Not right now.'

'Suspicions: Actions unaccounted for since night one.'

'I didn't take her death well,' Wyatt mutters.

After my reaction to Ravi's death, I hardly feel I can judge.

'I was inside my room since the first night. Shinjiro can attest to that.'

I nod.

'Motive: Probably wouldn't kill the woman he's been trying to bone for a decade.'

'Cross that out!'

I don't. 'Also, I'm pretty sure Ravi could take you.'

His nostrils flare, then he notices his murderer level. *'Four?'*

I smirk. 'Did it to mess with you. You're a one. No offence, but I don't know you that well. I had to at least give you a one. You don't come to half the summits, lucky sod.'

He unbuttons his collar, eager to move on. 'Next?'

'And you call me a moron.'

'You *are* a moron.'

'Fair.' I swing the pointer west, to a sketch of an ermine brandishing a knife.

'Province: Ermine.
Blessed: Eska Mustela.
Age: 25.
Blessing: . . .'

' "Unknown"!' Grasshopper sings.

'Suspicions: Visited Tendai night two. Witnessed wandering the ship alone.
Has not attended meetings or meals.
Motive: Hates everyone. Enjoys stabbing.'

'That's not true surely?' Wyatt looks a little peaky.

'The tundra people have a reputation for being a little . . .
anti-Dragon. Anti-anyone-who-isn't-them, really. She attends
even fewer summits than you, and barely engages when she
is there.' My hand throbs in memory. 'Trust me, she isn't
interested in befriending any of us. Bitching about Ermines
is a national hobby for fisherfolk.'

'What do they say?'

I count on my fingers. 'They're heretics with their own
religion. They fuck mammoths. They speak to each other in
"devil's tongues". I think they're saying Ermines have their
own language.' I'm pretty sure the mammoth fucking is an
exaggeration, but I suspect the language one is true.

'But that's illegal.' Wyatt clutches the bed. 'Only the offi-
cial religion and language of Concordia are allowed, by order
of the emperor. It encourages unity.'

'Of course.' I'm not sure about Bear Province, but I know
the ancient Crow and Fish languages were never truly
exspunged from existence. Ravi taught me whispered words
once, his tongue dancing around lyrical syllables.

My chest burns. I bury the memory.

'Murderer level: 3/5.'

I glance at Wyatt. 'Leofric's not wrong; she's suddenly
shown her face, and now her enemies are dropping like flies.
Combined with Ermine Province's infamous dislike of the

134

empire, I can't deny her suspiciousness. But I'm also sure if Eska was going around murdering people, I'd be first. I'd almost be offended if she *was* the murderer.'

'You're a unique kind of person, aren't you?' Wyatt says.

I move the pointer down to the long line that wraps along the southern border.

'Province: Ox (the Bandage).
Blessed: Jasper Bos (the Bastard).
Age: 14.
Blessing: Fire breathing.'

I spread my arms. 'Finally, a boy who isn't afraid to show his skills.'

'He sorta has no choice,' Wyatt says. 'Defending the Bandage from the Crabs every day.'

Grasshopper swings her legs, gnawing her pendant.

'Suspicions: Infamously hot temper.
Motive: Better access to divinium.
Murderer level: 3/5.'

I say, 'Apparently the Bandage is all kinds of fucked up. Jasper said he was here to suck up to the uppers to get more divinium to mend the tears. Maybe he realized the soft touch won't work?'

'Seems an extreme way to save everyone.'

I stare at the angry ox sketch. 'I don't put extreme ways past Jasper. But if he was killing, why not burn them to a crisp?'

'Too obvious?'

'Maybe, but Eudora's death was well thought out, executed with precision. Not an accident of rage.'

Not Ravi's though. Jasper would be the most likely candidate to kill someone if he discovered they were secretly half-Crab.

'Problem is, Eudora's death means if the emperor dies now the Bandage will likely fall. That seems a senseless thing for the commander to do.'

I move my cane to the far east.

'Province: Grasshopper
Blessed:—'

'Grasshopper!' she declares.

'You've just written "adorable".' Wyatt gives me a long look.

'Correct.' I scrutinize my drawing. It's challenging to make a six-legged insect look cute, but somehow, I managed it.

It's incredible she *is* this cute, considering her province. Grasshopper Province is an amalgamation of all the elements that make the others dangerous, bundled into one terrifying package. An inhospitable rainforest that regrows as quickly as you can cut it down, agonizingly humid, with a host of delightful murderous animals to boot. It's no wonder her region, despite its size, is the most sparsely populated.

'What's it like, living in the rainforest?' I ask.

'Sometimes when it rains our whole village gets swept away!' Grasshopper spreads her arms.

Despite this, her people grow an incredible array of crops – tropical fruits, cocoa, nuts, spices – but they're best known for their medicines. This child is fated to risk her life sending crops to people who have no comprehension of what it cost to grow them. Every lower province has trade quotas we must fulfil, for the 'united good of the empire'.

'Dee's sad?' Grasshopper asks. 'It's OK! We build new houses!'

I force a smile.

'*Age: 6*
Blessing: . . .'

It didn't feel right to expose someone else's Blessing. Especially not someone that adorable.

But Grasshopper prevents any awkwardness by proclaiming, 'This!' Then vanishes.

Wyatt gags.

'Right. That.' I write 'That' just in case someone gets hold of my diagram. We lower provinces need any advantages we can get.

Wyatt adjusts his hair. 'Wouldn't turning invisible be the perfect Blessing if you wanted to murder people?'

Grasshopper reappears and punches him in the arm.

'Good point.'

'She was with me the whole time. Also, she's six.' I look at Grasshopper. 'Hands over ears!'

'Right!'

'On the second day, I found the lock to her room broken, and her cabin wrecked,' I explain. 'I think someone went hunting for her the first night, or early the second morning.'

'She was targeted,' Wyatt says, his voice low.

'Considering we don't know when it happened, anyone could have done it. So it doesn't massively help us.'

I motion for Grasshopper to remove her hands.

'*Adorable level: 5/5.*'

I nod sagely. 'If I had to pick someone to be murdered by it would absolutely be her ladyship.'

Grasshopper claps gleefully. 'I'll kill Dee if he asks me to!'

Wyatt looks between us, speechless.

'Last and best of all . . .' I swerve the pointer to the western shoreline.

'Province: Fish.
Blessed: Yours truly.
Age: 22.
Suspicions:—'

'You missed out "Blessing",' Wyatt says.

I grumble and scribble in 'Blessing' beside the drawing of a suave fish. I almost write 'None' on instinct, but instead write 'Secret'. I know what it *should* be – controlling the weather. But I don't fancy being asked to demonstrate that.

Wyatt doesn't press the issue. Maybe I'm the only scion who dares ask another about their Blessing. Probably because I'm the only one *not* with one.

'Suspicions: Discovered Ravi night two. Last known
person to speak to Eudora.
Motive: Possible criminal mastermind.'

'You do seem to interact with the victims before they die,' Wyatt comments.

'Maybe my Blessing is death by proxy.'

He shifts; then he relaxes his shoulders. 'If I go, I won't hold it against you. It's a long time coming.'

I laugh. Then catch myself. I shouldn't be laughing. Ravi is dead and I'm laughing.

'You're allowed to laugh,' Wyatt says.

I press my lips together. 'Suffice to say, I didn't do it. Ravi was . . .' My heart pounds. 'He was . . .'

Something warm clasps my hand. Grasshopper, rubbing her little fingers against mine.

'I know you didn't do it,' Wyatt says softly. 'That's why I'm here.'

I return to the map. 'What we have are a lot of facts without much substance. Eudora's death doesn't make sense. How could anyone kill her and return in the seconds the lights went out? And almost everyone is unaccounted for when Ravi was . . . hurt.' I rest the cane against the wall. 'We need to start with the bodies. Get a proper look at them.'

Wyatt looks about as excited at the prospect of that as me. Our two lost loves laid out side by side. Quite the bonding experience.

An explosion of glitter bursts over Wyatt's head. A dragon appears, snow white with a long fluffy mane. 'Master Bear, this is your nightly alarm. You must return to your quarters.'

Wyatt's ears turn pink. 'I know, I know.' He shoos the dragon away and turns to me, apologetically. 'I have to . . . do some stuff.'

'Stuff that means you don't die?'

'You got it.' He massages his temples. He looks even paler than usual, veins popping blue against white skin. 'Don't start without me tomorrow.' I help him with the door, half tripping over my legs.

'You need help getting to your room?'

'What do I look like? A charity case?'

'No. You look swell. That greyish tinge to your skin really brings out your eyes.'

He laughs dryly, and then shuffles down the corridor.

I lock my door and return to the map, staring at those big red Xs.

'Dumpling.'

He's at my side in an instant. 'How may I assist you?'

'Can you hide this map from anyone who isn't one of us three? So if someone breaks in, they can't read it?'

'What would you like them to see instead?'

The possibilities. 'Anything. Naked portraits of the emperor.'

'Noted.'

'Also, can you alert me if my cabin is entered uninvited?'

'How would you like me to do that?'

'Anything. Slap me round the face with a fish while playing the harmonica if you have to. Just make sure I know.'

'Done.'

I collapse in bed. Grasshopper nuzzles into my side, arms locked around my torso. I could pretend I'm comforting her. But I know that's wrong. Because this time I'm the one shaking.

'Dumpling?' I whisper. 'Can you create smells?'

He drifts above us, glowing a faint green.

'Yes. Which scent would you like?'

I close my eyes. In the darkness, the night sky gleams with dancing colours. 'Smoke and lavender.'

Chapter Ten

Day Four – Feast of the Tortoise

Morning

'Maybe we shouldn't,' Wyatt says, hazel eyes upon me.

'We have to.' I study the door to Eudora's cabin. Leofric isn't guarding it any more, he's too busy with his vigil outside Eska's. I couldn't get close because Jasper was patrolling the perimeter as if it was the Bandage. I did notice that the handle was wrapped in chains. But I suspect being barricaded in a room away from everyone is far from punishment for an Ermine.

Wyatt rubs his arms, speckled with moles. 'I want to remember her the way she was – *alive.*'

If one of his brothers were here, he'd probably be parading Eudora's corpse through the ship with coloured streamers. Although, I'm not sure if being murdered is good for one's legacy. If Eudora had gone out wrestling a wolf, maybe.

I breathe out slowly. 'I'm not exactly jumping for joy at the prospect of seeing my ex . . . best friend looking like honeycomb, but their bodies could give us some clues towards the killer's identity.'

'Honeycomb?'

'You know – the holes?' I say.

Wyatt stares. '*Right* . . .'

Grasshopper tugs my hand eagerly. Goddess, that girl has bloodlust.

Wyatt looks like he's going to faint. His brow is wet with sweat.

I *really* don't want to enter the corpse chamber alone but . . . 'I'll go by myself.'

Wyatt's head snaps up. 'I'm coming.' He hobbles towards the door.

I kneel before Grasshopper. 'You keep watch outside.'

'Nobody's coming.'

I brush her hair away from her face. 'There are scary things in there and—'

'Dead bodies.'

'Yes. So—'

'I saw my first when I was two!' She holds up two fingers. 'I poked it with a stick. It went right through the skin!' She skips away and joins Wyatt.

I never thought cute things could also be terrifying until I met that girl.

I'm just joining them when the door springs open. Wyatt screams. I don't blame him.

Out strides Nergüi, jewels streaming down from a black headpiece like rain. 'Ganymedes.' They stop before me. 'You've come to see Ravinder?'

His name sends a hot lance of pain through my core. 'Yes.' I stare down at my feet. Being in Nergüi's presence makes me feel like a child facing a parent after their sin has been discovered – each waiting for the other to speak it into being.

'What were you doing in there?' Wyatt asks.

Nergüi doesn't turn to him. 'I needed to see her. To

confirm it. Dragons *are* mortal.' Their red lips twist into a smile. 'You have not taken me up on my invitation.'

'Invitation?' I squeak.

'In Ravinder's room on the second day. Our chat.'

I'll schedule that for just after the sea freezes over. 'I was a bit distracted by my best friend being brutally murdered.'

Their lips purse. 'This voyage is twelve days long. We are already on the fourth. Before these remaining nine days are over we *will* have this conversation.'

Wyatt tugs at his sleeves. 'Why don't we have it now?'

Nergüi's eyes do not leave me. 'Just Ganymedes and me.'

Goody.

Wyatt clears his throat. 'Why would—'

'How are your brothers faring?' Nergüi turns to him.

Wyatt licks his dry lips. 'They . . .'

'Because I know *exactly* how they are faring, and if you think my and Ganymedes' business is yours perhaps *your* business should also be vocalized to all of Concordia?'

Wyatt, Goddess bless him, makes a valiant attempt to hold Nergüi's gaze, but doesn't make it past their knees.

Nergüi returns to me. 'Nine days, Ganymedes.'

'Or what?' I whisper.

Their lips twist. 'I don't think that's a question you want an answer to.' They hold my gaze for a moment too long, then move towards me.

I wince, expecting a blade. Instead, they press something cold into my hand. A key.

'To the Dragon cabin. Do lock up for me.'

'How did you get this?' I ask.

'Tsk. What a dull question.' Then they turn, jewels clinking as they disappear down the corridor.

Wyatt doubles over, gasping for breath, while I silently congratulate myself for not shitting my pants.

'What did they mean about your brothers?' I ask.

Wyatt pales. 'All I know is one of them visited the Spider to demand they remove their spies in Bear Province.' He licks his dry lips. 'Well, it must have gone badly because since he returned, he's not spoken a word. He just sits still all day long. The only sounds he makes are his screams through the night.'

My blood goes cold. 'Why didn't I hear about this?'

He shifts awkwardly. 'We made sure it didn't get out. We're known for our strength. How would it look if the whole empire found out the Spider was able to badly harm the Bear Blessed's brother?'

It would make them look weak. Easy to take advantage of. A fearsome reputation is one of the only tools in Bear Province's scant arsenal.

Nergüi knew exactly what they were doing – sending a message to *stay out* of their business, while knowing they would never have to face any consequences for doing so.

His gaze catches mine. 'Don't meet with Nergüi alone.'

'No shit.' I shake out the tremble in my arms. After that, a room of corpses is almost appealing. 'Come on. Let's get this over with.'

*

When you live by the sea, death is a constant companion. People who drown all look the same – blue and bloated, soft flesh slipping away from bones. I'm accustomed to corpses. But Eudora doesn't look like those bodies. She lies atop her bed, hands crossed at her chest, still dressed in her glimmering scales. A sleeping dragon. She has a twinge of a smile, as if greeting an old friend. Perfect even in death.

Wyatt falls to his knees beside her. A trembling hand hovers over her cheek, afraid to touch her, even now.

The Dragon cabin could fit mine inside four times over. It's decorated to resemble the Emerald Palace, seat of the emperor. Everything is gilded or adorned with jade, including the four-poster bed with its silken sheets. Damask hangings cascade down the walls, and a fireplace burns green flame. It makes the room hot and humid. I imagine not the best place to store corpses.

'I never got to tell her,' Wyatt says, and I don't need to ask what.

Grasshopper rubs his back. 'They return to the earth, to complete the circle.'

This 'circle' is not anything I've ever heard a monk preach. It sounds dangerously like murmurings of a Grasshopper Province belief system beyond the Goddess, but I don't think Wyatt's listening. He's staring at Eudora the same way he did at the party – in utter awe. I'm tempted to ask how he can love a woman he only spoke to a handful of times. How he can seek revenge for someone who barely acknowledged his existence. Then I think it's better to say nothing.

'I'm sorry,' he whispers. 'I couldn't save you.'

'It's not your fault,' I say.

He grips the bed, body trembling. 'I'm an embarrassment to my family and province.' His words are like broken glass. 'If I do one thing before I die, it'll be to expose her murderer.'

I touch his shoulder, feeling his bones pushing against his shirt. There's nothing to this boy. 'You might want to look away.'

'You're going to undress her.'

'I have to check her body for clues.'

'I know,' he says stiffly, moving aside.

As I lean over the body, a strange smell washes over me – musty and acidic. I move her mint-green hair from her neck, exposing a reddish-purple bruise. Then I tug one strap of her dress down, brushing velvet-smooth skin. My hand jerks back. Blessed hells. I can't do this. She's the actual personification of the Goddess. How can I undress the Goddess?

'Ganymedes,' Wyatt says. 'Please do it. I can't.'

The last time I saw Eudora, she was smirking in the bathroom. A sunrise in human form. Now she's about to be stripped by a boy she only spoke to properly mere days ago, and another whose obsession would probably alarm her.

'I'll do it.' I run my hands down my face. 'Just give me . . .' I turn.

Her room has two beds. I didn't notice the one at the foot of hers. Maybe Leofric was supposed to curl up like a loyal hound. But now he won't. Because it's occupied.

I don't want to be closer to him; can't be closer to him. Yet my body drags me forward. As inevitable as two opposing poles – fated to eternally attract the other.

The thread wasn't cut after all.

Then I'm looking at the corpse of the man I love for the second time in two days.

Eudora looks as though she's sleeping. Ravi doesn't.

They've stripped him; his torso is bare and riddled with slashes. The blood crusts rust brown against dark skin. Seventeen stab wounds. *Seventeen.* Some are clean, but most are ragged and ugly. As if they were executed in a hurry, a mania.

They would have had to get close. And Ravi hated anyone in his space. It took him two years to work up the courage to hold my hand. They would have seen the terror in his eyes. He would have seen *them.*

146

I'd been holding on to a hope that that night was a shift of the eye. An illusion. Some scion playing tricks with a Blessing. Maybe I would find someone else here, or he would vanish beneath my touch.

But as I press my hand to his cheek, I feel him. *His* smooth skin. *His* plump lips. *His* long eyelashes. *His* bitten-down nails, an anxious habit.

It's him. It's Ravi. And he's dead.

Ravi hated anything to do with death. While the other Crows spoke solemnly about the souls trapped in their caves, Ravi tried to guide the spirits outside, crawling through tight tunnels with a torch. He couldn't stand the thought of a single soul suffering. He saw a fisherman gut a fish once and cried for hours. It seemed impossible that he could exist in this world and be that gentle.

But someone saw that sweet man and stuck a knife in him. Not once, but over and over again. Did he scream? Was he alone when the last vestiges of life left him? Was he cold? Ravi always felt the cold; that's why he wrapped up so tightly. Skinny arms hugging long legs.

Did he think of me?

I clutch the bed. I hate the world. I hate every person on this ship who isn't in this room. To turn him into *this*. This mound of flesh.

Grasshopper rushes to me, singing words of comfort – snippets of circles and rebirths and eternities.

Ravi got engaged to another, told me to stay away, that I was a risk to him. That I was of no value.

But it's not *that* Ravi I'm doing this for, it's for the *real* one. For the boy who trusted me enough to tell me his secrets, and who I trusted enough to tell him mine. For the boy who, for one moment in my insignificant life, made me feel important. Worthy of someone's affection. Worthy of anything.

I'm doing this for him.

I take his hand and kiss it. Long elegant fingers. His hands were always moving. Always warm. Now they're bone cold and utterly still.

When I turn, Wyatt is staring at me, eyes gleaming. He wipes them hastily.

Something brushes my hand. Ravi's fingers are beginning to lose the stiffness that sets in after death. I ease them open enough to glimpse something clutched inside. 'He's holding something.' I shimmy it out. It's a folded scrap of paper. 'A note?'

Wyatt dashes forwards. 'What's it say?'

My fingers are trembling so furiously I can barely unravel it. Ravi's hand was so firmly clasped around it that they must have missed it when they moved his body.

It might be a letter from the killer. A calling card.

Or it might be the very last thing Ravi wrote.

And for a moment, I think that maybe, just maybe, it might be a message for me:

My love,

I'm sorry the wedding can't go ahead.
But I walk to my death with open arms.
We will say our vows when we meet again in eternity.

Wyatt takes it from me, turning the paper over. 'This isn't . . . That sounds like . . .'

'He knew.' The words fall from my lips like lead. They fill the room, pressing in all around me.

He knew. He knew. He knew.

'He knew he was going to die.'

Yet the thing that hurts the most is that in his final moments he was thinking about *her* and not *me*.

I don't realize I'm crying until Wyatt awkwardly says, 'We shouldn't share this with anyone. They'll say he stabbed himself seventeen times.' He holds it out. 'You want it?'

I take it, though I'm not sure why. Maybe I just want to hold a piece of him. Even if it's jagged and painful.

'Who did he meet on the deck?' I ask numbly. 'And why would he go there knowing he was going to die?' Not only that – it sounds like he was content to die.

Wyatt scratches his neck. 'Maybe he . . .' There's nothing he can say. No explanation that fixes this.

'Everything we went through – he threw it away like it meant nothing.'

'I'm sure it meant something.'

'If it did, he wouldn't have left me alone.' And that's how Ravi wanted me. The last word he said to me. *Alone.*

Dragon's dick. I'm still crying. I slap myself across the face. Got to get it together. For the man who has betrayed me three times.

'Sorry to ask again.' Wyatt clears his throat. 'But Eudora—'

'There are no other marks,' a new voice says.

Grasshopper is the only one not to scream. She promptly disappears instead.

I didn't hear him enter, but standing at the door, trying to hide how pleased he is at terrifying us, is the monk – Shinjiro. 'Invisibility! What a delightful Blessing.'

'What are you doing here?' Wyatt clutches his heart.

Shinjiro pouts. 'I could ask you the same question, Wyatt dearest. Why haven't you been opening your door to me? It's rude to deny entry to the voice of the Goddess. Even worse to deny a friend. I was surprised to return to your room this morning to find it empty.' His words are as carefree as a trickling stream, but as with many things Shinjiro says, there's a sharp edge.

'I didn't . . . I wasn't . . .'

'What's that you said about her body?' I ask.

Shinjiro chuckles. 'You have an interest in corpses, Ganymedes?'

'These two maybe.'

He nods, as if expecting that answer. 'Very well. I'll tell you what I know. But let's do it somewhere slightly more *vibrant*. Perhaps with a spot of tea and a biscuit?'

Wyatt looks horrified, but as Shinjiro has yanked him by the collar, he doesn't have much choice in the matter.

The talk of food summons Grasshopper – she reappears and grabs my hand. With a 'Bodies and biscuits!' she drags me from the room.

Chapter Eleven

Day Four – Feast of the Tortoise

Afternoon

As I sit cross-legged on Shinjiro's mat, I realize two things –
I've been short-changed when it comes to accommodation,
and I've severely underestimated this monk.

Shinjiro's room is a monastic mountain haven in the
midst of a murder boat. While my room had illusions of
the sea, this guy has a real goddessdamn pond with *actual*
fish. A mini waterfall flows behind his woven-grass bed,
while rows of bamboo deer scarers 'clonk' against rocks.
An orange-scented breeze teases my hair, and in the distance songbirds twitter.

Shinjiro sits before me. A long chain hangs from his neck,
displaying the symbol of the Goddess – golden weighing
scales within a circle.

'How did you get all this stuff?' I ask.

Steam billows from his teacup. 'Anything is possible
through the grace of the Goddess.'

Right. Probably means he leveraged his 'unique' relationship with Dragon Province to bag himself a nice room.

I sip my green tea. After my last few days, I was hoping he'd slip in something other than tea leaves.

Shinjiro winks. 'Our special blend is for anointed monks only.'

I fucking knew it.

Wyatt sits stiffly beside me, untouched tea gripped in too-tight hands, looking like a man preparing to face his execution.

Grasshopper chugs her apple juice as she explores the room. There are distant crashes of metal and porcelain, but Shinjiro doesn't seem to mind.

'Before we get into that nasty business, I wish to enquire about your province, Ganymedes,' Shinjiro says.

'You do?' Nobody ever asks about Fish Province.

'I was concerned – my monks based in Crow Province informed me earthquakes have been reported in the south. They moved a great deal of the population north to safety.'

South of Crow Province would be north of Fish Province. 'We haven't had anything like that. A few storms but nothing unusual.'

He tucks a strand of pink hair behind his ear. 'That's reassuring. Ravinder was being cautious, I suppose. But if you experience anything, do let me know. Unusual weather is often a sign of discord.'

Before I can respond, Grasshopper leaps across my lap screaming, 'Bunny!'

Wyatt shrieks as a white blur speeds past.

'Oh dear.' Shinjiro holds out his arm. The fluffball settles upon it.

It's not a bunny, it's a bunnerfly. It has a rabbit's long ears, curious black eyes and pink nose. But it also has three things a rabbit does not – a long tail, and two feathered wings.

Shinjiro scratches its chin. It chirps contentedly. 'This is Bancha.'

'Bancha!' Grasshopper's grabby hands reach out. 'To eat?' Wyatt chokes.

'No, little one,' Shinjiro says softly.

She tilts her head. 'Then . . . to love?'

My heart swells. That's a good way to categorize the world – to eat or to love. Although sometimes things can be both. I smirk.

Shinjiro turns to me. 'The Goddess hears our thoughts, Ganymedes.'

Thankfully, her ladyship rescues me with more grabby hands.

'Be gentle.' Shinjiro lowers his arm. 'She comes from the Goddess. All things do. But she's special.'

Grasshopper places three stubby fingers on Bancha's back, stroking her with the tenderness of a mother.

'Anything with wings is sacred, as they can fly closer to the Goddess. But the rabbit is unique. It serves as prey to so many others. Without its sacrifice, all harmony would collapse. It's the lifeblood of the planet.'

'You could say the same of piscero,' I say.

He smiles fondly. 'There's a legend that piscero came from the moon. That's why their scales are silvery white.'

I try not to laugh at the image of a load of brainless fish flopping out of the sky.

'Bunnerflies are believed to be messengers of the Goddess.' Shinjiro casts the creature into the air. Grasshopper chases her, giggling wildly.

'Children's laughter is a wonderful noise,' Shinjiro says; then, to utterly decimate the pleasant moment, adds: 'We do not allow them to laugh in Bunnerfly Province.'

'Sounds . . . swell.' I gulp a mouthful of tea.

'I'm a little offended you haven't visited my cabin yet, dear Wyatt.' Shinjiro stirs his tea.

'You mentioned,' Wyatt mutters. 'Several times on the walk here.'

'I expected you—'

'Can we get back to Eudora's body?' He digs his elbow into my side.

I know a call for help when I see one. 'You said she didn't have any marks?'

Shinjiro shakes his head. 'Apart from the rope mark around her neck. I inspected her after her death.'

'Leofric was guarding her.'

'I anointed her body, so was able to examine her closely.' Which explains that strange smell. 'The Tiger was reluctant, but I persuaded him.'

I would give anything to have seen that showdown. There's always been an unspoken challenge between the two. One guarding the empress's body, the other her soul.

'There was nothing else? No stab wounds? Bruises?'

'Nothing at all.'

I narrow my eyes.

'It would be very foolish of me to lie about this, Ganymedes, when you could simply go across the hall and verify my words this instant. Do I seem foolish to you?'

I sit back, untensing my shoulders. 'No.'

'It's curious. If someone killed her prior to her hanging there would likely be a mark. Or sign of struggle. But that rope bruise is the only blemish upon her saintly skin. Goddess rest her soul.' He presses the golden scales to his mouth. 'I can see why it was surmised that she did it to herself.'

'Maybe someone strangled her?' I ask. 'Then put the rope over her neck. That would cover up the mark, right?'

'Unlikely. I studied the bruises thoroughly and they matched the rope's thickness. I saw no other marks that would indicate the force it would take to strangle someone to death.'

In the distance, Grasshopper leaps for Bancha, landing with a rather concerning crash.

'Maybe someone forced her to do it?' I say. 'Told her to put her head in the noose and fling herself off?'

'Preposterous.' He fills his cup, placing his hand over the lid of the teapot. 'That is not in her character. I did think it odd when suicide was deemed the cause of death but thought it more important to encourage peace at the time. But after Ravinder's death, there's no denying there is a murderous force upon this ship. Our Holy Mother held the virtues of our empire above all else – harmony and unity. She would not kill herself because she knew the effect her death would have upon Concordia. It is the very thing that the person who did this must be seeking.'

'And what's that?'

'Chaos.' He eyes me strangely, steam dissipating around him.

This motherfucker looks like he's about to accuse me.

'You think it's me?'

He chuckles. 'You are so delightfully to the point. Of course I considered you after your ... performance at the party.' He sweeps a hand towards my jewelled body. 'But it's illogical. Why serve a lukewarm cup of tea when you have a piping hot one almost ready?'

'Am I the hot tea?'

Wyatt sighs. 'He's saying there's no reason for you to have gone to all that effort to cause chaos with your costume if you knew the heir's body was gonna be swinging from the chandelier an hour later.'

Shinjiro places the teapot before me. 'Also, I trust anyone who befriends dear Wyatt.'

'Dear Wyatt' looks as if he very much wishes the ship would capsize at this moment.

'This person desires a different kind of chaos,' Shinjiro says. 'They want to tear Concordia apart.' He offers a jar. 'Anyone care for a biscuit?'

Grasshopper appears, grabbing fistfuls. Bancha seizes one from her hand. Bunnerflies also like biscuits, apparently.

Uncharacteristically, I turn down food. 'Can you elaborate?'

He grasps the scales around his neck. 'If you place all weight on one side of a scale, it will tip.' He demonstrates with his finger. 'But if you spread it out equally, everything will balance. A wolf pack will share a kill. Not because they are generous, but because they are stronger together. Alone, they could have the whole kill. But they would also be more at risk from predators. Exposed.' He smiles at Wyatt. 'Bear Province understands that. It's why they have such tight familial units. Everyone contributes because if they don't, they would suffer.'

Wyatt stares wordlessly at a biscuit clutched in his hands.

'The swarm!' Grasshopper declares.

'Yes, in Grasshopper Province they call this concept – and their units – a swarm,' Shinjiro says. 'Concordia is not a scale with two tipping points. It has twelve. We are what keep Concordia – an empire of such vastly varied places – balanced. We twelve, and our shared burden. The sliver of the Goddess's magic within us is not only remarkable because of the abilities it bestows, but also owing to the effect it has on the empire. It is sharing that burden which turned those animals from foe to friend.' He stirs his tea. 'Did you never wonder why we celebrate something that is slowly killing us? Because it unites us. Every province's Blessed is sacrificing themselves for one purpose – Concordia's survival. That concept is so powerful it has stopped our differing provinces warring against each other for a thousand years.' He leans forward, smirking. 'We're all in this together, right, boys?'

Wyatt looks sick. I nod very hard. Probably a little too hard. I'm not in this with them. I'll still be eating my way through my life's ambition when the Blessing pickles their organs.

'We have seen what happens when one province defies this order.' He sips his tea. 'The Crabs disobeyed the emperor's breeding laws. The Crab Blessed had a thousand sons and daughters.'

'I think that's just a turn of phrase,' I mutter, rubbing my hand.

'He did not ensure his children were raised with the Goddess's teachings. Instead, the child that inherited the Blessing was wild and dangerously powerful. He sowed his discord across Concordia, threatened our harmony, tried to seize power for himself.' He dabs at his mouth with his sleeve. 'What do you do when a healthy body has a diseased limb?'

'Cut it off?' I croak.

'And wrap a bandage around it.' He places his cup down. 'We have seen what happens when the scales tip. If even one of twelve were to step out of line . . .' He demonstrates with the scales again. 'We bear this burden so the emperor is not overcome with the Primus Blessing's power. But now we have no imperial heir. What reason is there to sacrifice our lives for someone who does not exist? Without that uniting force and shared trauma to bond us . . .'

'Chaos.' I finish. 'Every province for itself. A fractured empire. Fighting for independence.'

'Or, more likely, dominance.' He sits back. 'It is just a theory, and I'm known for flights of whimsy. Perhaps someone simply didn't like Eudora and Ravinder?'

'Impossible,' Wyatt and I say in unison.

His eyes flash. 'This is the first time a ruler's life has been taken. But it is not the first time an attempt has been made.'

I shift. I know what he's getting at. The same case of near-fatal stabbing that Leofric's mother failed to prevent. Because she was so distracted by Ermine Province, she failed to see the true villain, closer than she could have imagined. 'That assassin was executed.'

'Their heir still lives.'

Wyatt looks to me. 'You didn't mention that.'

I didn't even add it to the diagram. 'It was Nergüi's aveeg.' I use the gender-neutral Spider term for parent.

'Why did they try to kill the emperor?'

'We cannot be sure,' Shinjiro says. 'But I believe it was a grab for power.'

Nergüi and their province are lucky their dux acted alone. One person with one dagger. A spectacle was made of them, even within Spider Province. 'They're known as the "Shamed One".' A Spider had spat it at me when I dared ask about that rebellious history.

'Yes.' Shinjiro purses his lips. 'The outrage in Spider Province ensured they only had to pay monetary recompense and were not exiled beyond the Bandage. Unlike the Crabs, who formed an army to dethrone the emperor.'

He's overestimating it, in my opinion. It was the action of a lone lunatic, and the fallout was a mess. A shield shamed for suspecting the wrong province, and a body hung in the capital for twelve long months of decay.

'Why didn't you mention this?' Wyatt asks me.

I clutch the ground. I see Ravi's face before me, ashamed of the blood in his veins. Expecting me to hate him for it. And my father, disgust when he looks upon me, as if seeing his own sin etched into my skin.

'I won't hold the crimes of the parents against their children,' I say softly.

Wyatt's eyes do not leave me.

Shinjiro adjusts his white robes. 'It is only a theory: do with it as you will. I do not believe it wise to accuse baselessly. Doing so will only create more discord.'

I gulp my tea. The warmth eases the tension in my body. I'm so lulled by the peaceful surroundings I almost forget I'm supposed to be investigating. And this guy is almost as fishy as me. I need to be casual about it. Smooth. Detective Dee's first proper outing.

I rest one arm on my knee. 'So, Shinny J—'

'Never call me that,' he says cheerfully.

'So, Shinjiro, where were you the night Ravi was . . .'

'Murdered,' Wyatt finishes.

'I was outside Wyatt's—'

'No, you weren't.' Wyatt and I say at the same time.

Shinjiro chuckles. 'Aren't you two delightful? I must say, I'm a fan of this pairing.'

Wyatt gags on his biscuit.

Shinjiro sips his tea for a markedly long time. 'I left my vigil outside Wyatt's room for only a moment.'

'Why?' I ask. 'You seem a very dedicated man, and I know it wasn't during sunrise or sunset prayers. I was in the corridor around midnight, and you weren't there.'

Shinjiro glances aside. Unless I'm mistaken, there's a pink tinge to his pearl cheeks. 'I was in the restroom.'

Wyatt stares at Shinjiro, eyebrows narrowed. He doesn't believe him either. He's hiding something.

'Anything else?' he asks.

I click my tongue and point to him. 'What's your Blessing?'

Wyatt wails. 'You can't just ask people that!'

If Shinjiro is offended, someone needs to tell his face. 'You didn't tell him, Wyatt?'

'It's not my place to—'

'Blessings are a gift from the Goddess; they are not meant to be hidden.'

I like the cut of his jib. I'm nodding instantly.

'You seem enthusiastic to agree, considering your Blessing is so closely guarded everyone but Emperor Eugenios and your father were asked to leave when you showed him.'

My stomach squirms. Memories of that embarrassing display return. Me vaguely waving my arms as my father created storm clouds in the throne room. 'This isn't about me.'

'Wyatt.' Shinjiro moves the teacups aside. 'Why don't we show him?'

He opens his mouth dully. 'I don't need—'

Shinjiro's hand leaps out. Wyatt clambers backwards, hot tea spilling into his lap.

'You *are* being dramatic today,' Shinjiro sighs. 'Very well.' He searches his tea set and brings out a knife. Then he promptly stabs it through his palm.

Grasshopper hoots in celebration.

I stare as he yanks it out. Blood seeps down his skin.

Dragon's dick. I'm stuck in a room with a maniac.

'Observe – Her Blessing takes form.' As he presses his middle and forefingers against the wound, the skin knits together seamlessly.

I release a long breath. 'You can heal.'

'What gave it away?' He chuckles. 'If you are ever in need of such skills, do come to me.'

My chest aches. 'How good are you at it?'

'You'll have to give me specifics.'

'Can you heal a man who has been stabbed seventeen times?'

His expression doesn't move. 'I cannot cure death. That is the Goddess's realm. I can attempt to slow it, however. I have been attending to dear Wyatt since he was declared Blessed.'

Wyatt suddenly becomes very interested in his sleeve cuffs.

'He was always sickly. His family did their best to care for him, but nobody paid him much attention until he showed his Blessing. Now preserving his life is of the utmost importance.'

Because he was chosen by the Goddess and allowing him to die wouldn't be worth the shame it would bring, no matter which musclebound brother inherited his Blessing.

'I suppose Tortoise Province are currently in the shit then?'

Shinjiro's jaw tightens. 'They are paying a steep price, not only in the Goddess's eyes.'

I suspect he means that literally. A price that likely filled the coffers of Bunnerfly or Dragon Province. A price that would cripple Bear Province.

'You must remember – your lives are sacred. *Nothing* is worth risking them.' Shinjiro places the knife aside. 'Unfortunately, whatever is infecting our friend is beyond me. I can keep him stable, but I cannot root out the cause. But I'm determined. I *will* cure him.'

Wyatt glances to the door. 'We should probably—'

'Seeing as you seem resolved to miss your sessions with me, please ensure you're taking this.' He whistles and Bancha settles on his shoulder. In her paws is a vial of gleaming white liquid. 'I pay Wyatt visits as frequently as I am able, but my duties prevent these being as often as I would like. So, I prepare this medicine for him. It's infused with my Blessing.'

I decide not to linger long on what exactly that means.

He presses the tube into Wyatt's hand. 'A vial a day. If not, he suffers a mild case of . . . well . . . death.'

'I have plenty in my room.' But Wyatt takes it anyway.

'Why did you miss your sessions? You're usually quite fond of staying alive,' Shinjiro says.

'She's dead,' he mutters, as if that explains everything.

'It shows the Goddess disrespect if you—'

Wyatt throws down his hands. 'I don't want to talk about it.'

'I already knew you were dying, mate,' I say. 'No shame in it.'

He looks away, unwilling to meet my gaze.

It's bizarre to be around someone who would do anything to live, to prove themselves worthy of a legacy, to be part of *this*. Meanwhile, I've spent my life trying to fade into nothingness. I wonder if I'll ever be able to understand him.

The ship rocks with a terrible creak. Wyatt is thrown atop me, his face an inch away from mine. He smells different from Ravi. Fresh linen mixed with something sharp and medicinal. Is that cologne?

'You've certainly changed your tune.' Shinjiro smiles, bonsai trees crashing around him. 'Considering how often you tell me you loathe that "son of a bitch pissfish".'

Wyatt leaps off me. 'Sorry. I didn't . . . sorry.'

'It's OK.' He has freckles. I never noticed before. A strip across his nose.

Shinjiro clasps his hands. 'Enough ogling each other. Let's go and find what that rather concerning ripping metal noise was, shall we?'

*

The scene outside is half hilarious, half terrifying.

Everyone has gathered. Well, nearly everyone. I can't see Eska, though I believe she's the source of the commotion.

Leofric is pinned against her door. Muscles bulging as he presses his bulk against it. Jasper, eager to help, is instead hindering him and tangling in his tree-trunk legs.

The door emits a terrible creaking. The chains strain.

Cordelia (*goddessdammit, Cordelia*) has lowered to the ground, trembling hands pressed to her ears.

Tendai wheels up beside us, yawning. 'If she gets out, she'll likely tear the shield's limbs off.'

A slam answers from beyond the door.

'Would someone help?' Leofric's gaze passes from the girls and Nergüi, to Wyatt who is gripping the wall. '. . . Shinjiro? She's trying to escape!'

Another slam. The ship trembles.

'I must pass.' Shinjiro says politely. 'Keeping living beings caged up is against the Goddess's wishes.'

Leofric's eyes settle on me. 'Fish—'

But I never get to hear if he was legitimately going to ask me to help, as at that moment, the door explodes.

Jasper slams into the wall. Leofric lands in a crumpled heap at my feet, along with what remains of the chains.

Grasshopper promptly vanishes.

The door has been *eviscerated.* Ripped into shreds as easily as tearing into a loaf of bread.

And in that space stands Eska.

Oh, blessed Goddess.

It's not Eska as I know her – short and falsely adorably chubby. This is Eska after training with Leofric for a decade. She's tripled in size. Her muscles have torn straight through her sleeves, and her shirt is doing *remarkable* things to protect her dignity. She stands, huge and panting in the doorway, the icy innards of her room casting a freezing chill down the corridor.

'Fascinating,' Nergüi breathes, hushed.

Leofric clambers to his feet, but it's too late. Eska snatches his shirt, lifting him off the ground. All six feet seven of him.

'If you lock me in room again, if you even speak to me – I tear off arms,' she declares in clipped words. 'First.'

'Told you,' Tendai says.

Leofric's mouth opens and closes as he takes in all of her.

I'm doing the opposite – trying *not* to look. She's *magnificent* and I really don't think me getting hard is going to endear me to her right now.

'Pathetic.' She casts him to the ground. The floor cracks. Then she storms away, body shrinking as she moves through the ship.

The silence is so thick it could be sliced and served.

Instead, it's cut with laughter. Tendai wipes her tears with her headwrap. She's the only one not horrified (or turned on). And I realize she knew this would happen the moment they put Eska in a cage. Because she knew her Blessing.

I observe the hole Eska has blasted through her wall, the steaming hunks of metal all twisted and bent.

'Hmmm.' I tap my chin. 'I wonder what her Blessing could be?'

Leofric turns to me, hair wild. 'Shut up, Pissfish.'

Chapter Twelve

Day Four – Feast of the Tortoise

Night

'This is a terrible idea,' Wyatt says.

'You'll find that's a common thread with my ideas.'

Eska considerately left a path of destruction. After gathering ourselves, we follow it on to the deck with its – to be fair – charming tortoise sails, then down into the dining room.

The others were keen to leave Eska alone. But I'm seeking justice for Ravi. And although it's very possible I'm tracking a murderer, she's a stone I need to turn. I just need to stop imagining her with those rippling pectorals first.

Grasshopper has promptly vanished again. Probably for the best. I know from experience that Eska doesn't cope well with excitable children.

I track Eska to an unfamiliar place – the kitchen. I get the impression the emperor never imagined a Blessed would venture here, as it's lacking his usual *flair*. It is huge though, with twelve ovens, endless rows of cupboards and every conceivable utensil hung along the walls.

I peek around the corner. Eska is bent over a stove, prodding a dead piscero plonked in a pan. Hopefully not an omen.

'You said the first time you spoke to her she . . .' Wyatt trails off.

'Stabbed me. Yes.'

'That scar on your hand?' Wyatt eyes it.

'That's . . . No.' I track the raised line down the centre of my palm. 'She did stab me, but it didn't leave a scar.'

'So we're talking to her because?'

'Nobody else will.'

He glances at me curiously, then a deep, thickly accented voice makes us jump. 'I smell you, Fish.'

I freeze. I don't know if Eska's talking to me or her dinner. '*You*. Fish-boy.'

I stagger around the corner. 'How'd you know I was there?'

'Because you don't know when to shut idiot mouth.' She's retrieved a spare coat. Wrapped in so many fluffy layers she reminds me of Ravi. Except terrifying.

'We're just here to talk.' I spread my palms in a I-come-in-peace gesture. 'We're your neighbours, right?'

'Your stinking ocean borders my western side,' she growls, as if holding me personally responsible for the geography. 'His desert borders my east.'

Wyatt takes a swift step behind me. 'We should go.'

I clear my throat. 'Eska, I know you're—'

She twirls a knife. 'You know what we do with fish back home?'

'Keep them as beloved pets?'

She lifts the fish from the pan and plunges the knife into its belly. Its innards spill wetly on to the floor. 'Gut them. Now leave.'

Wyatt turns to go, but I grab his arm. 'We're not leaving.'

166

'We're not?'

Eska's eyebrow twitches. 'You know who else would not leave?'

'Who?'

She points the knife at Wyatt.

'Me?' he squeaks.

'Brother.'

'Oh.'

'Wanted hand in marriage,' she says. 'Travel all the way to Ermine kingdom to claim hand. I say no. He does not understand no. What happen when he return, Bear?'

Wyatt shifts from foot to foot. 'He . . . didn't have her hand.'

'I give him hand,' she says. 'His hand. In cloth bag he wear around neck.'

My honed instincts tell me that I should move the conversation away from dismemberment. '*Anyway*—'

'Even Ox understand "leave".'

'Jasper was here?'

'Bastard has what you call "death wish". Followed me since I left room.'

I hadn't spotted that. Does that boy fear nothing? What does he battle at the Bandage that makes facing down Eska in *that* form seem like a good idea?

Her lips turn down. 'He is dangerous man.'

I snort. 'He's barely a man.'

'A man is made by his deeds, not age, fish-*boy*.'

'Why's he dangerous?'

'He is desperate. Desperate men do *anything* to win.' The fish is still weeping innards. 'Shall I show you how I make him leave?'

'Come on.' Wyatt tugs my arm. 'The nice lady said leave.'

'Eska—'

'Say my mother name again, Pissfish, I cut tongue from mouth.'

'Ermine—'

'Leave.'

Trust me, I want to. But I won't find Ravi's killer by hiding behind walls.

'You know they all think you're guilty?' I say.

Eska stares. 'I was guilty day I was born Ermine.'

'Because you close yourself off to everyone.'

'Because we don't play their games,' she says. 'Because we don't live by their rules. Don't bow to green-haired princess.' She spits in the pan; it sizzles. 'How can she understand what it is to live in the tundra? To hunt the mammoth?' She slams the fish into the pan.

'I know it's hard – living in the ice lands—'

'You know nothing.'

Wyatt flinches as she storms towards me. In a flash, the blade is at my gut. 'You live in little houses by seaside.'

'Agreed.' I nod quickly. 'But I think I understand more than they do.'

She eyes me but does not say anything, or drop the knife.

'I saw a mammoth once,' I whisper.

She snorts. 'You saw baby.'

Baby? I remember it like it was yesterday, though I was only six. A single mammoth that had strayed too far from the tundra, separated from its herd or desperate for food. It killed five people before it finally had enough fishing spears in it to give up the fight.

'Adult mammoth size of house,' she says.

It's rumoured that the mammoth originally came from beyond the Bandage, that centuries ago a herd broke through.

'And you live side by side with them.' I say. 'That takes bravery.'

'Not bravery. Strength. For Blessed ceremony, I kill one singlehandedly.'

My stomach almost drops out of my arse. *'Singlehandedly'*?

My own ceremony is a memory my subconscious has filed away in the folder marked *So traumatizing you'll be reliving this over and over until you die.*

'I think they'd respect you if you'd just speak to them,' I say softly. 'If they understood—'

'We tried. For hundred of years we play their game. We hunt mammoth for them. Send them furs and meat and tusk. But they always want more. So, we kill more mammoth. And more mammoth, until there is none for us. My people die in the freezing wastes, bellies empty. What did Dragon do for Ermine then, little fish?'

I meet her icy gaze. 'Nothing.'

'While you bow your heads and send them nets full of fish, Ermine knew – it takes strength to survive. It takes strength to say "no".'

The concept is bizarre. Fish Province takes great pride in fulfilling the quotas. Even when we have little to eat ourselves. Saying 'no' to the emperor would be like telling the waves to stop.

She raises her chin, defiant. 'Now mammoth stalk the snow in great herds. Now we build houses from their bones. Now my people thrive. Because we know what it means to be strong. Only strong survive in ice lands.' She eyes Wyatt. 'This one would be left out in snow to die.'

Wyatt unsuccessfully attempts to shrink behind my back. He is quite a bit taller than me.

He's lucky he was born in Bear Province, where families being able to protect their infirm is a matter of pride.

Meanwhile, Ermines abandon newborns in the snow for a

day and a night. If they survive, they're deemed strong enough to join the tribe. Thanks, *Mum*.

'I do not care if they like me,' she says. 'We are stronger without them.'

'I know you didn't do it,' I say, forcing the tremble from my voice. 'You didn't kill them.'

The tip of the knife skims my belly. 'I tell you I kill mammoth and you think I cannot slay your skinny Crow and green-haired princess?'

The fish sizzles in the pan.

I lick my dry lips. 'Of course, you *could* do it. But you don't kill for fun, or political reasons. Else we'd all be dead. You kill to survive. Just like you said – what's the use in overhunting the mammoth?' Because although Eska hates Concordia, it serves her province as she needs it to. It keeps the world outside away from her people. Keeps them safe. The mammoth are not their enemies. The mammoth are their neighbours. Ermines kill only when needs must. 'I know where you come from. I know what it demands. You wouldn't kill like this.'

'I stabbed *you*.'

'Because I frightened you.'

She scoffs, but I know it's true. A girl from the ice, taught to always be alert, always wary – approached by a bouncy thirteen-year-old Ganymedes Piscero, eager to prove he *totally belongs here*. The stabbing is almost understandable.

'They think you did it,' I say. 'They look at you and see a monster. The Blessed their mothers warned them about. But I know that's not the case. I know it wasn't you.'

I do know. I'm almost sure. But I need her to confirm it.

She lowers the knife. 'If it was me, you would all already be dead, and I would be wearing your skins.'

'I don't doubt it!'

She scowls.

'Did you see anything, on the night of . . .' I trail off.

'Ravi's murder,' Wyatt whispers.

I see the question register, the way her eyes, for the briefest moment, dash aside. 'I see nothing. I was in cabin.'

She's lying. She was with Tendai. But I'm not sure how far I can press Eska without receiving a bellyful of steel. She definitely shared her Blessing with Tendai; I wonder what else they shared.

'Do you suspect anyone? For example – random choice – Tendai?'

If she feels some type of way about Tendai, she does an impressive job of disguising it. 'I suspect everyone. Eventually, they *will* destroy each other. That is why I do not have to do anything but wait.'

Ignoring that creepiness.

'They pretend to be in harmony. But I have been watching for a long time. I watch them from the corners of every summit. I watch them when they think they not being watched.' She places the knife into her belt but does not remove her hand from the pommel. 'They lie. They *all* lie.'

I nod.

'Except you.'

'Thanks—'

'Too stupid for lies.'

'Oh.'

She returns to her fish. The salty scent of it reminds me of home. 'If I were you, I would hide rest of trip. They target weak ones.' She picks up her meal and shoves it into a canvas bag. 'I am going to find safe place. Before monk preach about Goddess to me again. Or someone tries to kill.' She says both with the same level of loathing, and then strides towards the door.

I take a step forward. 'Es— Ermine!'

She freezes.

'If something occurs to you, or if you just want to chat or *anything*, you can come to me. We're neighbours, right?'

Silence. I wait for the knife to come hurtling for my soft underbelly.

But then a noise, a deep reverberating sound. She's laughing. *Eska is laughing.*

'You are funny, Fish,' she says. Then leaves me speechless.

*

That night, I dream of my Blessing ceremony.

I didn't want to do it. *Really* didn't want to do it. I'd already lied to the senate. Lied to the emperor. Worst of all, I'd lied to my mother.

My mother – who could read me like the fisherfolk read the waves – knew something was wrong. I was her smiley, playful child, but when I told her about my sudden 'miraculous' Blessing I was still and cold. As if my body had already begun to separate from my soul.

She took me away from my father and ran her hand through my curls, whispering, '*Diðu mir, parlskan. Diðu mir verteikann.*'

My mother spoke in forbidden syllables. A language a thousand years of empire tried to erase. And it did erase it – from books and law. But it could not steal it from the whispers of mother to child, in the folklore retold in quiet rooms, hidden by the swell of the ocean.

Tell me, little fry. Tell me the truth.

I had told her everything before then. All the boys and girls I wanted to kiss. The way the night lights made my heart feel big and full. How, sometimes, the sea spoke to me in a voice like hers, beckoning me beneath the waves.

But I could not tell her this. That her husband was

unfaithful, her child unworthy, and that both bore a lie so terrible it could destroy her home and people.

And she knew. *She knew.*

Some walls are built slowly. Scowls and cruel words adding to them – brick by brick. But the wall between my mother and me appeared in an instant.

I walled off my truth and my heart, and whenever I wanted to tell her other things, to speak words in a language only we two shared, all I saw was the wall.

The lie took many things from me. But that one hurt the most.

They covered the bridges connecting the islands of Fish Province with reeds the day of my ceremony. They laid down seagrass and kelp. They placed a pearlescent crown of shells atop my head. All I had to do was walk as people sang and cheered.

The relief was palpable. I had been late, but finally the Goddess had deemed me worthy. In Fish Province, the Blessed's soul is intertwined with the piscero. A Blessed guarantees the migration, ensures bountiful waters. They would not come without a Blessed. And without the piscero, we were nothing.

I was the child who would ensure everyone's survival.

But all I felt was the lie, sitting in my gut like a piece of rotting food. I wanted to vomit it out so everyone could see. Then I would cast the crown back into the ocean. It did not belong on my head.

But at the end of my walk, my father stood at the altar, face hard as stone, and I knew he would rather that lie poison me from the inside than his ugly truth be unveiled.

My mother was beside him, blue shells woven through seafoam hair, smiling placidly. But I knew what she really felt, because I felt the same.

All I wanted to do was *scream and scream and scream.*

My mother did not come to me after that day. She did not curl her body around mine on stormy nights, running her fingers through my hair. She did not share any more words of the language in which the sea whispered to me.

Instead, she avoided me like an unwelcome guest. A stranger in her home.

And I deserved it. I learned to live with it. I maintained that wall around my heart. Smiling when all I wanted to do was scream.

Until Ravi.

Chapter Thirteen

Day Five – Feast of the Elephant

Morning

As the heir of fisherfolk I should be comfortable on water. After all, our province is 90 per cent water, with floating islands serving as the only 'solid ground' other than the shoreline. But I slept awfully last night. Granted, that could be because of the raging murderer stalking the ship. But it's certainly not helped by Cordelia's nightly wanderings, wailing '*Lysander! Lysander!*' like a love-struck ghost.

'Goddessdammit, Cordelia.' I rub my aching eyes.

I wanted to burn Ravi's death note. Convince myself I'd read it wrong, that he was thinking about *me* instead of *her*. But he wanted Cordelia to have it, and I'm nothing if not loyal.

I leave Grasshopper curled up on my bed and try Cordelia's cabin. No answer, so I go exploring. First, I search the deck, the elephant in the sails watching my every move. Then I take the stairs to the empty dining room. I pray nobody else is awake. I don't fancy getting murdered doing *this* errand.

It strikes me how utterly quiet the ship is. That must be the emperor's magic. It feels as if it's barely moving.

Then – music. A sweet melody drifts mournfully through the ship. It sounds so much like Cordelia's nightly lament I'm sure I'll find her at the source.

I follow it through the wide corridor leading out of the dining room. I must be underneath the bow by the time I find the right room.

I stagger to a stop, gaping like the gormless piscero I am.

Every wall from floor to ceiling is lined with books. Books with gold spines, clothbound volumes with curling pages and tomes bigger than my head. Wheeled ladders are dotted around, and jewels plunge from the ceiling like stalactites, emitting soft blue light. I weave through the shelves and discover a strange golden contraption with spinning dials. There's even a map of Concordia, painstakingly embroidered in minute detail.

In a nook of the library Cordelia sits before a grand piano, slender fingers dashing across the keys. The blue light reflects off her golden hair, making her appear like an ethereal being, shelved and catalogued with the other curiosities of this room.

There's lots of music in Fish Province, like the shanties fisherfolk sing to ease their cold tired bones on long voyages. But I'm not fond of sad music. Sad music breaks the illusion that everything is fine. It conjures images of the darkness of the sea, and the back of my mother's head.

As the song ends it lingers around me like an unwelcome ghost. All I can think to do to break the spell is clap.

Cordelia nearly leaps out of her skin. She lurches back from the piano, skinny legs wrapped around the stool.

'Sorry!' I hurry to settle her back. 'Didn't want to interrupt.'

Her face is beetroot red, but she recovers quickly, adjusting her velvet skirt so it lies flat. 'Th-That's quite all right. I just wasn't aware you were there . . . Is that your Blessing? Are you very quiet?'

'There are several people here who can attest that's not the case.' I laugh. 'A heads-up, I wouldn't go around asking that. People get prickly about Blessings.'

She gasps, her mouth forming a perfect 'O'. 'I apologize! It's just all *so* interesting. And I'm rather far behind. I'm not used to lacking knowledge.'

'If I *was* quiet I think a lot of people would call that a Blessing.' I smirk, perching on the edge of a table. 'But the Goddess isn't that good, apparently.'

She giggles, and then clasps her hand over her mouth. 'Pardon me!'

Blessed hells, who has whipped this girl into apologizing for laughing? Although she's from Tortoise Province, where excessive *anything* that isn't learning is forbidden.

She crosses her hands over her knees. 'My father encouraged me to do the Twelve, but I declined. I regret that now. I would know so much more about you all.'

The Twelve is what Tortoise youth call their year-long tour around Concordia. A pursuit to further their own knowledge without contributing anything. I've seen them in the winter, shivering in their suits and bowler hats, observing us from a distance as if we're peculiar wild beasts they do not wish to engage with.

'Do you come here often?' I say, immediately regretting how much it sounds like a pickup line. 'I mean – it's dangerous, with a murderer on the loose.'

She glances aside. 'I know it's foolish, but I come here to play in the mornings. It clears my head. Admittedly, it's just been the same song over and over but . . .'

'For Ravi?'

'Ravinder?' Her blue eyes widen. 'No. It was my brother's favourite. They do not favour music in Tortoise Province. They say it's a frivolous pursuit that benefits nobody.' Her

177

fingers skim the keys. 'But I felt as if . . . only through music could I express myself. As if I could be understood through the melodies. Lysander always listened to me play.'

'He was good like that. He knew what to say to make people happy.' No doubt helped by his Blessing. Being able to see people's greatest desires probably cuts out a lot of small talk.

She smiles distantly. 'He wasn't like anyone I've ever met, certainly not from back home.' She nibbles her lip. 'Can I show you something?'

'Sure.'

She reaches into a satchel and unveils a book. It's not the biggest I've seen today, but it's certainly the oldest. The leather has remnants of gold embossing, but it's almost entirely worn away from centuries of being handled. I suspect the only thing stopping it from falling apart is the golden padlock attached to the cover.

'This has been passed down through Tortoise Blessed since records began. We must bring it everywhere, guard it with our lives.' I notice a key around her neck, gold like the lock on the book. 'Only the Tortoise Blessed may read or write in it . . . but as you're a Blessed, I'm sure it's OK.'

Wondering how many other sacred 'Blessed only' traditions I've decimated, I watch as she flips through pages of inked passages.

'These are writings from every Tortoise Blessed. We are to note down our insights for future duces. Each will build upon the wisdom of generations past.' Her hand freezes. 'This is *his* page.'

Written in swooping, beautiful letters is a single line: 'Be open to all others.'

I smile. 'That's very Lysander.'

She returns the smile. 'I don't know how he was real. How someone that good could exist in the world.'

My heart twinges. I fight the urge to crack a joke and destroy the serious moment. Jokes won't help me understand these people. And I *must* understand them – for Ravi. Talking to Eska demonstrated that.

'What's it like?' I ask. 'Growing up in Tortoise Province?'

She glances shyly over her glasses. 'You actually want to know?'

'I wouldn't ask otherwise.'

'You and Ravinder are similar,' she says and before I can contemplate *that*, continues, 'My parents treated us more like projects than children. I was . . . an emotional child, and emotions are discouraged. They tried to mould me into the perfect submissive girl who did not express or feel anything. Achievements are applauded in Tortoise Province. Not people.' She runs her fingertips over Lysander's words. 'But my brother knew who I was. He *saw me*. One time, when I was locked up studying, he broke me out. He took me to a secret room, a place in our estate even my parents did not know. He managed to sneak a piano inside. How does a boy sneak in a *piano*?' She laughs lightly.

'I was able to play whenever I wanted. Far away from the house, where nobody could hear or punish me. "Never stop playing," he said. "Yours is a song that deserves to be heard." He had so many hopes for me. But I have other concerns now. Other burdens.' She closes the book. 'But I still want to play for him, even if he cannot hear me. This song makes me feel like he is with me. I know it is . . . nonsensical.'

Goddessdammit, Cordelia, why do you have to start talking so much damn sense?

I know what it is like – to live two lives. To have two selves for the purpose of survival. 'It makes perfect sense.'

A whisper of a smile. 'Thank you. Nobody understands. The monk keeps trying to persuade me to pray with him. But when I pray, all I hear is silence. My brother never answers my prayers. At least this way, I hear his song.' She cleans her glasses on her skirt. 'I apologize. I've spoken about myself at length. It is a little lonely here. N-Not that everyone isn't welcoming. It's just . . .'

Bollocks. I'm supposed to hate her, the man-stealing vixen. But it's impossible to not see the truth of who she is: an emotional, passionate woman who has been told to *not be* her entire life. Then, when barely of age, she's thrust into *this*. And she's Lysander's sister. Talk about living up to a legend.

I'm going to have to be nice to her. Not only that – I *want* to be nice to her. *GODDESS. DAMMIT. CORDELIA.*

'How did Lysander . . . ?' I don't want to say 'die'. I still can't say 'die' about Ravi and I'm afraid the word will shatter this china doll.

She swallows hard. 'He got into an . . . altercation. He was stabbed.'

A shudder runs down my spine. Striking a blow against a Blessed is like stabbing the Goddess herself. But Lysander broke every rule underpinning his province, and there's only so many times you can shake a nest until the bees get angry.

'The monks are making your province pay for failing to protect him, aren't they?'

She nods. 'As they should. I would pay the price a thousand times if it would bring him back.' Her eyes glaze. 'When I fell he was always the one who helped me up. It feels unreal that he's not here. And I am.'

I know that feeling. Like your soul has been split in two. The before and the after.

I study her, this woman that Ravi loved. The way her narrow shoulders sag, her flute-thin wrists, the sadness wrapped around her, as visible as her layers of velvet and silk.

Oh, Ravi, do you always choose people who need saving?

'Well, now you have his Blessing,' I say. 'That's part of him, and it picked you.'

She fingers her blouse. 'I'm his only sibling so it passed to me. But sadly, I cannot be him.'

'Then don't. Be Cordelia. It's the only thing you can be – yourself.'

I expect her to be horrified, but instead her back straightens. 'That's exactly what I'm going to do. And it's what you do too, even if *everyone* dislikes you for it. I admire that.'

Ouch. True. But . . . ouch.

'Sorry! I'm terribly awful at conversation. It's why the library is safer. I can't offend anyone in here.'

'You like this . . . stuff?' I gesture around.

'Stuff?' she repeats, making the word sound ridiculous. 'You mean books? Of course. I'm a Tortoise – I *love* knowledge.'

'What kind of knowledge?'

'*Anything.* I fear I drove Ravinder a little mad, but I want to know everything about *everything.*' She spreads her arms wide, spinning in place. 'Tortoises believe that true progress can only occur by building upon the mistakes of the past. That is what our book is about. That's why it's *vital* I learn what I can.'

'I remember you holding Jasper hostage at the party. You were asking him about the Bandage?'

She leans in eagerly. 'It's incredible – don't you think? – to speak to the *actual* commander of the Bandage? Do you know it runs over a thousand miles long? It's the largest man-made object in Concordia.'

'Not exactly man-made. The emperor maintains most of it.'

She raises a finger. 'Initially perhaps, but the emperor's power drains. Most of the Bandage is maintained by the divinium now. And that barely keeps it together. No wonder we lose Ox Blessed quicker than any other – it's cracking *all* over. Especially near Grasshopper Province . . .' She buries her face in her hands. 'Oh, Goddess! I've rambled on and bored you! Ravinder is so patient and . . . *was* so patient. I forget that other people—'

I place a hand on her shoulder. 'Don't forget to breathe.'

She takes two deep breaths.

I can see why Ravi fell for her. He loved people who were enthusiastic about things. Because he spent his whole life hiding what he was passionate about, and the kind of person he truly was.

When we were sixteen, he asked me to show him the Bandage. We journeyed to where it juts into the sea. He stood, legs trembling, and placed his hand against the luminous green wall. We remained there for what felt like an eternity – the two of us in that tiny rowing boat, at the farthest edge of Concordia. When I asked about it later, he changed the subject. I know now what that child of two worlds was trying to hide. Why he wanted to simply lay a hand upon the Bandage. To feel it. If only for a moment.

Ravi never wanted to draw attention, so he pretended to be someone else, someone inconsequential. Cordelia with her unfiltered words and dumb pretty face would have entranced him. And then his open heart allowed her to be the person previously only Lysander let her be. Ravi always found his happiness in other people's.

I understand. I get it – why he loved her.

Goddessdammit, Cordelia.

'I have something for you.'

'What is it?' That curious smile again. No idea I'm about to hand over the equivalent of a suicide note.

'It's . . . something I found on Ravi's body.'

That shuts her up.

Her trembling fingers brush mine as she takes the note. When she finishes reading, her hand drops. 'Thank you for bringing this to me,' she says softly. 'It seems he knew something we did not.'

'Do you have any idea what that was?'

She pushes up her glasses. 'Ravinder was a private person. As much as he encouraged me to be myself, I felt like I never truly knew the *real* Ravinder.'

So he didn't tell her his origins. It shouldn't make me happy. But it does, a little.

'What is it, Fish?'

'Huh?'

'You're smiling.'

The awkward moment is saved by a rush of quick footsteps. Cordelia shrieks, swatting at the air like a startled cat.

Grasshopper emerges with a *pop*.

'Dee left the swarm!' she proclaims, finger pointed accusingly. 'People who leave the swarm don't come back!'

'Sorry.' I ruffle her hair. 'Didn't want to wake you.'

She pouts but accepts the ruffle.

'Ganymedes?' Wyatt is gasping as he rounds the corner. 'What are you doing . . . ?' He takes in Cordelia, the note hanging from her limp hand.

'Bear.' She greets him with a curtsy. 'I do not believe we have met. I am Cordelia. Lysander's sister.' She still says his name with a little pain. Maybe that's how I'll always say Ravi's from now on.

'Howdy . . .' Wyatt says awkwardly. Goddess, this boy is useless in social situations. That's what you get when you stay holed up inside dying all day, I guess.

Cordelia holds out her hand. 'How do you do?'

Wyatt ignores it and turns to me. 'You should've told me you were coming here.'

'Are you my keeper now?' I poke his stomach and hit bone.

'Grasshopper was screaming at my door. People are being *murdered*. I thought . . .' He glances over; Cordelia is staring, hands clasped at her chest.

'Am I interrupting? I – um – hoped I could ask you some things about your province, B-Bear?' She steps forward. 'Do you still maintain the cattle farms? I heard there are unique ways you tame horses, and that they are passed down orally, rather than in books? And what about—'

'Maybe later.' He grips my wrist and tugs.

Cordelia wilts. 'I know my brother wished to put the past behind us.'

Ah. So that's why Wyatt is acting like Cordelia shat in his sandwich.

Tortoise and Bear Provinces have always been mismatched. Tortoise with their love of learning and pursuits of the mind, and Bear who live and die by their bodies. But this didn't reach an apex until our grandparents' generation.

Tortoise Province – with their infinitely innovative brains – made a proposal: to build railways across Concordia. This would not only help bridge the divide between provinces, but also allow quick movement, especially of trade. Most provinces were on board, but Bear Province were *furious*. They'd been running cattle across their desert aided only by horses and their rippling bodies since time eternal. It's their culture, their way of life, and they weren't exactly keen on Tortoise barging in and laying down tracks across the grazing grounds. So, they said no.

A few months later, a terrible plague swept through Bear Province. Horses died in their thousands. They failed to complete the cattle run for the first time in history. The

resulting food deficit meant the entire empire had to eat piscero, even the nobles. The horse plague was so widespread
and sudden the cause couldn't be determined. But you can
guess who Bear Province blamed. Without horses, they
would need the railway. But Tortoise underestimated the
stubbornness of Bears. They never factored in the chance
that Bears would rather die alongside their rotting animals
than give up one iota of their traditions.

Tortoise didn't understand that in the wild southern provinces, traditions are all we really have.

The resulting clash was the closest Concordia has come to
war since the Crabs. The emperor had to step in to stop it
spiralling out of control.

You just *do not touch* Bear Province's horses.

Wyatt glares at her openly. 'I've come to reclaim
Ganymedes.'

'Oh. A shame.' She tucks her hair behind her ear. 'Perhaps
another time? I know there's this *history* between our provinces, but it is all rather silly.'

Wyatt stares coldly, as if 'silly' is a 'silly' way to describe the
near destruction of his people's livelihood.

Cordelia retrieves her book, and then disappears behind
the stacks.

'Wyatt, what—'

He holds up his hand, waiting for the door to close. 'Why
were you talking to her?'

'To give her the note.'

'You shouldn't have come here alone.' His grip on my
wrist is *very* tight.

'I'm a big boy.'

'In case you've forgotten, there's a murderer on this ship,
preying on people who wander around alone.'

'I think I can handle Cordelia.'

'You know what Tortoises are like,' he snarls. 'They put their *progress* before people's lives.'

I roll my eyes. 'Cordelia is a grieving—'

'Promise me you won't go wandering around alone again?'

Grasshopper stands beside him, echoing his pouty expression. I'm outnumbered.

Damn. Bears get *very* protective of their packs. I lean into him with a shit-eating grin. 'Are you jealous?' Ravi never got jealous. I kind of *like* that idea. I don't linger on that confusing emotion for long.

His eye twitches. 'Just promise me. No more lone library visits?'

'Fine.' I hold up my hands. 'I promise. Lest I be buried beneath an avalanche of books while Cordelia plays me a sonata.'

*

I'm almost back at my cabin when the last voice I want to hear slithers down my neck.

'Ganymedes.'

Nergüi. They stand before the deck-side doors, a tabard of jewels draped across their shoulders.

'There are eight days remaining.'

'What?' I breathe heavily, clutching my chest. Someone needs to put a damn bell on them.

'For our conversation. The sooner we are able to talk privately the better.' They finger a jewel at their neck.

I swallow hard, summoning my courage. This is a chance; I have to seize it. For Ravi. 'W-What did you mean when you said the party would be legendary? Did you already know about my outfit?'

Nergüi's storm-grey eyes flicker over me. 'Do you really think that you can keep *any* secrets from me, Ganymedes?'

My chest seizes. *They know.* They absolutely know.

Is that what Nergüi wants to talk about? Using my missing Blessing as leverage? Blackmailing me?

If so, that's the last fucking conversation I want to have. I'd rather go back to Eska and tell her that her province sucks.

'You like collecting strays, don't you? Do you feel, perhaps, they cover up your *lack*?' They drag the word out.

Lack. Lack. Lack.

Breathe, Dee.

'I think it's time for that chat, don't you?'

I break away from their gaze. Wyatt not-so-subtly shakes his head. He looks as peaky as I feel. Grasshopper glares at me. I know what she's thinking: *Don't leave the swarm.*

'I can't,' I mutter.

Nergüi's smile twitches. 'I'm afraid I'm not a patient person. When I get frustrated, my tongue starts wagging. All sorts of dangerous things tumble out. An unfortunate habit.' They reach out, tugging me close enough to smell their perfume. It's too sweet, as if they're slathered in honey. 'Who do you trust upon this vessel?'

I swallow hard. 'Grasshopper and—'

'The correct answer is "nobody".' A red flash of a smile; then they release me. 'Eight days. Next time I will not ask so nicely.'

Chapter Fourteen

Day Five – Feast of the Elephant

Afternoon

I distract myself from the urge to throw myself overboard to avoid Nergüi's rendezvous by updating Detective Dee's Diagram of Deduction. There's depressingly little to add in terms of breakthroughs, but I do have Shinjiro's Blessing: 'Healing', and Eska's: 'Incredible strength' (I leave out 'which gives Dee pleasurable twitches'). I add Shinjiro's 'shitting' alibi, and also record the lack of wounds on Eudora's body. At the last minute, I add 'Dangerous man' to Jasper's section, as I can't discount anyone who Eska believes that about.

'We need more information,' I groan, pulling at my hair. 'This is impossible.'

'Stressing out isn't gonna help.' Wyatt tugs my hands down. 'When was the last time you bathed?'

I blink. My cabin has a bath in a cramped washroom. But I haven't used it. I've also been wearing the same clothes for five days, which probably means I don't smell the sweetest. It's to Wyatt's credit it took him this long to mention it. 'I don't like baths.'

'Yeah, they ain't the best. But I think *someone* needs to chill out a little.'

I sheepishly run my fingers through the mess of my hair. 'Maybe . . .'

'Let me take you somewhere that can help.'

Wyatt leads us into the depths of the ship, beneath the level of the dining room and library. The air is heavy and moist. Grasshopper clutches my hand.

We follow Wyatt into a narrow room covered in white porcelain tiles painted with green dragons. There are rows of wooden benches against the walls, and hooks with fluffy white towels.

Wyatt turns to me. 'Clothes off.'

'You're quite forward.'

He glares through to the back of my skull. 'Towels on.' He forces a bundle into my arms.

Grasshopper has already flung off all her clothing and is screeching, 'Naked! Naked!' while pattering around on bare feet. I catch her in a towel and wrestle it around her before she flies away again.

I'm hesitant to take off my clothes. Not that I'm shy, I have way too many other insecurities to be worried about the softness of my thighs and belly. They're just my *only* clothes, and if the others were taken in an elaborate prank to get me naked this would be the climax. I can still investigate naked, but I suspect it may be off-putting for the other scions.

I undress, watching Wyatt from the corner of my eye. He's all elbows and sharp edges. Not a lick of fat on him. As he bends, the bone of his spine presses against his back. His body seems to be eating him from the inside. When he's wearing clothes and scolding me for exploring alone, it's easy to forget he's dying.

When he glances over, I look away and wrap a towel

around my waist. Side by side we look ridiculous – a wilting stick of celery paired with a dumpling. People made the same jokes about Ravi and me. Except he wasn't awkward edges. He was long and elegant, like a lily.

When I look back, Wyatt's eyes are upon me, lingering on my stomach.

'Are you checking me out?' I run a hand down my chest.

His head snaps up. 'Shut up.'

Blessed fishcakes, he actually was.

'Come on.' He darts away, ears gleaming pink.

When Grasshopper and I catch up with Wyatt, he stands before two huge doors. A wisp of heat escapes from the bottom, it smells like . . . peppermint?

'I dunno why we have those baths in our cabins, when this ship has the best darn bathhouse I've ever seen.' Then, with my help, Wyatt opens the doors.

'Bathhouse' seems an inadequate word. The room is a maze of waterways and canals, cutting through what must be at least half the length of the *Dragon's Dawn*. The whole place is carved out of white stone and marble, with the only light emanating from the water itself. The main pool glows blue. But there are also smaller pools – a hot spring billowing steam, and a jacuzzi of pink bubbles scented like cherry blossoms. The water of the main bath is so clouded with fragrant oils I can't see the bottom. It looks as deep and as endless as the ocean.

Grasshopper launches into the air with a delighted squeal, towel abandoned to fate. She lands with an almighty splash, and a wave of jasmine envelops me.

Wyatt chuckles. 'Shinjiro says warm water helps my condition.' He dips one foot in, wincing at the heat. 'Come on, we deserve a break.'

I don't move. I'm still in the doorway, staring at the clouded water.

'Ganymedes?'

In the muffled distance Grasshopper is laughing, and Wyatt is calling my name, but everything is silenced by the fear. The terror seizes every part of me; it tears through my body with ice-cold savagery. First it seizes my tongue; then my vision darkens; and, finally, my legs shake.

And the water beckons like an old friend, speaking my mother tongue.

I close my eyes, try to breathe, but *it* has control of my lungs now. I can still hear the water. Still see those vast empty depths. It rises around my legs, my stomach, my chest. Higher and higher. Until it's just me and the darkness. Me and nothingness. Me and oblivion.

'Ganymedes?' Someone grips my bare shoulders. When my vision focuses, Wyatt is before me, panic dancing in hazel eyes.

Grasshopper has stopped laughing; her head pokes out of the water.

'What's wrong?' Wyatt presses a hand to my forehead.

I move my aching arms and feel stone. I'm on the floor. I try to speak, but my breath catches in sharp bursts, like a fish gasping on air.

Even if I could respond to Wyatt's question, I'm not sure I would. Because the answer is pathetic, even by my standards.

Comprehension dawns on his face. 'You're afraid of water.'

'I'll let you make one joke . . .' I rasp. 'Here're the tools: fish, Fish Blessed, homeland is ninety per cent water; also, fish is our main export. Knock yourself out.'

But Wyatt isn't laughing. 'I'm sorry. I wouldn't have brought you here if I'd known.'

How could he have known? How could anyone?

'How do you bathe at home?'

'Filtered water system.' I massage my throbbing head. 'It trickles down like waterfalls. Don't have to submerge.'

His chin juts out defiantly, as if I've just set him a challenge. 'This way.'

I don't have the strength to protest. He slings my arm around his shoulders and leads me to the side of the pool.

He pulls out a wooden stool and places it five feet away. 'Too close?'

'Great . . . stool . . . placement.'

'Stop making jokes.'

If that's his idea of a joke Bear Province must be fucking grim.

He lowers me onto it, facing away from the water, then dashes off, shoulders set and determined.

Grasshopper rubs my back. They have tsunamis in her province, so I must seem like a child to her. 'I'm scared of lots of things too.'

Wyatt reappears, dragging a bucket across the floor. The water sloshes over the side.

'Wyatt, you don't have to—'

'Quiet.' With great effort and a rather concerning rattle of breath, he empties the bucket over my head.

I yelp at the sudden heat. 'I wasn't ready! My hair!'

He studies me. 'Anything's better than the mess it was.'

'You just don't know style.'

'Round two.' He's off again, plunging the bucket into the water with those matchstick arms.

Grasshopper hands me soap that smells like sherbet – obviously ill-suited to the hunk of pure man I am – but I'll do it for the kid. As Wyatt empties the next bucketful over my head, I scrub the soap over my body. Purple bubbles float around me.

'You could ask your dragon,' I say as Wyatt struggles back with the third bucket.

His chin raises again. 'Back home, people do almost

everything for me. If there's something I can do myself, I'm gonna do it.'

He can *barely* do it himself. I know his province measures your worth by what your body can achieve, but I wish he'd stop pushing his so hard. Sweat pours from places I didn't even know *could* sweat, and his limbs are shaking furiously. But the boy is so damn stubborn I know there's no point arguing.

Five buckets later and smelling like a candy cane, I'm squeaky clean.

Wyatt lies splayed on the soapy tiles, clutching his chest.

I want to thank him, but I'm so embarrassed I only say, 'Don't bust a lung.'

He looks at me upside down, hair stuck to his forehead. 'Don't tell me what to do.'

I snort, and then poke Grasshopper's nose as she paces from foot to foot. 'Go play, your ladyship.'

She tears away, butt naked and shrieking.

Wyatt's chest rattles with wheezed breaths. I can see the outline of his ribs, could count them if I wanted to. His hands are raw from carrying the bucket. Is there a part of this boy that isn't fragile?

I drive my nails into the stool.

I've never told anyone.

I *could* tell him.

I want to tell him.

Wyatt's the only person since Ravi who has treated me with kindness, who wasn't looking for something else out of it. Carrying a bucket. A truly selfless act – something that cost him more than it gave.

'When I was fourteen, I almost drowned,' I say.

He pushes himself up but doesn't look directly at me. He's

good like that. I'd curl into a ball if he looked at me. 'All Fish Province kids come out of the womb swimming. Literally. We're born in water.'

Wyatt, a son of deserts, looks horrified. Maybe people give birth on horseback in Bear Province.

'We're left to swim alone from an early age. But one day, there was a storm. The worst I've ever seen.' And then I'm back there.

Most storms howl, but this one screamed. It rocked our house. The water thrown so furiously against the windows one of them smashed.

I wanted my mother to hold me and whisper words of comfort. But she sat alone, watching the storm, so serene I started to suspect she was controlling it.

My father was away, probably deep into his flavour of the month. I wanted his Blessing then, more than ever. To tell those winds to stop. Then, finally, they did.

'Suddenly it went completely calm,' I say. 'I'd never seen the water so still. It barely rippled when I entered it. Like stepping into a mirror. I learned later that's what they call the "eye of the storm".'

My mother would have known. And she still let me climb down that ladder into the water. She watched me and she knew.

'I was outside for less than a minute when the storm returned. The wind picked up and the water with it. It seized my body, flinging me out into the ocean. I couldn't even see the stilts of our houses.' I wrap my arms around myself. 'I tried to kick, but it felt like wading through jelly. The more I fought, the more it dragged me under. The world turned from blue to black and I couldn't swim to the surface. I had no idea where the surface *was*. I was dead. I knew I was dead.'

Wyatt crawls closer.

'Just as the world began to slip away, a hand reached out of the darkness and grasped mine. That's the last thing I remember before I was on the shore. Sand against my back. And his lips against mine.'

Wyatt's eyebrows fly up.

'Breathing me to life,' I explain. 'Though I maintain he enjoyed it.'

'Who?'

I sigh. 'It was Ravi. Ravi saved me.'

His cheeks flush. 'He was with you?'

'He was visiting. He was fascinated by the ocean.' *And the Bandage.* 'Since that day I just . . . I can't go into water. Not even a bath. It brings it all back. I know it's lame – I'm a literal fish out of water.' I point to him. 'You could have made that joke. The fact you didn't was becoming awkward.'

'Not to alarm you, but we're on a ship and generally ships float on water.'

'I'm fine being *on* water. Just not in it.'

He pushes himself up. 'Sounds like I'd better train my bucket-carrying muscles.'

I laugh.

A small smile softens his features. 'Thank you for telling me.'

'Thank you for not laughing.'

He runs his fingers up his arms. 'People have . . . incorrect opinions about what weakness is.' Before I can respond, he hastily says, 'I better wash myself, eh?' Then darts away.

The guilt is already crawling across my skin.

I'm a coward. I was so close to telling him the truth. Instead, I lied. The one thing I'm good at.

I turn on my stool, watching Wyatt washing his face.

I'm not scared of water. Not really.

I did almost drown – that part is true. But I wasn't afraid. And I didn't fight. When the ocean dragged me under all I felt was *relief.*

Because if the water won then it would be over.

195

The great expanse of blackness, chipping at my consciousness, stripping parts of Ganymedes away, until there was no difference between me and it.

The utter nothingness of it. The sweet oblivion.

I didn't go into the water to drown. But when I *was* drowning, I was grateful. It was a gift. An opening and an ending.

The end of living with this coral version of my mother, cutting me with her sharp edges.

The end of the knowledge of what I was – not strong enough. Not worthy enough to bear the Goddess's Blessing.

The end of a life where nobody cared if the sea claimed me.

The water would wash it all away. And the world would be better for it.

Then Ravi fished me out. He was sobbing so hard he could barely breathe. I had to calm *him* down after he saved my life.

'Don't do that again, Dee.'

The only time he was ever mad at me. As if, somehow, he knew that I'd wanted it.

'Promise me – never again.'

He held me to his chest, clutching my body against his, as if it was the most precious thing in his life. As if he would tear the world in two to save me.

I realized then there was one person who cared if I lived. One sweet boy who would cry if I died. And by the Goddess I would do anything to stop that. I never wanted to see him cry again.

So, from then on, I avoided water.

I'm not afraid of it because I'm afraid of drowning. I'm afraid that if I go beneath the surface, I won't want to come back up.

And I do not break promises.

Chapter Fifteen

Day Five – Feast of the Elephant

Night

I decide focusing on solving the murder of my ex-best-friend-sort-of-almost-boyfriend is the best way to repress my possible suicidal tendencies.

The impossibility of Eudora's death convinces me discovering everyone's Blessings will aid our investigation. Problem is most wouldn't reveal their Blessings to their dearest friends, and I've been distancing myself from them for almost a decade.

'There must be another way.' I pace my cabin. 'Like Eska. Maybe if they think they're in danger they'll use them.'

Wyatt leans against the wall. 'Maybe. But not all Blessings are like that. And if it goes wrong, they'll hate us even more.'

I groan. My eyes are glazing over when someone knocks on my door.

Shinjiro stands in the doorway, Bancha perched on his shoulder.

Grasshopper appears instantly, short arms reaching for the bunnerfly.

The monk's gaze darts over my shoulder, towards Detective Dee's Diagram of Deduction. 'You certainly decorate your room in an *interesting* fashion.'

'That's not—' I block the view, but then remember my command to Dumpling: the naked emperor portraits. 'We all have our tastes. Mine happens to be senile old dudes.'

His lack of surprise makes me worry about my reputation. 'Clearly. Is dearest Wyatt with you?'

'Dearest Wyatt' likely hid the moment he heard Shinjiro's voice. 'He . . . err . . .'

He smiles. 'I'm doing the rounds – inviting everyone to a dinner party tonight.'

'A dinner party? On a murder ship?'

'Yes!' he says without hesitation. 'All this business of people eating separately is driving walls between us at the very time we should be in harmony. Dinner will be served in the dining hall in thirty minutes. Do come, Ganymedes. I'll be awfully upset if you don't.'

With that sugar-wrapped threat, he moves on, very bravely knocking on the remains of Eska's door.

I can't help but think his invitation is tinged with slight someone-is-going-to-fucking-die-at-that-dinner-tonight vibes. But while I'd usually avoid any chance of being in a room with these people, right now I have a very good reason to get to know them.

'Is he gone?' Wyatt's voice echoes.

I crouch. 'Are you under my bed?'

A shuffle. 'I'm not *not* under your bed.'

I offer him a hand, smirking. 'Come on, we've got a dinner party to attend.'

*

By the time we enter, nearly everyone is assembled. That chillingly empty seat at the head, Leofric at the right of it, looking as pissed off as when Eska flung him aside like a child; at least he's finally changed out of his damn tiger print. Nergüi sits opposite him with that all-knowing smile, making me not want to eat anything served tonight. Cordelia looks as though she wishes to devolve herself into a black hole of nothingness (relatable). Tendai is next to Nergüi – trying and failing to look unbothered by this. Jasper, perpetually grumpy, sits beside Tendai, and then there's Ravi's seat next to Shinjiro's. Empty.

That empty seat is why I've been avoiding the dining room, and it hurts just as much as I feared. A sharp burning in my chest.

Eska's seat is also unsurprisingly empty. I wonder what bunker she's hunkering down inside.

'Come in.' Shinjiro rises to greet us. Bancha winds her tail around his neck, watching Grasshopper warily. 'Take your seats.'

Wyatt freezes as he notes his placement. I don't blame him – he's next to Jasper, within perfect singeing range, and the Bastard doesn't look as though he's slept. Grasshopper sits beside Wyatt as he perches on his seat. The carved bear is huge around his skinny form.

If the Crabs hadn't been exiled, I'd at least have someone to look at. As it is, there's nobody opposite. And Eska's empty chair is stuck between me and where Ravi should be.

Fuck this. I'm not sitting next to two empty chairs like some chump.

I drag my chair across the room with an ear-splitting screech.

'You can't do that,' Leofric says sharply. 'The order is decided by—'

'I don't care.' I plonk the chair beside Grasshopper. 'Does it really matter which side of the table I sit on? I'm still bottom, OK?' I resist the urge to make a sex joke, which frankly deserves a medal.

Leofric throws me a look that makes me very glad there's a large table and several meat shields between us.

'That's nearly everyone! Wonderful!' Shinjiro claps his hands.

It certainly doesn't feel wonderful. The atmosphere is a little *stretched*. Even Grasshopper is sitting quietly, fiddling with her pendant. I pat my lap and she scrambles into it.

'You can't do that either!' Leofric snaps.

'Fine.' I climb into her chair, tugging her on to my lap.

'Do you think this is funny?'

'A little. It's just a chair, lion tiger.'

'Do *not* call me that.'

I pick at my teeth. 'It's literally your name – *Leo*-fric Tigris.'

He slams a fist down. 'These chairs are representative of our earned place. When the Crabs rebelled, my ancestors saved this empire. Thus, my place at the right-hand side is *earned*. What have you *earned*, Fish? What have you contributed to give you any value below rank bottom?'

A lance of pain.

Of no value.

Wyatt wrings his hands, whispering, 'Just sit in your chair, Dee. Please.'

I shuffle back. 'It fits my fish arse perfectly. The fact I've not earned it makes it *even better.*'

Leofric twists in his seat. 'You should listen to the Bear, Fish. At least he knows when the best thing a person can contribute is silence.'

Wyatt goes still.

The room hushes.

Wyatt's neck bobs. Something swallowed. Some word. His

entire body is sinking inwards, away from the others. At the party, he would have chopped off a testicle to be near these people, to be acknowledged by them; now he's trying to become as invisible as Grasshopper.

I clench and unclench my fists. Kiss-arse Wyatt was annoying, but I'd prefer he be naive and hopeful than ashamed of himself, even for a moment.

I lean across the table to Leofric. 'I'd rather listen to Wyatt all day than hear one more close-minded opinion leave your narcissistic lips. Prick.'

A united draw of breath.

Leofric's body tenses. 'You *insignificant* little—'

'Thank you all for coming,' Shinjiro says with such calm it shuts even Leofric up.

Wyatt stares at me, utterly speechless. I can't tell if he's horrified or delighted. 'Why did you say that to Leofric?' he whispers.

'He was being a dick to you.'

'But he's the *shield.*'

'A shit one. And still a dick regardless.'

Before he can respond, Shinjiro continues. 'As the voice of the Goddess, it is my role to ensure her message is heard even in the heat of chaos. That message is harmony. We exist as one united empire. And without even the smallest piece we would fall apart.'

By the way Leofric is glaring at me, I suspect he would like to break that smallest piece in half.

Shinjiro presses his hands together. 'This voyage is intended to strengthen our bonds. It's been too long since we dined together.'

'And why might that be?' Tendai scoffs. 'It's somewhat hard to strengthen bonds when one of us has murdered two Blessed. They may be sitting *right here.*'

Silence descends like a sheet of ice.

Glances pass down the table.

'Congratulations on ruining the mood, *sister*,' Nergüi says dryly.

'Someone had to say it.' Tendai shrugs. 'Or are we going to pretend we're all friends?'

'You never pretended that,' Nergüi bites back.

A chair screeches. Cordelia has risen. 'M-May I . . . be excused? I do not wish to . . .'

. . . dine with a murderer.

'I'll escort her back,' Leofric says.

'If they're leaving . . .' Tendai begins to wheel away.

Shinjiro places a hand on Cordelia's arm. 'Please. There's no need. I know tensions are high, but that is why I have brought you together.'

Reluctantly, Cordelia lowers into her chair.

Shinjiro strokes Bancha's head. 'Death is not a sin in itself. The Goddess takes whom she deems ready. But *murder*, the untimely taking of someone's life, especially when that life is of a Blessed – this interferes with the Goddess's plans. It upsets the balance.' He throws back his head, hair gleaming like pink silk. 'It would be noble for the one responsible to step forward. Then we can find a way past whatever is plaguing them, together.' He holds his cup above his head and rises. 'Will you stand with me, lost soul? Let the grace of the Goddess and the wellbeing of our nation compel you.'

If anyone else had stooped to such desperate odds to squeeze out a confession, I would have found it pitiful. But this is Shinjiro, and he uttered his speech with all the confidence that someone would jump up and say, 'Sorry about all that murder, old chap. Won't happen again.'

As it is, nobody moves.

'What a pity.' Nergüi throws back their drink. 'Though I suppose that was *rather* a long shot, Monk.'

Shinjiro's smile does not falter. 'Food then?'

Multiple dragons appear carrying various dishes. Just as I'm about to spoon my paneer curry, a voice stops me.

'Is there poison in this?' Tendai looks at her lilac dragon.

Everyone freezes.

'What?' She shrugs. 'You *really* didn't consider poison at a dinner party?'

The dragon shifts her bowtie. 'No poison, Mistress. Despite attempts, all food is prepared by the servers, and we cannot harm Blessed.'

'What do you mean "despite attempts"?' I ask.

Dumpling zooms before me. 'A request was made to poison food. It was denied.'

I grip the table. 'Who ordered that?'

'Requests between Blessed and their servers are—'

'*Whose food?*'

I somehow know the name he will utter. The person who already escaped one attempt on her life.

'Mistress Grasshopper.'

Grasshopper – completely oblivious – makes a 'mhmmm' noise, waving a gravy-covered spoon.

Prickles run up my back. Nobody is looking at us, they're all suddenly interested in their meals. One of *them* wanted to poison her. When they didn't succeed in killing her in her room, they tried a new tactic. One that preyed upon her love of food.

'Grasshopper is staying with me.' I raise my voice in the silence. 'I'm not letting her out of my sight. So, I'm sorry to ruin your valiant quest to kill a six-year-old, but *nobody* is touching her while I still breathe.'

No one responds. I didn't expect them to – after all, she's

from a lower province. Grasshoppers die all the time and nobody cares. I push my bowl away; I've suddenly lost my appetite.

'Threats won't stop them,' Jasper huffs, adjusting his uniform. 'They're a murderer. A monster. I know all about monsters. I fight them every day. Monsters don't stop until they're slain.' He says monsters but he means 'Crabs'. 'Unless we find the murderer, everyone on this ship is gonna end up dead.'

'Except the murderer.' Nergüi stirs their mutton soup. 'They'll be doing rather well, I imagine.'

Jasper leaps up. 'Listen—'

'No, *you* listen.' Nergüi's spoon clatters. 'This is *not* the same as the silly wargames you play at the Bandage to overcompensate for your sordid parentage. Blessed are being killed by other Blessed. Can your tiny mind understand the repercussions of this? This is not exiles fighting for survival. This is someone who wishes to alter the course of empires.'

Jasper shakily lowers himself back into his chair. He stares at his plate, red eyebrows knitted together.

Silence. Just the clink of utensils. Cordelia sniffs.

'*You* would know all about that,' Tendai says, bringing a spoonful of goat soup to her lips.

Nergüi's smile dips. 'As would you.'

'Whoever is doing this shows no consideration for how it will affect all our people. Someone cold and calculating.' Tendai fixes her gaze on them.

'Suddenly *you're* concerned with the woes of common people?' Nergüi twirls their noodles.

'I always have been.'

'You're not concerned with anyone but yourself. That will be your downfall.'

'Is that a threat?'

'Just a warning, *sister*.'

'I need your warnings like a kick in the head. And you can keep your "sister" too,' Tendai says. 'Now weave your web somewhere else, Spider, before you catch something that bites back. Now *that* was a threat.'

Nergüi delivers a red-lipped smile, then spoons noodles without a word.

'Good soup,' Shinjiro says with a slurp.

I can't bring myself to eat. Wyatt is similarly struggling, making half-hearted prods at his steak.

Grasshopper moves our plates closer. 'Nobody should go hungry. No matter who they are. That's what Momma says.'

I force a spoonful down for her. This sweet girl. Who here so desperately wants to kill her they tried not once, but twice? Will they ever stop trying?

'I'm not doing this any more.' Jasper, after entering a staring contest with his mutton, has finally located his backbone. He leaps to his feet. 'Sitting around, hoping someone will politely admit to their crimes. We have to *do* something before it's too late.'

'Sit down,' Leofric's voice booms. 'It is not your role to—'

'I am commander of the Bandage.'

'Exactly. This is *not* the Bandage.'

'Please.' Cordelia stands, a glass of orange juice clutched in her trembling hand. 'If Lysander were here—'

'He's not here. He's dead.' For a boy who sees death every day, Jasper struggles with the word; it leaves his lips like a pained breath. 'For all we know the person responsible is killing everyone on this ship.' He glares at Leofric. 'Why do you never believe me when I say action must be taken?'

Leofric rises slowly. 'This killer wants mayhem, boy. And you are giving it to them.'

But Jasper – full credit to him as he's half Leofric's

size – continues in earnest. 'We know who did it – Eska. The most likely poisoner is the person who *never* attends meals. She's cooked her own food since the voyage began. Her province believes they don't need to abide by our rules. Concordia is founded on us all working together, and they *don't help us*. She targeted the Crow because it would disrupt the flow of divinium. The Ermines think they're strong enough to face the Crabs alone. They want to destroy the rest of us. Pick us off one by one. She should be locked in the dungeon!'

I'm sure it's a metaphorical dungeon.

I *hope* it's a metaphorical dungeon.

Tendai subtly rolls away from the table. Stuck next to that fire-starter, I don't blame her.

Leofric's jaw tenses. 'I've noted your opinion. But lest you forget, in the All-Mother's absence, I am in control.'

Jasper throws his fists down. 'You're not in control of anything, even before you let her get murdered. You and your precious empress let the Bandage fall apart. Grasshopper Province is a mess, and you know it. I've lost hundreds of soldiers guarding that break. You're letting the Crabs in. Just like you're letting the Ermine run riot on this ship. Don't you see? She's hunting us.'

'Sit down, this instant. Final warning.'

Then I realize Tendai might be the wisest person in this room.

Jasper is trembling so furiously he's rocking the table. Plates and cutlery *ting* together, like the build-up to a crescendo.

Shinjiro retrieves his teacup, eyes upon the shuddering boy.

'You're not gonna do anything,' Jasper says. 'Are you that afraid of Eska's Blessing? Who will you blame when there's none of us left? Your mother almost got the emperor killed, and now you—'

Leofric smashes his glass against the wall. 'Do not utter another word, unless you wish to regret it.'

'I tried to stop them,' Jasper says, voice high and strained. 'I threw so many men at that break, but it wasn't enough. So, you blame *me*. You punish me by giving us no divinium.' His eyes swing to my outfit and I shift uncomfortably. 'We're protecting all of you, dying in our thousands. And you just look away, living your lives, pretending it's fine. No wonder Eska knew she could kill you. All of you are *blind fools*.'

Grasshopper's hand clutches mine beneath the table.

Leofric's mouth has gone very small and white. Cordelia is frozen, still clasping her orange juice. Nergüi seems the only one entertained, gaze passing between Jasper and Leofric, as if watching a particularly interesting play.

'You don't know how to act until it's too late,' Jasper snaps at Leofric. 'You're too worried about causing another war. But we've been fighting one for the last thousand years. I'll find her. I'll bring her to heel. Then at least one of us can protect the people we care about.'

'Just because your reprehensible father spread his seed as far as he could fling it, that does not change what you are!' Leofric yells, fury twisting his features into something unrecognizable. 'I am a son of greatness. I was born to protect this empire.' Sweat runs down his forehead, and I wonder if – with a dead empress at his feet – he's trying to convince himself. 'What authority do you have to defy me, *bastard*?'

It happens in slow motion, just like at the opening party. Jasper's body tensing. His mouth opening. The fiery crescendo.

I grab Grasshopper with one arm, and yank Wyatt with the other. As I crash to the floor, a hot rush of fire streams overhead. An almighty crack. Then a reverberating *boom*. Dust rains down. Grasshopper vanishes in a heartbeat and

Wyatt forces his body atop mine, burying my head in his chest.

The heat rolls over us, a great tidal wave of flame. I should be terrified. But all I can smell is Wyatt. Fresh linen and medicine. As his arms lock around my back, for the briefest moment I feel safe.

Someone screams.

Cordelia.

I leap to my feet for her. For that stupid girl. *Goddessdammit, Cordelia.* But if Ravi loved you, then I have to save your life. No question about it.

But Cordelia doesn't need saving.

As a fiery torrent spews from Jasper's mouth, Leofric flings Cordelia aside as easily as swatting a bug. The fire hits the wall, destroying whichever unfortunate emperor's portrait was hung there.

That's when Nergüi finally backs away from the table.

I'm used to Leofric having a face like a slapped arse. But the fury that takes control of his features – twisting and morphing them – is unlike anything I've ever seen. He stretches out his arm, and a dash of black leaps into reality. My eyes struggle to understand. It *looks* as if the ink of his tattoos has bled into the actual air.

In fact, that's exactly what's happened.

That awful tiger tattoo isn't just a tattoo. It's an actual goddessdamn tiger. It leaps forward, a blur of black, shifting like ink in water.

The beast bites a chunk out of the table leg. The cutlery and bowls slide to the floor in an avalanche of metal and porcelain. The tiger darts atop the tabletop, saucepan paws smashing through the broken glass.

Shinjiro is the only one who hasn't moved; he sits before

the lopsided table, sipping his tea and watching with measured eyes.

Before Jasper can create a lick of flame, the ink tiger leaps upon him, slamming him to the ground. It opens its mouth, black teeth bared in a silent roar.

Jasper's body goes slack. His eyes fix upon the beast. He opens his mouth, not to speak, but to gasp great trembling breaths. I've seen him annoyed. I've seen him furious. But never once have I seen that boy scared. In this moment, he's terrified.

Leofric watches without a lick of emotion, arms limp at his side. Strangely still.

I live close enough to the Bandage to know Oxen in all their agonizing dullness. There's only one thing they understand, one language they speak – power.

Jasper shakes furiously as the tiger digs its claws into his uniform. His small hands clench against the pain, lips curling back from his teeth.

'L-Leofric,' I stammer, heart thudding. 'Cut it out. He gets it.'

But Leofric doesn't respond. He's waiting for something he knows Jasper will give him.

Finally, with a whimper, like the fourteen-year-old he is, Jasper says, 'I'm sorry. I'm sorry.'

*

The dinner wasn't the most cheery to begin with, but it's well and truly soured after that.

'Up you get.' Shinjiro helps Jasper to his feet, examining his body. 'Ah, you see, you're fine. Just a few bruises. The Goddess truly has blessed you this day.'

Jasper doesn't seem to think he's 'blessed'. But he also

seems to have lost the ability to speak. He fingers the tattered remains of his uniform, eyes wide and unblinking with awe.

Leofric seems unbothered about revealing his Blessing. I suppose you don't have to be bothered by much when you can summon a demon tattoo tiger whenever someone pisses you off.

Cordelia is shaking furiously as she flees, constantly checking behind as if the beast is stalking *her*. Unfortunately for Cordelia, Leofric does just that, accompanying her with an 'I'll make sure she's OK.'

Jasper follows shortly after, still in a daze.

'Wonderful dinner.' Nergüi dabs their mouth and lays the napkin delicately atop the mess of crockery. 'Let's do it again sometime, hm?' Their eyes fix upon me. 'After all, there are only seven days remaining.'

I swear I actually *feel* my organs shrivel.

They're trailed by Tendai who seems the least surprised of everyone, looking at Shinjiro with a well-what-did-you-expect? expression.

I coax a terrified Grasshopper out of her invisibility with the food that was mercifully spared. She buries her face in my stomach and doesn't stop shaking until I wrap my arms around her.

I glance across the gently smouldering dining room to Shinjiro. 'Sorry about your dinner.'

'Never mind.' He picks up a piece of broken china. 'We get to clean it away, what a treat.'

'You and I have very different definitions of a treat.'

'In Bunnerfly Province cleaning away mess is a form of prayer. Of cleansing the soul.' He plucks shards out of the rubble. 'Just like resolving disputes or repairing broken things. All these activities encourage a return to states as they should be. A form of balance.' He hums as he cleans. 'These things are not truly broken. If we gather the pieces they can be put back together.'

I shrug at Wyatt, and we help him, retrieving the broken pieces and piling them up.

'It's a shame Lysander isn't here,' I say, cracking my back. 'He always kept Leofric on a leash.' Perhaps a *literal* leash, considering what I suspect their relationship was. The pairing is an unlikely one. A high-strung boy who would rather walk on hot coals than break a rule, and the Tortoise scion who, I suspect, was making grand progress in breaking them all. But that was Lysander. He was utterly enchanting. It was hard not to get caught up in his idealism. Even for someone like Leofric, whose entire life has been dictated down to how many times he can piss in a day.

Maybe that was *why* Leofric liked him.

Shinjiro hums something that might be agreement. 'But it *was* a thrill to see Leofric's Blessing confirmed, wasn't it?'

Note for the record: Shinjiro may terrify me even more than Nergüi.

'Thrilling's one word for it. I know Tiger Blessed are supposed to have a powerful Blessing but that's . . .' Before tonight, I found my father the most intimidating man alive, and all he can do is make it drizzle.

'Considering his duties, it makes sense. Many Tigers throughout history possessed Blessings designed to strike fear in those who intended harm against the leader. Or even to swiftly dispose of them.'

'You say that like he had a choice in what his Blessing is.'

'Not a choice per se.' He brushes a porcelain shard from his robes and adds it to the pile. 'It does not fall to us to choose our destinies. I did not ask to be blessed by the Goddess; she simply deemed it so. But there are choices that are ours. There are ways in which we can shape things.' He looks across the broken table. 'Do you think it is a coincidence that firebrand's Blessing manifested in flames? Or that mine chose to heal? The Goddess's magic interweaves with our being, it sees our core, what makes us who we are, and manifests itself based on that. The magic is hers, but it expresses itself through us.'

I stare. 'You mean that Blessings are based on the people who have them?'

'It is not so simple as that.'

Grasshopper steps before him, looking up hopefully.

Shinjiro holds Bancha out. Unexpectedly, the animal allows the child to sit with her in her lap.

'So, Blessings are personal, unique to the person?' I ask once she's settled.

'You must have felt it when your Blessing emerged – how essential it was to you? How it embodied a part of your soul that you had not understood until that moment?'

I cough. 'Sure. But still . . . elaborate?'

Having reclaimed the shards, he brushes away the remaining mess. I have no idea where he even got a brush. 'Blessings emerge when our souls cry out for them. That is why they are so closely matched with the core of our beings. Tiger Province even deliberately place their heirs in dangerous situations, hoping to *force* the Blessings to emerge early.'

I've heard the stories: tying up six-year-olds in lions' dens; locking them in burning buildings.

'But the Goddess only appears when she is needed. When the time is correct. I, for example, lived in discord for many years. I grew up with my sisters and brothers; we were nursed by the same monastery mothers, taught the same teachings. Our lives were identical. But whereas my siblings were content, I felt a great disconnect within me.' He pauses, watching Bancha nuzzle Grasshopper's chin. 'Then I realized what it was. I understood the unbalance. My physical body was not in harmony with my soul.'

'Not in harmony?'

He clasps the broom. 'It is not upon me to question the Goddess or her choices. But I knew my body and my soul were pulling two different ways. My soul was male, but I did not feel that my body matched accordingly.'

'*Ohhh.*'

His eyes meet mine. 'I had been bleeding since I was born, though nobody could see it. My body was an open wound, one I needed to heal. One I needed to set right. My Blessing emerged then.' He gently touches his face. 'I was able to heal my discord. Now, my body and soul are balanced. My Blessing helped me understand my purpose – to ease others whose bodies cause them suffering. I have been closing wounds and purging sickness since that day. Or trying to.' He smiles at Wyatt, who shuffles behind me. 'Wyatt must have told you his story?'

'No, actually.'

'Wyatt!' Shinjiro brandishes the broom. 'You can trust Ganymedes. Besides, we should be celebrating the Goddess's gifts. Not hiding them.'

Wyatt fiddles with his collar. 'I . . . I didn't want . . .'

Now I *need* to know.

I turn to Shinjiro eagerly.

'When he was a child, a bull got loose on the farm, charging towards him.'

Wyatt is already groaning.

'Then . . . Wyatt, you can finish the story.'

I doubt it. He's got his hands pressed over his ears, whimpering gently.

'He yelled at the bull to stop. And it stopped.'

Wyatt removes his hands. Speechless. 'You . . . you told him.'

'*You can speak to animals?*' I screech.

'He speaks to animals more than people.' Shinjiro chuckles. 'I sometimes wonder if using the Blessing so much is worsening his condition. Tell him why it's your Blessing, Wyatt.'

Red has flooded his face from the tips of his ears to his neck. He's practically luminous.

Part of me wants to tell Shinjiro to stop the torment, but a louder part is insatiably hungry for information about Wyatt (*not sure why* . . .) and my stomach always makes my choices.

'He has many brothers, but they're often absent on the cattle runs,' Shinjiro begins. 'That leaves Wyatt alone for months at a time, isn't that right?'

Wyatt's face is buried in his hands; a gleaming red forehead is all I can see.

'Alone apart from . . . the animals,' Shinjiro finishes.

Suddenly it's less funny, and my heart hurts a bit.

Wyatt lowers his hands, but he doesn't meet my gaze. 'I didn't have any friends. Lying in bed, useless, all day and night, watching my strong brothers growing closer, sharing stories of journeys I would never take. I just . . . I just wanted someone to talk to.'

Damn. How had I never noticed how alone he was? I concentrated so entirely on Ravi, I never thought to look at Wyatt, who was suffering just as much.

My words at the party return to me: '*He probably only spoke to you because you're easier to manipulate than your brothers.*'

I'm such a dick. Wyatt should've punched me.

Shinjiro continues, 'Blessings emerge when we need them most. I needed to heal, and Wyatt needed company. Even if that company was a horse.' He smiles. 'Ah! I just remembered! Bancha has been moody lately, can you tell me why?'

Wyatt yelps as the winged rabbit lands on his shoulder. 'I don't . . .' His breath catches. He looks as if he wishes Leofric's tiger would drag him out of this situation.

Suddenly it makes sense as to why Blessed are so reluctant to speak about their Blessings. If it was the same as their parents' it would be like inheriting their nose or eye shape – yours, sure, but not *personal*. But if it's based on your core? It's like someone glimpsing your soul.

Because my father and I had to pretend to possess identical Blessings, I assumed everyone else was the same. Shit. If I hadn't stubbornly avoided learning about Blessings, I probably wouldn't have made that assumption.

'Please?' Shinjiro sticks out his bottom lip. 'A favour? For all these years of keeping you alive?'

I steel myself not to laugh at whatever chirpy noise is about to emit from Wyatt's mouth, but he simply says in his normal voice, 'What's the matter, Bancha?'

Silence. Bancha sniffs Wyatt's nose.

'So?' Shinjiro leans forward.

'She . . .' He scratches the back of his neck, avoiding my gaze. 'She doesn't like what you're feeding her. She wants more biscuits.'

'I imagine she does.' Shinjiro holds out his arm and she flies to him. 'We shall arrange a biscuit feast for her highness.'

Wyatt stares at the floor, biting his lip.

'Wyatt,' I begin.

'Please don't,' he says, pained.

'This is amazing!' I leap before him, craning my neck to see his face. 'That's the coolest thing I've ever seen!'

His eyes flutter to me. 'R-Really? I always thought it was kind of lame—'

'*Nothing* about you is lame.' I grin, and his mouth snaps

shut. 'Once all this murdering is over, I got some fish I *gotta* chat with.'

I can't quite place if Wyatt is horrified or enthusiastic about that prospect. But I'm too busy imagining the epic adventures of Dee, Fish Whisperer, to worry about it. When I look back, his gaze hasn't left mine.

I cock my head to the side. 'What?'

'Nothing.' He looks away.

I can use this knowledge. If Blessings are unique to the individual, I don't need people to tell me what their Blessings are. All I need is to understand them enough to make an educated guess.

I wonder what Ravi's was. If it was such an essential part of his soul, I should know on instinct. But I have no idea.

I guess there were parts of Ravi that he kept hidden, even from me.

That should devastate me. But all I feel is numb acceptance.

'Ganymedes?'

'Huh?' Everyone is staring at me.

'Your Blessing.' Shinjiro smiles sweetly. 'We're all sharing.'

I'm sweating already. Incredible – the power one has to sweat. I need to escape this room. If Wyatt finds out – if anyone finds out – it'll all be confirmed. How unworthy I am. How worthless I am.

'Ganymedes?'

Lie.

I need a Blessing nobody can disprove. Incredible dance moves? Legendary love making?

'I . . .' A spray of glitter appears before me. A sharp harmonious melody. Then Dumpling slaps me. 'Is that a . . . fish?'

'You advised me to let you know if your borders had been breached.'

216

I nurse my cheek. 'What?'

'Someone is in your room, Master Fish.'

*

I'm not sure who is following as I run. Grasshopper is probably with me, and there's a strained, haggard sound which is likely Wyatt struggling to keep up.

I reach my door and grab the handle.

'Don't just go in!' Wyatt seizes my arm.

'But someone's in there!'

'Yeah – maybe the murderer!'

'Oh. Right.' I stare at the door.

Grasshopper jumps on the spot. 'Open! Open!' It's all very well for her, she can just disappear from whatever's inside.

'Be very careful.' Wyatt's brandishing a . . . what is that? A table leg? Should I have a weapon?

My hand closes around the handle. When I turn it, it clicks open.

Wyatt asks, hushed, 'Did you lock it?'

'Err . . . not sure.'

'Ganymedes!' he groans. 'Literal murderer! Remember?'

I swallow hard, and then push the door open.

The room is bathed in shadow. The only light is the crescent moon, casting a silver haze through the circular window.

'Blessed hells.' Wyatt lets out a long breath. 'It's a mess.'

'Well, yeah, but that's how we left it.' There's nothing out of place. Apart from the wardrobe door. It's slightly ajar. And I have no reason to open it – I'm wearing the only clothes I have.

I approach it warily, Wyatt beside me, wheezing as he raises the table leg. Grasshopper clings to my fish tail.

I slip my boot in the gap behind the door, then fling it open.

The fact that Grasshopper doesn't scream is the worst of all. She just vanishes. Wyatt steadies himself against the wall. The table leg clunks to the floor.

A body has tumbled out of the wardrobe. Eyebrows still knitted together, as if pissed off at me even in death. She could be sleeping, if not for the single trail of blood leaking from her mouth. Red against the ice blue of her hair.

My neighbour. My lifelong enemy. A woman who slayed giant mammoths. Dead in my wardrobe.

'Eska . . .'

Chapter Sixteen

Day Six – Feast of the Bunnerfly

Morning

Hot water prickles my skin. For a moment, the shock and pain empty my mind. Then last night's events return – the dead body in my wardrobe, the lifeless thud as she hit the floor.

I had fetched Shinjiro, and he checked Eska over.

'Dead for sure. No wounds except bite marks on her tongue. And nail marks inside her palms – most likely self-inflicted.'

In the present, Wyatt appears before me, concerned creases at the corners of his eyes. 'Are you OK?'

By the time I returned with Shinjiro, Wyatt was clutching Eska's hand, shoulders trembling with the force of his sobs.

His heart is fragile in more than one way, this Bear.

'I'm fine.' I force a smile and watch the creases vanish. 'Let's go over the main questions one by one.'

'Good idea,' he says, dashing across the bathhouse to fetch more water.

There's a screech followed by a loud splash, 'Again!' Grasshopper yells, followed by the pat-pat-pat of bare feet.

'Question number one – what the shit?' I say.

'Not a question!'

'Question number one – what was Eska doing in my room?'

Wyatt returns with a full bucket. 'You left it unlocked, for sure?'

'I think so . . .' I ignore his long-suffering sigh. 'Maybe someone's trying to frame me?'

'So, either someone forced her inside, or she went there of her own free will.'

I snort. 'You're her neighbour too; how often has she paid you a visit?'

His shoulders sag. 'Maybe I should have tried harder with Eska.'

'I bet your one-handed brother would beg to differ.'

But I *had* mentioned it to her, hadn't I? Told her she could come to me. I never thought she actually would, though.

'Maybe someone found her hiding spot?' I massage my head; then Wyatt tips another bucket over it. 'Ah! Warning next time!'

'Sorry.'

'Number two – how did she die? There were no wounds. It doesn't correlate with Ravi at all. He was stabbed seventeen times. But Eudora had no marks on her either, apart from the rope bruise . . . Maybe they knocked Eska out first?'

'But the tongue biting, and nail marks,' Wyatt says, moving back to the water.

'Shit. So she must have been awake.' *Forgot that annoying bit of information.* 'That brings me to number three – where did she die?'

'Your room, right?'

I rub my hands over my bare knees. 'Barely anything in my room had been touched. We've all seen her Blessing, and the hole it made of her door. This is a woman who takes on snow mammoths singlehandedly. She wouldn't go down without a fight.' I look up as Wyatt appears breathless before me. 'She must have been killed somewhere else, then stashed in my room.'

'That makes sense, else your cabin would be a crater.' His eyes travel, and I know he's reliving it. I shouldn't have left him with her.

'At least it's not Shinjiro. He was with us after dinner. He wouldn't have had the chance to kill her.'

Wyatt taps the bucket. 'Well . . . Eska wasn't *at* dinner. Maybe *that's* the reason.'

'Ugh. So number four – when did she die?' I wring out my wet hair. Eska had been warm. I remember because I never imagined that ice-queen to be warm. But unlike Ravi, she was inside the pleasantly ambient ship, wrapped in all her furs. So that doesn't really narrow down the time of death. 'If she was killed somewhere else it could have happened before dinner. That means it could've been anyone.'

Wyatt bites his lip. 'Tough one.'

'Except . . . Dumpling. He alerted me that my room had been entered after dinner. So even if she didn't die there, whoever put her body there did so after dinner, when every-one except me, you, Grasshopper and Shinjiro had left.' I almost feel triumphant; then a thought niggles my gut. 'Dumpling!'

He appears, shifting his bowtie. 'Master?'

'Are you able to pick up dead bodies? Move them to other rooms?'

His tail twitches. 'Which dead body would you like me to move?'

I groan as Wyatt upends another bucket of water over my head.

'So that's that alibi gone. Shinjiro could have asked his dragon to do it while he was with us,' he sighs. 'We're back at square one.'

'Dumpling, when you alerted me last night, was that because a *person* or a *server* entered my room?' I ask, grasping at straws.

'I cannot say,' he says solemnly. 'A server carrying out a command for their master would count as an intruder, just as much as their Blessed.'

Damn servers. I'm gonna strangle the emperor myself if I get out of this.

I turn to Wyatt. 'One more question – why? Shinjiro says chaos but who would want that?'

The image of her body returns. The blue of her braid across her light brown skin. Eudora's and Ravi's corpses had been chilling, but Eska's was like witnessing a mountain crumble to ruins.

She terrified me, and I really wasn't a fan of the stabbing. But she was my neighbour. I sat beside her in summits for years, both of us silent. Both of us shouldering burdens we could not speak of. Both of us building walls. Hers were just more obvious.

Wyatt crouches before me. 'What's our next plan?'

I push my hair out of my face. 'The only thing we know for sure is she was attacked somewhere else, or my room would be a steaming heap of metal. We should search the ship, see if we can find somewhere that looks like the fist of the Goddess slammed into it. There are some crime scenes you can't clean up.' I rise. 'Grasshopper! We're going—'

Then my world is pain.

I must have seen the water. Blacked out. The marble is hard against my back, and someone is holding me down.

'W-Wyatt . . . ?'

My head slams against the floor. Stars flash.

'You murderer!' Brown skin. Red hair. Jasper. Jasper is thumping my head against the stone like a child trying to crack a coconut.

Then I realize what the pain is.

I'm on fire.

I try to raise my hands, but he pins my wrists, breathing black smoke into my eyes. They stream with tears. My world turns grey.

In the distance, staggering footsteps. A yelp. Wyatt? I don't care about me, but if Jasper hurt him . . .

I kick out, but a wave of pain jerks me back against the floor.

For a moment, it stills. Jasper pants above me, eyes unfocused.

I cough, smoke tearing my throat raw. 'What – are – you – doing – you – bloody – madman?'

'I'm arresting you!'

'You're fucking killing me!'

His eyes swim, and the pain flares again.

My body jolts, legs kicking for purchase. For his body. For anything. Anything to make it stop.

A terrible noise escapes my lips, like the wail of a dying animal. Then the agony is all there is. The room vanishes. It's as silent and dark as the bottom of the ocean, this pain.

A screech. The ache ebbs. Blurred images push through the darkness.

Smoke rising around me. Grey as the heart of a storm.

Jasper flung back, swatting at something I cannot see.

My hearing returns in a blast of noise.

'Get off me, you little gremlin! You and your whole province are filthy animals.' Jasper's eyes are wild, completely unfocused. Great plumes of flame rise from him, seeping through his skin, from every pore.

He looks as mad as the emperor. All fire and pain and chaos.

'Dumpling!' I cry.

'Master Fish, how may I be of—'

'Kill him! Kill the fucker!'

'I'm sorry, my protocols mean that I cannot inflict harm on—'

'TEAR HIS EYEBALLS OUT!'

Then Wyatt drowns us all in a bucket of water. Jasper's flames extinguish in a poof of steam.

That is how Leofric and Shinjiro find us. Me, gasping against the floor, skin peeling off my precious, beautiful body, Jasper wrestling an invisible child, both frothing mad, and Wyatt on his knees, coughing up half a river and half a lung by the sound of it.

'Oh dear,' Shinjiro says, which just about sums it up.

Chapter Seventeen

Day Six – Feast of the Bunnerfly

Afternoon

There are times in life when things are utterly shit, no matter how you slice them. For example, being jump attacked (while wearing only a small towel) by a fourteen-year-old pyromaniac with anger-management issues and a long-held grudge after years of expert 'winding up', which in hindsight may not have been the smartest course of action against a fourteen-year-old pyromaniac with anger-management issues. These are the instances when one must stop and smell the roses. My roses are that not a single flame touched my hair.

'Tell me I'll live to break hearts,' I rasp as Shinjiro examines my body.

'I can heal wounds,' he says, Bancha's ears peeking over his shoulder. 'But growing hair back is beyond me. Luckily, the Goddess spared your mane.' His hand lingers on my leg, then he says, voice low, 'I must apologize. When you asked me about that second night – why I wasn't in the corridor – I must confess, I lied.'

I force myself up, arms trembling. 'What happened?'

He glances aside. 'I saw her.'

'Her?'

'The All-Mother.'

'You saw *Eudora*?'

He adjusts his robe. 'She looked so *real*, so I followed her. But it was a trick of the mind, most likely from lack of sleep. She vanished. If people were to find out . . . a monk of my standing . . .'

'I won't tell.' Why is he telling me this *now*? When I'm barely able to retain my own name?

'Are you done with him?' Leofric appears, glaring at me as if I set myself on fire to ruin his day.

'Nice to know you care, kitty cat.' I haven't forgotten his terrifying Blessing, but I have a Shinjiro-shaped barrier between us. 'Have you brought me some grapes?'

'He's ready.' Shinjiro removes his palm from my smooth skin. You'd never be able to tell it was a weeping mess just hours ago. 'My Blessing uses your life force as a power source,' he explains, helping me into my fakinium-covered clothes. 'That's why I can't raise the dead. There's nothing to sap energy from. So, you may be a little off balance.'

I've been sapped. I feel sapped. All floppy and sappy.

'You can leave him with me,' Leofric says, which sounds almost as appealing as another round with Jasper.

Shinjiro gestures. 'Is this quite necessary?'

I was carried out of the bathhouse unconscious and only came to when Shinjiro was halfway through healing me, so I didn't have a chance to examine my surroundings before now.

The walls are completely bare. Stripped-back stone, cold to the touch. The place is cramped, but almost entirely empty – just a wooden bench I presume to be some sort of torturous bed. There's a strange humming noise that seems to come from everywhere, but most disconcerting is the door, comprised entirely of iron bars.

'I'm in a cell,' I say hoarsely. 'A brig.'

It *was* a real dungeon.

'As I said,' Leofric repeats.

But Shinjiro wavers.

Leofric turns to him. 'You are the empress's moral guidance, and I appreciate your counsel.' He abso-fucking-lutely doesn't. 'But I am her sword and shield. I enforce her laws. With all due respect, this is my realm.'

Shinjiro frowns, but finally leaves. To my horror, another figure emerges from the darkness beyond the door, rubies gleaming like teardrops of blood.

Nergüi.

'What are you doing here?' Leofric demands. 'This isn't a—'

'I've been seeking a chance to speak to Ganymedes,' Nergüi says. 'Alone.'

Goddess almighty. They *never* miss an opportunity. To give them credit, me locked behind bars is perhaps the only time I'll speak to Nergüi one on one.

Leofric storms towards them. Nergüi doesn't even flinch. 'Not here. Not *now*.'

'I only wish to discuss—'

'Leave. Immediately.'

Nergüi shoots him a look so cold I actually shiver. Then they approach me. Long slender fingers wrap around the bars. 'You are yet to come and see me. I understand threats hold no sway over an *honest* man such as yourself, but perhaps a deal may tempt you?'

'A deal?'

Their grey eyes pin me. 'Agree to speak with me, and I will release you from this cell.'

227

'You will do nothing of the sort,' Leofric snarls. 'Who do you think you—'

'I know information the shield would do anything to keep secret,' Nergüi says coolly.

That shuts him up. He staggers back, staring at them wordlessly.

'He *will* let you out if I threaten to reveal this. All you have to do is accompany me to my cabin. Alone.'

Leofric looks as though he's attempting to swallow a live bee. Nergüi, meanwhile, is impossibly smug. And I need to pick between them.

Locked in a cell with the shield. Or a conversation with the Spider.

Wyatt's fearful face flashes in my memory. *'Don't meet with Nergüi alone.'*

Leofric may be vaguely terrifying, but he cannot hurt me the way I suspect Nergüi can.

I shuffle back. 'I'll take my chances here.'

Nergüi's eye twitches. 'You're simply delaying the inevitable.'

Leofric slams his hand against the bars above Nergüi's head. 'Leave. Before I pluck off all your legs.'

Nergüi smirks at him, then sweeps from the room.

'Lion tiger,' I mutter. 'I feel like we just bonded.'

'Shut up.'

'You're still wearing her collar.'

He touches the iron bar at his neck. 'I'm still serving her. Until my work is done, I will not be removing it.'

I feel sorry for him, in some distant part of my body that isn't throbbing with pain. When we return, his life is over. His mother was reprimanded for letting her emperor get stabbed. But Leofric's empress died under his watch. He is f-u-c-k-e-d.

'Fish, I'm going to cut to the chase. I know it was you.'

Sympathy gone.

'Now Eska is dead you go for the next easy mark.' My voice cracks.

'Stop playing the victim.'

I look around, but I can't see much in the dim light. 'Where's Wyatt? Grasshopper?'

'The Bear is likely being attended to in the art gallery by Shinjiro. He suffered quite a shock. We have detained your accomplice in an adjoining cell.'

'Accomplice.' Revulsion burns my throat. 'A six-year-old.'

Something dark shifts behind his eyes. 'From a wild, lawless land. I heard they breed with the Crabs.'

I hope they do. Ravi was half-Crab, and if Grasshopper is the same, maybe I'll hop the Bandage now.

Flashes of a different place. A different day. Snow streaked with red. Triumphant cheers. A hand closing over my mouth.

My fingers trace the scar across my palm. 'Is it true?'

'What?'

'They say in your Blessing ceremony, you transport a Crab from beyond the Bandage, tie them up in the dark for days without food.' My throat aches. 'You release them in your capital square, blindfolded. Then *you* are unleashed upon them.'

Leofric's expression doesn't shift. 'They have a sword.'

'Very thoughtful.'

'Once we dispatch the Crab, we kneel before the emperor and mark ourselves.' He tugs down his shirt. Two red scars form an 'X' across his chest. 'We dedicate our lives to them with that gesture – to bleed for them, protect them from evil.'

'How brave.'

He nods. He doesn't even understand I'm being sarcastic.

229

That putting an emaciated, blinded human in a ring to be sacrificed is horrific beyond measure. That that person could be any of us, if not for the luck of being born one side of a wall.

'I'm going to extend an offer to you. I know you are accustomed to jumping to idiotic answers, but I implore you to consider it.' He lowers stiffly before me. 'If you confess to the murders, I will arrange it so once we return to the mainland, you will be stripped of your title. You will no longer be a member of the Blessed, or the dux of your province. You will live out your days alone.'

I roll his words over and over in my mind, looking for the catch. 'You're not going to execute me?'

The tiger across his arms ripples. 'As a reward for your compliance, I will not take your life. But you'll never have anything to do with us again.'

I understand his play. His legacy is screwed either way. But returning with the killer lets him cling on to a shred of respect. Might even save his life. He's desperate. Maybe he doesn't even believe it's me. He just needs a head on a platter.

But how did he know to offer *exactly* what I want?

'What will happen to Grasshopper?'

'That's not your concern.' He holds his hand out. 'Do we have a deal?'

Leofric has offered me everything. My reason for going on this ship. All I have to do is agree that I'm the murderer. One handshake and I'll have everything I wanted since my father shattered my life.

Then why is my hand so heavy?

Why don't I feel an ounce of relief?

Why do I feel nothing but dread?

I want to escape everything. But if I shake Leofric's hand, then Ravi will remain unavenged. And Grasshopper will be left alone with this man, and others like him, who believe your worth is determined by where you sit at a table.

I can't – *won't* – leave her with them. My wild girl, clinging to me and singing her gentle songs. To eat, or to love.

They will break her. Destroy her. As they did with Ravi. Strip all the softness and sweetness away. Leave her cold and cruel. Like him.

Then snuff out her life as casually as swatting a bug. And the only concern will be how it disrupts the trade from her land.

I can't leave her with them.

Leofric leans forward. 'Do we have a deal?'

'Sorry. You don't get to catch your fish today.'

Silence. I wait for the barbed words, to be told all the ways I'm useless.

Instead, his face morphs. The same transformation I witnessed in the dining room. He goes from irritancy to outrage in the blink of an eye.

Dread builds for a fraction of a second; then his fist drives into my stomach. 'You pitiful low-bred scum!'

His blow unleashes the pain muted by Shinjiro, like the breaking of a dam. I fall back, limbs spasming. Before I can stop myself, warm liquid trickles down my leg.

'You have *never* known your place!' Another fist. 'You should have listened to your Crow. He understood the role of the lower provinces is to *serve* Concordia.' He draws back, wincing as he holds his arm.

'I'm sorry,' I rasp. 'Did my bones hurt your hand?'

That earns me a kick in the ribs.

I bite back on a scream. I will *not* scream for him.

'It's because of you our empire is failing!'

A foot slams into my chest, winding me. I gasp for air through bruised lungs.

'It's *your* fault! Yours!' His voice cracks.

Shock turns my blood cold.

He's crying. The noise of his sobs terrifies me more than if he was screaming.

'All you do is take!' He grips his knees, hot angry tears streaming. Tears that have been held back for too long. 'Dead . . . because of you!'

'I didn't . . .' I gasp. 'I didn't kill her.'

He's beyond listening. I try to crawl away. Desperate hands hauling my throbbing body across the cold floor. There's nowhere to go, but I need to get away from *him*. From the madness in his eyes. As if he will tear me in two to sate it.

Pain. A sharp stabbing in my leg.

My entire body seizes.

The tattoo tiger's jaws are clasped around my ankle, dragging me back to him. Him with his slack body. As if all life has been drained out of it. Tears falling from empty eyes.

There is something familiar about it – that stance.

'Shield!'

The tiger vanishes.

Shinjiro stands in the doorway, pink hair flared about his face. His furious expression is so foreign he looks like a different man. 'Acts of violence between Blessed are *strictly* prohibited. *Especially* using one's Blessing to inflict that violence.'

Leofric hastily wipes his eyes. He looks more than a little embarrassed. About the act itself, or because he got caught, I'm not sure.

But I know what I saw – grief. Grief so real and raw that even with all his discipline, it couldn't be contained any longer. How could I not see it until now? Because he hid it so expertly? Because I discounted him as a prickly dick? He's grieving for a girl he was born to protect.

Still doesn't excuse him almost tearing off my ankle though.

'What do you want, Monk?'

Shinjiro settles, patting his hair. 'I have discussed matters with the other Blessed. Were we on land, the truth of such accusations would be determined through a court of law, with the Blessed presiding.'

'Your point?'

'Well, we have seven Blessed here. Rather than you acting alone, surely you would prefer to take guidance from all our siblings?' Shinjiro's smile returns, as if it had never left.

Leofric goes still. 'I am perfectly—'

'I only ask as a matter of courtesy. We've already decided,' Shinjiro says. 'Bring Ganymedes to the art gallery. There we will *all* pass judgement upon his guilt.'

*

My wounds are still throbbing and my ankle hurts like a bastard, but Leoprick saw it necessary to shackle my wrists, so I have to awkwardly lean against the man who laid into my ribs minutes ago.

Putting an art gallery beneath sea level would normally be a terrible idea, but the emperor has added artificial sun to his. The room is flooded with so much light I'm momentarily blinded after my dark cell. Every wall of the arched room is covered with floor-to-ceiling portraits. Most are of previous emperors and empresses (because you can never have too many of those). But there are also depictions of all twelve Blessed from previous generations, standing side by side and looking utterly miserable. Which isn't dissimilar to the room's present occupants.

Cordelia paces from portrait to portrait, while Tendai sits with her chin in her hand, already dozing. Nergüi eyes my bruised body like a spider sizing up a particularly delicious fly. Wyatt stands alone in the farthest corner. As he notices me, his eyes widen in wordless horror.

Did Shinjiro lie about my hair? I can't check because Leofric—

'Stop it!'

I turn towards the source of the yells.

Jasper. That mad bastard. Unchained, unbound and holding *my* girl. Matching shackles around her tiny wrists. She's flailing wildly, filling his face with a mouthful of lilac curls.

'Grasshopper!' I yell. 'It's OK!'

She strains against her chains. 'Dee! Help me! Dee! Dee!'

Leofric storms towards her, dragging me with him. He seizes her chin. 'Quiet, gremlin.'

She falls silent, her small body trembling.

I'm in ball-kicking distance. I could do it. One swift kick and I'd only have to pay for it with a light tiger mauling. I *will* do it if he touches her again.

Tendai sighs. 'Can we get this over with?'

'Patience.' Leofric drags me beside Grasshopper.

'Hey, little lady,' I whisper. 'I won't let them do anything to you, promise.'

There are tears in her eyes. Oh my fuck, there are *tears*. But her bottom lip sticks out too – stubborn, furious, affronted. And Jasper's arms are covered with bites and scratches.

That's my girl.

'It seems our Tiger brother has reason to suspect Ganymedes of heinous acts.' Shinjiro steps out from behind me. Somehow, he already has a hot cup of tea. 'Namely, the murder of the All-Mother, and the Crow and Ermine Blessed. We are to listen to the evidence and pass judgement.'

My skin crawls. This isn't a trial. It's a mockery. Almost everyone in this room has already passed judgement on me.

They passed it the day I was born a Fish. They passed it every day I dared speak up when I should have been silent. When I reached out to Ravi with love, instead of joining their mockery.

I have felt their judgement burn into me with every disapproving glare and barbed word for the past decade. And now they have finally been given a way to wield it.

It doesn't matter what I say. I was damned long before I entered this room.

Shinjiro stops in the centre. 'Please present your case, Shield.'

Leofric observes Shinjiro with thinly veiled hate. Then he's all clipped, calm words. Nothing like the beast in the brig. 'I had my suspicions regarding the identity of the assailant of Her Majesty, but now I believe I possess enough information to draw a conclusion.'

'It's going to be *reeeeal* awkward for you when you're wrong in front of all these people.' If I don't channel my hopelessness and frustration into jokes, I'm going to *actually* kick him in the balls. My jokes are keeping his balls unkicked.

He ignores me. 'I initially suspected the Ermine, owing to her province's reputation for independence. But after careful consideration, I believe that was an incorrect assumption.'

'You mean after her corpse turned up?'

I yelp as he twists my shackles tighter.

'These murders have one thing in common – they are wild. They are unhinged. And they are chaotic.'

'That's three things,' I say dryly.

Another twist. The shackles nip my skin.

'Do you not find it peculiar that they occur now? What is different on this voyage, compared to our other summits?'

'This brat.' Jasper shakes Grasshopper.

'Exactly,' Leofric says.

My head shoots up.

What?

The shock registers strangely. I laugh. With my raw throat it sounds impressively demonic. 'That's your big play? You're blaming a six-year-old?'

'Before she appeared, our meetings were harmonious,' Leofric says.

'Wrong.'

'Anyone can see how deranged she is.'

'Also wrong. She's six.'

'We've all witnessed her Blessing,' Leofric announces. 'She uses her invisibility to sneak up on her prey, attacking them before they can defend themselves.'

'You're wrong!' I cry. 'She uses it to hide from *you*. 'Cause you terrified her on the first night. Why would Grasshopper poison her own food?'

'It was the Fish's server who claimed so.' Leofric speaks as if I'm not the one who asked the question. 'He likely commanded the dragon to say that to avoid suspicion.'

'I'm honoured you think I'm that smart.'

'We all know the chaos that is rampant in Grasshopper Province, where the Bandage is weakest. I hear they *breed* with the monsters outside.'

'If that's true,' I say through ragged breaths, 'then these *monsters* are preferable to whatever inbred gene pool you crawled out of.'

He hits me. My head snaps back.

'*Shield*,' Shinjiro says. 'Violence against—'

'I know!'

I spit blood. 'Tigers kill Crabs for sport. Blindfold them and celebrate their deaths.'

The silence that follows my words practically screams: *They don't care. Nobody cares, Dee.*

'If I had my choice, Fish' – Leofric's breath tickles my ear – 'I would throw your whole useless province out to meet the Crabs you love so much.'

I would gladly go. But I can't do that to my province. They deserve better.

'I apologize.' Cordelia raises her hand. 'I understand what you say about Grasshopper. But what is . . . Fish . . . doing here?'

Still doesn't know my name. *Goddessdammit, Cordelia.*

'I believe they've teamed up. Fish isn't brave enough to pull this off alone, though he hates us enough.'

'I don't hate you.'

'You have always pushed us away. Avoided engaging with us. Escaping at every opportunity.'

I can't deny that. But it wasn't for the reasons he believes.

'It would just be like Fish Province to piggyback on someone stronger like Grasshopper Province. After Ravinder realized how pathetic you are, bottom feeder, you needed someone else to leech off.'

I laugh dryly. Bottom feeder is supposed to be an insult, but I do like bottoms and food, so I don't entirely hate it. Plus, hearing Leofric say 'bottom' is worth it.

'He's wanted to cause chaos since he got here.' As he shakes me, my jacket rattles. 'Look at this damn outfit! He's worn it every day! Was it not enough to mock us at the party? Must he do it throughout the entire journey?'

I could tell them it's fake. But they wouldn't believe me. It's because of one of *them* that I'm wearing it. I've asked every morning for Dumpling to fetch my clothes, and every morning he's refused. Whoever sentenced me to this fabulous fate is in this room now, probably lapping it up. Styling it out is the only choice I have.

'He was the last to speak to the imperial heir, and he could have easily summoned his old friend to meet him on the deck. He was likely furious at Ravinder for realizing how useless he is. We saw the state of his corpse – that was an emotional attack.'

'I wouldn't,' I whisper. 'I would never hurt a hair on his head.'

'And Ermine – those two provinces have loathed each other for centuries. If there's any doubt remaining, her body was found inside his wardrobe.'

That draws their attention. Tendai's purple eyes fix on me, searching for something.

'I know that looks bad.' I lick my cracked lips. 'But—'

'He's pretending he was framed,' Leofric growls. 'But we don't all have fish for brains. He chose the targets; *she* did the killing.' He points at Grasshopper.

'I don't kill people!' Grasshopper stamps her feet. 'Only bugs, and frogs, and mangoes and—'

'Just like you lower provinces to believe the only way to deal with your problems is to eliminate them,' Leofric says. 'Even you must see it, Monk. How he is an ill-fitting piece. Since he came among us, he has done nothing but encourage chaos. He pushes back against all our traditions.'

'Because they're stupid and cruel,' I say.

'He weeps for the Crabs, as if they're human.'

'They *are* human.'

He seizes my shackles, dragging me to the centre of the room. 'You see – he *is* chaos.'

'So you set your dog on me?'

'I'm not his dog!' Jasper rages.

'I asked him to capture you.' Leofric's gaze falls on him. 'The burning was not specified.'

'He's a murderer. And a pain in my backside,' Jasper spits. The change in the boy since he witnessed Leofric's

Blessing is alarming. But he comes from the Bandage, where they put a sword in children's hands before they can hold a pen. Where the first words they are taught are 'yes' and 'sir'. Of course Jasper would bend to a display of power.

I'm just not sure I like this new team. Very anti-Dee.

'So, what do you say?' Leofric thrusts me forward.

I stagger, tripping over my own tired legs. When I look up, all eyes are upon me.

And I feel thirteen again. Walking into a room where I do not belong. Terrified that they would realize. That they would look upon me and find me lacking.

I feel the great gaping hole in my core, where a Blessing should be, and pray to the Goddess they do not see it.

'Nergüi?' Leofric says.

Their eyes have not left me since I entered. *They* see the emptiness. 'Fish and Grasshopper Provinces have long been untrustworthy and wild. I agree with the shield.' Usually everything Nergüi says feels deliberate, but there's hesitation in these words. Why would they say that? Don't they want me alone, away from Leofric? Nergüi is one mystery after another.

'Cordelia?'

'I . . . I do not . . .' As she wrings her hands, Leofric's gaze digs into her. 'Th-Though I suppose we must rely on the facts. And the facts point to Fish's guilt.' If she actually paid attention to emotions, she'd remember my reaction to finding Ravi's body – the way it took two of them to drag me off him. Then she would know, in her core, I would never hurt him. 'Perhaps if they're locked away I will be able to sleep. I have been having terrible trouble sleeping.'

Goddessdammit, Cordelia.

'Tendai?' Leofric asks.

Her eyes glaze over. 'They're Fish and Grasshopper Blessed. Why do I care?'

'Taking that as a yes. Shinjiro?'

He sips his tea.

'Shinjiro,' I say, breathing quickly. 'You were with me and Wyatt when we discovered my room had been broken into.'

'I don't know that for a fact,' he says coolly. 'You could have killed her earlier, then asked your dragon to pretend someone had broken in.'

Leofric is already smirking, but then Shinjiro states, 'Abstain.'

'You can't abstain.'

'It is only the Goddess who may judge our souls. It is right I remain impartial.'

'But you're the one who arranged this whole farce!' Leofric rages.

He strokes Bancha's tail. 'Abstain.'

Leofric spins to Jasper. 'Ox?'

'I'll return her to her cell.' Before the sentence is even called, he's dragging Grasshopper away.

She wails, her voice echoing, 'Dee! Help!' as if I'm the only person in the world who can.

'Stop!' As I turn, Leofric seizes my shoulders, holding me back. 'She didn't do anything!'

'Ox,' Leofric says. 'Wait until I command you.'

Jasper freezes.

Grasshopper's siren wail grows. 'I don't want to go back! Dee!'

'Jasper,' I say, my voice like gravel. 'You're the commander. You are *not* his to command.'

Jasper twitches. Muscles pulse in his lithe arms.

'It seems we've come to a consensus. The Fish and the Grasshopper are guilty,' Leofric's voice booms. '*Now* you may take her away.'

Jasper turns.

'Wait!' I yell. 'Let me say goodbye! Let me calm her down. For Goddess's sake, have some mercy.' I strain against Leofric's grip but it's useless. He's stronger than me. Everyone in this room is. Why did I think someone of no value, no Blessing, could ever succeed against the might of power on this ship? How did I ever think *I* could protect her?

She's crying for me, and I can't help her.

I taste salt. I'm crying too. I'm standing here, crying, and doing nothing as a brute drags a terrified child into a dungeon.

Ravi was right the first night – I am of no value. Not to anyone.

'You didn't ask for my vote.'

The room falls silent. Jasper halts.

A lone figure has stepped forward. His body trembles furiously, but he stares straight at Leofric, chin raised, defiant. 'You didn't ask for my vote,' Wyatt repeats.

'You're outvoted, Bear.'

'I can still speak, can't I? Or is that right taken too, along with my vote?'

'Make it quick.'

Wyatt clenches and unclenches his hands. 'Did you ever wonder why Ganymedes, Grasshopper and Ravinder – before you found a use for him – distanced themselves from you?'

'Because they're incompetent?' Tendai says casually.

'Because you're bullies.' Wyatt's voice is iron. He flings the word like a curse. 'All of you upper Blessed are bullies. You judge people before you know them. Their worth is measured by what you can gain from them. Ravinder was nothing to you until blue gold was discovered in those mountains. Then you cooed over him, making him feel valued and important before you bled him dry. From the moment we walked in, you treated us like something you fished out of your scum bucket. No offence,' he adds, with a quick glance to me.

'None taken,' I whisper.

He wrings his hands. 'Grasshopper and Ganymedes and . . . and me. We know what we are to you. Lesser. Nothing. Worthless. You're so awful to anyone who isn't you that you terrified *a six-year-old girl* into not being able to sleep in her own room. You're blaming them for one reason and one reason only – they're not you.' He gasps a wheezed breath. But when he recovers, he jabs a finger at Leofric.

'You have no proof but your own ignorant bias. I discovered Eska's body with Ganymedes; I was with him the whole day. He didn't do it.' His lips curl down. 'The way you act towards us is disgusting. I've met pigs with better manners.' He looks at the ceiling, thin chest rising and falling. 'I spent so long fighting for your acceptance. I thought it would give me worth, pride. So, every summit I nodded and agreed with your stupid ideas because all I wanted was to belong. Because I was lonely. More than anything I wanted to be one of you. I thought it would solve all my problems. You know what I realize now?' He lowers his head, hazel eyes ablaze. 'I will *never* be one of you. And thank fuck for that.'

Silence.

My heart is hammering so hard I can hear it. An escalating *thump thump thump*.

Then Wyatt, that dying boy with barely an ounce of muscle, approaches Leofric and asks: 'Are you going to let them go, or do I have to take matters into my own hands?'

Leofric is dumbstruck. He observes Wyatt the same way he would if a candelabra had suddenly spoken. An item diverging from its purpose.

'Let him go, Leo!' Cordelia dashes forward, awed eyes

upon Wyatt. She clasps something in her hands, twisting her fingers around it – the key to her book.

Lysander's words return to me: 'Be open to all others.'

I could kiss that dead golden heir, because *finally* Cordelia is listening to him. Suddenly the china doll is steel. 'Let them both go.'

'But we already voted.' There's a slight shake in Leofric's voice. 'He was found guilty.'

'Wyatt presented new evidence,' Shinjiro says, smiling at Wyatt. 'It's only correct we consider it. He claims to have been with Ganymedes all day. This gives the accused an alibi, because I certainly do not think it likely dear Wyatt would be lying to defend the All-Mother's murderer. As fond of her as he was.'

'Well, I'm convinced.' Tendai yawns. 'Count me in. I'm switching.'

'You're only doing that to piss me off,' Leofric snaps.

'So what? I'm still doing it.'

'That's three against three,' Wyatt declares.

'And that's enough,' Shinjiro says.

'What?' Leofric snaps.

'A hung jury means the scales of justice are balanced. Balance is something that should be respected. It is the very virtue underpinning our empire.' He sips his tea. 'We do not condemn men unless the scales tip.'

Jasper looks to Leofric. 'Uh . . . should I . . . ?'

The Tiger has gone strangely still. He sizes Wyatt up, tattoo rippling across his bare shoulders. 'Release her.'

While Jasper obeys, Leofric unlocks my shackles. He tugs them off so roughly they bite into my bruised skin.

'Humph!' I say. Then 'Humph!' harder, to really drive the point home.

'Dee!'

I catch Grasshopper in my arms, and though I'm far too weak and she's a bit too big, I lift her up so she can rest her head on my shoulder. I hold her until she stops trembling. 'All better?'

She nods. 'Don't leave again. Promise?'

It wasn't exactly my choice to leave, due to being on fire, but there's no world where I don't make this vow. 'I promise.' I place her down. 'Wyatt?' My voice trembles on his name.

He rushes to my side, offering an arm. I take it.

'Now.' I turn to the room. They're all staring at us. Those glittering, powerful heirs unable to look away from a gremlin, a pissfish, and a dying boy. 'If you don't mind, we are busy people with important places to be. After all, I have several more murders to scheme.' I hit them with a dazzling smile and leave them in my wake.

Chapter Eighteen

Day Six – Feast of the Bunnerfly

Night

I should be returning to the investigation. I should be updating the map. Adding a 'goddessdammit' before Leofric's name and a 'crazy bastard' before Jasper's. But as I navigate to my room, Grasshopper starts sniffling. Wyatt has gone strangely quiet. When I ask if he's OK he stares past me – wide-eyed and pale. Like a man who has undergone a mortal shock to his core.

Fuck this. I almost died today. *Fuck all this.*

That's when I call Dumpling.

'Master Fish?'

'Are there any empty rooms on this ship?'

'Several – the ballroom, the lounge, the—'

'Take us to the one farthest away from those twats.'

We follow Dumpling into the bowels of the ship, me limping on my aching ankle. I examined it earlier. Although there's no blood it still throbs like a bitch.

For a horrified moment, I fear we're returning to the brig,

likely still stained with my bodily fluids. But Dumpling turns in the opposite direction. 'Welcome to the engine room.'

I leave Wyatt outside, mute and unmoving. Grasshopper accompanies me because of course she does.

I wasn't aware a ship powered by the emperor's Blessing would have engines, but apparently even he needs a helping hand. Dumpling leads us through a dark maze of brass and iron. Whirring comes from every direction while dragons dart about, tinkering with dials and pipes.

It's hot, but not uncomfortably so. It's the warmth of a blanket after being outside in the cold. The engines muffle the sound of the ocean, so it's easy to forget we're on a ship. It could be just us three, in another place, in another time.

I follow the tight passages until I reach a room spacious enough for what I've got planned.

'I'm going to need your assistance again, Dumpling.'

He clasps his paws. 'How can I help, Master Fish?'

*

I find Wyatt exactly where I left him. When I help him to his feet, his entire body is trembling.

'You're going to have to speak again eventually, you know that, right?'

He nods mutely.

As Wyatt and I stagger through the engine room, we cling to each other for support.

Dumpling has transformed the space.

The cold grey light has been replaced by thousands of fireflies, hovering like tiny golden stars. The machines are hidden behind folds of midnight-blue fabric and soft music pumps from nowhere and everywhere.

A table strains with delicacies from every province – from

enchiladas oozing with cheese to a sushi boat as long as I'm tall, and of course, booze. Lots of booze.

Grasshopper explodes out of a mountain of candyfloss. 'Party!'

Wyatt looks to me, eyebrows knitted. A silent question.

'Because we deserve it,' I say. 'Because we might die, and I'm not having my final memory be Jasper fucking Bos setting me on fire. We can get murdered tomorrow. Tonight, we party.'

Wyatt's shoulders hitch. I prepare for a scolding for being irresponsible when we should be chasing murderers. Instead, a tiny smile tugs at his lips. It grows gradually – the right side surrenders first, then the left. Finally, it floods his face. Before this moment, I don't think I've truly seen him smile. 'I-I did it! I actually did it!'

'Uh, you're going to have to clue me—'

'I stood up to them,' he says, breathless and giddy. 'I stood up to *all* of them! For years I've done everything to make them like me but then they hurt you and I just got so mad. I didn't care what they thought of me. I just wanted to tell them how I really felt, and it all came out. It came out! I said it!' The golden lights glow in his hazel eyes like flames. 'I did say it, right?'

Goddess. He's cute. 'You said it.'

'I said it!' He seizes my shoulders, smiling brilliantly. 'Fuck them! Fuck them all!'

I chuckle as he spins on the spot, hollering to the ceiling.

'Fuck them!' Grasshopper says.

He winces. 'I'll stop yelling that now.'

'Probably for the best.'

'I haven't been to a party before,' he admits, pulling at his shirt cuffs. 'What do you *do*?'

I wrap my arm around his shoulder. 'Let Dee be teacher.'

We start with the food. Wyatt's a weakling, nursing his stomach after two helpings. But Grasshopper matches me plate for plate. She's the eating buddy I never knew I needed.

'I guess you just eat . . . cow, in Bear Province?'

Wyatt lies on the floor. He's removed his shoes. The sight of his white socks feels scandalous, despite the fact I've seen this man dressed only in a towel. 'Braised cow for breakfast, seared cow for dinner, mashed cow for dessert.'

'Mashed . . . ?'

'A joke.'

Wyatt's making jokes. He must still be delirious on his bout of backbone.

'Dumpling, play faster music!' I command.

'Deedee! Music!' Grasshopper echoes.

Dumpling and Deedee make a damn good double act. A catchy guitar and drum riff plays.

I turn to Wyatt, smirking. 'Now, we dance.'

I might as well have asked him to leap off the ship. 'I don't—'

'I know not everyone can have *my* natural rhythm.'

'Seriously.' He scratches his elbow. 'I don't dance. Ever.'

'Dancing makes your heart happy.' Grasshopper hops from foot to foot.

'I've seen Bears dance.' Granted, when they're drunk.

'I'm not like other Bears,' he mutters.

I can tell I'm dangerously close to hitting something raw, so I back down.

Grasshopper doesn't offer me the same mercy. She drags me – staggering on my throbbing ankle – to the centre of the room, where the fireflies are thickest.

We unleash a manic, rhythmless dance. Grasshopper sings in a language that sounds like drumbeats. Her province is unique that way – they keep their memories and stories safe within music, where empires cannot touch them.

She cackles as I toss her in the air. Ignoring the complaints from my ankle, ribs and pretty much everywhere, I spin her upside down.

'Make me fly!'

I thrust her above my head, running around the room. Then I hurl her to the ground and tickle her until she screams mercy.

It takes thirty more minutes of dancing before she finally tires. She staggers towards candyfloss mountain, and face-plants it, fast asleep.

I turn back to Wyatt, laughing.

He's staring straight at me, hands clasped to his knees. When our eyes meet, he glances away.

My stomach flutters.

How long was he watching me?

I'm soaked with sweat as I approach the drinks table. I grab a bottle of whisky and two shot glasses, then flop down in front of him.

'I'm *not* dancing,' Wyatt says.

'I know.' I lie down, catching my breath. 'I might murder myself if I continue anyway.' I thrust a glass at him. 'Kid's asleep. Let's drink.'

His hair is still untidy from his earlier bout of glee. 'Why?'

Because I don't know if I can face you looking at me like that unless I'm shit-faced. 'Because I say so.'

To give Wyatt credit, he knocks it back, doing his province proud. Maybe Bears nurse their infants on whisky.

Eventually, I'm tipsy enough to face him.

Never before has anyone defended me. Let alone in a room of Blessed. Even Ravi, who fought the ocean to save my life, hid behind me whenever they said cruel things.

249

Where did this boy come from?

He was there all along, of course. But I never so much as glanced at him. Now, I want to know every damn thing about him.

His features are suddenly fascinating. The strip of freckles across his nose. The shape of his collarbones, pressing against too-pale skin.

I need to find out who he is. Who he *really* is. And why I feel this force drawing me to him. Like a fish edging towards bait. This boy from a world so different to mine. Sea and desert.

I sit up. 'Let's play a game.'

'A game?'

I set the two shot glasses before us. 'It's called "Goddess Knows".' I fill both glasses with the amber liquid. 'We make statements in turn; if they are true for us, we drink. By that I mean – the Goddess knows it is true.'

He frowns. 'Why would we do that?'

'Because it's fun.' *And you're a hazel-eyed enigma, and I need to know more.* 'Easy one to start – Goddess knows I'm my province's scion.' I down my drink. He does the same. 'Now you go.' I fill the glasses.

He smiles slyly. 'Goddess knows I'm afraid of water.'

'Low blow.' I pout, but then drain my glass.

He tops it up.

'Goddess knows I hate the summits.' We both drink to that. He was always so eager for the other Blessed to pay him attention, I never considered he was loathing every moment too.

As I fill our glasses, Wyatt's long fingers close around his. 'Goddess knows ... I'm lonely.' He downs it without a second glance.

'Who isn't?' The alcohol hits the back of my throat with a sharp tang.

I already knew he was lonely. Only a lonely person has a

Blessing that allows him to talk to animals. But the sad slope of his shoulders makes my chest hurt, so I hastily top up the drinks. 'Goddess knows I stand up for my friends.'

He smiles. It's incredible, the way a smile softens his features. We drink together.

'Goddess knows Detective Dee's Diagram of Deduction needs a better name.' He pokes me with his toe as he drinks.

'That's not an objective truth.'

He gives me a long look.

'It's a bare-faced lie.'

'Fine. You go.' He shuffles closer, his foot still pressed against my leg. It could be nothing. It's probably nothing.

He's close enough that I can smell him. Just like before, fresh linen and medicine. That cannot be natural.

I fill his glass. 'Goddess knows I wear cologne.'

He sighs, and then swallows his drink.

'Why? To impress Eudora?'

'Maybe, at first.' His fingertip traces the rim of his glass. 'I figured if I at least smell nice then maybe it'll distract people from all . . . the rest of me.'

My heart crumples. Before I can stop myself, I squeeze his foot. 'You don't have to wear it. Not with me.' I let my hand linger. 'Besides! Nobody is going to notice how you smell when you're standing beside me.'

A flicker of a smile. When our eyes meet, I pull away. The whisky is going to my head, and I don't trust my hands anywhere near him.

But his foot is *still touching my leg*. That can't be an accident, can it?

Calm your tits, Dee. It's just a bloody foot.

'Goddess knows . . .' He speaks so softly I have to lean in. '. . . there are worse things in Concordia than what lies beyond the Bandage.' He drinks.

251

He said it in a roundabout way. In a *safe* way. But I understand his meaning.

I raise my whisky, but before I down it, he says, 'Goddess knows I've met a Crab.'

My glass stills, the rim brushing my lips.

His foot moves. A tiny movement. Toes rubbing against my inner leg.

I tip the whisky down my throat.

'Shall I down another?' As I reach for the bottle, he holds it in place.

'When?' he asks.

'Why do you want to know?'

'Because I've never heard anyone talk about Crabs like you did at that trial.' There's a weight in his words. An unspoken thing. He too has sat at night, watching the green-blue glow of that wall and wondering, just *wondering*.

'I was fifteen.' I rub the scar along my hand. 'I found them in a cave. The same cave . . .' I shouldn't be talking about this. If it gets out, I'll be publicly whipped. Worse.

Wyatt edges closer. 'How many?'

'A girl and her little brother. Starvation thin. Hair the colour of flames.' The story tumbles out in fragments, but I feel as though I'm listening to someone else tell it. 'She pressed a knife to my throat, yelling words in a language I'd never heard.'

'What did it sound like?'

I close my eyes and recall the guttural noises – somehow harsh and lyrical at once. 'Like the wild. All the terrible parts – storms and hurricanes. But the good parts too – sunrises across empty plains, trees that grow so high you can't see the top.'

A low breath whistles through Wyatt's teeth.

'I looked into her eyes. But I didn't see aggression. Only

fear. I knew that fear. It was built from experience. Someone had made her fear us. And I realized then all the stories I'd been told since I was a child were wrong. These weren't monsters. They were human.'

Three simple words. They should not cost so much.

'They didn't trust me. But they were ravenous, so when I offered them food it overcame the fear. I went back and forth with packages.'

'How long?'

'Weeks.' I can barely believe the balls on my fifteen-year-old self – climbing that steep incline, packs of bread, fish and water strapped to my back. 'They learned I wasn't a threat, so they started to tell me things.'

'You didn't speak their language?'

Heat rises to my cheeks. 'No. But . . . I'm good at them. I guess. Languages. I picked up enough to understand. They told me about the world outside. About trees that move when you don't watch them, and creatures with wings the size of houses. How the Bandage seems to draw them in. How it seems to draw everything to it.'

A crease appears between his eyebrows. 'What happened next?'

I pour another drink, throw it back. 'One day the cave was empty.'

'They left?'

I cradle my glass to my chest. 'It was snowing. I thought that was why I couldn't find anyone – nobody outside or in their boats. But then I went to the marketplace and everyone had gathered there. And . . .' I press the coldness of the glass against my palm. 'Fisherfolk know how to tie all sorts of knots. Nooses.' My voice breaks on the word.

His hand is upon my knee. A soft touch of warmth. 'You don't have to . . .'

'The snow was red with blood, so they didn't just hang them. And everyone was cheering. *Everyone.* The old women who had taught me to play chess. The little children who cried when their toys broke. They cheered like that moment was the most wonderful thing that had ever happened to them.' My breath catches. 'I'd been holding in a scream for two years and all I wanted to do was release it. But then a hand closed around my mouth, and strong arms dragged me away.'

His thumb traces little circles atop my knee.

'"I had you followed, Ganymedes," my father said. "Your soft heart will be the death of us."' I hear his words clearly even now, as if I'm still standing in the entrance of our home, the cold chill nothing compared to the ice of his voice.

'The only reason you do not hang beside them is because you are my sole heir.'

I turn my palm, showing Wyatt the ugly, raised scar. 'He had never beaten me in all my life. Not once. I was too important to beat. Too vital to be scarred. But that day he made me hold out my hands, and he hit me with a cane, over and over again. He did it without a hint of rage, as if it was a simple thing. A task that needed completing.' As I run my finger along the scar, an echo of pain shudders along it. 'Fifty lashes. I counted every one.' I stop the story there. I pretend that's the ending. I do not tell Wyatt that fifty wasn't enough. That I wished my father had continued until every last drop of blood was drained from me.

He squeezes my knee. 'It wasn't your fault.'

I should've told them to run. Should've scared them away, instead of giving them a reason to stay. But I had underestimated my sweet, good neighbours. I hadn't realized that loyalty did not just mean sending fish and saying prayers. Loyalty also meant hate. Indiscriminate, unquestioning hate.

I force a smile. 'What makes you so interested in Crabs?'

'I have a lot of time to think.' His hand slips from my knee. 'When you're trapped in a place, all you can do is dream about being somewhere else. I would like to see it someday – the world beyond the Bandage.' He draws his knees to his chest, as if afraid he'll shatter.

I want to say, *I'll take you. I'll show you.* My hand reaches out, but stops short of him. Instead, I refill our glasses. 'Goddess knows I've had a crush.'

'What are we, twelve?' He raises his glass.

'On a man.'

His glass stills. Then he downs it.

Interesting. Maybe I was wrong about that foot.

He snickers at my expression. 'What?'

'It's just . . . you're full of surprises.'

'They encourage us to have same-sex relationships. To stop those pesky bastards.'

Sure. But I didn't know he had ANY relationships.

'A human man, right?'

He hits me. 'Drink.'

I swallow, then fill the glass again.

'What are you then?' His words are slurring. 'Gay?'

'Play the game.'

'Goddess knows I'm gay.'

I raise my glass. Then place it down.

'Goddess knows I'm . . . straight?'

I snort. Don't even raise the glass.

'Goddess knows I'm . . . bi?' He stares at me, then sighs and throws back his drink.

I raise mine. 'Goddess knows I'm iconic.' I swallow as he kicks me in the shin.

'That's not fair.'

'Goddess knows,' I say solemnly. To be fair, most Blessed

are usually a *little* gay – apart from the shields, who don't get to fuck anyone. Opposite-sex couplings are forbidden until after the pilgrimage, but once we become dux, we must produce at least one heir. No objections. 'Have your parents got a bride picked out for you? Insurance in case you couldn't convince Eudora to marry you?'

His body goes still. 'Unfortunately.'

My heart sinks, which I choose to ignore. My father has done nothing of the sort. I suspect he will abscond the second I return and leave me in the shit he has shat.

'Gotta pass on that magical seed.' Wyatt fills our glasses. 'Goddess knows I have magical seed.' He swallows, wincing.

Dragon's dick. My seed isn't magical. But if he finds out, he'll know it all. How useless I—

Shit. He's staring.

I throw back my whisky. It burns my throat. Or maybe that's the deceit. I hastily refill the glasses. 'Goddess knows I've lied to you.'

That makes it better, right?

Wyatt drinks too. He sets his glass down with a dull clunk.

'Seems like we both have secrets,' I say.

'I'll drink to that.' He giggles and throws back his glass, but it's empty.

'We already did.' I poke my foot into his stomach.

He seizes my leg, tugging it playfully. 'Goddess knooooows . . .' His words are slurring even more than mine. 'Someone I loved died on this ship.'

The world rocks. I pour another glass, but it topples, the amber liquid flooding the floor. I swig from the bottle instead.

'You need to drink too.' I swing the bottle towards him.

He doesn't take it. His smile has vanished. 'No, I don't.'

'Eudora died.'

256

'I didn't love her,' he says, as easily as declining Shinjiro's biscuits.

'Yes, you did,' I slur, crawling closer. 'You went on about marrying her all the time. To secure your legacy. So when you die your brothers can throw your corpse a party.'

'I wanted to marry her,' he says. 'But I didn't know her. She didn't know me. I wasn't in love. I understand that now.'

I lower the bottle.

He runs his hands over his knees. 'I don't love her. I never did. I was a fool. Clinging to someone I thought would fix everything. Thinking that by marrying an upper I would advance and prove myself worthy. It was all I cared about.' His gaze meets mine, amber flames trembling in the darkness of the room. 'I'm sorry. I'm really *fucking sorry*, Dee.'

My heart thumps in my throat. Something about that look is familiar. It makes me feel tingly all over. As though I would do something reckless to see it again.

As though maybe, someday, I might tell him my entire truth in a cave on a cliff in a storm.

I stand, swaying in place, then hold out my hand. 'Let's dance. You're too tipsy to protest.'

I pull him to unsteady feet. His hand is clammy in mine.

We're both so drunk we can barely remain upright. He's falling into me and me into him, smelling of booze and freshly laundered sheets. I probably smell like melted flesh. Sexy.

I clasp his hands, those pale slender fingers. And all I want to do is close the distance between us. The space between our bodies. That final wall.

I swing him a little too vigorously. He falls into me, long legs tangled in mine. His chin knocks against my cheek.

'Thank you.' His words tickle my ear.

'For getting set on fire? For a fish, I'm pretty good at it.'

257

His hands sweep up the back of my neck, his thumbs pressing into my jawbone, angling my chin up to face him. 'I wouldn't have spoken up without you. I'd still be that weak man, nodding at everything they say. Thank you, Dee.'

My stomach twists. A pang of something, too quick to place.

Concern floods his face. 'Sorry. Can . . . can I call you . . . ?' His hands are cupping my cheeks. Where are mine? Clasped around his back, clinging to his skinny shoulders, terrified he'll flee.

He called me Dee.

Then I realize what that pang was. I've felt it before. Once. Only once.

Oh, shitting fishcakes.

I'm in love with him.

I love Wyatt.

He hasn't moved. I could count his freckles from here. I *want* to count his freckles.

'Ganymedes?'

I chance a glance into his eyes. Yup. There's that pang again. Inevitable, terrible – and wonderful.

Love.

'You can call me Dee.'

His face beams with a smile and, predictably, I love that too.

Chapter Nineteen

Day Seven – Feast of the Ox

Morning

The whole being in love with Wyatt thing was a product of way too much whisky. An intoxicated flurry. I'm not in *love* with him.

As Grasshopper and I enter the lounge for breakfast, he glances over, hair sticking up at odd angles. 'Mornin'.'

He looks like absolute shit.

My stomach cartwheels anyway.

'What's wrong?'

Oh, nothing. Except I'd literally chew off my arm to look at your face. 'Hung-over.'

'Ah. That's what this is.' He sips orange juice. 'I thought my tastebuds had exploded.'

The dining room is off limits since the *fiery* dinner, so now the lounge is being used for meals. It's far better – no long table with assigned seating. Instead, there are smaller tables dotted about with plush leather seats. A fire crackles in a gilded fireplace, casting flickering shadows across the walls. For some reason, everything smells like cinnamon.

Grasshopper launches into a chair and orders a plate of syrup-drenched pancakes.

I sit gingerly next to Wyatt. My ribs are covered in ugly purplish bruises, but at least my ankle hurts a little less. 'Dumpling, something hot and greasy.'

Wyatt leans towards me. 'I'm surprised you're up this early.'

'Lest you forget, there're murders to solve. I've been studying Detective Dee's Diagram of Deduction.' Partly because I couldn't sleep and partly because I now not only have to solve it for Ravi, but also to ensure Wyatt doesn't become the next victim. Love is so inconvenient.

'Any deductions, Detective Dee?'

My chest tightens. My name sounds *amazing* in his Bear Province drawl. The poetic way he twists a single syllable.

'Dee?'

Dumpling reappears with a plate of eggs and bacon. 'Yeah.' I glance around the empty lounge. I didn't pass anyone on my way here either. The corridors were eerily quiet. I guess now they don't have Eska to blame, nobody wants to wander the ship alone. 'Just a small thing – I assumed Cordelia inherited Lysander's Blessing. But Shinjiro said Blessings are unique to the person. So, I changed her Blessing to "Unknown".'

Wyatt groans. 'That sounds like a step back.'

'We need to determine what Cordelia, Tendai and Nergüi can do.' If the Blessings are based on the person, then that means getting to know them better. 'That should help the investigation, especially if they're using them in the murders. Only three Blessings left!'

'And yours.'

I choke on my bacon. I *will* tell him. I'm going to tell him. Eventually. Maybe. Probably.

But I told Ravi, didn't I? I told him; then he left me. Wyatt will do the same. Anyone would. And I wouldn't blame them.

He touches my arm. Those damn eyes are upon me. Who knew devastation came in hazel?

I shift. 'Well, you haven't seen my cock yet, and my Blessing is entirely contained to that area.'

He laughs.

That's right, funny boy. Keep telling your jokes.

'I did catch a glimpse when you got attacked in the bathhouse.'

Act casual. 'And . . . ?'

'Your personality is large enough. I think a big cock would be overkill.'

Take. Me. Now. He's perfect.

His hand casually rests on my arm. But I know what it's saying – *You tell me when you're ready.*

I have to save him. I have to crack this damn thing. Today.

I fling up from my seat. 'Come on! We have murders to solve!'

Wyatt looks up blearily. 'Can we solve them after my coffee?'

'Grasshopper!'

She leaps to attention, knocking Wyatt's coffee from his hand.

'Onwards! Dee's Diamonds!'

'Dee's Diamonds!' Grasshopper cheers.

Wyatt sighs. 'You are *not* calling us that.'

*

Alongside trying to crack these last three Blessings, I resume our original plan – before I was rudely set on fire – of finding somewhere Eska could have been tamed into submission.

I start with the cabins, but they all appear normal. The only one with a crater through the doorway is Eska's. I knock on all of them but only Tendai answers.

'Fish.' The door opens a sliver. 'You made me come to my door.'

I put on my most charming grin and prepare to *woo*. 'Tendai, you're—'

'I only sided with you in the trial to annoy the Tiger and Spider. Rest assured, you're still very irrelevant to me.'

'Noted.' I swing on my heels. 'Why are you locked inside your room?'

'Because people are being *murdered*.' She stares at me long and hard. 'You're a real-life moron, aren't you?'

I'm not sure how to answer.

'Never mind.' The door closes in my face.

Grasshopper blows a raspberry at it.

Wyatt squeezes my shoulder. 'Don't take it personally – she's always ignored me as well. She's only interested in herself.'

I assumed she hated me. It's kind of nice to know she ignores Wyatt too. Bonding.

I doubt I'll be having a heart to heart with Tendai anytime soon, so we continue our search.

We've already cleared the brig, dining room, lounge, art gallery and bathhouse, so I head to the library. It looks the same as the last time I was here. If anything, it's a little neater. Has Cordelia been tidying?

Almost on cue, her mournful song drifts through the bookcases. As I approach her, Wyatt grasps my wrist and shakes his head.

'Why not?' I whisper.

'Because she's . . . Tortoise Province.'

'*She* didn't kill your damn horses.'

'Fish! Bear!'

We yelp as Cordelia appears before us.

'Apologies!' Her hand flies to her mouth. 'Are you quite all right?'

'Fine. Fine.' I adjust my hair.

Grasshopper clutches my waist, hiding her face in my belly.

'Thanks for vouching for us yesterday at the trial.'

'It was nothing.' Cordelia's so naive she has no idea she's speared her province in the throat by doing that.

'Your speech was rather impassioned, Bear. In Tortoise Province you'd be arrested for such a logicless argument.'

Wyatt grunts in response.

'Do you mind if I ask you some questions?' I say.

She claps her hands. 'Like a quiz? I love quizzes!'

Really? HER, Ravi?

'Did you hear anything the night Eska was killed? After the feast?'

She taps her chin. 'I must admit, the events at the feast rattled me. I'm not used to such flights of emotion.' I visualize her family dinners, the muted silence and grey gruel. 'At least, not in the upper classes.'

'Upper classes?'

She blinks. 'But of course, you lower provinces wouldn't understand. Tortoise Province rewards those who achieve great feats but does not do the same to those who do not contribute to society. *Those* people are more likely to engage in the fighting I witnessed last night.'

She's talking about the poor. I know Tortoise Province has castes within castes, but I never imagined the attitude to be so prevalent that even this china doll can express it as if complaining about a spell of rain.

'Don't worry!' she says upon seeing my horrified expression. 'The lower classes are comprised only of those with *deep moral failings.*'

Well, that's a relief.

Wyatt clenches his fists, clearly trying very hard not to punch her, so I twist the conversation back. 'And what happened after the feast?'

'Oh yes! Leo escorted me to my room. He's sweet like that. Probably because of my brother. They were very close.'

I wonder if she knows whether they ever banged.

'Leo made sure I was OK, then left.' She pushes her glasses up. 'Then I went to sleep. Or tried to, at least. I've been sleeping terribly.' She doesn't need to tell me that – her wandering and wailing wakes me up every night. 'I didn't hear anything though.'

Well, that probably means the fight didn't happen in my room. Though Cordelia sleeps so far away in her hallowed upper heights maybe the noise wouldn't travel.

'Where did Leofric say he was going?'

'He didn't say.' She bites her lip. 'But he's so loyal. I wouldn't worry about Leo.'

She clearly has no clue he beat the shit out of me yesterday. My ribs ache at the memory. I wonder if Tortoise Province would regard *that* as a *'moral failing'*, or only those who fuck for fun.

'If you didn't put the Ermine there, I wonder how she got in your room.' She clutches her satchel, whispering like a naughty child. 'I read a fiction book once where there was a hatch in a room. It was concealed in the floorboards. Have you checked for secret doors? They can be quite well hidden.'

Hm. Maybe I chose the wrong sleuthing partner.

Wyatt's glaring at her openly. I step between them. No need really – Cordelia's totally clueless. Imagine being so content in your own world you have no idea when people hate you. I know every single person who hates me.

Grasshopper looks up with orb-like eyes. 'Time to go.'

'Just a moment.' I ruffle her hair. 'Cordelia, when you got your Blessing, was it the same as Lysander's?' I know the answer of course.

His name is a total mood kill. Her eager face crumples. 'No. It seems I am not worthy to bear a Blessing like his.'

Not worthy. Maybe *that* was Ravi's type. The unworthy.

'Does that come into it? Worthiness?' I'm not sure I want to know.

'The monks certainly believe so. But . . . I do not know.'

'Really?' *That's a first.*

'After Lysander . . .' Her breath catches at his name. 'After he got his Blessing I barely saw him. I wrongly blamed the Blessing for that. I was so grumpy about the whole thing I refused to learn about them.' She fiddles with her hair. 'Ironically, now I'm surrounded by Blessed. Perhaps there's a book in here about them?'

If I could, I would get to know this girl – the intimate parts of her soul, how her curious mind works. As it is, I don't have time, so instead I ask: 'What Blessing did you get?'

Wyatt's head falls into his hands.

Cordelia smirks. 'When I ask people that, they tend to walk away from me. Quickly.'

'I don't see you walking.'

'I'll tell you . . . if we can trade?'

My skin prickles. That's a Tortoise for you. Always gathering knowledge.

I could lie. But then I'd have to keep it up for the rest of my life outside this ship and—

'My Blessing.' She steps forward. 'For yours – Bear.'

Wyatt gags. 'M-Mine?'

'You are *such* a mystery.' Her blue eyes study him in a way that makes me want to, ever so slightly, tattoo my name on his forehead. 'Bear Province is *so* terrible at chronicling anything – no offence.'

The pulse in Wyatt's cheek indicates he very much does take offence.

'But I would be delighted to know more! And a Blessing relates to someone's core being, correct? Why don't we skip all the steps?'

I look at Wyatt, summoning my finest puppy-dog eyes.

'I . . .' He tugs his shirtsleeves.

I shake him playfully. 'There's nothing to be embarrassed about.'

'You know it?' Cordelia spins to me.

'Kinda.'

She does a little jig. 'Oh, goodie! We shall swap! Shall I go first?'

I wish I could, but Wyatt is boring holes into my skull. 'Sorry. It's not mine to tell.'

Her body sags. 'I understand. It's a very private thing. Perhaps we can talk another time, Bear? My brother was trying to overcome the differences between our provinces. It would be an awful shame for his efforts to die with him.'

'We should go.' Wyatt grasps my arm a little too hard.

Before Wyatt drags me away, I say, 'You should go to your room. Nobody should be wandering around this ship alone.'

Her hands drop. 'But this is the *library*.' As if a library is a portal to another realm where serial killers don't exist.

'Still. Let's not lose two Tortoise scions in one year, hm?'

Wyatt doesn't release his grip until we are clear of the library.

'You complain about them ignoring you, but when she asks questions, you blank her!' I sigh. *Inter-province politics are so dumb.*

His fists clench. 'Her province almost destroyed mine. You can't just forgive things like that.'

266

I clasp his arms. 'She isn't her province. We're all people. Individuals. Everyone deserves a chance. If we keep blaming each other for stupid shit that happened years ago, not only will *nothing* ever change, but we'll also tear this empire apart.'

Something lingers behind his gaze. His hand raises to my face, fingertips brushing my cheek. 'It's like none of this has touched you.'

I open my mouth, but the sound of raised voices interrupts us.

We tear apart, following them to the doorway of an unfamiliar room – considering the chess tables and stacks of cards, probably the games room.

Nergüi and Leofric are in the far corner. He looms over them in what looks like an attempt to intimidate. Nergüi, however, doesn't appear to be someone who *can* be intimidated.

'Listen,' he hisses. 'You must—'

'You can't order me around. Last I checked I wasn't a member of your military police.' Nergüi flicks their ashen hair. 'You will simply have to trust me.'

'I *don't* trust you,' he bites back. 'I know what you're planning. What you are. Snake.'

Nergüi fixes him with a gaze that manages to be both casual and cutting. 'You call me a snake, but I know what you shields do. I'm not the only one who works in the shadows.'

Leofric steps back, breathing heavily. 'I'm watching you.' As he turns, I duck behind the door. He's in such a rage he doesn't even notice us as he storms away.

'That was . . . strange,' Wyatt says.

'It sounded like he was accusing Nergüi.' Is Leofric just going through us all in turn?

'We should ask Nergüi where they were the night of Eska's death too.' Wyatt moves towards the door. 'Plus, we have to work out their Blessing.'

Fuck no. Nergüi already tried threats and bribery; I don't want to discover what comes next.

I grab his sleeve. 'Not them.'

'If we speak to them together—'

'Nergüi's just . . . I feel like they can see into my soul.'

A whisper of a smile. 'Why are you hiding your soul?'

I try to answer, but every response lodges in my throat.

'It's OK.' He squeezes my hand. 'You don't have to show your soul to anyone you don't want to.'

Marry me.

We track Leofric to a room on the same level as the baths.

I think it's a gym. Training room? I don't know. It has mats, swords and bows, and rows of stuffed dummies. Apart from the brig, it's the most functional room on this ship. Clearly the emperor expected the shield to want somewhere normal to train.

Leofric is unleashing hell upon some unsuspecting dummy. He carves great slashes across it with a sword almost as long as I'm tall.

My entire body throbs at the sight of him. And not the way it does around Wyatt.

Grasshopper shakes her head furiously as I try to approach.

'It'll be OK,' I whisper. 'I got you as my back-up, right?'

She considers this, and then promptly disappears. I'm not sure if that's comforting.

'Leofric,' I say.

He yells out, sticking the dummy over and over. His body is like a raw nerve, all tensed, bulging muscles.

I don't discriminate based on appearance, but there's something about skinny men that makes my heart flip. Muscles mean they can throw me across the room if I say something stupid. Which is often.

'Leofric.' I raise my voice.

'Do not presume to use my name, Fish.' He doesn't look up.

'Fine . . . *Tiger.*' I roll the word on my tongue.

He wipes his brow. 'Where's the gremlin? You should put her on a leash.'

I resist the urge to knock his teeth out. Mainly because I suspect that would break my fist before his teeth. 'I'm not here to discuss her ladyship. I was hoping to ask you some questions.'

He swirls the sword, cutting the air. 'Is this an act to try and clear your name?'

'If you'd just trust me, you'd realize I'm trying to find the culprit. And save your neck with it.'

'You think I need *your* help? I am the shield of—'

'We know exactly who you are. You showed that yesterday.' Wyatt leaps to my defence, staring down Leofric – a man who could snap him in two – as if facing a kitten.

'I thought you were different from the rest of your kind.' Leofric's grip around his sword tightens. 'But I see all Bears are the same – they have an inflated sense of their own importance.'

Pot. Kettle. Black.

'Answer Dee's questions.'

Leofric glares. My man – I mean, *Wyatt* doesn't budge.

I usually prefer soft men but there's something about Wyatt becoming protective that makes me want to tear off his clothes and ravish him right here.

'*Dee?*' Leofric repeats. Some of that daydream must be lingering in my gaze as he grimaces. 'Goddess, Bear. I thought you had better taste than that, what with your previous obsession. *That* would be like fucking a baby seal.'

The silence is razor sharp.

Wyatt raises that defiant chin. Leofric is taller, but Wyatt is like a coiled spring. 'You *will* answer Dee's questions.'

Leofric looks down at him, that tightly wound ball of newfound confidence. He clears his throat, and unless my eyes trick me, takes a step back. 'One question.'

I could ask him if he killed Eska. Too obvious. Could ask him why he thinks Nergüi did.

'Hurry up.' He returns to the training dummy, jabbing his sword into its unfortunate heart.

There's something out of place in this room: an elaborately framed portrait. I edge closer. It's Eudora. She looks perfect, of course. All poised, posed perfection. But it doesn't capture what I saw the first night – that sunrise in the bathroom mirror.

'Did you put up this portrait of Eudora?'

Wyatt turns to me with a look of *I knew you were stupid, but that was pretty fucking stupid.*

But I'm watching Leofric. The way his body swings to face the portrait, the casual lowering of the sword. I watch the way his eyes study her likeness. 'Yes. In Tiger Province it's mandated that every household has a portrait of the emperor. Eudora never became empress, but it felt appropriate.'

'Eudora would like it,' I lie. 'When are you going to take the imperial collar off?'

He raises his sword. 'I said *one* question, Fish.'

I sigh. 'Maybe you shouldn't be alone? There's a murderer—'

'I'm aware.' The tiger ripples across his shoulders. My ankle throbs in response. 'Get out.'

'Right-o.'

I leave him to his hacking and exit the gym.

Grasshopper reappears with a *pop.* 'I untied his laces.'

'That's my girl.' I poke her nose.

'We're lucky we saw his Blessing at the meal.' Wyatt leans against a wall. 'Because there's no chance he's gonna open up to us.'

'I'm OK with that.' I put my hands in my pockets 'Guy's a nutter. Set his tiger on me.'

'He did *what*?' The steel edge to Wyatt's voice is thrilling.

'Just a little ankle nibbling. But I'm fine.' I tug up my trouser leg to show my disappointing lack of awesome scar.

He pouts. Maybe he'll go back and yell at Leofric some more. As sexy as that prospect is, I'd rather not have two of us nursing injuries.

'Besides, I have padding.' I grab my stomach.

He pokes it. But instead of drawing back, his hand lingers there. 'I happen to think baby seals are cute.'

'Only cute?' I whisper, leaning into him.

His eyes track down my body. 'I don't know how to respond to that in a way that doesn't sound very wrong.'

I feel something *stirring*, then remember Grasshopper is here, and hastily back away.

'Pity you wasted your question,' Wyatt says.

'Mhm.' I continue through the ship.

It *was* a foolish idea. But as soon as I saw that unfeeling hunk of muscle, I remembered what I'd witnessed the day before in the brig – that uncontrollable grief. The way he was bent double with the pain of it. I hoped by asking about Eudora, I'd see it again, even an echo of it. I wanted to see *him* again.

But there was nothing. When I mention Lysander's name, Cordelia practically wilts. I still can't voice Ravi's murderer into existence. How can Leofric so closely guard his face? How does he put his grief in a box? I don't know if that's suspicious, or just Leofric being emotionally stunted. Maybe I'll never understand someone like him.

After giving the kitchens the once-over, we emerge on to the deck where an ox stampedes across the sails. We go up to the stern deck to check the ballroom (untouched since Eudora's murder), and then up again to the shrine.

271

The space is a mirror of Shinjiro's room. Piscero swim in crystalline ponds overlooked by white cherry blossom trees. There's even a little bridge leading to the main shrine – a great golden scale with twelve balances. Each holds a collection of coloured pebbles, corresponding to the different provinces. Everything is symmetrical, perfectly balanced down to the number of fish in each pond. No fighting happened here.

Shinjiro kneels before the shrine, dinging bells and praying to the Goddess while Bancha flies in circles above him. 'Please provide your obedient servant with guidance in these darkest days.' *Ding.* 'Discord walks amongst us, though I do not know their name.' *Ding.*

I'd hoped to obtain more healing juice, but Wyatt tugs my arm, anxious to leave, and I'm too soft on him to say no.

'Why are you so afraid of him?' I ask.

'I'm not "afraid" of Shinjiro. He just always wants to talk about my duty and illness and . . .' Wyatt glances aside, words trailing. He doesn't need to finish them.

Eventually the only place we haven't searched is a place on the upper stern deck I didn't know existed.

'A greenhouse.' I blink. 'On a ship?'

We have plenty of waterfalls and rockfaces back home, but we lack the lush flora of Crow and Grasshopper Provinces. This space has plucked the most astonishing plants from those provinces and encased them in glass. Spiralling trees grow high into the domed ceiling, and luminous flowers snake across the path. As we walk, more blooms emerge, bursting into colour at our feet like fireworks.

It's beautiful in a cultivated way. The same way a watercolour is beautiful. The beauty of considered brushstrokes.

Grasshopper spins in place. 'It's like home! All hot and green!' Before I can catch her, she dives into the foliage, plucking dubious berries.

'Don't go far!' I yell.

'It tastes like home!' her little voice calls back.

Wyatt sniffs a pink lily. 'This is *incredible*.'

I inhale a heady mix of honey and rose. 'I guess you don't get many flowers in Bear Province.' I follow him to a weeping willow, pushing aside its drooping branches.

'Nope. Just lots of sand. Some lakes. And the grazing grounds, of course.' His fingertips linger atop the petals of a blue rose. 'Do you think flowers grow . . . beyond the Bandage?'

His words bridge that unspoken divide. Bringing a thing we discussed when drunk into the light of day. And with it, everything else that happened last night.

Just like that, I'm completely exposed. And I don't *entirely* hate it.

I pluck the rose and tuck the stem behind his ear. My hand hovers over his cheek. A featherlight touch upon his skin.

As Wyatt gazes down at me, the sun moves behind him, filtering through the willow's leaves and accenting him in gold. Then my world is him. The awkward smile softening his sharp features. The blue bloom against the mahogany shine of his hair.

You are beautiful, I want to say. *And I don't think anyone has ever told you that you're so much more than just a Blessing to pass on.*

His gaze locks with mine. Flecks of gold gleam in his eyes.

Kiss him, a dangerous little voice says. *Kiss. Him. Now.*

But it's not me who moves.

In a moment, his body is against mine, chest to chest. He cups my chin, drinking me in, as if I'm something to be marvelled at. Me. In a greenhouse bursting with the natural wonders of Concordia, he's looking at *me*.

'Dee . . .' His thumb brushes my lips, teases them apart.

273

I'm stirring again. So is he. I can feel him hardening against my thigh.

We can't fuck in a greenhouse. *We can't.*

I can't hear Grasshopper; she must be all the way over on the other side.

Good.

I close the distance. I surrender my mouth to him. Dry chapped lips against mine. My body curls into his, knowing what it wants before I do. *Him. All of him.* I moan the tiniest, weakest moan.

His smirking lips tug my mouth. I know what he's thinking – *that noise means he's mine.*

As he tugs at my jacket, eager and ravenous, I grasp his hair, tipping his head back. I run my tongue along the silk-soft skin of his neck.

My hand brushes the flower. A chill shoots down my body.

Someone else wore a flower, once. White against the black of his hair. Smoke and lavender. Night lights in dark eyes.

I wrench his hands away, flinging myself back.

Wyatt freezes, reaching for me.

What the hell am I doing? Putting flowers in his hair? Who do you think this is, Dee?

I can't do this. I can't let him get close. The moment he tears away that final piece he will realize the truth, just like Ravi.

Of no value.

He lowers his hands, hurt in his eyes.

I bite back on the guilt, trying to ignore the ruin I've made of his lips, the taste of him on my tongue.

I shouldn't feel guilty. I'm saving him from wasting time on someone like me. Some legacy that would be.

A tear rolls down his cheek, but he's not crying. It's blood.

'You're bleeding.'

He touches his temple. 'I didn't notice.'

'The thorns.' Blessed hells. How much pain is this boy in to not realize when he's being speared?

Because he's dying, Dee. You moron. And you have to push him away before the last thing he does is fall in love with a lie.

'Here.' I take the rose and throw it to the ground. 'Better finish the search.' I turn from him.

His hand closes around my wrist. 'Wait.'

Pain spikes in my chest. Maybe *he's* the murderer and that's his modus operandi – make my heart as broken as his.

'*Please*—'

He tries to make me face him, but I look down, away, anywhere that isn't those eyes.

'What are you afraid of?'

Everything. I'm afraid of everything. But right now, I'm terrified of the way you crash through my walls, as if they're not there at all.

'I . . . I just—'

A scream rips through the greenhouse. *Grasshopper.*

I tear away from Wyatt, dashing into the foliage.

I don't need to run for long. She's standing alone in the centre of the greenhouse before an enormous tree, thicker than the three of us standing side by side.

But we're not alone.

Vines entwine skinny wrists, pinning him to the trunk like a grisly ornament. Red hair falls over boyish features. He looks so young.

He *is* young.

'Jasper.' I fall to my knees beside him, tilting his chin up.

I know he is dead then. Not because of the blank red eyes. Nor the heaviness of his head. But because, for the first time since I have known him, Jasper is cold.

Chapter Twenty

Day Seven – Feast of the Ox

Afternoon

I draw a red cross over Jasper's ox. We didn't exactly get on. And he did try to kill me the once. But he also sat towards the bottom of the table. And as much as he sucked up to the others, I know why – he wanted to prove himself. Because he was not only a lower province, but also a bastard. And deep down, he made me think of my own bastard sibling, wherever they are, set to inherit a Blessing they didn't ask for.

'You OK, Dee?' Wyatt asks me from the bed, looking peaky.

Grasshopper has recovered worryingly well from seeing her fourth body in seven days and is gorging on her berry hoard.

'I'm fine.' I run my fingers through my curls.

I knew me discovering yet another corpse didn't look great, so I ran to Shinjiro. Let him deal with Leoprick. But that meant I left Wyatt alone with a body *again*. I returned to a mirror of Eska's scene. Wyatt clutching the fourteen-year-old, his shoulders shaking with sobs. All I wanted was to hold him. But I couldn't. I can't. I can't hold him.

But I *can* protect him. In more ways than one. First, I need to solve this damn thing.

I study the slice of pie which is Concordia. 'I don't think Shinjiro was right about the killer wanting chaos. This doesn't look chaotic at all.' I gesture to the red crosses. 'It looks like they know *exactly* who they're targeting.'

'How so?'

I turn to Wyatt. 'Don't you think the south looks a little crowded with X's? Three out of four deaths have been from lower provinces – Eska, Jasper and Ravi.' I check that Grasshopper is still busying herself with her hoard. 'Also, they targeted Grasshopper, not once, but twice. That means five out of six attempts were on Blessed from the south.'

Wyatt rubs his chin. 'Roughly eighty per cent.'

'If they really wanted utter chaos they'd kill off the big players – the upper provinces who hold the most power. Or kill randomly, indiscriminately. I think someone's deliberately targeting the lower provinces.' If true, all the more reason to solve it now. Because that means only Wyatt, Grasshopper and I are left. I study the names of those remaining. 'It must be someone from the upper provinces.'

'What's an upper?' Grasshopper asks, teeth stained berry red.

I smile. 'It's not important.' Because, despite everything, this girl is still innocent about some things, and I want to keep her that way.

'They've always ignored us, discounted us,' I say. 'But I never thought they felt strongly enough to *kill us*.'

'Why would they murder people who are providing them with food?'

Good point. We're not a threat to them. We *barely* bother them. It would be like targeting your own butler.

I scan the portraits, trying to recall what I know about these people.

Tendai – refuses to engage with anyone, calling me *'irrelevant'* at the party. The uppers hold disdain for her for reasons I still don't know. Then there's that midnight visit from Eska on the second night, which makes me wonder if maybe she *does* have connections she's hiding.

Nergüi – the opposite of Tendai, all too eager to engage with me. Appearing in Ravi's room with that red-lipped smile the day of his death; visiting Eudora's body to check that Dragons *are* mortal. The heated discussion with Leofric. For some reason they want me alone, and they're willing to threaten me with my darkest secret to ensure that happens.

Cordelia – Ravi's bride who appears out of nowhere, wearing her grief like a badge of honour, walking the ship at midnight hours screaming for a dead man. Her eagerness to know *everything* about *everything*, but especially Wyatt and me. As if we are curiosities. Puzzles to be solved.

Shinjiro – a mystery wrapped in a pleasant smile. His keenness to gather people together and watch as chaos tears through them, despite professing to be an enemy of that same chaos. The lie about his absence the second night, and then the second explanation – that he saw *Eudora*. I have no idea if he's telling the truth about anything.

Then there's Leofric. He who has the most to lose from Eudora's death. He who tried to maintain order, but – when he thought nobody was watching – attacked me, an injured man. *'You pitiful low-bred scum!'* The outrage when I dared sit in the wrong seat. A chair I had not earned.

'Leofric hates us the most,' I say. 'He lost it in the brig.'

Wyatt wrings his hands. 'I'm sorry, Dee. I won't let him hurt you again.'

My chest clenches around his words. I hastily continue: 'But that's all Tigers really. I've not met one that *doesn't* treat me like shit.' My eyes flicker up the map. 'Then there's Eudora. He doesn't have anything to gain from her dying. His legacy will be destroyed, even if he manages to cling to his life. He still wears her damn collar everywhere, as if she's not lying dead in her cabin.' I slump down to my knees. 'My head hurts.'

Ravi was right to reject me. I really am too dumb to team up with. Poor Wyatt – he had no idea.

Wyatt kneels before me. 'Let's think about Jasper. What clues can we glean from what happened to him?'

I massage my forehead. 'Judging from the coldness of his body we can assume it happened last night when we were . . .'

I risk a glance. His awkward grin spears straight to my heart.

'. . . we were busy. So we can't account for anyone's movements. Like Eudora and Eska, there were no marks on his body. But the strangest thing about his death is where it happened. The greenhouse is such a random place for him to be, especially at night.'

'You think he was moved?' Wyatt asks. 'Like Eska?'

I swallow hard. 'I don't think so. Those vines were holding him against the tree. Why do that other than to stop him struggling? Because if I know anything about Jasper, he would have fought like hell. He was killed in that greenhouse, Wyatt.'

'But that doesn't—'

'I know.' It doesn't make sense. We've seen his Blessing all too close for comfort. The smouldering remains of the dining room can attest to that. He would have burned straight through those vines. 'The greenhouse was perfect. Not a petal out of place. Just like my room. We searched the entire ship today: did you see anywhere that looked like Eska had unleashed hell in it?'

'No.'

I press a knuckle to my temple. 'I think we've been looking at this all wrong. We assumed Eska must have been killed somewhere else and moved. But what if she *was* killed in my room? And what if Jasper *was* killed in the greenhouse?'

Wyatt pushes his hair out of his eyes. 'Then they were both unconscious.'

'You're the one who reminded me about the marks inside Eska's mouth, and on her palms. She was awake. So was Jasper – why tie him down otherwise?'

'Then why is this ship still floating?' he asks. 'If those two were awake they would have fought back, and if they did the *Dragon's Dawn* should be at the bottom of the ocean.'

Jasper wouldn't have just rolled over and died. This was a boy who commanded armies, who criticized Leofric for inaction. He wouldn't have died without a fight. Someone should be burned to ash right now. But they're not. And they *knew* they wouldn't be.

The back of my neck tingles. One possible answer. The only one that makes sense. 'They didn't use their Blessings.'

'Impossible.' Wyatt's head snaps up. 'Unless Jasper trusted the killer?'

'But that would mean Eska trusted them too. Eska didn't trust *anyone*; you heard her yourself.' I rise, pacing the room. 'If you were attacked, and had a Blessing that could save your life, you would use it without question.'

'Then why didn't they?' Wyatt rises.

'Because they *couldn't*.'

'Why not?'

I breathe deeply. 'Fucked if I know.'

He throws up his hands with a sigh.

'Have you ever . . .' I clear my throat. *Have to ask this very delicately.* 'Have you ever wanted to use yours, then not been able to? Like if you're scared or startled?'

He snorts. 'Of course not. You know how they work.'

Except I don't.

'Never?'

'No. I've always been able to use mine. It comes as easily as breathing. And trust me, I'm scared a lot.'

I turn on the spot. 'Then it wasn't any fault of *theirs* that they couldn't use their Blessings.'

'A-Are you saying the killer found a way to immobilize their Blessings?' He looks utterly horrified, as if the concept of not having a Blessing is the stuff of nightmares.

'It's the only thing that makes sense.' I flump onto my bed. 'But I have no idea how.'

Wyatt perches beside me. 'At least it's something.'

'Someone was able to stop those two volatile heirs from using their Blessings. We need to find out how.' That means facing the thing I don't want to. The thing I've been trying to escape for the past decade. The thing I should know everything about, but instead know nothing – Blessings.

Chapter Twenty-One

Day Seven – Feast of the Ox

Night

'My brain's not big enough,' I moan into the open book.

'That's why we're here.' Wyatt gestures around the library. 'To expand your brain.'

'Wyatt, the fact you believe my brain capable of that reflects very poorly on yours.'

He rolls his eyes.

The library is strangely quiet without Cordelia's song. She must have listened to my advice to stop wandering around alone. Now she's not here, I kind of miss it.

I turn to Wyatt. 'You're the one always stuck at home. Didn't you read anything about Blessings?'

The sudden hurt behind his eyes makes my chest ache. 'I spent most of my time talking to animals. And they don't know much about Blessings either.'

I reach for his hand. Fingertips brush skin. 'Sorry. I didn't mean . . .' I draw back.

'I know.' He returns to his book. Beneath the table, his foot nudges mine. Probably an accident.

I ignore the fluttering in my stomach.

I bitterly regret the years I avoided learning about Blessings. From ages seven to thirteen 'Blessing' was all I heard. *'Does he have his Blessing yet?' 'When will he get his Blessing?' 'A bit late for his Blessing, isn't it?'* I became so sick of the word my brain switched off at the mention of it.

'Shinjiro knows about Blessings.' I take a sip of water to keep me awake.

Wyatt's book hits the table. 'Absolutely not! He'll just talk endlessly about the Goddess's gift, in metaphors. Trust me – books are better.'

I'm not sure Grasshopper agrees. She's currently tearing out pages and giggling maniacally like some sort of paper serial killer. I already checked that book, thankfully. I'll have to hide the corpse from Cordelia though.

I stare at the endless shelves. I'll never get through them all. I may as well just stab myself now and save the killer a job.

'Dumpling.'

Glitter rains down on my book. 'Master Fish?'

'Are there any instances in history where a Blessed's power stopped working?'

Dumpling chews his tail. 'I'm here to attend to your needs and answer questions regarding the vessel. I am afraid I cannot answer—'

'Just leave.'

He vanishes with a bow.

I attempt to concentrate on the book before me: *A Blessed's Blessing usually passes to their heir between the ages of seven and nine. In rare cases, the Blessing has appeared in heirs as old as eleven.*

Wow. So fucking old.

After this point, the original Blessed no longer possesses their Blessing. The Blessing takes on a new form in the heir.

Thank the Goddess the emperor was so senile by the time I 'inherited' my Blessing he didn't question that my father and I possessed identical Blessings.

I skip through the pages, but then stop. 'This says most Blessings are active by nature – Blessed need to be conscious to use them. But in rare instances, Blessed can use them passively.'

'That doesn't help us. We know Eska was awake.' Wyatt flicks through his book. 'Listen to this: "Originally, the nature of Blessings had to be declared publicly in the interest of safety. It was only after opposition from the Blessed that this law was revoked. The Blessed argued this was an invasion of their limited privacy, as Blessings are uniquely attuned to a person's innermost self."'

'It would be helpful if they brought that law back,' I say.

'You sure? You seem pretty protective about yours.'

Heat blazes in my cheeks. 'I . . .'

His foot knocks mine again. I risk a glance and am rewarded with his crooked grin.

For the love of all that is blessed – stop *being so wonderful.*

I divert my attention to my book. *Shields have consistently produced the most impressive Blessings, usually consisting of physical might, intimidation and, when required, the capacity to dispatch enemies swiftly. Whereas the southern provinces are known to produce Blessings which aid farm and trade, such as influence over elements.*

Maybe *that's* why the emperor didn't find my identical Blessing unusual. Considering my province's belief that the Blessed ensures the piscero migration, weather control is probably a common Blessing for Fish.

The words begin to blur. There's something I'd much rather study at this table.

I can look. I'm *allowed* to look.

Wyatt's absorbed in his book, butterscotch hair falling

over hazel eyes. I watch his lips silently mouth the words, remembering the way they felt against mine, that sudden hunger, as though if he didn't have me the world would shatter. And the way my body responded in kind, leaning into him. No hesitation.

I've always given excuses when things started going that way with others – that I suddenly felt ill, or my father was expecting me. They all accepted them because they were commoners, and I was the scion. Never before have I got so close. Never before has the *want* of my body almost beaten back the fear, the terror of unmasking that final part of myself.

Wyatt is a polished blade – captivating but also terrifying in its potential to inflict harm. This boy who has been bedbound for most of his life. So lonely that his Blessing emerged in the ability to talk to the only things around him. Animals. A boy who dreams of the world beyond the Bandage. A boy who will not see that world unless I unmask this killer.

'It's hard to concentrate.' He lowers the book to his lap. 'With those golden eyes on me.'

I leap up, spilling my water.

As I hurry to clean it, he touches my arm. 'Dee, I don't want to rush you.' His thumb brushes my inner wrist. 'We'll take things at your pace. As slow as you like.'

My heart thumps in my throat. 'Thanks.'

'But have some mercy and don't look at me like that unless you plan to do something about it.'

Holy shit.

I reclaim my arm before I *do* do something about it. 'H-Have you found anything?'

'Nah.' He waggles the book. It looks like a gardening journal. 'I was hoping there'd be something about a magical herb or mushroom that can stop Blessings. Sadly not.'

I sit down with a groan. 'Blessings aren't *normal* enough to be documented clearly. What kind of magic passes on to a child at *random*?' My eyes scan over to . . . 'Grasshopper!'

She looks up, half a page hanging from her mouth.

'Not for eating!'

She spits out the saliva-covered page. 'To love?'

'Apparently.' I turn to Wyatt. 'What did your parents tell you about your Blessing?'

He looks down. 'I-I didn't—'

'They arranged a marriage as soon as he got it.'

Wyatt leaps up, gripping his chest. 'Sh-Shinjiro! Where'd you come from?'

The monk grins like a child who just pulled off a successful prank. 'They are rightly concerned with Wyatt producing a child as soon as the pilgrimage is complete. And before a demise I aim to prevent.'

Rules dictate that Blessed must delay procreating until after the pilgrimage. I understand why Wyatt's parents are antsy about it – if he dies before he has a child, their province will be ruined, and not just in reputation.

But still, I won't be *super* upset if that wedding happens to fall through . . .

Shinjiro presses his hands together. 'I will be partaking in the fertility ceremony once I return. I'm thirty now, so time is of the essence.'

I don't hear much beyond the words 'fertility ceremony'. I have a thousand questions.

'What are you doing here?' Wyatt rasps, sweat gleaming on his forehead.

'Looking for you.'

'Shinjiro.' I move towards him. 'You know all about Blessings, right?'

'Blessings are the Goddess's power taking form in humans. They are what unites the twelve diverse—'

'I know,' I say impatiently. 'But is it possible a person could be prevented from using their Blessing? Like it just stops working?'

His brow furrows. 'Have you been having performance issues?'

I gag. 'No! Not me! I'm top-notch. Just wondering if it's possible? It would explain why Eska and Jasper didn't seem to use theirs to defend themselves.'

His brow furrows. 'No. A Blessing *is* the Goddess's will. There's no power in Concordia that can stop it.' He takes my half-empty glass and approaches a nearby potted plant. 'Think of the Blessing as the water. You can pour the water out.' He does so and it absorbs into the soil. 'Now, you may claim the water is gone. But the water still exists. It's soaked into the earth. And the plant will consume it and it'll become part of the plant.' He turns back to me. 'A Blessing cannot be erased from existence. It must *go* somewhere.'

'But do you know if it's possible to *take* a Blessing away from someone?'

'Why would you want to do that? The Goddess speaks through the Blessing – showing the world who is worthy to bear it. That is why protecting our Blessed is of the utmost importance.' His tone is a *little* accusatory.

'I don't want to!' I wave my hands. 'I'm just wondering if it's possible.'

'The only way for a Blessing to leave a body is when it passes to the next generation. As your father's did to you.'

'There's no other way?'

'When someone dies. A Blessing needs a live host.'

Duh. Then it passes to a sibling. It must be mayhem in Crow Province. Ravi had sisters who he barely knew, and Eska had an army of siblings. The Bandage must be shitting . . . 'Wait.' My head shoots up. 'Jasper was a bastard, and his father died young. Did he even have any siblings? What happens when a Blessed dies and they're an only child?'

Shinjiro's eyes flicker away from me. The silence stretches so long I fear he's meditating, then he finally says, 'Blessings come from the Goddess. To her they return.'

About as clear as mud, that. Wyatt wasn't wrong about asking the monk for a straight answer.

'Thanks for your help,' Wyatt says, edging away.

Shinjiro swipes his arm. 'Something has been troubling me. I require a friendly ear. Would you accompany me to my cabin?'

Wyatt looks as if he'd rather join Grasshopper in eating the library. 'I'm sorta busy. Dee needs—'

'I think it's wise, Wyatt,' Shinjiro says, smiling broadly. 'If we talk alone.'

I see how it is. Nobody ever trusts the Fish.

'It's OK,' I say. 'I have a brain to expand.' *And I can't do it with you and your freckles here.*

'Wonderful!' Shinjiro links his arm through Wyatt's.

The look Wyatt gives me makes me worry he may never forgive me. But I'm concerned about how pale he's looked recently, the tremble in his arms. Also, I'm pretty sure Shinjiro won't murder the boy he's dedicated his life to curing, especially with two witnesses to them leaving together. 'We shall speak later, Ganymedes. Also – the little one appears to be eating a book.'

'Don't distress him too much,' I say, wrestling the paper from Grasshopper.

'No promises!'

*

Movement. Muted blue light. Someone is snoring. A child.

I must have fallen asleep in the library.

More movement.

I squint into the darkness. Nothing. Nothing. Then something.

A shape. The outline of a man. He moves towards me, fading in and out of blurred vision.

His black hair gleams like ink. He's close. A breath away. I know those eyes.

'Ravi.'

A soft smile. Like witnessing an eclipse – a place where the sun and moon meet.

He probably wants to explore the beaches again. Or row out to where the Bandage juts into the ocean. Something about it makes me uneasy – the cold green glow. But I'll go. For him.

My head falls forward. Something fluffy envelops me. A blanket, maybe.

The last thing I see is him. Watching. Smiling. I don't understand why that smile, which always warmed me, now makes my heart ache. Why an eclipse now feels like a blade. Like seventeen stab wounds.

Then darkness claims me.

Chapter Twenty-Two

Day Eight – Feast of the Crow

Morning

I wake up nauseous. Probably a result of sleeping face down on a book aboard a ship. Or maybe it's the guilt.

What do I even feel guilty *for*? Dreaming about a dead love when I'm in love with an alive one?

Or the more worrying and likely true reason – I feel guilty for loving Wyatt. For cheating on a dead man. A dead man who loathed me when we last spoke and wrote a suicide love letter to his fiancée, who *is not me*.

You found someone, Ravi. Why do I feel like trash for doing the same?

Aren't I allowed someone new?

Grasshopper drags me to the lounge. A stack of buttermilk waffles I don't remember ordering appears before me. Everyone else is here too, so at least nobody died in the night.

They're all eating their breakfast in complete silence. Leofric is the only person looking at anyone, and that's with obvious suspicion.

When Wyatt moves his chair closer, I become very interested in my waffles.

'You look terrible,' he says. *Pretty rich from a guy whose veins I know intimately.*

'I was in the library.'

'All night?'

I can't sit here staring at waffles all day.

I look at him.

Blessed fishcakes. I love him.

I love the wild way his hair sits. I love the strip of freckles across his nose. Most of all, I love the way he looks at me – as if *I'm* that beautiful sunset, and if he glances away, even for a second, I'll vanish behind the horizon.

Guilt burns in my throat. I cough into my apple juice.

'Are you OK?' He touches my arm.

No. Yes. I don't know. 'Fine.'

He leans closer, but when Shinjiro approaches, diverts his attention to his porridge.

The monk studies Wyatt over the steam billowing from his tea. He looks different somehow; there's something about his posture – he's not quite as perfectly poised.

'What happened to you last night?' I ask Wyatt. 'You didn't come back to the library.'

'I was . . . err . . .' His eyes dart to Shinjiro.

'With Shinjiro? All night?' I glance between them with a jealous pang.

His ears turn pink. 'It's nothing. Really.'

Sure. Nothing. Absolutely nothing that could cut the tension like a knife.

'Ganymedes,' Shinjiro says.

Wyatt's head snaps up. 'Don't.'

'I simply wished to say good morning.' He raises his teacup.

Wyatt's leg shakes. I want to squeeze his knee, but the guilt stops me. Instead, I think a change of topic may be his saviour. And I know exactly who to poke.

I look across the room. 'What did you do with Jasper's body?'

Leofric runs a hand down his face. 'I put the bastard with the others.' He sounds like a beaten man.

'I've already performed the anointing,' Shinjiro says softly. 'Poor child.'

'That room must be getting quite cramped.' I stab my waffle.

Leofric glares, though struggles to conclude that this is a personal insult. 'In around four days, we'll reach the mountain. Then we can contact the mainland.' I know what he's really thinking: *Four days until I'm fucked.*

'It'll probably be a ship of corpses by then.' I stretch. 'Unless you've got another suspect? Who haven't you accused yet? You already got the six-year-old.'

Despite looking as though he wants to strangle me, Leofric doesn't answer, which is a pity as I could really use a confession.

Cordelia scoots to the edge of her seat. 'Th-There is a rowing boat. Hanging on the side of the ship. P-Perhaps we could launch it and—?'

'That boat is tiny, designed for paddling to shore.' Leofric dismisses her suggestion. 'The ocean would kill you before the murderer does.'

'Besides, who will be joining you?' Nergüi waves their fork. 'You can't handle the boat alone – how unfortunate if your companion happened to be the culprit.'

Cordelia's eyes widen in horror.

'Everyone should lock themselves in their cabins,' Leofric says. 'We can take our meals there for the remaining journey. Nobody leaves.'

I think of Grasshopper's cabin, the twisted metal of her handle. Whoever the killer is, locks certainly won't keep them out. 'Great idea. The murderer can go from room to room and kill us in isolation without anyone realizing.'

'Then what do *you* suggest, Pissfish?' Leofric snaps.

'We could wait in this room until we reach the mountain,' Shinjiro answers, before I'm able to come up with a snappy comeback. 'Though that means we will have to offer our prayers here instead of at the shrine.' He smiles at Cordelia.

Nergüi fixes their eyes upon Tendai. 'Four days with my sister? Splendid.'

The murderer wouldn't even have to do anything. We'd all kill each other.

'We can't do that!' Wyatt breathes quickly. 'What about pissing?'

'You want me to urinate in here? With *him* watching?' Leofric points at me.

I scoff. 'I've seen your cock, Leofric. I don't need a second viewing.'

'When in the Goddess's name did you see my cock?'

'Lysander described it to me.' I smirk.

Leofric flies to his feet. 'It's clearly him – he's deranged.'

'Says the guy who used my body as a training dummy.'

Cordelia pushes her glasses up. 'Wasn't the Ox found in the greenhouse? That's next to the shrine.' She sneaks a glance at Shinjiro.

The monk chokes on his tea. 'Let's not make baseless accusations.'

'It wasn't baseless,' Leofric says. 'You *did* have a reason to be there at sunset, Monk.'

'What are you suggesting I did?' Shinjiro asks. 'Heal him to death?'

'If you're gonna start pointing fingers' – Wyatt raises his voice – 'everyone should state where they were after the trial.'

'Everyone will say they were in their cabins,' Cordelia says.

'Not me. I was with Dee,' Wyatt responds.

Leofric laughs dryly. 'Convenient how you get so close to him *this* trip.'

'What're you trying to say?'

'That the only explanation I can conceive for why you'd spend time in that Pissfish's company is because he's the only one dumb enough to give you an alibi.'

'Dee's not dumb!' Grasshopper yells. 'Dee's nice!'

'Cool your heads.' Nergüi speaks calmly. 'Getting worked up accusing each other will only play into the killer's hands. Haven't you almost been assassinated before?'

The silence informs us – no, just Nergüi, actually.

'So!' Tendai places her spoon down. 'It seems someone tried to murder me last night.'

Everyone turns to her. I'm on my feet, like an absolute goon, but it feels right.

'Calm down, Fish.' She rolls her eyes. 'That's one thing Nergüi and I have in common, perhaps the *only* thing. People have been trying to murder me as long as I've lived so I'm quite adept at surviving such attempts.'

'You're sure someone attempted to murder you?' Leofric's body has gone strangely still.

'I didn't hallucinate it, if that's what you mean. It's tempting to take it personally, but it seems this time I was only next on a list. If I'm going to die, I'd at least like it to be because of something I've done.'

Right on brand, Leofric says, 'You spend all day alone; you don't have any alibis. How can we be sure you're not the murderer, and you're making this up to throw us all off?'

'I suppose you don't.' Tendai wheels towards the door.

'But here's a little advice for the murderer – I'd rotate me to the bottom of the list if I were you. Else your continued failed efforts will only slow you down and I'd hate to be a barrier to someone's productivity.'

Then she leaves the room in deathly silence.

Chapter Twenty-Three

Day Eight – Feast of the Crow

Afternoon

I'm a tad annoyed Tendai inconsiderately got herself targeted and ruined my lower province theory. But to be fair, they *do* all seem to hate her.

My knowledge of Tendai is as good as Wyatt's knowledge of anyone not covered with fur. I almost wish she loathed me as much as she does the upper provinces. She nothings me. *Nobody* nothings Ganymedes Piscero.

Who is this woman, capable of resisting my charms? A statue. An iron-clad warrior. A legend.

'Are you gonna stare at her door all afternoon?' Wyatt nudges me. 'Or are you gonna knock?'

'I'm working up to it.' I unclench my hands. Of course, Tendai could be lying about the attempt. She could be the murderer. But there's also a chance she's not. In which case I need her information, because I'm severely lacking it. 'I need to endear myself to her. I need to find out what she knows.'

His hand brushes mine. 'When you're just being *you*, without all the stupid jokes, nobody could resist you.'

My legs almost give way. 'I thought you liked my stupid jokes?'

'I like you *despite* them.'

'KNOCK KNOCK!' Grasshopper screams. Before I can grab her, she slams her tiny fists against the door.

What's my play? *I know you nothing my existence but tell me who tried to kill you please and thanks?*

The door opens a crack. Tendai's face appears. 'Fish.'

I stick my foot in the gap. 'A girl like you must get lonely.' I cock my goggles. 'All cooped up in that room. I bet you could use a dose of vitamin *Dee.*'

Her purple eyes are upon me. She doesn't look completely disinterested.

My goddessdamn charm is going to cinch this.

'No need to be *koi,*' I say. 'Let me inside and we'll have a *fintastic* time.'

Wyatt cackles.

Tendai massages her temples. 'If I wanted to fuck chubby white men, I'd wander down to the Fish Province docks.'

The door rattles against my foot.

'Just in case I haven't made myself clear over the last decade . . .' She purses her lips. 'You are *nothing* to me. As insignificant as a flea. At least fleas carry diseases. You're not even worthy to carry disease. You're an irrelevant smudge of a man who amuses only himself and contributes nothing. I've met selfish Blessed, and I've met hateful ones, but I've never met one so *inconsequential.* Now get your foot out of my door.'

Wyatt isn't laughing any more. He's gone strangely quiet, glaring at Tendai with a mixture of loathing and something far more dangerous.

She doesn't know me. None of these upper Blessed do. Not really.

I grasp the handle. 'How about you listen to me for once, you self-obsessed snob? The only reason I'm nothing to you is because you never look beyond your own selfish nose to consider anyone else's existence. You lock yourself up, then attend summits to make sly remarks and fight with Nergüi, and think that makes you not like *them*. You're exactly like them. You treat me just like they do. You're *everything* you loathe.' I fix her with a fierce glare. 'You really want to piss them off? Then you're going to need me as an ally.'

I brace myself for the door to slam into my foot. But it doesn't. Instead, she says, 'What do you want, Ganymedes?'

She's never said my name. Not once.

'I want to know what happened to you last night.'

She studies me, weighing my worth in those purple orbs. I've felt it before, the few times she's deigned to look upon me. That same penetrating gaze – searching for something. 'Come inside. Quick. Before anyone sees you.'

I slip inside, Grasshopper trailing me, but when Wyatt approaches, Tendai pushes the door to.

'You let Grasshopper in,' Wyatt objects, his stricken face peering through the gap.

'Because she's six. And cute.'

Wyatt's mouth drops open. 'We're solving this toge—'

'I know exactly who this cloud-headed moron is – a useless fish who causes disaster everywhere he goes.'

I 'humph' a bit, but don't object too fiercely. She's not exactly wrong.

'But he didn't commit these murders,' Tendai continues. 'He's not capable of it. And to put it frankly – I don't trust you, Bear.' She slams the door; then she turns to me. 'If you let that man in, our conversation is over.'

Grasshopper looks at me with wide eyes. 'Swarm.'

My heart aches. I know what it is for a boy you love to close a door between you.

'Your choice,' Tendai says.

Goddessdammit.

I press up against the door. 'Go to the library, Wyatt. See if you can find anything about . . .' I eye Tendai. '. . . that *issue* we spoke about yesterday.'

'Dee—'

'*Please*, Wyatt.' I fail to keep the tremble from my voice.

Silence. Then fading footsteps. Who knew footsteps could sound so sad?

'Heart-breaking, truly,' Tendai says.

I bite down on whatever smart retort leaps to my mouth. It'll be worth it in the long run. I'm trying to save his life, after all.

Tendai's room is a kaleidoscope of art and colour. The floor is an intricate mosaic of porcelain tiles, and the walls a waterfall of woven fabrics. Shifting blades of light move across the room through stained-glass windows.

On one hand, it's breathtaking. On the other, I'm already getting a headache.

I affix my best grin. 'Why does a gorgeous girl like you need a taste of—'

'Drop the act. This'll be quicker if you do.'

Damn. Why does the way she talks to me ever so slightly turn me on?

Her eyes track down my bejewelled form. 'This is all business.'

'Gotcha. Business.' She *definitely* just checked me out. First Wyatt, now Tendai. I must be irresistible in this outfit.

'I'm beginning to regret my decision. I knew you were boring, but I wasn't expecting you to be this slow.'

My body goes rigid. '*Boring?*' I'm many things – possible

narcissist, possible anxiety-ridden mess who uses humour to hide his insecurities, but boring? Ganymedes Piscero?

'Settle down. It's because you're boring that I trust you.'

'And why is that?'

She clutches her armrests. 'Because of my Blessing.'

Play it casual. 'And that is . . . ?' I lean against a table, but my elbow knocks a vase. It wobbles, then falls – smashing into hundreds of pieces.

Tendai raises one eyebrow. 'I see this is going to be a *long* conversation.' She hands a bundle of papers and bright chalks to Grasshopper, who is currently clinging to my legs. 'Knock yourself out while the adults talk.'

She's easily won over, my ladyship. She sits obediently on the floor, colouring with careful, considered strokes. She looks like a different child.

It makes sense that Tendai can handle wild children. Elephant Province has only ever produced female Blessed, and, as a result, values motherhood more than any other province.

'How much do you know about me, Ganymedes?'

I crouch to gather the pieces of broken vase. 'The upper provinces seem to hate you. You didn't get an invite to the golden heir's funeral either.'

She grins, as if this is some great achievement. 'Do you know why?'

'Not really.' I scoop up the remaining shards. 'Something to do with the Funnel? My father said you raised the toll.'

A twitch of a smile. 'Sit down. I'm going to tell you a story, and I'd rather you be eye level.'

I take a seat on her bed.

'I hope your limited knowledge extends to knowing the Funnel's purpose?'

'A trade route to Dragon Province,' I say. 'Avoiding the impassable mountains.'

She nods. 'That wasn't always the way. Elephant Province was originally a place of great renown in the arts. Once trade became important, the other uppers – *Spider Province*,' she adds with disgust, 'realized how vital the Funnel was. Controlling the trade route put your fingers in the coffers of the provinces who wanted to use it.' She looks down, golden powder shimmering on her eyelids. 'It took many years, the occupation of my land. They do not come with swords and flags in Concordia. They come with open palms and promises of unity. They inserted themselves in positions of influence, and over the years they climbed and climbed, until nobody could stop them placing their friends in any spaces which became vacant.' She fingers a brass circle dangling from her ear. 'I will give Spider Province this – they know when to act. Spiders *never* miss an opportunity to be on top.'

I edge forward. 'Spider Province took control of Elephant Province?'

'In all but name. We had our Blessed. But our councils were filled with foreign faces. People that cared only for the wealth they could squeeze from a strip of land.'

I clench my fists atop my knees.

'Have you never questioned why there's such a divide in our empire? Though they pretend there is not.' She rests her chin in her hand. 'Spider put itself in a position where it could set the price. It could reward its friends and punish its enemies. And when I say friends, I mean provinces that could benefit them. And when I say enemies' – her eyes fix upon me – 'I mean provinces that could not.'

'The lower provinces.'

'That's how provinces like Tortoise and Spider got rich, while others stayed poor. Of course, none of this wealth found its way back into Elephant. A province of creativity and beauty became plagued by famine. Homelessness.

Starvation.' Her mouth twists. 'My province could not fight back – we were ruled by the ones choking us.'

'I had no idea,' I breathe. My tutors conveniently left *that* out, though I suppose Elephants are not the ones writing the history books.

'Those being exploited do not always realize it. Especially when they're told how dearly they are serving their empire.' Her eyes flash up at me. 'Don't give me that piteous look. You really think yourself free?'

I clear my throat. 'All we do is send them piscero, fulfil our quotas. They wouldn't—'

'And what if you didn't? What if to stop *your* people going hungry, you kept the fish you caught? What if you said "no"?'

I shift beneath her gaze. 'We wouldn't say no.'

'Just because they are not sitting on your councils does not mean they do not rule you.' She smirks. 'They would *make sure* they got what they demanded. They would take your pretty little beaches without hesitation. They would let your people starve to fill their own bellies. And there is nothing you could do to stop them.'

I wish I could say she's wrong. But I know she isn't. None of the lower provinces have a choice about their own lives. Not really. Ox children fated to become meat shields. Crows dying in the dark, their lungs black with coal dust. Fisherfolk, braving violent storms – because *this is our role. This is our value.*

'What about Ermine?' I ask. 'They said no.'

'And the only reason their province isn't currently occupied by Dragon or Tiger or whoever got there first is because it's a hellscape that only Ermines know how to survive.'

'Then what happened in Elephant Province?'

'Here's the thing about the powerful: nothing is ever enough. They got greedy. After a thousand more deaths, my mother started asking questions.' She observes me above steepled fingers. 'What do you think they did to her?'

My throat is bone dry. 'Killed her?'

'Perish the thought. She died of a mysterious illness. Very sudden. The week after her Blessing passed to her only daughter.' She gestures to herself. 'A timid thing "confined" to a wheelchair. A far more malleable and obedient option.'

'I'm going to guess that was a bad judgement.'

She points at me. 'So you're not a complete moron. I was seven years old when I became dux of a region on its knees. You know what I did to these people who bled my nation?' She adjusts her headwrap. 'I kicked them out.'

'The whole council?'

'Everyone who was not loyal. Every spider in elephant's clothing. Every courtier who smiled at me with liar's eyes.' She speaks slowly. 'Now, Ganymedes, how did I know who to get rid of?'

I try to imagine her, that small girl. Her mother's death still fresh. She would need a weapon, against those spiders, to survive. 'Your Blessing?'

'That's two in a row. I'm an empath. Of sorts.'

'You sense other people's emotions?'

'Only the negative ones. I feel contempt between people. Animosity. It enabled me to determine who amongst my advisors had bad intentions. I removed the bad eggs and rebuilt my province.'

'They just left? But you were seven.' I glance at Grasshopper, who has moved on to her next masterpiece. A year older than her.

'No, they did not leave. I asked nicely, and they laughed. So I gathered the leaders together for a meeting – the prominent figures with the most influence.' Her hands run over the wheels of her chair. 'Sadly, before I arrived, the building collapsed. It was apparently structurally unsound. There were no survivors. A *terrible* accident.'

My legs go numb. *Ah.*

'After that, people became a little wary of Elephant Province. Rumours spread of a dangerous Blessing. They left en masse.' She presses her hands together in mock prayer. 'The Goddess finds a way.'

I study her. That short woman in her wheelchair. The splash of purple hair against dark skin. No wonder the upper Blessed loathe her. She cut them off at the throat. They never saw her coming. I can only imagine how it crippled their economies, to lose control of the Funnel and have *her* set the price. No more favours for friends – she doesn't have any.

More than that, it's just plain humiliating. Flagrant disregard for Concordia and its facade of unity. It's the biggest 'fuck you' I've ever heard of.

And I'm intensely jealous.

'I don't know much about Blessings,' she says, 'but mine saved my life. Now Elephant Province has begun to rebuild. Colour is returning. Soon we will be known as artists again. For that, I must be thankful to the Goddess.'

Shinjiro was right. The Blessing takes the form you need. Tendai's soul cried out, and it helped her throw out the trash.

But the cost was the Blessing itself – to only feel negative emotions from others. To only have the things you fear confirmed.

What kind of person would that make a child grow into? Wary. Untrusting of everyone. Tendai.

I move closer to her. 'It couldn't have been easy to live with that. If I only felt negative things . . .' Only ever felt the times Wyatt or Ravi had unkind thoughts about me . . . 'It would make the world seem very unwelcoming.'

So that's why Tendai hides behind closed doors.

She tightens her headdress. 'It's protected me from those who intend harm. There's a hell of a lot of animosity on this ship. But that's no different to every summit. The hate behind sugared words. The lies upon lies. "Concordia" indeed. Then there's you . . .'

Oh, Dragon's dick. What has she sensed from me? Did she also sense something she didn't like from Eudora? Ravi? Eska? Jasper?

She plants her hands beside me on the bed. 'You're unique. I've never encountered anyone like you before.'

'N-No?'

'You don't bear an ounce of hate for anyone here. You never have.'

Oh.

'How in the Goddess's blessed name does a boy grow up amongst this shower of bastards and not loathe a single one of them?'

It's hard to hate others when you despise yourself so entirely. Tendai's right, I don't *hate* anyone here. They've treated me awfully, but I deserve it, so how can I hold that against them?

'You're a strange man, Ganymedes Piscero,' she states. 'Worse – you're a *good* person. An actual good person. *That* is what makes you boring.'

'Thanks. I think.' I scratch my neck.

She passes fresh paper to Grasshopper. 'Hate's a strong emotion. It makes people act stupidly, rashly. That's something I can use to my advantage. Don't look at me like that,' she says as I furrow my brow. 'It's for the good of Elephant Province. I will do anything to help my people thrive. If a province hates another, I can feed that fire. So, for the past decade you have been of complete disinterest to me. A good man cannot be twisted to my advantage. A good man is a boring man.'

I curl a strand of hair. 'I'm going to make you eat those words.'

'But now, a good man is exactly what I need.' She clasps her chair. 'You didn't kill anyone. A person incapable of hating others does not stab someone seventeen times.'

'True.'

'I wanted to stay clear of the whole ghastly murder plot – let them destroy each other.' She flicks her hair back. 'But someone tried to kill me last night. So now I'm involved, aren't I? I won't massively mind helping you solve it if it means I survive this thing.'

I lean forward. 'Your Blessing – is that how you survived last night?'

'Sometimes the hate dashing between people is so dense it's hard to pluck apart. Like trying to spot individual brush-strokes in a finished painting.' She rubs her forehead. 'But last night a spike of ill intent roused me from my sleep. I pushed the table against the door, then hid beneath the bed. They broke the lock but didn't make it past the table.' She levels her eyes at me. 'I know that malice. I'd recognize it anywhere. Have no doubt, they intended to kill me.'

'Did you see them?'

She shakes her head. 'I was under the bed and they didn't enter the room. But I did hear voices.'

'Male? Female?'

'Couldn't tell. But the intruder stopped trying to get inside the moment they spoke. Then I heard footsteps. They sounded like wooden sandals.'

Shinjiro wears those. All monks do. They make a dis-tinctive *clonk clonk* noise. I doubt Tendai has got that detail wrong. I'm just not sure if it incriminates or vindicates him. 'So, you're going to help me find them? Who has ill intent here?'

She snorts. 'How long is a piece of string? There's a reason you're the only person on this ship I can trust. Apart from the child. They don't tend to have true contempt for anyone either.' She slips a finger beneath Grasshopper's chin, lifting her head. 'No. She's clean. You're as complex as a six-year-old, Ganymedes. You should be very proud.'

She's compared me to a truly awesome six-year-old, so I don't feel that bad.

'I can't tell you for sure who was outside my door. But I do want to strike a deal.' She clasps her hands. 'You like solving mysteries, right? I haven't neglected to notice you wandering the corridors, poking around dark areas.'

'I don't *like* doing it. I have to do it.' For Ravi. And Wyatt. And Grasshopper. That list keeps growing.

'Well, I have a mystery that needs solving. You solve it and my Blessing is yours.'

'Mine?'

'You can ask me about any two people and I'll tell you how they feel towards others.'

Motive. One key thing I'm lacking. I need this.

'Fine.'

'In return, I need you to find the answer to a question which has confounded me all my life. One which may ensure the survival of my province. You must find this out *alone*. I don't want that Bear getting involved. And I will know if you're lying, Ganymedes.'

My breath hitches. 'What do you want me to find out?'

She leans in; then she utters the worst words I've heard in my life: 'What is Nergüi's Blessing? Bring me this information, and I will give you mine.'

*

'Dee!' Wyatt rushes over the moment I emerge from Tendai's room. Sadly, I'm cock-blocked by Grasshopper who slings her arms around him.

'You didn't go to the library, did you?'

He has the decency to look a little guilty. 'I was worried.'

He was worried. Someone is worried about me.

'What did Tendai say?'

I want to tell him everything. I *really* do. But Tendai asked me not to talk to Wyatt about it, and I can't lose this chance. 'I can't tell you,' I say as Grasshopper finally releases the poor boy.

'Oh.' His body wilts.

I take his hand. It's cold and clammy. 'It's not my choice.' *Please believe me. I would tell you anything. Almost anything.* 'I have to do this alone.'

'Y-You think I'll be a hindrance?'

'No!' I clutch his face. 'Never. You're not a hindrance, you hear me?'

His cheeks flush with warmth. 'I hear you.'

'I had to promise her. She doesn't trust anyone. Her Blessing's messed her up.' I press his hand to my heart. 'Can you trust me with this?'

His chest shudders; then he smiles sweetly. 'Of course, Dee.'

If we get out of this alive, I'm gonna climb the Bandage myself and bring you back a dragon.

'Wish me luck. I need to finally have that chat with Nergüi.' The thought alone makes my bowels churn.

His hand stiffens. 'No. Not them.'

'I have to. It's part of the deal.'

'I don't want you alone with them.' His voice is high and strained.

'Trust me, it's not exactly my idea of a fun time either.'

His other hand closes around mine, still pressed to my

heart. 'Forget the deal. We'll find another way. My brother was never the same after—'

'We're running out of time.' *And it could be you next.* 'You said you'd trust me. I can deal with the Spider.'

I wish I felt as confident as I sound.

He rolls his neck, as if working out a knot. 'Fine. *Please* be careful.'

'You know me! Mr Cautious.' I lean into him, grinning.

His eyes drink me in, in that dangerous way. Then he pokes two fingers into my cheeks. 'You have dimples. Did you know?'

'N-No.'

'Smile again.'

I do so, feeling strangely exposed.

His eyes light up, like an artist studying brushstrokes. 'They're like a gift your smile gives me.'

Then he has the gall to turn around, after saying *that*.

I clasp his wrist. 'Wait, Ravi.'

His body goes still.

I did not just say that. I did not just call him Ravi.

'Wyatt!' I correct quickly, rubbing his wrist.

He doesn't turn to me. But I see the slump in his shoulders and hear the resignation in his voice as he mutters, 'I'll be in the library.'

Chapter Twenty-Four

Day Eight – Feast of the Crow

Night

When I was five, I climbed a tree to escape a feral dog. I stayed there all night, the beast circling below, until my father sent people to look for me. Aged thirteen I faced the emperor and lied through my teeth. Neither of those things come close to my abject terror at the prospect of being locked in a conversation with Nergüi. Which is probably why I've been stalking them from a safe distance for the past two hours.

They are dressed suavely today – a red suit framing slender arms, ashen hair cut bluntly around dagger-sharp cheekbones. Devastatingly beautiful, like a tsunami.

They saunter across the deck – not slow, but not hurried. That's what unnerves me about Nergüi. They're always in control of their emotions, even when people are dying around them.

Nergüi has a thousand names – the schemer, the weaver of shadows, the maestro of whispers. I have no idea who they really are.

Grasshopper waits beside me, chewing on fudge. She's

unnervingly good at sitting still. Like a cub taught by a lioness, something instinctual kicks in when hunting prey.

Not hunting. Just . . . stalking. A spot of harmless stalking.

I run my hands down my face. What am I going to say? *Hello, I've been avoiding you since I was thirteen as I suspect you know my deepest secret, which would destroy my entire province, but do you fancy telling me about your Blessing?*

I hate Tendai, I've decided. See if she senses *that.*

Nergüi climbs the stairs to the shrine. I follow at a distance, hiding behind a cherry blossom tree.

We have company – Shinjiro kneels before the golden scales, dressed entirely in black.

Nergüi slinks forward. 'What are you praying for, Monk?'

Shinjiro presses his head to the ground: a final whispered prayer. Then he rises and faces Nergüi.

His eyes are red. His hair unbrushed. The sun is setting, but I get the distinct impression he's been here since midday. Now I realize why he looked different at breakfast – he's barely holding his shit together. Honestly, I'm surprised it took this long.

Nergüi raises their voice: 'Didn't you hear me? I said, what are you praying—'

'For salvation,' he murmurs, without a smile.

'For whose soul?'

'For all souls that are lost. For the souls I was unable to save.'

'The only soul you should be praying for is your own.'

Shinjiro sighs, moving past them. 'I do not know what you are speaking—'

Nergüi blocks his path. 'You know exactly what I'm speaking of. Ensure they are *long* prayers, Monk.'

His fingers sweep over the collar of his robe. 'All are forgiven if they are truly sorry. The Goddess is merciful.'

'Convenient for you,' Nergüi says. 'People are asking a lot of questions. Are you concerned about what they may unearth?'

Shinjiro raises his head to the heavens. 'There is nothing I fear.'

'Liar.' Nergüi drags the word out on their tongue, savouring the taste.

'I have lived with my guilt. I carry it every day. I will never allow myself to forget.' The corners of his mouth turn down. 'What do you do with yours? Hide it in a box? Cover it with whispers and threats?'

'I have no guilt.'

'And that is what separates us. Now you must excuse me; there is someone who needs my guidance.' Shinjiro storms away without looking back.

Nergüi stands alone. The dying sun silhouettes their profile – the sharp nose, the curve of their chin.

It sounded like they were accusing Shinjiro. If he was a problem, Wyatt would've told me.

Although Wyatt *is* terrified of him.

Wyatt.

What happened with Wyatt forced me into action. If I'm tracking Nergüi I don't need to think about my colossal fuck-up. Or what that fuck-up actually means.

And there's that guilt again, gnawing my gut.

Wyatt loves me. I feel it in the way his eyes behold me, as if I'm a marvel. A miracle.

And I love him back.

So why did I say Ravi's name? Is it possible to love two people at once?

I rest my head against the tree, breathing deeply.

Get it together, Dee. First confront the person you're terrified of; then worry about your competing loves.

A familiar *pop* awakens me to the world. When I push away

from the tree, there's one less Grasshopper and one new person. They're shrouded in darkness, a shadowed figure against the horizon.

Shitting hell. Nergüi's spotted me.

'Uh.' I cough. 'I wasn't being a creep. I was just . . . I want—'

As they step forward, my words snap off.

It's not Nergüi.

Ravi stands before me. His black silken hair. His slender fingers.

I've officially lost it. I close my eyes. Open them.

He's still there.

The growing night floods his skin, enswathing him in the darkness he used to hate.

I'd almost forgotten how beautiful he is – was – *is*. That smooth brown skin. Those eyes – pools of obsidian black. The lean, elegant length of his body.

'Rav—'

He turns.

'Wait.' I reach for his hand, but he moves with wide strides, picking up speed as he dashes down to the ballroom.

'Wait, Ravi!' I chase after him, adrenaline powering my body. I need to get closer – touch him, prove he's real. This isn't a dream. He's *real*.

'Dee!' Grasshopper tugs my arm. 'Spider person!'

Nergüi can wait. If Ravi's alive, then none of this matters. We can run away together. Fuck all this, like we always said we would.

Guilt. Someone else's name whispered in my heart. I silence it.

'Ravi!' I'm sprinting, but he's always a step away, a dark shape twisting through the corridors. Like trying to catch a shadow.

He runs down the stairs into the cabins; then he stops and turns at the centre doors to the deck.

We stand feet apart, my heavy breaths piercing the silence.

Even now I feel it, the thread stretching between us – his heart to mine.

He is my other me. Half of my soul. My reason for living. The only one who cared if I drowned. The one who pulled me from the water.

Our gazes lock.

I have looked upon those eyes a thousand times. I looked upon them when they only existed in the corners of my mind, stopping me from stepping into the sea, even when it called to me in my mother tongue.

Never before have I looked upon those eyes and felt the terror I do now.

'Ravi,' I whisper. 'How?'

The door behind him opens. The wind whips at his hair and clothes. He's going to leave me again.

I take a step.

'Dee!' A small desperate voice. Grasshopper tugs my arm and gestures to the . . .

My gut drops.

There's a body at the base of the stairs to the dining room. Pale skinny arms sprawled limply across the carpet. Brown hair falling before freckles.

Wyatt.

My world freezes.

Ravi turns for the door.

If he leaves – if I lose him – I might never see him again.

But then there's Wyatt. Lying on the floor.

'Dee!' Grasshopper pulls my arm.

My legs are stuck. Torn two ways. Into the dark with Ravi. Or a different path. Unknown, terrifying, but exhilarating.

His lips against mine in the heady heat of the greenhouse, a single voice defending me in a room of Blessed, and everything my heart needs to mend.

After all, every storm must end.

As I turn to the stairs, Ravi leaves my vision. The door to the deck clangs shut, and he's gone.

'*Wyatt?*' I fall to my knees beside him, turning him over. He's as light as a doll.

A trail of blood leaks from his mouth, just like Eska.

My shoulders tense.

Not him. Anyone but him.

'Wyatt?' I shake him as Grasshopper sits at his side, whispering soft songs into his ears.

I have to check his pulse. I know this. But I want to live here a moment longer – in the version of reality where he is not dead.

But as I bring my fingers to his wrist, I feel a distant, weak heartbeat. Stubbornly holding on. 'Grasshopper, get Shinji—'

A groan. Wyatt's eyes roll as he tries to focus on me.

'It's me! Dee!' I grasp his face. He's scorching hot.

His body shakes furiously, bucking beneath me like a wild horse. He clings to my jacket. 'D-D-Don't . . .'

I grasp his back. His shoulder blades press against his shirt. 'Help me with him.' Grasshopper tugs his hands as I wrap my arm around him and haul him to his feet.

He gasps disjointed words, 'Not him. Don't take me . . . to . . . him.'

'He's a literal healer.'

A weak hand turns my face, forcing me to look in his eyes. 'Not him. Promise.'

'What happened? Were you attacked?'

He mutters into my shoulder: 'Worried . . . Followed . . . Passed . . . Don't . . .'

He's been following me. I'm an idiot. Of course he wouldn't have left me. You do not leave someone you love in the jaws of a spider.

As I take a step, he doubles over, coughing and retching. Blood seeps from his mouth, tracking red down his chin.

'Wyatt . . .'

He smiles distantly. 'Welcome . . . to . . . dying . . .' Then his body goes limp.

I want to scream. I want to collapse.

But Wyatt needs my help. He'll never forgive me if I take him to Shinjiro. Plus, something about the terror in his eyes at the monk's name is making my spine tingle.

He hasn't been attacked. If he had, he'd be dead like the others. He's dying of his illness.

His scent washes over me – fresh linen and medicine. *Medicine.* The vials. His cabin.

I haul him up the first step. His legs drag on the ground.

Grasshopper flitters before me, her face drawn and anxious.

I lug him up two more stairs. He's still awake, muttering and drooling down my jacket. That's blood, drool, piss, and shit now. Only one more bodily fluid for the bingo.

I stagger up more steps, praying nobody sees me with what looks like a corpse.

'You . . . nice . . . smell . . .' he giggles.

If Wyatt is giggling things are on the brink of collapse.

I make it to his cabin, breathless and drenched in sweat. As I lean him against the door to search for his key, it gives way. I grab him before he falls straight through. His door was unlocked. And *he* gave *me* a hard time.

I drag Wyatt inside and place him on the bed, throwing his long legs over the end.

I press my hand to his forehead. Scorching hot.

'Dee . . .' Wyatt cups my cheek.

My stomach squirms pleasurably. How can he cripple me with one word?

Blessed hells.

'Medicine!' I proclaim, leaping off the bed. 'Grasshopper – keep an eye on him.'

She does just that, leaning over him unblinkingly.

As expected, Wyatt's walls display an expanse of plains and deserts. It's unexpectedly beautiful – the great majestic emptiness of it. But there's something mournful about it too. Something terribly lonely in the distant sound of horses' hooves and the press of heat. As if I'm standing alone at the end of the universe.

'Baby girl . . . Dee looks after you. Doesn't he?' Wyatt croaks.

He's calling her baby girl now. Got to move.

I rush to the only thing which could possibly contain medicine – the drawers near the bed. Shinjiro gave him a vial of the stuff. A vial a day to keep him alive. He must have –

I freeze. The drawer is full of them – stacked vials neatly labelled with each day, and another set labelled 'back-ups'. They're *all* here. Every single one. Even the extra Shinjiro gave him.

'How long haven't you been taking your medicine for?' I ask, my voice rough and jagged.

But I can tell how long. 'Night One' is untouched.

He looks at me like a drunk man being posed a complex maths equation.

'Wyatt, you *have* to take it! Shinjiro said—'

He blinks. 'Who?'

With a groan, I snatch a random vial and storm towards him, nudging Grasshopper out of the way. 'Thank the Goddess you're not dead already.' I uncork the vial and bring it to his mouth.

'No!' He hits my hand. The vial flies across the room, smashing against the wall.

'You're taking it!'

'Don't want to!' He flails his arms like a petulant child.

'Grasshopper, hold him down.'

Commanding that of a six-year-old would usually be laughable but Wyatt is delirious and entirely lacking muscle, so it works rather well. She restrains his arms while I grab another vial.

I climb atop him, pinning his torso between my legs. Then I uncork the medicine and lower it to his lips.

'Swallow.' I tip the bottle.

He splutters. The liquid pours over the sides of his mouth and down his chin.

My hand trembles furiously. 'Come on, drink it. You have to.'

'Can't!'

'Drink it!' I scream.

Grasshopper stares at me, releasing Wyatt's hands. Only then do I realize I'm crying.

Wyatt goes completely still.

I press my forehead against his. 'If you don't drink it, you'll die,' I breathe, tears streaming down my cheeks and settling on his. 'I know you think you want that. I did too, once. Then someone saved me. Someone made me take a breath. Someone wanted me to live.' I take his face in my hands, cradling it like a work of art, as he does mine. 'I want you to live. So, swallow it. Live. Just a little longer. For me.'

He's silent. Hazel eyes transfixed upon me, as if by a spell.

I tip the gleaming liquid into his mouth.

He doesn't take his eyes off me as he swallows. His fingers skim down my legs, intertwine with mine. They fit together perfectly. As if our hands were created to hold each other's.

'You're *everything*,' he says. Then he passes out.

Chapter Twenty-Five

Day Nine – Feast of the Bear

Morning

I spent the night in Wyatt's cabin, jerking awake frequently to check he hadn't died in his sleep. He didn't stir once, didn't even mutter a word. But his heart didn't stop beating. I should know – I slept with my head on his chest.

I did pick up some useful information – Wyatt bites his nails. His legs are too long for his bed. And he has forty-two freckles on his face.

I've made the choice. Wyatt over Ravi.

I will always feel a softness in my heart for Ravi. For what he did for me when there was nobody I could lower my walls around. But the fact I couldn't guess Ravi's Blessing kept snagging at my heart, like a loose thread. Now I know why – it's proof I didn't *entirely* know him. There are parts of Ravi I will never know.

Wyatt is different. I want to know *everything* about him. I want to share everything. I will. I swear. Once this is over.

He wakes mid-morning. His bleary eyes settle upon me,

sitting next to him on the bed. My hand is in his hair, brushing it away from his forehead.

'Dee . . .' The sweetest smile lights up his face.

'Morning, you.' I kiss him softly.

His hands track up my back, tugging me into his chest. His lips brush my neck.

'Steady on, big bear, we got a kid in here.'

He jerks back, clasping my shoulders. His eyes dart around the room. 'What are you doing here?'

'You passed out last night. I carried you here. I didn't want to leave you in case . . .' *In case you died, to be honest.*

'I was ill,' he blurts out. 'I remember coughing and feeling dizzy and . . .' He pushes himself up, holding his head. 'Do I look . . . OK?'

I pull his hands away from his face. 'Why haven't you been taking your medicine?'

'I . . . I . . .' He grips his chest with a wince, unleashing a coughing fit.

The noise rouses Grasshopper. She looks up, hair wild about her face. 'Bear is OK?'

'I'm fine.'

'Do you need more medicine?' I move to the drawer, but he grabs my arms.

'No.' He sways to his feet. 'I-I need to rest.'

I clutch his shoulders. 'Then rest. I'll look after you.'

'You can't.' He's gone the strangest shade of green. His hands fly to his mouth.

'Then we should go to Shinjiro. Maybe—'

He jerks away. 'Absolutely not!'

'Why are you so afraid of him?' I ask. 'You wouldn't even let me take you to him last night.'

He opens his mouth, but no words escape.

'Wyatt, if he's dangerous—'

'He's not,' he rasps. 'We just . . . We don't know what *anyone* on this ship is capable of.'

'But he's been healing you for years.'

'I don't trust anyone . . .' He gasps a breath. '. . . not in this room. Neither should you.'

He's probably right. I should be more cautious. But how am I meant to solve anything if I don't speak to people?

'We'll talk later . . . Just . . . right now you have to leave.' He grasps Grasshopper and me, dragging us to the door. 'I don't want you to see . . .' He falls against the wall, clutching his chest.

'I don't want to leave you alone,' I say. 'I'm worried about you.'

His eyes soften. 'Thanks for bringing me back. I . . .' He bites down on his pain. 'But when it gets like . . . this . . . need to be . . . alone.' He's ashamed. He can't meet my gaze. As though I'd judge him for daring to be ill. Or think him weak. Have others treated him that way?

I would never think him weak. He's the strongest person I know.

'I'll be fine.' He doesn't *look* fine. He's scalding hot and soaked with sweat. He looks like a man preparing to take a shit made of solid gold.

I really don't want to leave him, but I also know what it's like to want to hide the weak parts of yourself. I turn to the door, then freeze.

The lock and handle. They're completely twisted up, broken like Grasshopper's. That's how I got in without a key.

'Wyatt . . .' I run my fingers over it. 'How long has your lock been broken?'

'What?' he gasps, his body shaking furiously. 'It's not important right—'

'"Literal murderer", remember?' I glance around the

room for something, anything to help secure the door. With no better options, I tug at Wyatt's belt, unbuckling it.

'I'm not exactly in the mood.' He tries to fight my hands, but I bat him away.

I pull the belt free and hand it to him. 'Tie it around the handle, then your bedframe. Keep it shut.'

He barely has the strength to hold the belt. 'I need . . . rest. A few hours.'

I nod wordlessly, and then take Grasshopper's hand. As we exit, he closes the door behind us.

*

The lounge is empty. I haven't seen a single person since I found Wyatt last night. The silence has a heaviness to it, a weight pressing in around me. Grasshopper cheerfully munches her way through six bowls of luminous cereal, but for the first time – possibly in my life – I'm not hungry.

Living by the sea, death always surrounded me. The ocean gives and the ocean takes, that's what the fisherfolk say. We take life from the ocean, and it takes lives from us. We give the empire our fish and receive the serenity of knowing we're doing our duty.

After a life spent *seduced* by death, I've never really feared it. She was an elusive temptress. A whisper in my ear urging me to step into the ocean.

But now, death feels like a foe I must face. And the bitch is everywhere. She's taken my first love and stalks this ship in a guise I must unmask. And even then – even if I unveil her – she lingers within Wyatt too. She invaded him before I even knew him. Clawing through his veins and grasping his heart.

I hear death in the rattle of his lungs, feel her in the tremors of his hands. How can I defeat death when she got there before me? When she's had years to feast on him?

I have to beat death twice to win. And those are unlikely odds.

Someone tried to break into his room. He's *already* been targeted. Death has staked her claim all over my love.

I spoon my sad-looking porridge.

Pull it together. One step at a time. Beat her once, then find a way to beat her again.

Footsteps. Cordelia enters the lounge. She looks like a spectre herself – grey eyebags magnified by her glasses, golden hair limp around pale cheeks.

She sits, head in her hands. 'Ly?'

A golden dragon appears. 'Yes, Mistress Tortoise?'

'Water. And crackers.'

Goddess. What a depressing breakfast.

'Add a little jam at least?' I suggest.

She blinks at me. 'Fish. Didn't see you.'

'I *am* hard to miss.' I wink, gesturing to my lightly soiled clothes. I hope I cleaned all of Wyatt's blood off.

'It is comforting to see someone else who isn't hiding in their room.' She smiles distantly. 'Are you not afraid?'

'Nope.' Not for *me* anyway.

'You must have quite the Blessing.'

I clutch my knees. 'And you.'

'I *am* afraid. But death took my brother, and he was far stronger than me. I do not believe I can escape it if it wants to claim me too.' She hangs her head. 'When I was a child, Lysander was the only one who paid me any attention. When he got his Blessing, I was jealous. Jealous of the world. That they would get to have him. That he wasn't just *mine* any more.' She sighs softly. 'Now, if I die, at least we'll be together. I won't have to share him with anyone.'

'That's not a reason to give up.' Does everyone on this ship want to die? Is that it? Did they all just walk up to the murderer and politely request to be killed? It sure would explain a lot.

'I am *not* giving up.' She moves to place her elbow on the table, but slips and slams her chin into it.

Ouch.

'Bad night's sleep?'

'I was late to bed. I finally relented and went to sunset prayers with Shinjiro. He's locked in his room like the others, too scared to even go to the shrine now. But he said he'd make an exception for me. He has been hearing my cries through the night. But prayer didn't help.' She rubs her eyes, staring across the room. 'I keep seeing him. I see him *everywhere.*'

'Your brother?'

She nods. 'It used to be only at night but now . . . I'm not mad. I know he's dead but . . .' Her eyes swim with tears. 'You believe me, don't you? I'm not making it up. I've seen Lysander every night on this ship. He enters my room. I can't sleep.'

'Dead people don't come back,' Grasshopper says, playing with her necklace. 'They stay in the ground.'

Cordelia gasps, utterly horrified. 'How could you say such a thing?'

'Words are born in my head, then escape from my mouth!' Grasshopper turns to me, beaming with pride, but I've frozen in my seat, staring at Cordelia.

'Dead people don't come back.'

I grip my armrests. 'Cordelia, what does he do – your brother – when you see him?'

'Looks at me, gestures like he used to. Like . . . he wants me to climb out of a window with him. Go off on some adventure.' Her breath catches. 'But when I approach him, he flees.'

My mouth goes dry. 'Have you ever caught up with him? Touched him?'

'No matter how fast I run he's always out of reach.'

I sit back in my chair, releasing a long breath.

I'm such a moron. How could I not notice the similarities? Cordelia's been chasing ghosts since this voyage began, and last night I almost abandoned Wyatt to follow a dead man.

'I don't think you're crazy. I think someone else is involved.'

Her eyes go wide. 'Impossible. Who can raise the dead?'

'They're not raising the dead.' I stand, dragging Grasshopper away from her seventh bowl. 'Stop following Lysander. Stay in your room. I mean it this time. It's not him or his ghost. It's a Blessing.'

'A Blessing?' Her head snaps up. 'Whose?'

There's only one person it could be. Because Cordelia certainly isn't tormenting herself. I could tell her. I almost tell her. But there are still so many questions, and I need to get my answers, even if that means finally facing the person I fear most.

Chapter Twenty-Six

Day Nine – Feast of the Bear

Afternoon

I'm ready to face my fears. Completely and utterly ready.

That's why I've been standing outside Nergüi's door for twenty minutes. Because that's what 'ready' people do.

I could go straight to Tendai – I know Nergüi's Blessing now. But I'm not here to swap information with the Elephant scion. I'm here to solve a murder, and my gut tells me the Spider's wrapped up in it. I'm just not sure if I'll be the one unravelling information out of them, or the opposite.

'Knock knock!' Grasshopper squeals.

I wrestle her hands to her sides. 'This is a door I have to knock on myself.'

She seems to understand the gravity of the situation and settles down.

I raise a hand and take a deep breath.

Then he's there, beside me. That long body. That frame of dark hair. Those eyes.

I turn to Ravi. His stare digs into me, unblinking.

'It's a good imitation. But you got one thing wrong,' I say, my voice echoing in the corridor. 'He stopped looking at me, at the end. He couldn't hold my gaze for longer than a second. But you couldn't have known that, Nergüi.'

Nergüi appears in the corridor behind an unmoving Ravi. 'Are you sure about that?' Their hair is long today, sprouting in twisted horns above their head. 'I studied him quite closely.'

I quirk an eyebrow. 'How closely?'

They laugh dryly. 'I'm asexual. Any study of your dear Crow was purely informative.'

Grasshopper retreats behind my legs, but I regard the fact she isn't invisible as much-needed support.

'Could you get rid of him?' I gesture to 'Ravi'. 'He's distracting.'

They wave their hand, and he vanishes like smoke in the wind. 'You worked it out. I've been trying to decide if you're a moron or a genius. I think that just settled it.'

'I'm a genius?'

'A moronic genius. The most dangerous of all.'

I don't feel dangerous. I feel like a fat little fly dangling in a web.

'It took you seven days to come to my door. Are you ready, Ganymedes?' they ask.

I swallow my terror, force my lips to move. 'Yes.'

*

I didn't think anything on this ship could glimmer more than Nergüi. I was wrong. Their cabin has them beat.

It looks as if the entire room was carved out of a diamond. Every surface is reflective, casting my own slack-jawed expression back to me in distorted hazy colours.

'Is that real ruby? And sapphire?' I gesture to the walls.

They incline their head. 'Why wouldn't it be?'

327

My stomach almost drops out of my arse. This room is worth more than the entirety of Fish Province. Like its occupant, nothing is out of place – from the immaculately made bed, hewn out of what I have no doubt is actual amethyst, to the rose-quartz dresser placed before a nonsensical mirror – as if the room did not already offer enough reflection.

The cabin is cold, detached and utterly devoid of emotion. It's Nergüi.

The only thing that gives it any character is the constant thunder of rain.

'Let's make an agreement.' Nergüi clasps their hands at their waist. 'We will not lie to each other throughout this conversation. Deal?'

A deal with a spider. A spider who I suspect will know exactly when I'm lying. But one whose information I need.

'Deal.'

Nergüi takes two quick steps forward.

Grasshopper dashes before me, flinging out her arms. 'No!'

Nergüi observes her, half smiling. 'This one would die for you. Don't you find that strange?'

'Swarm,' Grasshopper says quietly.

'Not really,' I say. 'You all treated her like crap before you even knew her. I extended human decency.'

'And it's that simple to you?' Their grey eyes fix on me.

'It's that simple.'

Their lips purse. 'She cannot be here. I must speak to you alone, Ganymedes.'

'She's six.'

'She's still a person.'

I stoop before Grasshopper. I won't get her out of the room, but she will, thankfully, go to the toilet without me. 'I need you to stay in the bathroom, OK?'

'Don't need to—'

'Only for a little while.'

Her bottom lip pushes out. 'They'll hurt you.'

'I'll be fine,' I say, but Grasshopper stamps her feet.

I glance at Nergüi. 'She likes bunnerflies.'

A flood of them flutter into existence, white fuzzballs whizzing into the bathroom.

I shouldn't be insulted by how fast Grasshopper loses her concern for my wellbeing. She skips into the bathroom, giggling manically.

Nergüi closes the door. 'You should be more cautious. Ask more questions, even if only in your head.'

'She's six.'

'I became dux aged six.'

That must have been after their parent's failed assassination attempt. A child Grasshopper's age inherited *that* legacy. The sole heir of the 'Shamed One'. 'Then you know what it's like for people to hate you for what you've inherited.'

Incredibly, that shuts them up. They stand at a distance, but their image reflects all around me, so I feel as if I'm facing twenty Nergüis.

I shake the tremble from my arms. I came here for answers, and I know a secret about them, a secret I'm sure they want to keep. It makes me feel a little more powerful. A fat fly with a tiny shield.

'How long have you been conjuring images of the dead?' My voice doesn't betray how shit scared I am.

'Around the same time I inherited that throne.' Their words are clipped, emotionless, as if talking about someone else's life. 'But it is not only the dead I can summon.'

'Live people too?'

A small nod.

'Are they dangerous?' I ask.

'They can't stab people seventeen times, if that's what you mean.'

'How about no times at all? Can they bleed the life out of someone and leave no mark?'

A flash of a smile. 'Now you are asking the right questions. To the wrong person, sadly. My creations hold no sway in the physical realm.'

I study them for any sign of a lie. But Nergüi is as cold and unyielding as the jewels entombing us.

I clench my fists. 'Then why are you summoning them?'

Nergüi's fingers dance over the jewels at their neck, twisting a ruby. 'I tried everything to persuade you to speak with me. Threats, bribery. Who would have guessed that instead you would follow *him* to my door? You really did love that Crow, didn't you?'

Their words pierce through my shield like a blade.

'Why him? He abandoned you the moment he got a whiff of attention from the uppers. Also, I spoke with him on occasion – he was awfully dull.'

Dull, my arse. They didn't know Ravi at all.

I grit my teeth. 'He was the only one who treated me like a human.'

'You're not human. You're Blessed. *Isn't that right?*'

I try to ignore the intonation on that question. Nergüi never outright said they knew. Just hinted that something was amiss. Maybe they don't know. Maybe they want to prise the truth out of me.

Maybe.

'I know you were tracking me. You're about as subtle as that outfit you insist on wearing.' They turn their nose up. 'I don't like people following me.'

Because you're the one usually doing the following.

'So I used the Crow's image to get you here . . . and here you are.'

I swallow hard. 'You're playing with people's emotions.'

'They're the best things to play with,' they say matter-of-factly. 'Emotions cause people to lose control, to lose perspective.'

I wonder if they've ever felt an emotion in their life. They're like a mirror. Displaying an image of humanity, but beneath the surface, there's nothing but cold hard rock.

'You've been using them. Summoning figures people trust and attacking them.' It would explain everything – why Eska and Jasper did not defend themselves. They wouldn't. Not if they saw someone they trusted. And Nergüi would know who to pick; they have a legion of spies to root out that information. 'Who did you summon for Ravi?' I can't fight the tremor in my voice. 'Was it Cordelia . . . or me?'

They tap their red fingernails against their chin. 'Interesting. You're close. But not quite there.'

I clench my fists. 'I saw Leofric yelling at you. He worked it out, didn't he?'

'Of course not,' they scoff.

'You deny it?'

'Explicitly.'

'You said you wouldn't lie.'

'I'm not lying.' They tuck a curl of ashen hair behind their ear.

I suspected they'd twist words to their advantage. But they aren't aware of what I know about Cordelia. 'Explain to me then – why you have been summoning images of Lysander?'

They pause. 'Why do you think?'

I feel like my questions aren't my own, let alone my

answers. Nergüi doesn't look worried at all. I'm a toy to them. A curiosity to be poked and prodded.

Just like Cordelia.

'Because you think she's weak. You want to manipulate her and drive her mad.'

'One of those statements is false.'

I throw down my hands. 'Cordelia's mourning. You're tormenting her for your own twisted pleasure.'

Their eyes cling to me. 'The Tortoise may attempt to deny it, but she is ruled by emotion. That is her flaw. Her parents knew it; that's why they tried to beat it out of her. *That* is what will lead her to destruction, more so than my creations.'

'They certainly don't bloody help.'

'What do you propose?'

'Stop summoning Lysander. Leave him in the earth so she can move on. She has it hard enough coming into this mindfuck.'

They consider my words. 'You *like* her, don't you? The woman who stole your love?'

'It's not her fault Ravi loved her. All she did was love him back. I can't blame anyone for that.' I glance down.

They release a long breath. 'You're too soft, Ganymedes. You look for friends in the wrong places. Everyone here is weaving a web – the monk, the shield, even that Bear who follows you like a lost puppy. At least I am honest about it.'

A bubble of rage swells in my chest. 'You think you understand people, but you don't. You never get close enough to.'

'Don't you think it strange how that boy has never paid you any mind before, and now he's all over you?'

'Wyatt isn't—'

'I know Bears. They do not invest their time in anything not worth their while.' They speak slowly, pounding every syllable into me. 'They believe they belong with the uppers. They have been trying to climb that ladder for generations. The things his brothers have done would make your skin crawl.'

'What does that have to do with Wyatt?' I snap, hating the fire in my voice. 'I'm hardly the one to help someone up a ladder when I'm at the bottom of it.'

Their eyebrows quirk. 'Everyone needs a leg-up.'

'Is that why you did *something* to one of his brothers?'

Their head cocks to the side. 'Is that what he told you?'

My heart thumps.

'People tell all sorts of lies to protect their provinces. I suspect he didn't want you speaking to me alone and finding out about his brothers' *exploits*. After all, he needs you.'

'He wouldn't—'

'Here's my advice – never forget what that boy is. *Bears hunt fish.* And I certainly would not lower my defences around my predator.'

They're wrong. Wyatt adores me. He wouldn't use me.

But Ravi adored you too.

I feel a snag of something. A part of my heart. A thread, beginning to unravel.

They smile, almost sympathetically. 'It's peculiar that a man can sleep soundly on a ship where people are being murdered without a working lock on his door.'

My stomach twists. I know what they're doing – trying to make me suspect my closest allies. 'I trust Wyatt.'

'I thought we agreed not to lie to one another.'

Heat rises to my cheeks, pounding in my head.

'If I possessed a secret which could destroy my province, I would build a wall around myself. A solid cage around my heart. And I would not let pretty smiles and sweet words chip it away.'

The ground rocks beneath me. *They know.*

Nergüi shrugs. 'Just some advice.'

If Wyatt is trying to root out that secret, he could use it to wreak devastation. Throw my province over the Bandage. Take over the fishing grounds. With control of the piscero and cattle, not even the uppers could ignore Bear Province. They would have what they always wanted – power.

I bite down on my cheek. I can't let Nergüi spin their web around me. 'Why should I believe anything you say? I know what they say about you. That you'd do anything to be on top. That you trade in secrets, through a web of spies. That you're a spider, through and through.'

The thunder of rain follows my words.

Nergüi's eyes finally leave me. They remove their head-dress, placing it atop a mannequin near the dressing table. The wig follows, revealing cropped hair. They sit at the table, click open a vanity and then pluck out a sponge pad.

'I remember a time before the shame,' they say, pressing the pad to their face. 'It comes to me in whispers of memories. In the scent of dry leaves, in birdsong. That is how I know there was a time I did not live in fear.' They drag the pad along their cheek, removing a thick layer of make-up. 'Do you know the legends about Spider Province?'

'Which?'

'Remember when the monk spoke about how the Dragon line must remain pure, unblemished by the blood of other provinces?'

'Yes.' It was the second day, when I asked what would happen if the emperor were to pass without an heir.

'As he often does, he lied. The blood is not "unblemished". Five hundred years ago a Dragon heir fell in love with a Spider Blessed.'

I know this story. They had two children. Twins. One

inherited the Primus Blessing, the other was banished to Spider Province. The Dragon bastard was disguised as a trueborn heir, and the real parentage of the Spider bastard hidden so they could never challenge the throne, despite both twins being blood of the Goddess. 'That's just a folk tale.'

They drag the pad down the other cheek, scrubbing it clean. 'That's what the monks want you to believe. It is a truth they have woven into legend.' Their reflection stares back from ten surfaces, daring me to question them. 'In Spider Province, this "legend" is as real as the stars. A truth passed from parent to child. Because writing it down would mean death. All Spiders live with this knowledge in their hearts. I am blood of the Goddess.'

I don't know if I believe it, but all that matters is that *they* do. And to have that as a part of your identity – the belief that you have been wronged in some great way that needs righting – suddenly Spider Province's attitude makes more sense.

'My aveeg would sit me on their lap, telling me how the blood ran through our veins. How Spider Province had been stripped of the power which was its birthright. Thrown into a hole to be forgotten about.' They dab their lips from red to nude. 'They also told me how the emperor was rapidly fading. How they, far wiser and more powerful, would be a better ruler.'

I shift, staring at their reflection.

'My aveeg believed they were destined to rule,' Nergüi says. 'Now they are known as the Shamed One.'

'Because they tried to kill the emperor.'

'No,' Nergüi says swiftly. 'Because they failed.'

My eyes narrow.

'Spider stands apart from other provinces.' Nergüi removes

the black liner from their right eye. 'We do not yield to mean-ingless rules. We strive to defy them. We do not allow the constraints of family or duty to limit our potential. We revel in the individual. People who step out of line are vilified else-where. In Spider, they are our heroes.' They move to the other eye. 'My aveeg would have become a Spider paragon if they had succeeded. Instead, they *failed*. In a province that prides cunning, nobody could loathe them more than us.'

'And you?'

Their hand stills, hovering above their left eye. 'When my aveeg was hanged for their failure, they broke not only their neck but also all stability in my life. I went from heir of a glorified province to the blood of a vilified criminal. I was greeted by only hate and suspicion. The punishments dealt by our cousins in Dragon Province were crippling. Then, my dear Elephant sister cut us off from our most valuable source of wealth – the Funnel.'

'Because your aveeg killed her mother.'

'Yes. They were a fool to underestimate Tendai because of her inability to walk. As if the restrictive shell of a body is more important than the infinite possibilities of a mind.' Nergüi removes their eyeliner. 'The trade our province relied on was lost. We had no way to ship our jewels to the capital. No way to pay the fines. And nobody to help us – we were poison.' They place the pad down. 'My province entered a depression so fierce parents smothered their children to stop them dying from hunger. Thousands perished – their bellies swollen with jewels. Everyone looked to me because I was our leader. And I was six.' Nergüi turns to me, their face completely bare. They look like an entirely different person. 'We made a deal when we entered this cabin. I promised you the truth, Ganymedes. Allow me to show it to you.'

The room darkens. The mirrored walls distort, and

suddenly I'm not in Nergüi's cabin any more. I'm surrounded by pillars of rock, stretching as far as the eye can see. The marble at my feet is inlaid with crystals, and before me sits a throne. It's almost completely transparent, if not for the white glow pumping from its heart.

It's a throne made from diamonds. A throne fit for an emperor. Or someone who believes they should be one.

'This is Spider Province,' I say, hushed. '*Incredible.*'

'Did you really think *my* Blessing would be limited to images of people?' Nergüi smirks. 'Dream a little bigger, Ganymedes.'

A lone figure appears before the throne. So slight in the vastness of this room, dwarfed by that diamond chair.

I would recognize those steely eyes anywhere. But they are thin. Gutter thin.

Nergüi. Aged six.

The real Nergüi stands behind their younger counterpart, lips twisted in disdain.

The child's mouth moves, but older Nergüi speaks the words, '*I hate you.*'

The child falls to their knees before the throne. Tiny fists pound the floor. '*I hate you!*'

A figure appears behind them, summoned out of shadows. A person a little older than Nergüi now. Their aveeg.

The child's body tenses. Hate floods their face. '*You.*' They lunge, hands clawed, teeth bared, like a wild animal. But they pass through the image.

Their aveeg turns. Their face is a perfect mask, just like Nergüi's.

The child screams, lunging again. Again. Again. But every time they pass through that silent figure. They beat the floor until their fists are torn and bloody. Nergüi doesn't need to speak the words any more. I know what that child is screaming. '*Why have you done this? Why did you leave me? I hate you!*'

It goes on for minutes. Hours? The pain of that child, the screamed words to an illusion in a room where nobody can hear them. Where nobody will ever know.

They fall to the floor, curling into a tight ball, shuddering with tears. They mouth one word over and over: '*Aveeg. Aveeg.*'

I want to hold that child, tell them they are not defined by a parent. By what *they* did. But I can't. Because then I'd be a hypocrite.

Nergüi's voice bounces off the stone: 'I summoned their image every night for six months. Every night I went to bed hungry. Every night after I buried my people. Every night after begging duces below me for help. Every single night I screamed at my aveeg. And every night they did not answer.'

Nergüi steps through the illusion and stops before me – eyes red, cheeks wet with tears.

They are still the same person. Still that child screaming at an image that cannot hear them.

'I didn't know,' I whisper.

'I knew, if I was to rebuild that which my aveeg destroyed, I would have to play their game. And I would have to play it better.' They do not wipe their tears. 'All I had was distrust and a legacy of shame. So I used that. I became what they believed I was. I clawed my province out of the dirt and back into the elite.'

'By using spies,' I whisper. 'By manipulating and black-mailing.'

'I knew they would never respect me. But they *could* fear me. A man can fight a tiger, but he cannot fight a shadow. He cannot fight a dark rumour that takes root. You call me a coward because I whisper from the darkness instead of wielding a sword? My whispers saved my province.' They look at the quivering child, taking no care to hide their scorn.

'I will *never* be that child again, sobbing on a cold floor, utterly powerless.'

But you're wrong, I want to say. *You're still that child. You've just encased them within a cage of diamonds.*

'Now you know me,' they say. 'You understand me.'

I nod mutely. I don't even fear them, not in this moment.

'I have shown you my truth. Will you do the same?'

My breath catches. It's true – they shared something intimate. Something I know they have not shared with anyone else.

'You're the one who told me to build a wall around my heart,' I say, my voice shaking. 'Why would you risk showing me this? I could use it against you. Blackmail you or destroy your reputation.'

They settle their shoulders, observing me with that unfamiliar bare face. 'Because there is no risk in it. None at all. Not after tonight.'

They know I won't use it against them. They know I won't be *able* to use it against them. Because something is going to happen *tonight.*

I fight back tears. 'Why are you doing this?'

Their jaw quivers. 'I have never had a friend. Nor a confidant. Only temporary allies. I have remained behind the safety of my walls, and I do not regret it. But I cannot say I have never felt a desire to climb over them. Do you not feel the same, Ganymedes?'

My breath catches in my throat.

'Despite what you've heard, I'm not merciless. I'm not wasteful. Everyone deserves a chance to show their truth. This is your chance.'

I open my mouth, but no words escape. I stare at the shuddering child. At the exposed throat Nergüi has shown me.

Perhaps this is why I have always feared them – because I

339

felt an unspoken connection. The most unlikely connection in the world. Both of us carry wounded children. Children who scream, but only the silence answers.

My throat burns. 'It was raining. Storming. The night Ravi and I climbed to a cave on a cliff.'

Nergüi's illusion changes. The sobbing child is replaced by two others, their images uncertain, shifting, as if viewing the scene through a pane of frosted glass. Hand in hand they climb, white hair and black.

Ravi falls, and younger me rushes to help him. He's so gentle, that Dee. He handles Ravi like crystal. There's love in even these blurred movements.

I was right. Nergüi has always been watching me.

'We entered the cave.'

The room darkens. The two figures – the white and black – huddle together.

'He wore a flower that day. A white one. In his hair.'

The bud blooms, flashing brilliant light.

'And the night lights were in the sky.'

The room floods with dazzling colours.

'There's an old fisherfolk tale, about secrets told beneath the night lights. Ravi told me his.'

The black figure moves closer to the white.

Nergüi's gaze pins me.

'It's not mine to reveal,' I say.

Nergüi does not push. This is, after all, not about Ravi.

'And I told him mine. My deepest secret.'

The boy who is me takes the other's hand. He leans closer, as close as he can.

'What did you tell him?' Nergüi asks.

The white figure shifts; purple light streams above his head.

'What did you say?' Nergüi's voice is not cruel. It is, if anything, gentle. Encouraging. A little desperate.

The truth lingers in the boy's mouth. I feel it on my own tongue. The weight of it.

'Ganymedes.'

'I can't.'

'You can. You must.'

I want to say it. Nergüi already knows. What difference would it make to speak it now?

'You can say it.'

I can't. I'm not strong enough to face it. To utter it into existence, even to someone who already knows.

Those little words have defeated me.

I lick my lips, failure sitting in my gut like a stone. 'I told him I loved him.'

The scene vanishes as quickly as snuffing a candle. The mirrored room returns. Nergüi faces me, their face twisted with fury and betrayal, like the child they claim to no longer be.

'That was your chance. Your last chance to share your truth. You are a coward.'

I am. They tore down their walls for me, and I'm still hiding behind mine.

They fling the bathroom door open. Grasshopper bounds out, face falling as she looks upon me.

'Get out,' Nergüi commands.

I grasp Grasshopper. As my hand reaches for the door, Nergüi speaks again, their words as hard and cold as diamonds. 'You will regret it, Fish. Of that I am certain.'

Chapter Twenty-Seven

Day Nine – Feast of the Bear

Night

Tendai studies me over a pyramid of fingers. 'You better be here to tell me Nergüi's Blessing.'

I pout. 'Is that what passes for a welcome nowadays?'

'Tell or leave.' She smiles at Grasshopper. 'You can stay, sweetheart.'

'Why does she get to stay?'

'Because her presence doesn't irritate me.'

'Yay!' Grasshopper throws her hands in the air.

I sit on Tendai's bed. I haven't faced what happened with Nergüi yet. But I do know one thing – if Nergüi believed there was no danger in unveiling themselves to me, it's because they knew I would never be able to use it against them. They said as much themselves – '*There is no risk . . . Not after tonight.*'

Murder is an effective way to keep your secrets safe.

I'm just not sure if Nergüi is the one responsible, or knows who is. They are the Spider after all. If anyone could unearth clandestine murder plots, it would be them.

'Just tell me already.' Tendai glares.

It's kind of nice – having information one of the uppers would kill for. I *could* lord it over her for a few days, but I don't have a few days. I don't have any days.

'I got their Blessing.'

'How?'

'I'm smart.'

She gives me a long look.

'Also, they used it on me.'

She massages her forehead, and then leans forward eagerly, like a child hungry for dinner. 'Out with it.'

'They can create illusions – people, places, scenes – but you can't touch them. They don't interact with the real world.' I believe Nergüi about that. Neither I nor Cordelia managed to catch our lost loves.

Tendai settles back in her chair. I thought she would cheer, maybe stretch to a smile. Instead, she looks contemplative. 'So that's how they do it.' There's another mystery there, but I don't have time to unravel it.

'I think if you two just talked it out you'd stop clawing at each other's throats. You're very similar.'

'We are *not* similar,' she snarls.

'You were both born into shitty situations. Both built your provinces up out of ruin through sheer force of will.'

'You want me to break bread with someone whose parent killed my mother, then arranged for assassins to kill me?'

The heat on my neck prickles. I don't need Tendai's Blessing to know danger is near if I venture down this path.

Grasshopper shakes her head. That's all the confirmation I need – my girl's attunement to danger is second to none.

I slap my knees. 'So! Can I get my payment now?'

'No.'

I leap up. 'We had a deal.'

'I need you to do one more thing.'

343

'I don't have time. Something's going to happen tonight. And that something likely involves me and a grisly death.'

Tendai doesn't appear concerned. 'This'll only take a moment.'

Like I have a choice. I've already played my hand. 'What is it?'

'Strip. Take off your clothes.'

'Why?'

'Whyever not?' A smirk tugs her lips.

'Is this because I said you and Nergüi are similar?'

'Strip.'

Tendai says I have no malice, but right now I feel a spike of it. But then her deep purple eyes settle upon me. It's kinda hot – the way she knows I'm going to do it. The absolute control.

Why is it that I want women to beat me up and men to gently embrace me?

I won't linger on that and its potential parental overtones. 'Look away, Grasshopper.'

I unzip my jacket – nice and slow. Once I'm free, I cast it to the floor with a flourish. Might as well own the moment. Tendai rests her chin on her hand, eyes scanning my body. I shimmy my butt as I lift my shirt over my head. Then, with great fanfare, I whip down my trousers and pants.

Tendai buries her face in her hand. 'Goddess! Fuck!'

'What?' I gag, covering my precious parts.

'I was joking!' she shrieks from behind closed fingers.

'Oh.'

'Put your clothes back on!'

I do so.

She uncovers her eyes. 'You're unbelievable.'

'Catch a look? What do you think?'

'Cute. For a chubby guy.'

'Wrong – I'm cute *because* I'm chubby.' I clutch my thighs.

344

She smiles deviously. 'You're fun. We'll play again some-time. Now, we had an agreement. I'll tell you how two of our delightful travel companions feel about the others. Do you have two names for me, big boy?'

Big boy? Is that a joke? Or am I . . . ?

'The NAMES.'

'Right.' *There's business to be done, big boy.*

I know I should be using this opportunity to fish out peo-ple's motives. But there's a name I have to say for my own peace of mind, though it sticks in my throat.

Tendai drums her fingers.

I croak one word: 'Wyatt.'

My heart thuds against my chest. A collision of anticipa-tion and guilt. I should trust him. I *do* trust him. But Nergüi's words burrowed into me. I just want to prove them wrong. That's all.

'You don't trust him. Wise.'

Goddess, they're so similar. 'I do trust him.'

'Of course. That's why you said his name.'

I glance away. Maybe there are *some* things about Wyatt that trouble me. And maybe I find it hard to believe someone like him could fall for me. Maybe I do think him wanting some-thing else out of it – like power – makes much more sense.

But once Tendai tells me he's safe, I'll let him in. Allow him to peel away that final piece. Tell him the things whis-pered in a cave on a cliff in a storm.

'He's a strange one. At the opening party his contempt for you was so strong I sensed it from across the room. What the hell did you say to him?'

Mentioned he was dying fifty times. Told him Eudora didn't love him. 'I was a cunt.'

'Well, after the party that completely changed. Since then the bear cub has shown contempt for *everyone*.'

My heart seizes. 'E-Everyone?'

'Everyone who isn't you, Fish.' Her gaze passes to Grass-hopper. 'And her. I've never felt such a shift from contempt to – well – not a trace of it. Not once. Since the party. That's why I wouldn't let him in. I don't trust someone who can change their whims so easily.'

Despite Tendai's suspicion, my heartbeat settles.

Wyatt wasn't lying about his intentions. He told me himself – after Ravi's death, he realized I couldn't have been the one who killed Eudora. He wanted to partner with me because he trusted me.

As I should him.

I wasted a name for nothing. For my insecurities. The next one needs to count.

'Your second?'

I skim the possibilities: Leofric clearly loathes me; Nergüi has other secrets I'm sure they're not telling me; there's been something *off* with Shinjiro since the journey began; and Cordelia is just a goddessdamn mystery.

Picking a random name won't work. These provinces have so much bad blood that contempt is probably hanging around every summit like a bad fart. I need to identify someone who is capable of killing mercilessly. Who loathes *all* of us enough to do it. And there's one person who can help me identify them.

'Has anyone shown ill will towards Grasshopper?'

Tendai blinks. 'Sorry to tell you, Fish, but most hate her based on her province. That doesn't narrow it down.'

'I don't mean passing contempt. I mean something deeper.' Enough to try to kill her within one day of meeting her. A six-year-old.

'It's not as simple as that. Sometimes feelings spike if someone does something to anger them, like you and Bear at the party. But you can't put contempt on a scale.' She closes

346

her eyes. 'I can't gauge how intense the feeling is unless something significant happens. And that hasn't occurred since your little friend showed up.'

My shoulders sag. Another name wasted. Maybe if I drop my trousers again she'll let me have a third.

'There is *something*,' she mutters. 'Something unusual regarding Cordelia. She doesn't have contempt for anyone. The little dove is similar to you that way – dull.' She fiddles with her earring. 'Except when it comes to . . . Yewande.'

'Who?'

'Hi!' Grasshopper thrusts out her hand.

Tendai stares at me open-mouthed. 'Did you never ask her name?'

'Err . . . come to think of it. No.'

Her head falls to her hands. 'Regardless, Cordelia has shown contempt for the little bug since this ship set sail.'

How is that possible? None of us knew Grasshopper until nine days ago. Right?

Grasshopper plays with her pendant. I need to talk to her, but not here with Tendai's eyes upon my neck. I set aside Cordelia's strange contempt for later examination.

'One more question,' I say.

'I said two.'

'You've seen my dick.'

She grimaces. 'That was hardly a reward.'

Farewell, big boy.

'Go on, if it'll make you leave quicker.'

I grin. 'Why did Eska come to your room?'

She coughs. 'What? When?'

Wasn't expecting that.

'The second night. She entered your cabin around midnight.' I stare her down. 'When everyone accused her, you didn't speak up. You were her alibi.'

Her jaw tightens. 'Eska was a big girl. She could take care of herself.'

'Clearly not.'

She taps her fingers on the arm of her chair. 'If you really must know, we were meeting up for . . . relations.'

'Relations?' I repeat. Then gasp and cover Grasshopper's ears. '*You were having sex?*' I whisper.

She laughs. 'You're adorable, Fish.'

I *knew* everyone was fucking behind my back. Who's next? Have Nergüi and Shinjiro been getting it on?

Tendai adjusts her headwrap. 'I enjoy partaking in anything that makes *them* uncomfortable, and Eska hated them as much as me.'

A love affair based on hate. How heart-warming.

'It was purely physical. Nergüi wound me up at breakfast, so I wanted to have some fun. The Ermine blew me off initially,' she says. 'But I guess she changed her mind. Perhaps she was impressed by how few shits I gave about Eudora dying. As for me . . . you're not the only one who likes strong women, Fish.'

'I'll say,' I scoff. 'I'm amazed you managed to get that close without being stabbed.'

Tendai stares blankly. 'You have *no idea*, do you?'

'What?'

'Eska liked you.'

My arms drop. '*What?* No, she didn't.'

'Maybe "liked" is too strong. But she hated everyone else ten times more. "Can't trust them," she said. Couldn't even trust me, beyond a tumble. "Thank fuck my neighbours are a coward and a fish," she told me. At least with you she knew where she stood. At least with you, you're so dull and transparent, you're not hiding anything.'

The thought of Eska sort-of-maybe complimenting me is so foreign I actually stagger backwards.

She trusted me. That's why she was in my room. I wasn't being framed; Eska came to me for help because I was the only person she thought *would* help. But someone killed her there.

Eska wasn't lulled by a mirage of someone she knew. There would be no reason for her to go to me for help if she thought she was safe, or with someone she trusted. She wasn't safe, and she knew it. I was right – she couldn't use her Blessing.

'Does that answer your question?'

I nod weakly. 'Y-Yeah.'

'Then leave.' She gestures to the door. 'I'm barricading myself in for the rest of the trip. Nobody gets in. Not even you, big boy.'

I'm aware she's saying it to send me into meltdown. But it works, the tease.

*

It takes me ten minutes to summon Wyatt to his door, during which I have approximately five heart attacks. He appears in the gap, looking like total shit. I mean – he's Wyatt, so my heart still leaps at the sight of him. But I can't ignore the greyish tinge to his skin.

'You're taking your medicine, right?'

He trembles against the door. 'I only have to take one vial a—'

'Take ten!'

'It doesn't work like that.'

Grasshopper rushes forward, fists clenched before her. For a moment, I think she's going to punch him. Instead, she opens her hand, revealing a bundle of leaves and herbs.

'They'll make you feel better,' she whispers. 'Momma gave

349

them to me in case I got poorly. But you need them more. When you get sick it makes Dee sad. Then I get sad.'

Wyatt's body wilts. The herbs won't do anything for him; they're a common cure for colds. But his face softens, and he takes them anyway.

Grasshopper nods, satisfied. Then retreats behind my legs.

Wyatt looks at me. 'Is that why you're here?'

The ghost of his smile lingers. It makes me want to feed him soup until he's all better. 'I spoke to Nergüi.'

'Alone?'

'I had Grasshopper.'

If possible, he looks even peakier.

'They're planning something tonight. Something bad. I'm going to lock Grasshopper and me in my room. And . . .' *I want you there* is what I wish I could say, but the words stick. 'You can come too.'

His eyes travel.

'Grasshopper's right, we're stronger together.'

'The swarm!' she agrees.

'Maybe that's why we've survived this long – because we've been a swarm.'

He licks his lips.

'Wyatt?'

He starts, as if suddenly remembering I'm there. 'I have to rest tonight.'

'Rest in my room.' I reach for his hand. 'If something happens—'

He jerks away. 'I-I don't like you seeing—'

'I don't care what you look like!' I say, more angrily than I mean. 'All I care about is that you're safe.'

'I'll be fine.' He doesn't look fine. He looks one strong gust away from tumbling over the side of the ship.

'How long has your lock been broken?' I ask in a small voice.

He freezes. 'Since the third day.'

'Why didn't you tell me?' I squeeze his hand, but it hangs limply. 'Someone broke into your room, Wyatt. They tried to *kill you*.'

'I didn't want to worry you. Besides, I asked my dragon to put in a new one,' he explains quickly. 'But it's one of those ones you pull across, so I can only lock it when I'm inside.'

I had been so shocked by the broken lock I hadn't spotted that when I concocted my ingenious 'belt lock'. 'But—'

'I'll be fine.' He forces a smile. 'I'm stronger than I look.'

Grasshopper shuffles forward. 'Heart-bonded people shouldn't be apart. Your hearts are meant to be together. Or they'll get sad, and break.'

Wyatt's eyes meet mine. My chest aches – my heart fighting to close the distance.

I want to tell him that she's right. That I'm meant to be close to him. That every moment of separation I feel like a fish wrenched out of water. That when I'm near him, everything slots into place as perfectly as the way our fingers lock together. And I can be just *me*. And almost feel as if he would accept me fully. All of me.

Instead, I say nothing. And the moment passes.

'I'll see you tomorrow. Promise,' he says; then he closes the door between us.

*

I lock my cabin door and push the drawers against it. My delicate frame can't quite handle the wardrobe, but I do manage to drag the bed over. I ask Dumpling to bring some food, then hunker down in my bunker.

I hate Bear Province and their fucking strength complex. How they've made that boy feel as though surviving death every day isn't enough. That he has to do something stupid to be worthy. I'd feel a lot better with Wyatt here, in my arms, than alone in his room.

Grasshopper munches her way through a mountain of chocolate and marshmallows, short legs dangling off the bed.

All Tendai's information did is create more questions. Why would Cordelia hate a child? *Only* a child? Why not me? I'm far more hateable.

This whole time Grasshopper has been by my side, and I didn't notice. If Cordelia hated her before this journey began, there must be a reason.

'Grasshopper.' I sit next to her. 'Or would you prefer Yewande?'

'Grasshopper loves Grasshopper because Dee calls me that name!'

'Good.' I pop a marshmallow into my mouth. 'I'm going to ask you some questions, OK?'

'Will you give me sweets?'

I stare at the pile surrounding her.

'More sweets.'

'Deal.' I hold out my hand, and she shakes it, businesslike. Her eyes are already wandering, dreaming of promised delicacies, so I get straight to the point. 'Where did you meet Cordelia before?'

'Haven't met her before ship.'

'You must have. You know Cordelia, right? Golden hair? Tortoise Province?'

'All Tortoises look the same,' she says through a mouthful of chocolate.

She's not wrong. They're all tall, skinny, blonde and beautiful. If you're into that conventional kind of beauty.

'You've met other Tortoises?' As far as I'm aware, their tour of the twelve involves observing Grasshopper Province from a safe distance and fleeing at the first sign of danger, which doesn't take long.

'Boy. Tortoise boy. He gave me presents.'

There's only one person that could be. The only Tortoise who would treat a Grasshopper child kindly – Lysander.

'When did you meet Tortoise boy?'

'When I was five.' She thrusts out her palm, fingers splayed.

'You went to Tortoise Province?'

'Nope! He came to Grasshopper Province.'

Why in the Goddess's blessed name would Lysander go there? Although hadn't Wyatt said something similar? Lysander visited him too.

'He was nice to me, and Momma and sisters and brothers. Shook my hand. "How do you do?"' she mocks in a plummy voice.

'What else happened?'

She lowers the chocolate, staring down at it silently.

'Grasshop—'

With a *pop*, she vanishes.

'Grasshopper?' I call. 'No need to be afraid. It's just you and me.'

She pops back, crouched in a corner. '*That* happened.'

I go to her, brushing the hair from her face and rubbing her trembling limbs. 'What happened? You can tell me.'

She clutches the pendant around her neck. 'Grasshopper go poof.'

What in the hell does that mean?

She pops out of sight again, then returns.

'You disappeared? Your Blessing came?'

She nods mutely.

I always assumed a Blessing emerging would be a celebrated

event – Goddess knows it would be in Fish Province. But Grasshopper's face is drawn and terrified.

Shinjiro said Blessings come when we need them. That means something happened while Lysander was there which meant Grasshopper needed to disappear.

If he hurt her, I'll travel to the afterlife to punch that golden heir.

'What were you hiding from?' I whisper, trying to keep my voice calm. 'Why did you disappear?'

She buries her face in her knees so all I can see is a poof of lilac hair. 'Friends came to visit.'

'Which friends?'

'Friends who gave Grasshopper this!' She thrusts out her pendant.

I study it – the strange material, the care that went into it despite the use of rudimentary tools. Something beautiful from something ugly. Something human from something wild.

I think I know what 'friends' she means.

'Did they have orange hair?'

She nods. I drop the pendant.

Crabs. Crabs are her friends. Good enough friends to make her a gift.

'They come through hole in wall,' she says. 'We give them food.'

'For how long?'

'Since I was born. Momma says humans should help each other. A big swarm is stronger.'

I try not to hug her, or linger on how wonderful Grasshopper Province is. My people hanged the Crabs who asked for help, while Grasshoppers have been secretly feeding them for generations. They would be exiled or killed if ever discovered. But they did it anyway. Because humans should help humans. Regardless of which side of a wall they were born on.

I take Grasshopper's chocolate-smeared hand. 'So, your friends came when Tortoise boy was there?'

'Tortoise and his friends got scared. Got mad.' She swings her arm. 'Used swords.'

'They fought them.'

'Friends fought back. Knives everywhere.'

I can imagine. Lysander and his entourage coming face to face with 'monsters'. It must have been a melee.

'It was really scary,' she whispers. 'I couldn't run away. So I went poof.'

I rub her arms. 'You did good. Clever girl.'

'I should have stayed,' she says, eyes gleaming with tears. 'Because I hid ... Because I hid ...' With a *pop* she's gone again. 'They died.'

'Who?' I ask the emptiness.

'*Lots.*' The word is so haunted I don't ask her any more questions.

That's why Cordelia hates Grasshopper. Because her brother died while visiting her province. And she blames a six-year-old for it.

*

Grasshopper snoozes, curled up on the bed. She eventually drifted off in my lap as I stroked her hair.

I've spent the last hour or so adding everything I've learned to Detective Dee's Diagram of Deduction – notably Nergüi and Tendai's Blessings, and the circumstances of Lysander's death.

I almost have every thread I need to knit it together. And I *must* knit it together. If I survive tonight, I need a name by the time the sun rises.

So I begin at the start:

355

Eudora was killed the first night, during the few seconds when the lights went off. No wounds apart from the rope mark around her neck.

Ravi was killed the second night, seventeen stab wounds. He knew he was going to die. He wrote a death note to Cordelia.

Eska was killed the fifth night. No wounds, apart from the marks inside her palms and her mouth. She came to my room for help because she couldn't use her Blessing.

Jasper was most likely killed on the sixth night. His body was in the greenhouse. No wounds. He also couldn't use his Blessing.

I stare at the red crosses: Eudora, Ravi, Eska, Jasper. Someone also broke into Wyatt and Grasshopper's rooms. There have been attempts on the lives of every lower Blessed, bar me, though I suspect that's imminent.

Someone's hunting us. Someone who can kill without a trace.

Lysander's death must be tied to this somehow. It would explain why someone would hate Grasshopper enough to attempt to take her life. But Cordelia doesn't seem—

My eyes stop at a different portrait.

Cordelia was not the only person to love Lysander.

The angry tiger glares at me.

No. Leofric is Eudora's shield; it makes no sense for him to kill *her*. And I saw his grief in the brig. You can't fake that.

But not in the gym. Not when I mentioned Eudora's name. He didn't even twitch. Would he have reacted if I had uttered Lysander's name instead?

I close my eyes and recall the image which has been haunting me. The way he keeled over, sobbing as if his soul were leaving him.

'Dead . . . because of you!'

My body goes cold. There's a reason that image of grief has stalked me. Something about it never felt quite right, and

I think I know what. I *recognized* that grief. It's the same one I've been battling since I found Ravi's body on the deck.

Duty cannot produce grief like that – not so raw and all-consuming. Only love can. And Leofric only ever loved one person. Lysander.

I clench my hands to stop them shaking.

Something about Jasper's death has niggled me – the location. The greenhouse was such an unusual place for that fiery boy to be. Unless someone drew him out there. Someone Jasper trusted, or *respected*.

After being pinned by the tiger at the dinner party, Jasper had stood in his tattered uniform, utterly awestruck. He had obeyed, without question, Leofric's order to capture me. He would have gone to the greenhouse if Leofric asked. I can't think of anyone else he would have gone there for.

But that still doesn't explain why nobody could use their Blessings, or why they died without wounds. That tiger made such a goddessdamn mess of the dining room it's been out of bounds for days. Hardly invisible. Jasper's ruined uniform can attest to that. I remember Shinjiro helping him up: *'Ah, you see, you're fine. Just a few bruises.'*

But claws and teeth don't bruise, do they? They rip flesh. I felt them myself – the dagger-like pain in my ankle as I tried to crawl away.

I tug up my trouser leg and stare at my perfectly smooth ankle. Not a mark.

Not a mark on her.

Oh fuckballs. I was so distracted swooning over Wyatt I didn't notice how unusual it was that a bloody tiger bite didn't leave a mark.

The book I read said shields' Blessings usually consist of 'physical might, intimidation and, when required, the capacity to dispatch enemies swiftly'.

Could swiftly also mean invisibly? Is *that* what shields do? It would make sense. I'm sure an empress would have hordes of enemies – all the better if their deaths could be passed off as unsuspicious. Especially in an empire which holds unity above all else.

Nergüi had said something like that too: '*I know what you shields do. I'm not the only one who works in the shadows.*'

Blessed hells. The emperors and empresses gave themselves a goddessdamn assassin.

If the Tiger Blessing affects physical objects – like Jasper's clothes – but not organic ones – like human flesh – it could easily kill without leaving a mark. It could even, if needed, break locks. Or tear a room to shreds.

My chest goes tight.

One death doesn't fit the narrative. Why kill Ravi with blades and fury when you have a Tiger who can tear flesh apart invisibly?

One possible reason – if Leofric discovered Ravi's secret, perhaps killing with his Blessing wasn't enough. If he was truly racked with grief over Lysander's death, he'd want the Crab to suffer. To bleed.

I stare at the sketch of the tiger. He loved Lysander, but what's the motive for the murders? I loved Ravi and I didn't go mad with revenge, killing everyone who isn't him. Why *Eudora*? Why the lower provinces? I know he's obsessed with rank, but does he really hate us enough to eradicate us like a plague?

And why oh why did *nobody* use their Blessing?

Footsteps. My head snaps up.

Shuffling outside my room. Then my door handle twists.

I freeze, lungs burning as I hold my breath.

More footsteps. The handle stops.

Then one gasped sound. One word of genuine shock: '*You.*'

The voice vanishes, and the rest of the night is still.

Chapter Twenty-Eight

Day Ten – Feast of the Ermine

Morning

Someone is pounding on my door.

Grasshopper shoots up, but I hold her back.

'Go away!' I yell. 'Or I'll pound . . . you.'

'Why does that sound like a treat?'

'Wyatt?' I drag the furniture away from the door, sweating with sudden exertion, and then open the door a crack. 'Get inside. Nergüi's out to get me.'

I've been thinking about the *'You'* I heard outside my room all night long. It *was* Nergüi's voice.

I think.

'I doubt it.' Wyatt wrings his hands.

'What do you mean?'

'I think you'd better see for yourself,' he mutters.

I tell Grasshopper to stay but it's pointless. We follow Wyatt down the cabin corridor.

'Take medicine?' she demands, tugging his shirt.

'Of course, my lady,' he says with a bow, and then turns to me. 'You barricaded your room well. I'm impressed.'

'Are you OK?' I ask.

'Huh?'

'Your sickness. Last night you went really weird.'

His eyes drift. 'Sorry. I just didn't want you to see me like that.'

I grasp his shoulders. 'Wyatt, you could vomit down me and I'd still think you're the most beautiful thing I've ever seen. Inside and out.'

'Untrue,' he says, ears gleaming pink. 'You own a mirror, right?'

His hair is particularly untidy this morning, as if someone has been making love to him all night, and his shirt is untucked. Maybe there's a little Bear Province wildness in him after all. I don't hate it one bit.

He stops before the deck doors. 'Prepare yourself.'

He opens the doors. And I'm not fine. I'm not fine at all.

Today is the Feast of the Ermine. The sails should be displaying a curious white creature.

Instead, they're stained crimson.

Before us hangs a mess of ropes, knotted and tied together – a great web spreading out across the *Dragon's Dawn*'s wingspan. And in the centre, wrapped up and presented like captured prey, is the Spider themselves.

Nergüi.

My legs go numb. Wyatt clamps his hand over Grasshopper's eyes.

Nergüi said that there was no risk in unveiling their truth to me. Is *this* what they meant? Did they, like Ravi, know they were going to die?

No. Last night someone tried to get into my room. A turn of a handle. That voice, that gasped *'You'*. It was Nergüi. That did not sound like a person at peace with their fate.

Nergüi came to my room. And there is only one reason for

them to do that. It's the same reason they knew there was no risk in telling me their secrets – they *were* planning to kill me.

But they didn't. They didn't get past my door. Because someone was waiting for them.

Perhaps Leofric intercepted them. Took the chance to get another kill. But that doesn't feel right.

I'm sure the shield is responsible for the other deaths: they fit so perfectly with what I know his Blessing is capable of. So how probable is it that Nergüi also happened to be planning to kill me on the same murder cruise?

No. Far more likely would be if somehow Nergüi got involved in Leofric's plot. Nothing happens without the Spider knowing about it, after all. And that might explain why they were arguing in the games room. He wasn't accusing them, they were co-conspirators.

If they were working together, it wouldn't make sense for Leofric to murder Nergüi, especially when they were on their way to get rid of me.

But who else would kill Nergüi? Who would have a reason to slay them at the very moment they came to my door to carry out their bloody plan?

Someone who wanted to stop that plan. Someone who didn't want me to die.

That same someone protected me last night, and *this* is the result.

Nergüi's corpse doesn't look anything like Eska, Jasper or Eudora's. Great ugly gashes mar their body, a ring of dried blood around their throat. They've been brutally attacked.

Just like Ravi.

These two deaths stand apart. They don't fit the narrative. There's only one explanation.

These are not Leofric's kills.

I sink to the floor, grasping the deck. My head pounds the

same words over and over: *Two murderers. Two murderers. Two murderers.*

Wyatt's hand brushes my shoulder. Squeezes.

Nergüi meant to kill me last night. Someone stopped them. Stabbed them. Displayed their body. It's not subtle, it's practically screaming – 'Don't hurt Dee.'

Only one person has protected me on this ship. Facing down Leofric when he was ready to throw me to the dogs. Holding me to his chest when Jasper's flames raged overhead. Refusing to come to my room when I told them a killer was on my trail. The only person I told about Nergüi.

I stare up at Wyatt. His untidy hair. Hastily buttoned shirt.

'Were you outside my room last night?' My voice trembles.

'Is that really the question you want to ask?' His gaze is unnerving, searching mine, willing me to say something else.

His feelings changed so suddenly. After that first night.

'Ask me, Dee.'

I don't want to ask him anything. I don't want to know. Because if he killed Nergüi then he killed someone else too. The two deaths that match.

Ravi.

He hates everyone who isn't you.

Suddenly I don't know the boy clasping my shoulder. A friend? A lover? An enemy who would lay hands on Ravi?

A boy who would do anything to prove his legacy. A boy with a history of obsessions, whose feelings change like the wind.

And yet, even now, something draws me to him. The intensity of his gaze. Magnetic. Like two poles eternally fated to draw together.

'So it's true.'

I don't even notice the deck has filled until Tendai speaks.

She stares up at her archnemesis without a hint of victory. Just acceptance. 'Whoever beat me to it, congratulations.'

Shinjiro grasps Cordelia's arm. She's bone pale and trembling like a leaf – a mirror of when we stumbled upon Ravi.

Leofric stares straight at me, not even trying to hide it. Consideration. Suspicion. His gaze confirms everything. He knows Nergüi came to my room last night to kill me, but instead the Spider is up there. And I'm here.

I push aside Nergüi and Ravi's deaths, and focus on what I do know – Leofric killed at least three people.

I need to accuse him while everyone's here. He'll be outnumbered.

'I have something to say,' I state.

'It'll have to wait.' An orange dragon appears in a blast of glitter. It hovers before Nergüi, checking their bloodied neck for a pulse. 'Mastress Spider is dead.'

'So you should be gone,' Tendai says.

'Servers cease to exist once they complete any outstanding commands,' she says, adjusting her bowtie. 'Mastress Spider had one final order for me to carry out upon their departure.'

'What's that got to do with us?' Leofric grunts.

The dragon rubs her paws together. 'Everything. Please gather in the lounge.'

Chapter Twenty-Nine

Day Ten – Feast of the Ermine

Afternoon

It's midday by the time we assemble in the lounge. We didn't all come willingly, but the other servers wouldn't comply when Tendai attempted to return to her room. Nergüi, as usual, accounted for every possibility.

The seven of us sit cramped around one table.

'We shouldn't be gathered like this,' Tendai grunts. 'Knowing Nergüi, they've set a powder keg to explode to take us all with them.'

Pretty rich coming from her.

Cordelia looks on the brink of projectile vomiting, twisting her hands around the key at her neck. Leofric grips the table, blue veins matching his hair. I clutch Grasshopper – my last raft in a tumultuous sea – while Wyatt sits beside me, his face a mask.

'No need to worry,' Shinjiro says, patting Cordelia's eternally twisting hands. 'Nergüi's likely just wishing us a fond farewell.'

'When have you ever known Nergüi to do *anything* that wasn't for their own benefit?' Tendai hisses.

Silence. The hair on my neck prickles.

Leofric leans across the table and utters a guttural, 'You little shit.' To my surprise, he's not talking to me, but to Wyatt.

Wyatt looks up. 'What's that?'

'My mother warned me about your lot. That Bear Province think themselves worthy to sit with the uppers because they transport some stinking cattle. But I didn't think you foolish enough to—'

His words snap off as Cordelia touches his arm. 'Please, let's not fight.'

Leofric keeps his gaze upon Wyatt, the same way a cat watches a mouse.

Actually – no, it's the opposite – the way a mouse watches a cat. Wary, unblinking, terrified the creature will strike if it looks away. And it's not the first time. It reminds me of when they faced each other in the gymnasium, that small step back.

For some reason, Leofric fears Wyatt.

Nergüi's dragon reappears. 'Now you are gathered, I can fulfil my mastress's last command.' Her voice is candyfloss sweet. 'Upon their death I am to recount these words.' She clears her throat. When she speaks again, it's with Nergüi's chillingly calm tones: '*It appears one of you has killed me. Congratulations. You have outfoxed me. Or, more likely, overpowered me.*'

If it was Wyatt, he doesn't appear ruffled. His face is agonizingly blank, even with Leofric's smoulder burning holes into him.

'*I have garnered a reputation. Some of it is unwarranted, but most isn't. I have spies. And I have secrets. More secrets than you could imagine. The things I know about every one of you would turn your hair white.*'

Bit late for me.

'*They* will *turn your hair white.*'

Shinjiro places his teacup down with a soft clink.

'*I present you with a choice — spill your blood here today, or I will spill your secrets. The things you think nobody knows. You're wrong. I know them. Choose.*'

I clutch my seat.

The secret nobody knows.

Yesterday, Nergüi pleaded with me to reveal my truth. They tore down their walls and assumed I would do the same. Then when I did not — '*You will regret it.*'

If I had stripped away my mask like they did, I suspect this threat would not apply to me.

I could have escaped it. Nergüi gave me a chance. But I was a coward.

'You can't do this!' Leofric reaches out his arm. In a flash, the tiger leaps across the room, lunging for Nergüi's dragon. But when the beast lands, the dragon has vanished.

Leofric stands unmoving — arms still at his sides, eyes empty.

I know that stance. I recognized it in the brig when he used his Blessing. I've seen those heavy arms before, at the opening party after the lights went out.

The dragon bursts back into existence, paws planted on hips. 'Oooh! That's *very* naughty! We're under the emperor's protection — striking us is like attacking the Dragon himself!'

The tiger leaps again. The orange dragon disappears, then reappears above our heads. 'It won't work. Now stop being so silly!'

The tiger slinks back to Leofric. He slumps forward as the ink bleeds up his arms.

'Y-You can't harm us,' Cordelia says. 'Dragons are forbidden from harming a passenger.'

'I'm not harming you! *You* are harming you. I'm just giving you a choice. You don't *have* to choose the grisly option,' the dragon says gleefully. '*Buuuut* if you don't spill your blood, I will spill your darkest secret. One each. The worst one.'

Oh fuck.

A hand upon mine. Wyatt's kind eyes. 'Slow your breathing. You're going to have a panic attack.'

'I . . . can't . . .'

He smiles sweetly. He has no idea what I am. A fake. A disappointment from the day I was born. I've been lying to him every single day. I'm not worthy to be here; Nergüi knew that.

'*You don't count, Yewande,*' Nergüi's voice says. '*I won't lower myself to harming a child.*'

Tendai snorts. 'Apart from when you set an assassin on me, aged seven.'

The table has fallen eerily silent. Leofric looks as if he may tear a chunk out of it. Cordelia's body has wilted. Shinjiro's teacup sits untouched.

Tendai, however, leans back, smiling broadly. 'I don't have a damn thing to hide. It's why Nergüi hates me so much. They don't have any secrets they can use against me.' She turns to the dragon. 'Do your worst.'

Nergüi's mocking smile on the dragon looks bizarre. 'In due course. Anyone else?'

'I'll bleed,' Shinjiro says simply.

'Got something to hide, Monk?' Tendai raises an eyebrow.

'Acute observation. How much blood is necessary?'

The dragon unveils a chalice, placing it before Shinjiro. '*Everyone who wishes to keep their secrets must fill this cup with some of their blood until it's full to the brim. You can work together for once in your lives. The more who bleed, the less you bleed. Isn't that harmonious?*'

367

Shinjiro glances around the table. 'Does anyone have a blade?'

Leofric produces one from Goddess knows where.

Shinjiro takes it, then draws back his sleeve, Bancha peering over his shoulder.

'Ahem!' The dragon somersaults before Shinjiro. 'My mastress was very specific with their conditions.'

The blade stills.

'You must *entirely* remove a finger.'

Cordelia releases a tiny wail.

Leofric leaps to his feet. 'They're a lunatic.'

'I told you – Nergüi was *murdered*. They're not going to let that go easily,' Tendai says, checking her nails.

Shinjiro clears his throat. 'I-I can heal us. We just need to . . . do it and then I'll—'

'I'm not cutting off a *fucking finger*,' Leofric snarls.

'Then let her reveal your secret,' I say. 'You have nothing to hide, right, noble shield?'

Nergüi had threatened him with this secret once already, in the brig. They said he would do anything to stop it getting out. If they're both involved in the murders, it all makes sense.

His gaze pins me, but I hold it. Then he places his palm flat on the table. 'Give me the knife.'

Shinjiro hands it over, pushing the chalice to him. 'Careful. If you cut where the base—'

Leofric slams down the knife, severing his middle finger. The dull *thump* sends a shudder through me. He throws back his head, neck muscles pulsing as the blood dribbles into the chalice.

'That's enough,' Shinjiro says. 'Give me your hand.'

A poof of glitter drowns them both. The dragon hangs upside down. 'Awfully sorry – did I not mention? The monk is *not* to use his healing. No no no!'

368

Leofric grits his teeth, slamming his fist against the table.

'He's in pain. I'm using it.' Shinjiro places his hand over Leofric's.

'If you do, *all* secrets will be told.'

Shinjiro freezes. 'I—'

'Don't.' Leofric snatches his hand away, cradling it to his chest. No wonder – I know what secret he's bleeding to protect.

'I'll heal it after,' Shinjiro says quickly. 'Once the dragon's gone they can't—'

'Then hurry up!' Leofric snarls.

Shinjiro takes the knife and places his hand on the table. Bancha curls her tail around his neck as he mutters beneath his breath. The anxious lines fade from his face. His chest rises and falls, slow and measured.

The knife flashes.

He cuts off his finger, as easily as slicing a carrot. You wouldn't know he's in pain if not for the sweat on his brow, the slight shake as he hovers his hand above the chalice.

I want what's in that tea.

'M-Me next,' Cordelia says.

'You have nothing to hide,' Shinjiro says, his breath hitching. 'Remember? Through prayer the Goddess will—'

'Give me the knife,' she whispers.

Cordelia isn't as calm as Shinjiro, or as rash as Leofric. She hovers the knife above her hand for what feels like an eternity. Eventually, she draws away.

'I-I-I can't . . .'

'Put your hand back.' Leofric takes the knife.

She nods wordlessly. But it takes another minute for her to follow his command, as if she's fighting every instinct.

'Look away,' Leofric says.

She whimpers, closing her eyes.

The knife plunges down. Cordelia sinks to the floor with a screech, writhing in pain.

Leofric goes to her, drenched in blood himself. He wrestles her hand to the chalice long enough to add a drop, then presses it to her chest. All that pretty lace stained red.

'Put pressure on it. It'll slow the bleeding.' Leofric slams the chalice before me, followed by the blade. 'Make your choice. And do it quick.'

The crimson liquid sits at the bottom of the cup, barely half full. The base is smeared with blood.

I already know I'm going to do it. I knew the moment my secret was held ransom. Nergüi didn't know everything about me after all. I would have cut off the whole hand.

Grasshopper wriggles. 'No.'

'It's OK.' I scoot her off my lap. 'Close your eyes.'

I place my palm against the table, then seize the blade.

'Wait.' Wyatt's hand closes around my wrist. 'Don't.'

'I have to.'

He twists my wrist. 'Whatever this secret is, it's not worth your pain to keep it.'

But it *is* my pain. This pain will be nothing compared to shouldering that secret for the last decade. Feeling it burn in every smile I give him. Feeling it sharpen beneath my skin when we kiss.

If it comes out, he'll abandon me. He'll know I'm only worth abandoning. Like Ravi.

I don't care if Wyatt killed Nergüi. I don't even care if he killed Ravi. Whatever he's done, I know it was to protect me. Because my heart calls out to his. And if he learns my truth, I might as well carve into my chest now and be free of it.

'You'll hate me,' I whisper, tears in my eyes.

His fingers close around mine. That perfect fit. 'There's

nothing that could stop me adoring you. You're the strongest person I know.'

My breath catches. The entire room is silent, bar Cordelia's whimpering. All eyes are upon us, and he doesn't care, his gaze is for me. Only me.

But he's wrong. I'm weak.

'I'm sorry.' I tear my wrist from his grasp, then carve the blade through my little finger.

I drop the knife as pain lances through my hand, but it's preferable to facing the hurt on Wyatt's face. I lean into it, a bodily distraction from the agony burning my soul. I hold my hand over the chalice. A single drop of blood falls, then the cup is torn away. Wyatt holds his own bloodied hand over it, the blade gripped in his other.

'Wyatt, you—'

'I will not watch you bleed.'

I bite back a sob, doubling over as pain courses through my body. Not from my hand. From this boy – this wonderful boy I do not deserve, who would bleed for me even though I just threw his faith back into his face.

I know Wyatt is accustomed to pain, but I expect him to show *something* of it as blood pumps from his open wound. But he doesn't even wince. He courts pain the way he courts death.

Grasshopper cradles my weeping hand. 'Does it hurt?'

'It's fine, don't worry.' I try very hard not to cry.

'Done.' Wyatt pushes the cup forward. The blood spills over the sides.

'Hurry!' Leofric snaps, kneeling over Cordelia.

As the dragon seizes the chalice, Wyatt whips off his shirt. He takes my throbbing hand and wraps it around the wound. He would give me the shirt off his back, bleed for me, and I still couldn't give him my final piece.

I fall into his shoulder, sobbing.

I'm nothing. Worse than nothing.

'Congratulations!' Party streamers explode overhead. 'You have filled the chalice with the necessary blood!' The dragon thrusts the cup high, then upends the gruesome contents over Tendai.

'*This is the blood of my people,*' Nergüi's voice rages. '*You flung my province into poverty. We died in our thousands. This blood is on your hands.*'

Tendai gasps, blood streaming into her eyes. 'Bullshit. I closed the Funnel to a monster. I didn't kill them. *You did.*'

The dragon gives a polite round of applause, and then continues: '*We are not so dissimilar, sister.*'

Tendai shudders, hastily scrubbing the blood from her face with her headwrap. No matter how she spins it she can't deny the truth – Nergüi got the last word. After all, there's no Spider left to argue with. All she has now is a legacy of death.

'Now!' the dragon says excitedly. 'Shall we get to the secrets?'

'You promised,' Leofric snaps. 'You said if we bleed—'

'*I imagine you are currently angry at me for breaking a vow. I imagine the Tiger is waving those big arms of his, as if he can beat a ghost into submission.*' Nergüi's voice says. '*Did you honestly expect me to keep to my word? Me? The Spider? One of you killed me. I'm telling all of your secrets.*'

Leofric's roars echo around the room. Nobody else moves.

'Here's a fun fact!' The dragon somersaults through the air. 'If you hadn't added your blood your secret would have been kept. There's no fun telling secrets people are happy to get out!'

A final fuck you from the master of shadows. Nergüi *did* know me. They knew I would bleed to keep that secret. They gave me two chances, and I blew both.

Terror writhes through my body. White-hot panic. Wyatt's arm tightens around me.

'Who first?' The dragon taps her chin. 'Eeny . . . meeny . . . miny . . . monk!'

Shinjiro's eyes flicker open.

Nergüi speaks from beyond the grave: '*This monk is the bastion of the Goddess. Her voice on earth. For all these years he has spouted her creed of balance and togetherness. It is the doctrine he preaches and the lie our nation was built upon. But her words should turn to ashes in his mouth.*'

Shinjiro's eyes turn down. He knows what's coming, just as I do.

'*This man of faith sent an assassin to kill me when I was ten years old.*'

Leofric's head snaps to him.

'*He nearly succeeded. I was found bleeding out on my bedroom floor. After that, I knew . . .*' Nergüi's voice uncharacteristically cracks. '*I knew Concordia's message of harmony was a lie. The voice of the Goddess was supposed to protect us all. But in striking me, a Blessed, he also chose to strike the Goddess.*'

No way. No fucking way. His Blessing is to heal. His *soul* wants to heal. Nergüi must be lying.

But it fits. If Shinjiro did this, and Wyatt found out, it would explain why he doesn't want to be near him. Why he's terrified of him. It would make you question everything you believed about him.

'You said Concordia needs twelve balances,' I breathe, nestled against Wyatt. 'Twelve Blessed.'

Shinjiro's face hardens. 'The Spider who tried to kill the emperor was a whispered curse. I thought by eradicating their bloodline, it would root out the discord.'

'Y-You punished my province for Lysander.' Cordelia is trembling. 'But you . . . you tried to kill a Blessed deliberately?'

'I was young and foolish.' His voice rises, losing all semblance of calm. 'I thought that one death – just one – might ensure a hundred years of peace.'

'If only you'd been successful,' Tendai says.

My head pounds. This goes against everything Shinjiro preached. Worse, I suspect it pushed Nergüi deeper into the shadows. How could they trust *anyone* after that? 'What did Nergüi do to you?'

Silence.

'They were a lone child. Their province was dying. What did they do to deserve this?'

His pink hair masks his face. 'Nothing.'

If anyone finds out, he'll be stripped of his title. Monks don't take kindly to *any* murder, let alone an attempted murder of a Blessed by the leader of the Church. The scandal would destroy them.

'Cordeliaaaa.' The dragon flits around her in quick circles. She's still crouched on the floor, shuddering over the mess of her hand. '*You have not been Blessed long, but secrets have a way of finding me.*'

Cordelia's uninjured hand clasps around the key.

'*Lysander is dead because of her.*'

The words shatter her. Cordelia curls inwards, like parchment tossed on fire. She wails, that same terrible noise as Leofric. The sound of a soul torn from a body.

'*She accompanied him to Grasshopper Province – hidden with the entourage, following her beloved brother like a shadow. But when the Crabs attacked, she froze – immobilized by terror.*' When the dragon speaks again, it is in Lysander's voice, his deep panicked words: '*Run, Cordelia! Run!*'

Cordelia presses her hands to her ears. 'No no no.'

The voice grows louder, until it's booming from every direction. '*Run, Cordelia! Run!*'

'Stop it!' Leofric yells. 'Stop using his voice.'

'*But you didn't run, did you? You never could do anything without him. So he had to protect you. It cost him everything.*'

Cordelia rocks, thin arms wrapped around her head.

'*When they found his body, it was draped over her. How long did it take to wash off his blood?*'

Cordelia doesn't sob now. She doesn't even scream. She's utterly silent.

'*If she had acted, he would be here with us. It's her fault.*'

I try to comprehend that – to combine my grief with guilt. I can't. The agony is too much. It's not possible for one person to bear it. No wonder she chased his ghost. No wonder she played his song. No wonder she locked herself in the realities before he got his Blessing, when he was still hers.

'We can pray for forgiveness.' Shinjiro speaks softly. 'I have prayed for mine.'

Cordelia's arms drop. She sits like a broken doll – pretty dress smeared with blood, golden hair hanging limply. 'I do not seek forgiveness.'

'Your turn, cowboy.' Nergüi's dragon spins backwards.

Wyatt tenses; he reaches to fiddle with shirt cuffs that aren't there.

I squeeze his leg.

'*We all know our little dying boy had eyes for the empress,*' Nergüi says. '*But nobody knows the extent of it. His family have been planning the match since his Blessing showed. His brothers blackmailed members of the senate for over a decade. When that didn't work, they used more violent means of persuasion. Wyatt himself sent over five hundred correspondences to her, within which he proposed thirty-two times.*'

'You little worm.' Leofric rises unsteadily. 'You could have killed every member of the senate, and she still wouldn't have married *you*. A bear can never be a dragon.'

My hand hasn't left his knee. I couldn't give one solitary shit about what his family pressured him to do, or who he *thought* he loved. None of that is his fault. I know who he really is.

Wyatt's shoulders relax. As if a stupid secret like that could ever stop me loving him.

The dragon darts away, trailing orange glitter until it stops before Leofric. He's drenched with blood, his own and Cordelia's.

'When the shield took his vow to serve the empress, he swore her his heart,' Nergüi says. *'Show them.'*

Leofric's arms move stiffly, pulling back his shirt to reveal that 'X' mapped across his heart. The one he killed a defence-less Crab to earn.

'A shield's loyalty to the empress is above all others.'

His arms drop. 'Don't. I will tear you apart.'

'You already tried that!' The dragon blows a raspberry.

I hold my breath. I don't need to unveil him. Nergüi will do it for me.

'He lied. He couldn't swear her his heart – it belonged to another.'

Leofric swings for the dragon. 'Lies!'

It reappears at his shoulder. *'How soon after you met Lysander did you fall in love with him? Did you rage alone, racked with guilt about the feelings you weren't allowed to have?'*

Leofric goes still. 'I didn't . . .'

He can't do it. He can't say he didn't love him. His mouth won't form the words.

'I found them together once. Naked and writhing. The shield was clinging to him like a child. Like nobody had ever held him.'

Leofric drops like a stone. His knees thud against the ground.

'How can you wear that collar, when you know you cannot swear yourself to her?'

I push away from Wyatt. '*That's* his secret? Please. As if we didn't already know that.'

'What?' Leofric snarls.

'You eye-fucked him for ten years. It doesn't take a genius.'

His mouth opens and closes. Even Cordelia doesn't look surprised.

Bugger this. Leofric may be more ashamed of love than murder, but I'm not letting him get away that easily.

I raise my voice. 'That's not the secret about Leofric that everyone should hear.'

'Ganymedes,' the dragon says.

My throat closes around the words. My name hangs above my head like a swinging blade. Or an empress from a chandelier.

Maybe Nergüi didn't know. Maybe it's something else. Like that time I consumed my weight in cheese. Or anything. Anything else.

But I know Nergüi saw me completely. I have always known.

Wyatt's fingers brush mine. I push them away. I can't feel his hand leaving mine when the dragon unveils me. That will destroy me.

'*He has been hiding this secret for a long time.*'

The silence between their sentences has a taste, a salty tang in the back of my throat. It tastes like the sea.

'*Ganymedes lied to every one of you. He even lied to the emperor.*'

I need to move. Get out of here. But I'm more still than I've ever been in my life. A prisoner in this body.

'*He lied to hide his father's bastards. He doesn't have a Blessing. He's not Blessed. He's nothing.*'

Nothing.

Nothing.

The dragon vanishes in a rain of glitter.

Every eye is upon me. Cordelia's pink mouth is ajar, an unspoken 'What?' lingering on her lips. Shinjiro's face falls, horror widening his eyes. Tendai leans forward, as if seeing me for the first time. Leofric lurches to his feet.

But I would rather watch their appalled faces all day than take one look at the boy beside me.

'I knew it.' Leofric is shaking, trembling with pure outrage. The force of it surprises even me. 'I knew there was something *wrong* with him. He's not one of us. He's *never* been one of us. He doesn't belong here. He's worthless.'

And nobody speaks up against him.

All the strange calm that stilled my body seeps out like water. I stagger back, my chair slamming against the floor.

He doesn't belong here.

Of no value.

For the first time in my life, I can't find a single wall to hide behind.

Then I'm running. I reach the door, fling it open and leap into the dying sun.

My vision blurs. I follow my feet through winding corridors, clinging to walls, dragging myself away. Always away.

Footsteps behind me. Someone screaming my name.

'Dee!' A small hand tugs mine. Grasshopper. 'You're hurt.'

'Let go!' No matter how hard I shake she won't release her grip. I'm so weak, I can't even fight off a child.

I stumble on. Cold wind tears at my skin as I emerge on to the deck. The ship is close enough to see the mountain now, thrusting out of the ocean like a blade of ice.

'Dee.' Another hand around my wrist. The strength of his pull makes me stagger to a stop.

'Get off me.' I won't look at him. I can't.

Wyatt's grip tightens. 'Stop running.'

'I can run if I want to.'

378

'Then I'm running with you.'

He's stupid. So stupid. 'Didn't you hear what Nergüi said? I'm not Blessed. I've lied to you every single day.'

'No, you haven't.'

What the hell is he talking about? 'Leave me alone, Wyatt.'

'Never.'

His words don't give me the comfort I expected. They bounce straight off me.

'I will never lea—'

I spin around, seizing his shoulders. 'Why? Why do you care so much? Why did you . . .' *Kill for me?*

He takes my bloodied hand, pressing it to his heart. That steady *ba-dum ba-dum ba-dum.* 'Because our hearts are bound.'

A sob racks my body. 'I don't deserve—'

'You deserve everything. You saw me, and you embraced me. *All* of me, when nobody else did.'

'But I don't have a Blessing.'

His hand closes around mine. 'You don't need a Blessing to be a miracle.'

My head shoots up. 'What did you just say?'

'You heard what I said.' His eyes meet mine.

He's cruel. Cruel for messing with me like this. 'I . . . I can't . . .' I struggle against his grip. Impossibly strong for a dying boy. A dying boy who should be breathless after chasing me. A dying boy who doesn't take his medicine and still lives. A dying boy who loathes me one day then loves me the next. 'Leave me alone.'

'I will never—'

'Leave me!' I free my wrist and run, not looking back. Not once.

When I fall against my door, Grasshopper is still with me, clutching my uninjured hand. 'Let go.'

She stares, eyes wide. 'Why?'

379

'Don't you get it?' I sink against the door, blood weeping from the sodden mess of Wyatt's shirt. 'I've lied to you. Pretended to be something I'm not. You're Blessed. You're special. I'm *nothing*.'

'Not nothing.' She places her hand over my heart. 'Dee.'

My legs weaken. I want to wrap my arms around her, hold her to my chest. So soft and warm. Loving anyone, regardless of who they are or where they come from.

Then I realize what this is: childish ignorance. And I am poison to her.

'Let go of me.'

'No.' She digs her fingers in. 'Swarm!'

'Grasshopper!' I prise them open.

'No!'

'Let go!'

'Swarm!'

'We are NOT a swarm!' I shove her.

She crashes to the floor with a dull thud.

I stare down at my hand. The cruel shape of my arm.

This is what I am. Not a miracle. A man who would push a child.

I unlock my door and stagger inside before she has a chance to follow. Then, for the first time since I boarded this ship, I am truly alone.

Chapter Thirty

Day Ten – Feast of the Ermine

Night

Grasshopper's still screaming my name. She claws at the door, slamming her tiny fists. It sounds like a siren. Like all my lies coming home to roost.

I dip my head beneath the water, but I can still hear her muffled squeals. I surface and stare at the bathroom ceiling. I asked Dumpling to return the sea to my walls, but it doesn't whisper to me the same way the real ocean does.

I have no experience filling baths so it's slightly too hot, making my skin feel raw and tingly. The blood from my finger has turned the water rusty brown. I'm still wearing my fakinium scales. I hoped they would drag me down and do all the hard work for me. No such luck – the bath is only a foot and a half deep.

Still enough to drown in.

I shift and the water spills over the side. Someone will have to clean that, or it'll ruin the floor. Dumpling won't be able to, of course. Dragons' fates are tied to their masters'.

The first time, I didn't realize I wanted to die until I was halfway through doing it. Until the nothingness welcomed me like a mother.

But then Ravi saved me, and I had someone to live for.

I was never scared of dying. I was scared I'd upset him. Scared I'd break a promise. I think that night we exchanged secrets in a cave on a cliff in a storm was the last time I was truly happy.

I push the memory away. It's not comforting any more. I've turned it over and over so many times I've sharpened the edge of it. All it does now is cut me.

Grasshopper screeches my name.

The water laps my chest. A spike of heat.

Soon everyone in Concordia will know my father lied. They'll find out about his bastards, and Fish Province will be exiled outside the Bandage, like the Crabs we hanged. I know those men and women – the little houses they've passed down generations. The routines they repeat day after day.

They will not survive the wasteland.

And I can't help them. I did this to them. If I were better, stronger, smarter, I would've carried this lie to my death.

I see that version of myself sometimes – that glimmering heir. Effortlessly fitting in with them. Nobody questions him. Nobody sees his *lack*.

But I will never be him.

Furious fists pound my door. My name rings out.

As I shift, more water floods over the sides. Ugh. The floor.

I close my eyes. 'Dumpling.'

'Master Fish?'

'Can you write a letter?'

'Of course.' The sound of paper crinkling. 'What should I write?'

'Write . . . "To whoever finds this, please mop the floor."'

'Is that all?'

I breathe deeply. 'That's all.' Glitter rain falls upon my face.

That's that then. All that matters now is this moment. This bathtub. This water.

All I have to do is die. Even a pissfish can manage that.

I push myself beneath the surface.

I didn't expect my body to kick or fuss or panic. But it's surprising how easy it is to release my bubble of breath. How eager I am, like devouring a food from childhood I've been desperate to taste again.

Beneath the surface, the great nothingness beckons. It's where I belong. The only place I belong.

A distant burning in my chest. My heart thumping furiously. *Ba-dum. Ba-dum.*

There's something *off* about those heartbeats.

Ba-dum. Ba-dum.

Something is . . . missing.

Ba-dum. Ba-dum.

Grasshopper.

She's stopped screaming my name. She would *never* stop screaming my name.

Ba-dum. Ba-dum.

Someone will help her. Someone else will.

But where was this 'someone' at the party when I stopped her tears? Where were they when she was in chains? Where were they when all she needed was one person to be kind?

I'm that someone. I'm the only someone.

I surface, spluttering for breath.

'Grasshopper?' I climb out of the bath, dripping wet. 'Grasshopper!' I fling open the bathroom door. The cabin is pitch black. How long was I in there? How long was she screaming while I did nothing?

I scramble with the key, drop it, and then grasp blindly in the dark. Finally, I find it and thrust it in the lock.

Please be outside. Please, Goddess, be outside.

She's not outside. 'Grasshopper? Are you there?'

Silence. No pops. No suddenly appearing lilac-haired girls, berating me for leaving the swarm. Just silence, and the howling night.

Terror roots me to the floor. The nothingness of the bath calls to me like a siren song.

It would be easy. Far easier.

I dash into the night. She *has* to be alive. She knows danger like nobody else. She would have run.

But where would she flee if someone was chasing her – if not to me?

I skid to a stop before a door, pounding my fists against it. 'Wyatt!' The door creaks open, revealing an empty room.

Broken lock. Not here.

I breathe heavily, pacing back and forth.

Think, Dee. If she was being chased, where would she run?

Somewhere she feels safe.

Where the hell's that? She's witnessed every awful murder with me. Nowhere is safe. Even the bloody greenhouse had a corpse in it.

An image stirs – Grasshopper shrieking with laughter as I held her above my head. The engine room. She was safe there. So was I.

I sprint down the stairs, falling down the last two. I race past the bathhouse, then descend into the pit of the ship, soaked with bathwater and sweat.

After wandering the silent ship, the noise of the engine room is an assault on my ears. I dart around the whirring machinery, retracing my steps until I find the open space we spent that one precious night.

It's completely empty. Long shadows twist over the bare walls.

'Grasshopper?' My voice echoes back to me. *Grasshopper.*
Grasshopper.

The engines whirr. I will go back to the bath, straight back, if Leofric's killed her.

A ragged breath.

'Grasshopper?'

Shuffling.

'It's me, Dee.' I step forward hesitantly. 'You need to appear for me, OK?'

I swipe at the empty space, but my hand passes through it.

She was screaming for help and you didn't come. She's probably goddessdamn terrified.

'I know I left you,' I whisper, eyes brimming with tears. 'I'm sorry, I'll never leave you again. You were right all along. We *are* a swarm.'

Pop.

I swing around.

A tiny, slumped form on the ground. Skinny arms flung over her head.

'Grasshopper.' I fall to my knees beside her, pulling her arms away.

My stomach lurches.

She's drenched with blood. *Drenched.* It runs down her face in crimson torrents. I can't even tell what's wrong with her, just that something is very, very wrong. I squeeze out as much water as I can from my jacket on to her face. It washes away enough for me to see.

Where there once was a wide, curious eye, there is only a ragged red hole.

My legs go numb.

She groans. 'Said you wouldn't leave.'

Relief rushes through me. 'I won't. I promise – *never again.*'

'It hurts.' She clings to me, little fists clutching my back, then her arms go limp.

I stagger to my feet, cradling her body to my chest. She's too big. I'm too weak. Don't care.

I force my legs to move. I climb the stairs two at a time, her head rocking against my shoulder. The ship seems to sway around us. Every step takes longer than the last.

Finally, I emerge at the cabins, weaving through the corridors like a drunk man. Shinjiro. Shinjiro will heal her.

I thump my aching foot against his door. Once. Twice. Thrice.

He does not come.

Shit. Where is everyone?

I sink to the floor, cradling her to me. I could sleep here. Just for a little while.

Move, Dee. If you don't, she'll bleed out and die.

A blade of white light hits my feet.

'Sunrise,' I whisper.

I know where Shinjiro is.

The corridor lurches as I rise. I fall into the wall, use it to guide me towards the deck. Why is everything moving so strangely? Why is my body so useless?

The wind outside hits me in an icy blast.

Oh, that's right. I cut off a finger. Blood loss.

I focus on putting one foot before the other. One foot. Another. One foot. Another.

Somehow, I'm at the shrine. I stagger across the pretty stone tiles, leaving a grisly crimson trail.

'Shinjiro,' I rasp in a voice that isn't mine. 'Shinjiro.'

The blood is at my feet again. I've turned around somehow.

Get it together, Dee. You need to go into the shrine, not out of it.

I look up. I haven't turned around at all. The trail is coming *from* the shrine. It leads to a slumped figure, white robes marred with a stream of red.

If I wasn't delirious from blood loss maybe I'd find the scene poetic, or eerily beautiful.

But I'm not in the mood for metaphors.

He's dead. That's all there is to it.

Chapter Thirty-One

Day Eleven – Feast of the Grasshopper

Morning

His name repeats on my lips. A delay in my body understanding what my mind already knows.

Grasshopper moans in my arms.

I can't help Shinjiro now. She still has a chance.

I flee from the shrine as though the killer is at my heels. He may well be.

On the deck, the mountain looms ever closer. The wind tugs at my sopping wet clothes. I skid into the cabin corridor.

I can't fix this girl, I need help.

Wyatt's gone, Goddess knows where. That leaves two choices: Tendai or Cordelia.

I know Cordelia isn't Grasshopper's biggest fan, but I don't think she's cruel enough to ignore a child bleeding to death. Tendai probably won't even open her door. She won't help unless I promise something in return. And I don't have time to waste.

I take a left, Grasshopper's slight frame growing heavy in

my arms. I stop outside Cordelia's cabin. But when I go to call her name, it lodges in my throat.

A niggling feeling. Something on the edge of my mind. Like trying to remember a forgotten song lyric.

Something about Shinjiro felt *off.* If I went back, I think I'd know what.

I shift Grasshopper to my other shoulder.

What was he even doing at the shrine? He's been locking himself in his room since that heated conversation with Nergüi on the eighth day. Cordelia told me herself – he was too scared to go to the shrine.

'But he said he'd make an exception for me.'

My heart stills.

If Cordelia asked, he would have gone with her to pray. He's been appealing to her since the voyage began.

I back away from her door.

Grasshopper moans weakly.

Tendai. Tendai first. Then I can unravel this mess.

I slam my body into her door. 'Tendai!'

Silence.

'Tendai!'

Her muffled voice speaks from behind the door. 'Boy, it is six a.m. Have you lost your mind?'

'It's Grasshopper,' I breathe heavily. 'She's hurt.'

'Not my concern.'

'Tendai!' I bash my foot against the door. 'She's going to die unless you open this damn door! For once in your life do something for someone else. Prove you're not Nergüi.'

That does it. The door opens and something hard presses against my stomach. A curved blade. 'Is that a fucking scimitar?'

Tendai nods. 'Murderer, remember?' Her face darkens as she notices Grasshopper. 'Inside, quickly.'

I dash in. She locks the door behind me.

'On the bed.'

I lay my precious bundle atop the sheets.

Tendai wheels over, pushing me aside. She checks Grasshopper's body, examining the wound. 'How in the name of the Goddess did this happen? Weren't you watching her?'

'I left her,' I whisper with such self-loathing Tendai doesn't need to add anything.

'The monk's dead then?'

I nod wordlessly.

'I knew something was going to go down after Nergüi's little show. The negative emotions were so rampant I could practically taste them.' She gestures vaguely. 'Bottom drawer. Medical pack.'

'Why'd you bring this?' I ask as I retrieve it.

'Spoken like a man not important enough to dodge assassinations.' She snatches it from me, then begins work. She uncorks a bottle and gently tips the liquid over the ragged mess of Grasshopper's eye; then she dabs it with a translucent ointment. Her hands move quickly, as if she's patched a million wounds. 'Had to learn to do this on my own. No doctors I could trust.' She lifts Grasshopper's head, wrapping a bandage around it.

The child winces. I take her hand. 'It'll be OK. You'll be OK.'

Tendai pushes away from the bed. 'Maybe. You're lucky you found her when you did. She'll need stitches. And rest.'

The relief almost sends me to the floor, but I know I won't have the energy to stand again. And there are things I must do.

'Can you keep her here?'

She glances at her door. 'I don't want anyone breaking in here to finish the job.'

'I need to check Shinjiro's body.' I need to work out what felt so *off* about it.

'You're going back out there?' She grabs my wrist. 'Are you dumb as well as stupid, cloud-head?'

'I have to.'

She releases a long breath. 'I know murderous intent when I feel it. If you go out there, you're going to die. Tomorrow we reach the mountain. Any idiot can see this is building to something – all of us dead probably.'

I clench my jaw. 'If I don't go, then we'll all die anyway. At least this way there's a chance.'

She studies me in that searching way. 'Oh hells.' Her hand slips away. 'It seems I was wrong – not *all* good people are dull.'

*

The shrine is almost exactly how I left it. The trail of blood, drying reddish-brown against the white stones. The only difference is the bunnerfly nuzzling Shinjiro's face.

I move slowly. My hand is starting to hurt – a distant throbbing pain. 'Bancha.' As I reach for her, she starts and flutters away.

I should chase her, but I don't have time.

I kneel before Shinjiro's body. There are no signs of a struggle, apart from the bells scattered at his feet. It's as though he was propped up against the scales by his killer.

I can't find any visible marks, despite the bloody trail. But then I lift his hand, pressed against the side of his stomach. A single wound leaks blood. A deep puncture – probably from a knife.

I clutch my knees. Leofric didn't do this, not with a shadow tiger that leaves no marks. Shinjiro bled out. A man who can heal with a touch bled to death.

I'd assume he was knocked out, but his hand was pressed right against that wound. He was trying to heal it, but he couldn't. Just like Jasper and Eska – Shinjiro couldn't use his Blessing.

And the final piece slots into place.

The bodies confounded me because their deaths made no sense. Most with no marks *and* the victims unable to use their Blessings.

But I was wrong to look at those two features together.

Two peculiar signatures – two Blessings.

Shinjiro said a Blessing is something immensely personal, the Goddess interacting with your soul. Cordelia had been coy about it, but Nergüi was right – she *is* emotional, and there were times her emotions overcame her. Notably, when she spoke about her brother. How, when he got his Blessing, he wasn't just *hers* any more. How she deliberately avoided learning about Blessings as a result.

The Blessing stole Lysander from her before his death did. No wonder *her* Blessing is to take them away.

I slump forward, pressing my palms against the ground. The two have been working together – Leofric unleashing his invisible destruction, and Cordelia ensuring they couldn't fight back. The perfect team. The perfect murders.

Why didn't I see it before? Leofric left Eudora's side the first night to comfort Cordelia. A shield *never* leaves their empress. Not for anything. They were each other's alibis the night of Eska's death. Nobody else can account for their movements.

Leofric saved her from Jasper's fire before I could get to my feet. He cut her finger off when she struggled. And that intimate way he held her when she was bleeding. They tried to hide it, that bond, but occasionally their walls slipped.

And I know what unites them.

'As usual, you are where you're not supposed to be,' a deep voice says.

I turn slowly. He stands at the entrance, all six feet seven of him. As Leofric's gaze meets mine, the respectable shield vanishes, and the monster from the brig is all that remains.

'You've been a bad kitty, haven't you?' I rise, ignoring the shaking in my knees. 'What *would* Lysander say?'

His name strikes Leofric like an iron rod. I recognize echoes of my own grief. The blade of a loved one's name.

I know what drew Leofric and Cordelia together. I know the weight of it, the power of it. One person with a tragedy is sad, but two united in grief have the potential to be wonderful, or terrible.

'He was too good,' he says through gritted teeth. 'He wouldn't understand what must be done.'

'He was trying to fix how fucked up this empire is. He was reaching out to us lower provinces. Wyatt, Grasshopper—'

'And it killed him.'

'So we deserve to die?' I step to the side, keeping him in my sights. 'Killing us won't make your grief go away.'

He stalks my movements like a cat. 'My feelings are nothing to do with it.'

'Bullshit. I know what loss does to a person.'

His face darkens. 'You have no concept of it.'

He's wrong, of course. I skim my fingers over the bark of a cherry blossom tree, edging sideways. 'This won't bring him back.'

'I know that.' He strides across the bridge. 'I'm finishing his work.'

'He wanted to fix the world. Not tear it in two.'

'Sometimes those are one and the same.' Then he leaps. But he hasn't realized how close I have edged to the exit.

I jump across the fishpond, water seeping up my calf. Behind me, Leofric crashes into something.

Then I'm running, the wind snatching at my wet clothes as I flee across the deck. I fling open the cabin doors and dart inside.

Fast footsteps.

He's already caught up. The man's a beast. My lungs burn; I can barely catch my breath. I steady myself against the bannister. I'll never lose him.

A smash of glass. Then a voice: 'Leofric!'

Cordelia.

His footsteps falter. I throw myself down the stairs, half crawling, half rolling. My body throbs as I land in a tangle of limbs.

I scramble across the floor, dragging myself down the next set of stairs. Something in my brain tells me deeper means safer, but I suspect I may be closing off my escape routes.

Finally, I find a door and crawl inside. I lean against the wall, hoarse breaths rattling my lungs.

Where the hell can you hide from a homicidal maniac?

The bathhouse, apparently.

I need to rest. Even this marble floor is appealing.

A distant thunder of footsteps.

Move. Hide.

I stagger dazedly towards a pillar. Pin my body against it. Sink to the floor. The best I can do.

The door swings open, slamming into the wall.

Silence. Maybe he didn't see me and moved on.

I glance around the pillar.

A shadow. A flickering shape stalking across the floor. The twitch of a long tail.

My body goes rigid.

The tiger moves slowly – the confident saunter of a beast that knows it has no predators.

I hold my breath, command every limb to still.

Leofric stands in the entrance, arms heavy at his sides, eyes blank.

The tiger presses its nose to the ground, whiskers twitching. Its head rises, black pits of eyes searching.

I duck back behind the pillar. Too late.

Huge paws slam me against the floor. Something cracks. Hot pain shoots up my spine and I cry out before I can stop myself.

The pressure on my chest releases.

I writhe, biting down on the agony.

'You're quick. Not quick enough.' The tiger has vanished. Instead, Leofric prowls around me with leisurely footsteps. He knows I'm trapped. He knows he's won.

'I made sure they were painless,' he says. 'Except for that bitch Ermine. She fought hard. But without her Blessing, she was *nothing*.'

I turn over and try to crawl, but he slams his foot on my back. The pain makes me howl.

'The Bastard was eager to get you back in chains. Didn't even question meeting in a greenhouse in the early hours. He did not like you, Pissfish.'

'Likes you a lot less now, I'd bet.'

He rolls his shoulders. 'The child almost got away. Vanished. Thank the Goddess Cordelia had that knife.'

He thinks Grasshopper's dead. Good. Dead means safe. 'I'm sure the Goddess would endorse you killing children.'

He forces his foot beneath me, flipping me over. 'Cordelia was meant to kill the monk, but she told me she had trouble. So I went to finish him and instead I find . . . *you*.'

Why would Cordelia say that? Shinjiro was clearly dead.

'Now.' He leans forward, his face hovering above me. 'You've got nothing to lose. So tell me – what's the Bear's Blessing?'

'Why the hell do you care?'

He breathes heavily. 'Because the person who tried to kill him was found on the deck with seventeen stab wounds.'

My body goes still. Leofric must see it – the confusion in my eyes. The horror.

Ravi tried to kill Wyatt.

Leofric laughs. 'It's almost charming – how stupid you are.'

'Ravi wouldn't,' I whisper. 'He would never hurt anyone.'

He snatches my collar. 'Maybe you two *did* belong together. You're as useless as he was.' He drags me across the bath-house, my boots squeaking as I kick for purchase. 'I don't *need* to do this, after Nergüi revealed your secret. But you've been pissing me off for a decade.'

He throws me to the floor. My head dips into empty space. The smell of peppermint. The gush of running water.

My chest seizes. 'No! Wait!'

But he's already upon me – strong hands grasp my collar and legs pin my arms. 'When I kill with my Blessing, I feel it. The crunch of bone. The taste of flesh. That is what it means to be a shield. You're no longer a person. You're a weapon. A blade. That's what I was to her.'

'But not to Lysander.'

The pain of that name loosens his grip. But then his fists tighten again. 'Now it doesn't matter if I leave a trace. There are some things you just want to feel with your own two hands.' He thrusts my head beneath the water. It washes over me in a wave of sudden heat, all the way up to my chest.

I didn't even have time to take a breath. I try to free my hands, wriggling them desperately, but his knees pin them to the marble. I kick out, but my feet only meet thin air.

It is an automatic response, I think. The shock made me fight. Then the darkness floods my vision, and the water embraces me.

I've saved her, after all. Leofric thinks she's dead. Grasshopper will be safe.

And there's nothing left for me. Only disappointment and shame.

But there's an itch in the back of my mind. Something I'm missing. The real reason for all this.

Leofric killed Eudora, and he isn't worried about the repercussions because he doesn't think there will *be* any. Cordelia's mad with grief, but she's also clever. She would not orchestrate a plan that leaves her and Leofric the only survivors of a massacre.

It may have started with grief. But that grief took root and grew into something bigger. Bigger than this ship. This is just the beginning.

And if I don't live – if I'm not alive to stop them – who will?

I need to live.

I try to raise my head, but Leofric forces me deeper.

My lungs burn; the final scraps of air vanish. The one time I *don't* want to drown is the one time I can't fucking surface. The irony is almost poetic. A poem nobody will write.

Dying doesn't feel peaceful this time. It's goddessdamn agony. The pressure in my lungs feels as if I'm being crushed.

I *have* to live.

A voice in my head. Or perhaps it's not in my head – these words in my mother tongue: *Respaðua. Respaðua.* Breathe. Breathe.

I breathe.

My lungs fill with air.

Not air. Water.

I breathe again. Water gushes in my mouth, filling my lungs with immediate relief.

Leofric stares down, distorted and twisted from above the water. He watches the bubbles disappear. His hands go slack.

He thinks I'm dead. But I'm not. Why aren't I dead?

As he rises, I kick out. My foot collides with his groin and he drops to the floor. I shoot out of the water like a goddess-damn kraken.

I scramble across the tiles, half drenched.

'You liar,' he growls, staggering to his feet. 'You *are* Blessed.'

I shake my head, wet hair hanging limply. 'I'm not.'

'How the hell else are you breathing underwater?'

I breathed underwater?

I breathed underwater.

'Fucking . . . shitballs.' No wonder it didn't show until now. Every time I entered water I wanted to die. And a Blessing doesn't come until you need it. Until your soul cries out for it. I sit, staring at the water.

Is that why you've been calling to me?

'Whatever. Even more reason to kill you.'

Pain explodes in the side of my face. My shoulder thuds against the marble. Leofric leaps upon me, bloody fist drawn back.

'Wait!' I struggle beneath him. 'No way am I dying now. I *just* got my Blessing!'

'Like I give a shit.' As he thrusts his fist forward, I jerk aside. His hand collides with the floor. He howls.

I claw at his face, scraping my fingernails down his flesh and leaving a bloody trail. He wants to fight like a goddess-damn tiger, how about this?

'You – insignificant – Pissfish!' He drives his elbow into my face over and over. I taste blood, but don't release my hands. If I'm going to die, I'm taking this motherfucker with me.

'Leo.'

He freezes. A slight figure moves behind him, footsteps echoing around the bathhouse. She stops before us, observing the scene with a quirk of her head.

'Cordelia,' Leofric says, gaping up at her.

She looks oddly serene, but as her gaze falls upon me a darkness passes over her eyes. 'You hurt him.'

He breathes heavily. 'You told me to. Said he knew too much.'

I try to focus my swirling vision. Something about her is off. The intensity of her eyes.

A thread. A pull. Between me and those eyes.

'Oh Leo, you are mistaken.' She bends down, cupping his cheek tenderly. 'I would *never* let anyone hurt Dee.'

A sharp metallic ring.

Leofric and I stare at the blade sticking out of his chest, Cordelia's small hand wrapped around the hilt.

He gasps. Once. Twice. Then slumps on to me, utterly still. The warmth of his blood seeps over my stomach.

Cordelia rolls him off me. She removes the knife with a sickening *squelch* and then cleans the tip on Leofric's clothes. 'Goddess, I *hate* blood.'

I scramble back.

'No need to be afraid.' Cordelia stands awkwardly, like a disobedient child expecting a scolding. Quick anxious hands tug at her sleeves. Her clothes are far too big, hanging off that petite frame.

My heart thumps. 'You . . . saved me?'

A small smile. 'Of course. That's what I do.'

'Why?'

She glances aside. 'You . . . You know who I am, right, Dee?'

Cordelia would never call me Dee. She didn't learn my name. This isn't Cordelia.

I had always assumed there was one murderer. But there wasn't only one. There wasn't even two. There were three.

Cordelia. Leofric. And someone opposing them.

Two little deaths that do not fit the narrative. That are not clean. Their bodies laid out in the open, almost as if to tell a story. Ravi. Nergüi.

I deduced that Wyatt likely killed Nergüi. But that never sat right. Why would he murder for me? *How* could he murder for me, that dying boy? And if Ravi was sent to kill him, I know who would win that fight.

After the party, his feelings completely changed.

Her gaze digs into me. Blue, hazel or obsidian black. The colour doesn't matter. I know those eyes.

There's only one person that would protect me. Only one person who ever cared if I died. Two slender hands reaching for me in the depths of the ocean. Screaming at me for trying to leave him. Clutching me to his chest, as if he would tear the world in two to save me.

Only one person.

'Ravi.'

Chapter Thirty-Two

Day Eleven – Feast of the Grasshopper

Afternoon

I should have known Ravi's Blessing. His whole life he has worn a thousand faces. The mute child, trying to be invisible at summits. The blushing boy, escaping into treetops with me. And the heir of a lifesaving discovery, speaking to the uppers as if he belonged.

Ravi has always been whoever he needs to be. It's his core. Because if he was truly himself, they would hang him for it.

Transformation has always been Ravi's Blessing.

So I'm not surprised when Cordelia's golden hair turns dark, when her body grows taller, button nose becomes long and curved, milky skin turns deep brown, blue eyes to black.

Ravi scratches his neck. 'Sorry for—'

I have energy, even after having ten shades of shit beaten out of me. He doesn't expect my fist connecting with his jaw.

He staggers back. 'I deserved that.'

I'm breathless, my body bent double. 'You lied to me. For eleven days you lied.'

'Strictly speaking it was only eight and a half.'

He blocks my next punch.

'I'm on your side. I only lied when I had to,' he says softly. 'Just enough to—'

'I *mourned* you! You watched me mourn you.' He had stood in Eudora's cabin, eyes brimming with tears, watching me bring his hand to my mouth.

His hands. Always moving. Wyatt wouldn't sit still either. Always tugging at those damn shirtsleeves.

He holds out his palms, one finger missing. 'I'm sorry, Dee. I never wanted to hurt you. I did it *for* you.'

My fists clench, but I can't raise them. I can't hurt him. I'm so weak to him. He's my sickness.

I pace, tugging at my hair. 'Goddess, Ravi. Fucking hell.'

'You're bleeding.'

I turn.

He stills, hand outstretched to me.

'You're going to explain exactly what you've done. All of it. Start to finish.'

He runs his hand through his hair; it falls in ripples of midnight black. 'Shall we sit?' He pulls up two stools. The same stools I sat on as he emptied buckets of water over my head.

'That's mine,' I say as he goes to sit.

'I thought you'd want to face away from the water.'

'I'm not scared of it any more.' In fact, I feel as though I need to face the water to get through this.

He smiles sweetly. 'Good. You're part of the ocean, you know, else you wouldn't smell like it.'

I ignore the heat rising to my cheeks. 'You've killed at least three people – Wyatt, Nergüi and Leofric. Tell me why.'

'That's not quite . . .' His eyes travel; then he sets his shoulders. 'I came on this ship with a purpose.'

'You knew what Cordelia and Leofric were planning, didn't you?'

His face lights up. 'You worked it out! I knew you would. You're smarter than anyone knows.'

I clutch my knees. '*Ravi.*'

'Sorry. Yes, I knew. I met Cordelia at Lysander's funeral and . . . fell in love.' He winces. 'No. I thought I did.'

'Because she was broken. Because she needed someone.'

'You know me better than I know myself,' he says, hushed. 'I believed I was in love, and she told me what she was planning. But she and Leofric still didn't completely trust me.'

'She was your fiancée, and she didn't trust you?'

'I'm a lower province.' The look on his face tugs at my heart. 'To prove my loyalty, I had to . . . kill one of you. That way I would also be implicated and couldn't back out or tell anyone even if I wanted to. I chose Wyatt.'

The pain twists like a knife.

'He was going to die anyway, so I thought . . .'

I can't believe what I'm hearing. My Ravi. My sweet boy who cried when he saw a fish die, talking about murder as if he was picking clothes from a wardrobe. 'A death isn't less tragic because someone was already ill.'

'I know!' His hands reach for mine, but as I flinch, they drop. 'I just . . . wanted to fit in. I needed to. For my province. The divinium was a gift, but also a curse. If I didn't fight for my place amongst them, they'd take me for everything. You know what they did to the Funnel, right?'

My throat goes dry. I'd never considered that. How the divinium put a target on Crow Province.

'You don't know what it's like to be amongst them, Dee. The way they speak about the lower provinces. About C-Crabs.'

I stare at my knees. I can't look at him. Not after the way

his voice cracked on that word. It must have been torment. In too deep to get out alive. They would have killed him if he hadn't agreed to take part.

'But you knew what they were planning,' I whisper. 'On this ship. With a six-year-old.'

'Yes.'

A chill crawls down my spine. Another version of him I do not know.

'I won't lie to you. I was set on the plan – ready to do it. Kill Wyatt and close my eyes to the rest. Just get through it.'

'So what changed?'

He shifts. The silence sits between us, heavy as a stone.

'What changed—'

'You.'

Our eyes meet. That same tug. It's still there.

'I saw you at the party.'

'I remember. What was it you called me? Oh yes – "Of no value".' The tremble of my voice betrays me. 'No risks, you said.'

'You are always my risk.' His fingertips brush my hand. 'I did *everything* to please those people. All I wanted was to make them happy, make them like me, accept me, even though I knew if they found out what I am – if they found out my father was a Crab – they'd kill me. But then you . . .' He chuckles, eyes sparkling. 'You unveiled that costume. Pure divinium. The thing they've been fighting over since it was discovered. The *looks* on their faces. You basically stuck up two fingers to all of Concordia.'

'That was the intention,' I mutter, glancing at my outfit. 'But . . . truthfully, it's not real divinium.'

His smile doesn't budge. 'You think I don't know that, Dee? As if you would ever do *anything* that puts innocent people in danger.'

404

A lump forms in my throat. I glance aside.

'Fake or not, all that matters is that you knew *they* would believe it was. Do you know how wonderful it was – after spending the past five years begging for a crumb of their acceptance – to see the scion of the lowest province tell them he doesn't care what they think?'

I did care. That's the irony. I cared very much.

I look up. 'Blessed hells, Ravi. Are you the reason I've been stuck wearing this?'

He fiddles with his collar. 'I liked seeing their sour reactions. Besides, you look great in it.'

I repress a smile. 'You could have left me a change of underwear.'

'Sorry.' He chuckles. 'I spent the past five years trying to forget you. I had to forget you. You were a threat against everything. But in that moment, you standing on top of that table, arms wide, smiling at them . . .' He runs his hands down his knees. 'I have given them everything. I have changed everything about me, for them, for their acceptance. But I realized then there was one thing they could never take from me. Couldn't corrupt or change.'

His eyes meet mine, swimming with tears. 'You made me realize what's important. Dee, I don't think I've ever stopped—'

'Don't.' I can't hear him say it. It'll break me. 'I asked you for help. You said I had to do it alone. You closed your door on me.'

'Please understand – if I suddenly started helping you, Cordelia and Leofric would've known right away. They would've killed us both – me for being a traitor and you for knowing their scheme.' He wrings his hands. 'When you came to me, I was a mess. I didn't know what to do. I just knew I couldn't let them hurt you.'

'Nergüi was meant to kill me. Weren't they?'

He nods. 'I don't know how Nergüi found out about it all. They weren't originally part of the plan. But by the time we met in Dragon Province, they knew and Cordelia wasn't happy about it.'

'I don't think there're many secrets that can be kept from Nergüi.'

He nods. 'Nergüi and I chose our targets shortly before boarding. Nergüi picked you right away. I guess they knew about you not having a Blessing. They were meant to do the same as me – one kill to prove their loyalty, to ensure they were also implicated. Cordelia didn't trust them at all.'

I snort. 'Wise.'

'I was to kill Wyatt the second night. They figured it could be passed off as a result of his illness. The most important thing was to avoid a panic, you see. They didn't know what most of the Blessings were, so they had to keep people's guards down,' he says. 'Nergüi noticed Shinjiro keeping watch outside Wyatt's room and used their Blessing to draw him away so I could complete the kill undetected.'

'They created a vision of Eudora.' I'd forgotten about that. 'So that's why Nergüi was in your cabin? They were telling you their plan to distract Shinjiro?'

'Yes, they agreed to help, though I wasn't aware of the nature of their Blessing. Leofric used his Blessing to break the lock, so I could enter Wyatt's cabin.' He runs a hand down his face. 'I don't know what I was thinking when I went there.'

'You were thinking about killing him.'

He winces the words away. 'He was lying in bed. But when I got closer, I realized he wasn't breathing.'

My hands fall to my sides. 'He was already dead?'

'At first, I thought Leofric had done it, because he didn't

believe I could. But then I found the medicine and put two and two together.'

The unused vials. At that point he'd have skipped a day. Maybe two. And one day without was enough to kill him.

'I saw an opportunity. I could use my Blessing. Pretend it was *me* who had been killed. A way out of the whole mess. I wouldn't have Cordelia or Leofric on my back. I could help you and they would have no idea.'

'You swapped bodies.'

'Yes, my Blessing extends to other bodies. I went to your cabin as Wyatt, but you weren't there.'

'I was on the deck, with Cordelia.'

'Mhm. I worked that out.' He clutches his hands. 'I needed you to find my "body". If Cordelia or Leofric did, they would've tried to hide it. They didn't want a panic, as I said. Also, I knew there'd be a clue there, somewhere. So, I carried his body on to the deck and I . . .'

My stomach twists. 'You stabbed him.'

'He looked like me. I thought it would make it easier, but – I closed my eyes. I couldn't . . .' His breath hitches.

I touch his knee without thinking, but then draw my hand back.

'I had to make them believe I'd been attacked, overpowered. I needed them to fear Wyatt – fear his Blessing – so they wouldn't immediately target him – that is, me – again.'

I rub my temples. 'So as far as they knew, you had gone to kill a dying boy with an unknown Blessing, but turned up massacred on the deck.'

No wonder Cordelia was hysterical at the sight of Ravi's body. No wonder Leofric stepped back when 'Wyatt' spoke harshly to him. They thought he had some kind of monster Blessing.

'That's why Cordelia kept asking for Wyatt's Blessing.' I speak low. 'She wanted to know what she was up against.'

'It was also why I wouldn't give it.' He clears his throat. 'Anyway, I left the body, then locked the stairway doors, to make sure you'd find it.'

I see it even now. That sprawl of black hair. Those empty eyes. 'Didn't you think what it would be like for me to find you like that?'

His shoulders slump. 'I didn't think it would hurt you as much as it did.'

How could he not know it would destroy me? That it would feel like losing a limb? That even now, with him sitting across from me, I feel a great gaping hole within me, a wound that will never heal.

'I managed to snap you out of it, even if it took a bit of manhandling.' He grins.

I fight the urge to return it. 'So, you didn't kill Wyatt. But what about Nergüi?'

His throat bobs. 'When you told me Nergüi was planning to strike, I didn't have a choice. I knew they were going to kill you. I'd waited as long as I could.'

'What happened?'

'I hid outside your room. When they tried to get in, I appeared.'

That must have been the source of that astonished 'You'. 'You appeared as yourself, didn't you?' That would explain why the unflappable Nergüi sounded shocked for once.

He nods. 'It was the best way to get them away from your cabin. They *really* weren't expecting to see me. I led them to the deck and tried to talk them out of it.' His breath shudders. 'I told them what I'd been doing. I . . . I pleaded for your life.'

My chest burns.

'But they called your death "necessary". Like you were

some insect that needed swatting. Nergüi said if I let them kill you, they wouldn't tell Cordelia and Leofric that I still lived. That I could escape and be free of all this. As if I'd *want* to. As if there would be any point in living if . . .' His breath catches. 'It was you or Nergüi. I picked you.'

I stare down at my hands. I wonder if I could do it – murder someone to protect him. I have no idea, and I'm so grateful I've never had to face that choice. 'It's a bit much, as far as romantic gestures go.'

He smiles gratefully. 'I swear, I'll only murder one person for you.' His eyes flicker to Leofric. 'Maybe two.'

I hold my head in my hands. 'I don't understand how you tricked me for so long, pretending to be Wyatt. You didn't even know him, did you? I certainly didn't.'

'And that helped me, admittedly.' He stretches his arms. 'I've only met him a couple of times.'

'But you told me his Blessing.'

'Not strictly true.' He coughs. 'I didn't tell you anything Shinjiro didn't already let loose.'

Goddessdammit, he's right. Everything came from Shinjiro. After all, he was the only one who really knew Wyatt.

'He worked it out, didn't he? *That's* why you were afraid of him!'

He bites his lip. 'Yes. He didn't know who I was, but he knew I wasn't Wyatt.'

It all adds up. Shinjiro demanding Wyatt use his Blessing on Bancha. Asking to meet with him alone. How, after that meeting, Shinjiro was a mess. He wore black. He wasn't dangerous, he was *mourning*.

'I was worried he'd reveal the truth and ruin everything, that's why I wanted to avoid him. Luckily, he has a policy of not intervening, and I promised I was acting with good intentions.'

I want to believe that, but it's hard to connect that soft boy with a man who would cut someone's throat, even if it was to protect me. 'He just believed that you were harmless?'

He shifts. 'I may have . . . also known some things he didn't wish to get out.'

He must mean Shinjiro's attempt on Nergüi's life, the secret he maimed himself to protect. 'Ravi, that's blackmail.'

'Sorry!' He waves his hands. 'Just the two murders and the blackmail. I swear that's it.'

I sigh and sit back, running over the facts, trying to make sense of it.

'Where did the note come from? The one in Ravi . . . Wyatt's hand?'

'Oh.' He smacks his head. 'My clothes don't transform with me. I took so much care dressing him, I didn't even think to check his hand.'

'Wyatt wrote it then.' My relief surprises me. 'It wasn't for Cordelia – it was for Eudora. He skipped his medicine on purpose. Her death was the last straw – he lost his chance to prove his legacy . . .' My words trail off. I don't know what's true about Wyatt, and what Ravi made up. 'The shaking, the sickness . . . was that all an act too?'

'No. Last thing I wanted was to go to my cabin every night to change back. I wanted to be with you.' His knuckles brush mine. 'But maintaining a body that long, as well as disguising Wyatt's as mine in the morgue, took its toll. I guess that helped the illusion, but it wasn't my intention to . . .'

Pass out on me. Or cough blood.

I run a hand through my hair. 'You should've told me it was you.'

He shakes his head immediately. 'No. Then you would have relied on me to solve the mystery. You had to work it out yourself.'

'Why?'

He catches my gaze, and says in the softest voice, 'Because you thought you couldn't.'

Heat floods my body. *This boy.* There's nobody like him in the entire world. I want to strangle and embrace him at the same time.

He scratches his neck. 'I've done terrible things. If you don't want to touch me – if you *can't* touch me, or look at me, or anything . . . I understand.' His eyes flash up at me. 'But know this – what happened when we were together, the person I was . . . the person I *became.* That was all me.'

And it only took four days for me to fall in love with him. I'm so predictable.

'Being Wyatt allowed me to be *me.* The me I've always wanted to be. I stood up to them!' He smiles widely.

I can't help but return it. No wonder he was spinning for joy. Wyatt standing up to them was an accomplishment. Ravi standing up to them is a goddessdamn miracle.

I still find it hard to separate the two men. But the *real* Wyatt died hating me. Tendai proved that. I lived a reality he didn't. Wyatt never loved me. And I never loved him.

It was always Ravi.

I study him, the familiar curve of his nose, his long slender limbs, his awkward grin. 'You're not the same Ravi I left in that cave.'

'No. Can you forgive me?'

Silence.

Being with them made him cruel and ruthless. The Ravi I knew would have never done the things this one has.

But he also cried over their bodies. He fell to his knees before Eudora, begging her forgiveness. He made me feel for the first time, since that same cave, that I am someone worth anything.

411

His body slumps forward. His eyes leave mine. Fingers limp in his lap.

I grasp his hand. Our fingers fit together perfectly, as I knew they would. 'I'm not giving up on you yet, Crow.'

He doubles over, crying great gasping sobs into my hand.

I rest my head against his. 'Ravi, promise me something?'

His eyes are red with tears, his face a ruin. 'Anything.'

'Be honest from now on. You don't need to change around me. I just want you to be you.'

'I promise,' he whispers.

I pull back, grinning. 'Don't suppose you saw what happened when Leofric was drowning me?'

'No?'

'I got my Blessing! It finally showed up!'

'That's nice, Dee.' Ravi's face doesn't shift.

'*Nice?* A tie is "nice". A painting is "nice". I just got my goddessdamn Blessing after years of thinking I didn't have one! Don't you care?'

He leans forward. 'I never cared.'

My cheeks flush.

'What made it appear?'

I look away. 'I-I guess . . . I really wanted to live.'

His hands grasp mine. 'Dee!'

I go to say, *That's not the cool part!* but his beaming expression steals my words.

'You are a *marvel*,' he states.

Glitter rains down on our heads. 'Master Bear.'

'Err – change that to Master Crow.' He directs the instruction to the white dragon.

'Master Crow, it's five thirty p.m.'

He shoots up. 'Right. We need to move.' Suddenly he's all business, all steadfast determination.

'We haven't discussed Cordelia yet,' I say, rising. 'What she's planning.'

'She'll tell you herself. I'm sure if anyone can squeeze it out of her, it's you.'

'Aren't I going to hide?' I assumed Ravi was going to store me away while he finishes his bloody crusade, but he just smiles.

'You're going to hide all right. I'm hiding you in plain sight.'

I cross my arms. 'Just tell me what's going on.'

He falls to his knees beside Leofric, stripping his clothes. 'Leofric came hunting for you earlier. Luckily, I spotted him and transformed into Cordelia. He was confused, saying they weren't meant to meet until six p.m. in the gallery, that I was supposed to be dealing with the monk.' He hastily unbuttons his shirt. 'So, I told him I was having trouble and he went to the shrine.'

'Cheers for that. You sent him straight to me.'

'Sorry. I had no idea you were there.' He strips off his shirt. I make an attempt not to look.

Not much of one though – I'm owed a treat after this fucking day.

'What does this have to do with stripping Leofric? I'm not really into threesomes.'

A devious little smile. 'Steady on, golden eyes. I have another date in mind.'

Chapter Thirty-Three

Day Eleven – Feast of the Grasshopper

Night

'You know, of all the sides of you, this is my least favourite.'

'I don't know.' Ravi adjusts his jacket. 'It's nice to have muscles for a change. And all ten fingers.'

He stands before the door to the gallery, a perfect replica of Leofric. We carried the real Tiger to the makeshift morgue, then disguised him as Wyatt. Ravi wasn't bluffing about the strain his Blessing has on him; he's already sweating.

'You really think Cordelia's going to buy it?' I eye the door.

He flexes his muscles. 'I know Leofric better than Wyatt. And it'll only be for a day or two.'

'It better,' I say petulantly. I just got him back. I wanted to stare at him a little longer. 'Just call me Pissfish and talk about order: she'll fall hook, line and sinker.' I force a grin, but my insides are churning. I'm about to enter a room with a murderer, and I don't have the faintest clue what's going on in her head.

Ravi gives my arm a squeeze. 'It'll be OK. Follow my lead.' He pushes open the doors.

The room is as we left it the day of the trial. Except instead of being full of people, Cordelia stands alone before a painting of the mountain. If she wanted to see the real thing, she could look outside; it's drawing closer every hour.

Shinjiro must have healed her and Leofric after I fled. What wonderful payback she gave him – a dagger through the stomach.

Ravi storms forward, hulking boots thundering across the polished wood.

'Leo!' Cordelia throws her arms around him. 'You're bleeding! Did someone hurt you?'

'Not my blood,' Ravi grunts. It's unnerving, how easily he wears his skin. 'Bear.'

Cordelia releases a breath. 'Good. What was his Blessing?'

'Didn't get time to find out.'

'I got the monk.' She starts counting on her fingers. Then her gaze falls on me, hovering in the doorway. 'Leo!' She darts behind him, using the shield as a literal shield.

I lick my dry lips. She may be a murderer, but watching her literally cower does temper my nerves a little.

'It's OK. He's not going to hurt you,' Ravi says.

I'm considering it. I could rip a painting off the wall and slam it over her pretty head. I don't really know why that's *not* the plan.

'Hi, Cordelia.' I try to sound as casual as possible.

Her eyes gape. She looks at Ravi desperately.

'The Fish stumbled upon me when I was finishing the Bear. He'd found the Grasshopper's body.'

'This is Grasshopper's blood.' I gesture down myself. 'Maybe a little of mine.' I waggle my four-fingered hand.

Cordelia clutches her chest. 'Why didn't you . . . deal with him – like we discussed?'

415

Deal with me. What an absolute cow. I'll deal with *her* in a second. I didn't listen to her shitty symphonies for days to be 'dealt with' like a nasty stain on her undies.

Ravi glares at me. 'I was going to. But he begged for mercy.'

Cordelia clears her throat. 'But he knows everything.'

'We agreed to keep the bloodshed to a minimum,' he says bluntly. 'No unnecessary deaths.'

'But he's a—'

'No, he's not,' Ravi interrupts. 'Remember what Nergüi said? He doesn't have a Blessing. Goddess knows everything else they said was spot on.'

She looks at me. 'So it's true? You do not possess a Blessing?'

I wonder if I'm fated to lie all my life. Now I actually *have* one I have to lie about that too. 'No, I pretended my father's Blessing was mine.'

'And the emperor believed that?'

I nod.

'Goodness.' She pushes her glasses up. 'He's even farther gone than we feared.'

'I thought an extra pair of hands would be helpful,' Ravi says. 'Even a Fish can be useful.'

It sounds like an insult, but my heart warms.

Cordelia fiddles with her bodice. 'Are you sure we can trust him . . . ?'

'No. But you know Fish – they're cowards. He practically pissed himself. He doesn't exactly pose a threat.'

Warm feeling gone.

Cordelia still doesn't look convinced. Her blue eyes dart from me to Leofric then back.

I take a deep breath. 'Listen, I've wanted out of this shitty "Blessed" role since I got it.' I lock my gaze with hers, refusing to break eye contact. 'Why do you think I wore this outfit? I wanted to piss you all off.'

Her eyes track down my form.

'I'm so *tired* of being saddled with this damn lie. So as long as you promise to tell my father I died with the others, then I'll let your plot play out however you want it to. All I want in return is to disappear.'

All the best lies are built on truth. And Cordelia hears it in the earnest tremble of my voice.

She observes me with a mixture of pity and disgust. Mainly the latter. 'Fine. I suppose that makes you dead, Fish. Congratulations.'

I resist sighing with relief.

'That's everyone now, correct?' She counts on her fingers, as if ticking off a shopping list. 'Ermine, Ox, Grasshopper, Bunnerfly and Bear. And although we hadn't planned it, Crow and Spider makes seven.'

Missed out Eudora. Not so smart are you, missy?

'Oh, but what about Elephant?'

'She's dead,' I say, probably a little too quickly.

'How? She seemed to know when—'

'I lured her out,' I say. Might as well score some murder points. 'Leofric pounced on her.'

'You *have* been productive. I did not expect that of you, Fish.' She smiles at me.

'I guess you don't always know people,' I reply dryly.

'So that's eight! That's more than enough.' Cordelia clasps Ravi's arms, jumping in place.

I have no idea what 'more than enough' means, but she is fucking ecstatic, as if she's just discovered some ancient text. Not eight dead bodies.

'We're going to do this.' She looks up to him, breathless. 'It's going to work. I can scarcely believe it.'

417

'We're going to change the world,' Ravi says simply.

'Improve it.' A crease appears between her eyebrows. 'Where's your collar?'

Ravi's hand flies to his neck. 'No point wearing it. Eudora's dead, and there's nobody to lie to any more.' The real reason is we couldn't get it off Leofric's body, no matter what we tried. We had to put a scarf around 'Wyatt'. I pray Cordelia is as squeamish as she seems and avoids the corpse chamber.

'You're sure Bear didn't hurt you?' She reaches for his face.

Ravi seizes her wrist before her fingers touch him, crushing the lace at her cuffs. 'I'm fine. Promise.'

Ah. Skin contact. *That's* how her Blessing works. No wonder 'Wyatt' didn't want to shake her hand.

Her face hardens. 'I know I am not my brother. But with Ravinder gone I will need someone—'

'I know,' Ravi says stiffly. 'Perhaps we should discuss this afterwards?'

She nods. 'Afterwards. We still have work to do, after all. But we're so close I can taste it!' She spins, her body squirming with delight. 'By the end of tomorrow, it will finally be done. It will be over.'

*

I get out of that room as quickly as I can, leaving Ravi to lie again to the same girl. I go for a wash, but my skin still feels gritty. I can't scrub out the gleeful way that doll said, '*So that's eight!*' as if it was a winning answer to a quiz, not the people she's killed.

I don't doubt her viciousness now. And I still have people to protect.

Tendai opens her cabin door for me instantly.

'You're warming to me,' I say.

Tendai scowls. 'You're letting in the cold.'

She locks the door behind me as I enter her room. Grasshopper is still lying in the bed, snoozing, but she has more colour in her cheeks, and Tendai has washed off most of the blood.

'Is she OK?' I perch on the bed.

'She'll live. But she's lost that eye for good.'

The guilt stings. I might as well have plucked it out myself.

I bury my head in Grasshopper's chest. She smells like icing sugar. 'I'm sorry.'

'Dee?' Grasshopper stirs.

I wrap my arms gently around her. 'I'm sorry.'

'I went *poof* but Tortoise hurt me.'

'I know.' Cordelia stabbed a child. Worse – she slashed at thin air, *hoping* a child would be there. They assumed she was dead. But they don't know how strong a lower province child can be. Grasshopper battles death every day.

'Why didn't you open the door?' Grasshopper asks.

My chin quivers. 'Because I'm a coward. Because I wanted to . . .'

'Disappear?'

I nod.

She wipes tears from my cheeks. 'I'm good at that.'

'The best.'

Her hand lingers on my face. 'You're not meant to disappear.'

'I think the Goddess agrees.'

She edges closer. 'You won't disappear, promise?'

'Promise.' I rub her hand.

'And you'll pay me back?'

'All the sweets?' I say.

'*All* the sweets.' She smiles a toothy grin.

419

I rise to leave, but she clings to my hand. 'I'll come with you.' She tries to sit up, but her body trembles and she falls back.

'You have to stay here and get better. Tendai will look after you.'

'You're going to be with your heart-bound,' she says sleepily.

'Something like that.'

'Heart-bounds are meant to stay together,' she whispers. 'Stay with him. He's always looking after you.'

My heart skips. 'Is that right?'

'He looks at you like I look at candyfloss.' She smacks her lips. 'I'm sleepy.' Then she's out.

I kiss her on the forehead.

'I'm on babysitting duty now?' Tendai crosses her arms.

'For one day.'

'Fine.'

'Are you going soft on me?' I smirk.

She glances to Grasshopper. 'Kids don't have the same strength of negative emotions as adults.' Her fingers skim the wheels of her chair. 'Being with them is . . . peaceful.'

I reach for her hand, but she slaps me in the chest. 'Ow!'

'Steady on. I'll look after Yewande. That doesn't mean you can jump my bones.'

'I wasn't going to!'

'Uh-huh . . .' She sounds unconvinced. 'Give me your hand. That gaping wound is pissing me off.'

I do so and she starts wrapping a bandage around it.

'What the hell happened out there?' Tendai asks.

'It's Leofric and Cordelia.'

She sighs. 'Figures.'

'You knew?'

'No. But I wouldn't have been surprised whatever name you said. They're all pricks.' She ties the bandage roughly.

I wince. 'Well, he's dead now . . . kinda . . . and she . . .'

She gives me an I-don't-really-care look. If I had expected some dramatic change of heart from Tendai regarding the people who threatened her life, I would be disappointed. Luckily, I hadn't.

'Don't open your door to anyone. Don't come out, no matter what happens. Pretend as if you're dead.' I clear my throat. 'I may have told her you're dead.'

'I can be dead.' She releases my hand. 'I just want this shit over with. I have a province to lead.'

'It will be. Soon.' I head to the door, but she catches my arm.

'What happened to you?' she asks.

'Huh?'

'I lied before – when I said you didn't have any contempt for anyone,' she says. 'You did have it, but it was a bubble, surrounding you and only you. Seemed a bit awkward to bring up that you hate yourself more than anyone.'

My cheeks burn. 'It's awkward to bring it up *now*.'

'I'm bringing it up because it's not there any more.'

I breathe deeply. 'I guess I found my Blessing?'

'You *found* it? Like an old sock behind a sofa?'

'I'm everything my father lied about now – a fully fledged Blessed.' So why do those words feel so empty? I have a goddessdamn Blessing; I should be bouncing off the walls.

'Well, something about you has changed.' Her hand drops. 'I suspect you're about to become very relevant, Ganymedes Piscero. Don't forget all the favours you owe me.'

Chapter Thirty-Four

Day Twelve – Feast of the Fish

Morning

I spend the early hours dismantling Detective Dee's Diagram of Deduction, placing Eudora, Jasper, Eska, Nergüi, Shinjiro, Leofric and Wyatt in a neat pile. I should be satisfied. I was too late to save them, but I *did* solve it.

But I'm not satisfied. Because even if I didn't get on with all of them, even if some hated my guts, every one of these deaths deserves justice.

And that justice starts and ends with Cordelia. I need to find out why she did this. Why so many people had to die for her to dance in the gallery.

As soon as the sun rises, I leave my cabin.

I expect to find her in the library, but instead, she's in a place I've barely ventured – the games room.

She stands before a table, pale fingers skimming over a chess set.

'Late night, or early morning?' I ask.

'Ah!' She turns sharply. 'Oh, Fish. Apologies, I was in a world of my own. My wits have been on edge this entire journey!'

I force a smile. 'I can imagine.'

'Oh!' She raises a finger. 'For the last few nights, I haven't seen Lysander at all. You said it was a Blessing that created his image, but I don't think that's correct. I believe that now everything is in order, he can finally rest.'

I consider telling her about Nergüi's Blessing, just to wipe that satisfied grin off her face, but I owe the Spider. Even if they did try to kill me, I still feel guilty about not unveiling myself when they lowered their walls. 'My mistake.'

'Not to worry!' Cordelia dips her head. 'I suppose it was awfully confusing for you.'

I bite down on my cheek. 'Well, Fish aren't known for our brains.'

This, for some reason, she finds hilarious. She giggles as I approach the chess set. It's a thing of beauty – all the province animals carved from ivory and obsidian. Dragon as king, Tiger as queen, Bunnerfly as the bishops, Elephant and Tortoise for rooks, and Spider and Ox as knights. Three of the remaining five provinces are represented by two pawns each, and Grasshopper and Fish by single pawns.

'Do you play?' I ask.

'Oh, yes.' She turns eagerly to the table. 'I've read all about chess. It is a game which sharpens the mind. Have you seen a real set before?'

My eyes flicker to her. 'I saw a picture once.'

'Wonderful.'

I expected to find a different Cordelia in this room. That she would tear off a mask and reveal a dark persona hidden beneath her doll face. I wanted to discover how she concealed her murderous desire beneath a guise of girlish innocence. But the Cordelia before me is the same person. The same sweetly curious, excitable bookworm.

423

It hurts more, somehow, to know there aren't two Cordelias. Just one.

But maybe it's to my advantage. I *do* know this Cordelia, after all.

'Why don't we play a game?'

'I'd love to!' she squeals. 'But will you be able to cope?'

I roll my neck. 'I'll get by.'

'Goodie. You can be white, it matches your hair, and you get to go first.'

We sit opposite each other. The room reacts, the light focusing to a spotlight above us. You've got to admire Emperor Eugenios's flair for the dramatic.

I take the first move, shifting a Crow pawn.

She quickly responds with her Grasshopper pawn.

I pick up another pawn. 'I've got to say, I'm impressed.'

'Oh, yes?'

'To be able to carry out all those murders.'

She shudders. 'I hate the word "murder". It is *so* loaded. Let's call them "sacrifices".'

I resist the urge to cram my pawn down her throat. 'Well, I'm impressed you managed to carry out those *sacrifices* without anyone finding out. How did you do it?'

'I shouldn't . . .'

'I can't wrap my head around it.' I tap the pawn on my chin.

Her fingers drum the table. 'Well, if you insist.'

I knew she wouldn't be able to resist gushing about her own genius. She's really not as complex as she reckons.

'Eudora, the first night.' I place my pawn down. 'That really confused me. How'd you manage to "sacrifice" her so quickly?'

'That's the one I am most proud of.' Her bishop zooms across the board, collecting my pawn. 'Leo really did

424

comfort me, that wasn't a lie. That's a vital lesson, Fish – it's easier to stick to as many truths as you can.'

'Thanks for the advice.'

She grins. 'You're welcome! After, Leofric found Eudora in the bathroom. He used his Blessing to dispatch her.'

She didn't even make it out of that bathroom. If I'd remained a few minutes longer . . .

Who am I kidding? I'd probably be dead too.

'He strung her body up from the balcony, so she was concealed behind the chandelier. Then he went down to the ballroom asking if anyone had seen her.' The words stream out, as if she's been dying to boast about it. 'I was asking Ox the most boring questions I could conceive of. He wasn't paying attention, so he didn't notice me hit the lights. Then Leofric released his Blessing. He tied Eudora up so the tiger only had to chew through one rope to send her body hurtling beneath the chandelier, where everyone could see it. Then I turned the lights back on, and ta-dah!'

'So, if we had looked up before then,' I say, edging my knight towards one of her pawns.

'You *might* have seen her. But she dropped five feet when Leo's Blessing cut that rope. I believe that is where the mark around her neck originated.'

Killed by her own shield. Did she realize the betrayal in those final moments? 'Very clever. You had us all fooled.'

Her cheeks blush, as if I'd just called her pretty. 'Grasshopper was supposed to be next, but her room was empty, and Leo had to quickly vacate it when the monk left the Bear's cabin for sunrise prayers. So I attempted another means.'

'Poison.'

'But my server refused. A pity. It was supposed to be a mercy. I did not wish for a child to live through the horrors I knew were coming.'

I purse my lips. 'Very considerate.'

'Then Ravinder's sacrifice went wrong.' She leans forward. 'What *was* the Bear's Blessing? It's been niggling at me.'

I move my Tiger queen over the board. 'He could turn into a bear.'

'My! That explains the state of Ravinder's body.' She clutches her Ox knight. 'If I had known, I wouldn't have agreed to send Ravinder there.' The grief trembles in her voice.

I can't look at her. She genuinely cared for him, and I can't get through this if I start pitying her. 'And Eska?'

She jumps her knight across the board, collecting a white pawn. 'We wished to prevent a panic, so the Ermine was easy to blame. Everyone already suspected her. She had no allies. I must admit, I was rather flustered when I saw her Blessing.' She twirls her hair. 'The original plan was for Leo to deal with the sacrifices alone. But when we saw *that*, I knew I would have to help. My Blessing stops other Blessed using theirs upon flesh-to-flesh contact.'

I try to look both surprised and impressed. 'Very cool.' Total lie. All her Blessing demonstrates is how self-obsessed she is. I move a Bunnerfly bishop.

'We planned to strike the fifth night, so the timing of the dinner was rather frustrating. But by pure chance we encountered her in the cabins.' Her knight darts forward. 'She went straight for Leofric but disregarded me. People often do. I gripped her ankle. She was *very* surprised, and ran, but I held on and was dragged along behind her. I must maintain contact for my Blessing to work,' she explains. 'Bad luck for you, Fish – she went straight to your room.'

Because she thought I would help. I would have, if I had been there.

'Leo then quickly dispatched her.'

She's omitting details. Leofric said he dragged that one out on purpose, long enough for Eska to create those nail and bite marks.

'We heard someone coming, so stashed her in the wardrobe.'

'Wyatt and me,' I say, claiming her Crow pawn.

'We knew people would be demanding answers, and we wanted to avoid anyone unleashing any more Blessings like *that*. So I'm afraid you were easy pickings, Fish. That's why Leo had Ox arrest you.' She pushes up her glasses. 'The trial was supposed to create the illusion that everything was under control.'

I swallow hard. 'But at the trial, you stood up for me.' It had endeared her to me immensely.

'I was worried about Bear,' she says swiftly. 'He was getting very passionate, and I didn't want him to hurt Leo as he had Ravinder.'

I try not to let the disappointment reach my face. I thought I'd got through to her, or Lysander had. Instead, even that move was calculated to ensure her massacre could continue.

'The Ox was easy; he came when ordered.' She picks up her other rook. 'It was my idea to use the greenhouse. I had been staking out the ship and nobody had set foot in there. What *were* you doing in there?'

Kissing your fiancé.

'Looking for signs of Eska's Blessing,' I say honestly. 'I assumed she'd been moved to my room.'

She smiles like a mother humouring a child. 'A very good try.' She places her rook. 'At this point we had three of the required deaths, but we needed six to carry out our plan. We were beginning to panic.'

I edge out another pawn. 'Why not kill us all in one go?'

'All at once would be madness, considering we weren't

aware what skills people possessed. We had to do it slowly, one by one, so we could control the narrative.' She drums the table. 'We decided to leave the monk until last, as he was doing a fine job of keeping the peace. I told Leo to put some pressure on Nergüi. They were meant to have dealt with you a while ago.'

So that's what that intense conversation in the games room was about. Leofric was ordering Nergüi to kill me. Gosh, that makes me feel *all warm* inside.

'I haven't the foggiest idea what Nergüi was waiting for.'

Nobody can be sure what went on in the Spider's head, but I think Nergüi was desperate to show their truth to someone, just once. And I was perfect – not only would I be dead by morning, but they also recognized a part of themselves in me: that sobbing child.

Nergüi just wanted to feel something genuine. One moment of connection in a life ruled by masks and whispers and shadows. Cordelia could never understand that.

'We could hardly wait for Nergüi all voyage, so I suggested Elephant next. She was always alone, after all.' Her queen pounces upon my knight. 'I kept watch while Leo used his Blessing to break her lock. But she had barricaded the door. It delayed us, and then the monk returned from his prayers. I distracted him while Leo's Blessing escaped. It was not difficult; he was obsessed with praying with me, so I appealed to that part of him.'

That explains why Tendai only heard Shinjiro's footsteps. Leofric's Blessing didn't make any sound, and Cordelia's cabin is on the right-hand corridor. The monk is the only person who would have passed Tendai's room.

'After that near miss I was rather stressed. But then Nergüi informed us they would be completing their sacrifice on the ninth night.' Her eyes flicker up to me. 'That didn't go to plan.'

'Wyatt was waiting.' I slide my rook forward.

'I suspected. The wounds were similar to Ravinder's.' Her queen lunges upon my rook. 'Ultimately, it did not really matter. In fact, after learning your secret, I believe that ninth night went better than I could have planned.'

My brow furrows. 'But Nergüi was on your side.'

'Nergüi is never on anyone's side but their own,' she says. 'I did not invite them to be a part of it. Somehow a whisper wound its way to them. When we reached the capital they took me aside and threatened to tell everyone if we did not include them. I expect they saw something they could get out of it.'

I suspect the same. Nergüi was sending visions of a dead brother to torment the ringleader of the plot they were part of. And if I know Nergüi, it wasn't to save anyone's life, but instead to send Cordelia overboard and claim the prize themselves. Whatever that may be.

'Why didn't Nergüi reveal your plot through their dragon?'

Cordelia shudders. 'I almost wish they had. I never wanted anyone to know what they revealed.'

And Nergüi knew it. They broke Cordelia and Leofric with those secrets. Their reactions proved the truth of them. They could have denied the murders.

'After Nergüi's *show*, the time for subtlety was over. We needed numbers, and quick.'

'You said you needed six, but you killed Wyatt, Grasshopper *and* Shinjiro.' I move my Ermine pawn.

She shrugs. 'We happened to find Grasshopper outside your room. We couldn't be sure the sacrifices of the monk and the Bear would be successful. So we took the chance the Goddess gave us. Insurance.'

Minimal bloodshed, my arse.

'I requested the monk pray with me at the shrine. He

eagerly obliged. I knew his Blessing was healing so I could take him on alone, while I told Leo to face the Bear.'

'And to deal with me.' I can't hide the sting from my voice.

She has the decency to blush. 'That was just part of the tidy-up. No loose threads.'

'I understand.' *I understand I'll be a loose thread that pulls your entire fucking plan apart.*

Once I find out what it is.

'And that's it.' She tucks a strand of hair behind her ear. 'What do you think?'

What kind of question is that?

But I know exactly the validation she wants. 'Very clever. I certainly couldn't think of something like that.'

'No.' She laughs, moving her knight. 'It took a lot of planning.'

'So why do all this?'

Her eyes flicker away. 'If I confessed the reasoning, it would not be pleasing to you.'

Yeah. I suspect that too.

I take her Fish pawn with my queen.

She leans back. 'Concordia's population has grown up surrounded by lies – everything the monk preached and the legend the Dragon recited at the start of this voyage. How we're stronger if we shoulder this burden together.' Her bishop moves across the board. 'I don't blame people for believing it. Lysander believed it more than anyone.'

'This is about Lysander? Revenge?'

'No,' she says a little too quickly. 'But it began with him. He was convinced if we improved the relations between provinces, the whole of Concordia would benefit.'

I nod. 'He was visiting the lower provinces.'

'He genuinely cared about them. He could see a better

world, he said. Where all provinces were truly united.' Her shoulders fall. 'But then *that* happened. *They* happened.'

She utters the word 'they' with such hatred that it nearly makes me bolt up in my seat. 'Crabs?'

'*Monsters.* They have no regard for civility, for law or order. They're not human.'

She's wrong. I've seen their humanity. I see it when I close my eyes. I rub the scar on my hand. 'You said this to Ravi?'

'Of course.'

Poor Ravi. If he didn't feel enough shame for his origin already, he had to listen to this tosh for the past six months.

'Because the Bandage was broken, they got through and *murdered* my sweet brother who only ever wanted to help people.'

So it's murder when it suits her.

'I'm doing this to ensure no more good men die like Ly did.'

I drag my Fish pawn forward. 'I just don't see the link between Lysander's death, and your . . . sacrifices.'

She nibbles her lip. 'You will when it is done.'

Her walls are flying up. I need to appeal to her nature. There're two things Cordelia loves: showing off her intellect, and feeling superior.

'Let's turn it into a quiz,' I say. 'You ask me questions and I'll try to answer.'

She taps her rook against her chin. 'Oh gosh. OK then!' Her piece makes a beeline for my queen. 'Question one – the Ox said something on this journey which was the wisest thing anyone said. What was it?'

Probably 'Fuck you, Fish'. 'You've got me there.' I move my queen.

She smiles that patronizing smirk. 'He said we have been fighting a war for a thousand years. He wasn't exactly *my* kind

431

of person, but he was right. We have been trying to protect Concordia from the Crabs by using the Bandage, and it's not working. Countless emperors have lost their minds trying to maintain it.' She spreads her hands. 'Every ruler has died raving like a lunatic, mind pickled by the effort of maintaining a wall that is not working. Even with the divinium, it's not enough. Sooner or later, it *will* break. And then *they* will be everywhere.' She sends her knight out to meet my queen. 'I'm afraid I'm going to take your queen very soon. A little advice, don't leave the big ones unprotected.'

'Thanks.' I move my Fish pawn forward.

'Question two – do you know *why* the Bandage is deteriorating?' Her queen slides across to mine.

'Because the emperor's power is failing.'

'And why is it failing?'

'Because of the Bandage?' I push my Fish onwards.

'Close enough. The Bandage is a huge object; maintaining it requires a great deal of his Blessing. I have a theory.' She says 'theory' but I suspect she believes there's little chance she's wrong. 'Those with Blessings die early, correct?'

'Sure.'

Her knight dashes out, blocking my queen's escape. 'It's like a slow-acting poison, killing us over time. But – and here's another question – which Blessed die earlier than any other?'

'Ox.' I edge my fish pawn forward. 'Because they have to fight on the Bandage.'

'Very good! The previous Ox Blessed leapt right over it. And other Oxen throughout history have committed similar senseless acts. I believe this occurs because they use their Blessings more than other Blessed.'

I can't deny that. I saw the madness in Jasper's eyes when he pinned me in the bathhouse. 'You think using it is what makes their minds deteriorate? Rather than simply *having* it?'

She cleans her glasses. 'Well, it does for the emperor – why not us also? He just has a greater amount of it so lasts longer. I know when I've used my Blessing a lot, I feel rotten.'

Ravi said the same. And I witnessed the effects of using it too much. The blood still stains my clothes.

'My theory is: the more a Blessing is used, the faster the deterioration of the host body. It can manifest in different ways, physical or mental, but I believe it is accelerated by use. Therefore, I believe it is the immense size of the Bandage which has contributed to its failure. The emperor simply cannot maintain it. Even with the Primus Blessing.'

'Fascinating.' I move my Fish pawn to the end of the board. 'Queen.'

'That's a pawn, silly.'

I smile. 'What does this have to do with the Blessed you sacrificed?'

'That brings me to question four – what happens to Blessings not passed on to children?'

'They pass to siblings.'

Her blue eyes fix on me. 'Incorrect. I will give you a hint. There's a good reason we are encouraged to produce natural heirs.'

My mouth goes dry. Shinjiro told me, *'Blessings come from the Goddess. To her they return.'* That's vague enough for Cordelia to feel smug. 'The Goddess takes them back?'

She smirks. 'That's sweet. But not quite right. They do not return to the *Goddess*, if she exists at all. They return to the source.'

'The mountain?'

She nods. 'After Lysander died, the Church needed to ensure a sibling took possession of his Blessing and I was the only option. The monk took me up the mountain, and there I was able to claim it. I was sworn to secrecy by Shinjiro.'

I don't need to try to look utterly flabbergasted: it comes naturally. 'But then *anyone* could claim it.'

'That's right. They could.' Something about the sharpness in her eyes makes my skin crawl.

I push away, my mind racing. The monks knew this, and they've been keeping it secret for Goddess knows how long. Is *that* why there's such a taboo against killing Blessed? Because if people knew, they could just target them, then claim the Blessing themselves. No wonder Shinjiro was so obsessed with keeping Wyatt alive. If those ambitious Bears discovered the truth, there would be chaos.

It seems the monk *was* hiding something after all.

'Question five – what would happen if many Blessed died before they passed on their Blessings?'

My throat is bone dry. 'Their Blessings would all go to the mountain source.'

'Which just so happens to be where this ship is heading.'

'Convenient.'

She giggles. 'I believe even you can work out what my plan is when we reach that mountain.'

I clutch my chair. 'You want to take the Blessings?'

'Yes, all eight. More than I estimated, which will be bene-ficial in the long term.'

Six would be enough, she'd said.

'It would pickle your mind, surely?'

'Weren't you listening? It's overexertion which does that. One person could house all the Blessings and not go mad; I believe they will simply be absorbed into, and boost, the Primus Blessing's power. Another way that fable is a lie.' She captures my queen with her own. 'See? I told you.' Her white

434

stack is piled high beside her, like bones. 'Final question –
why do you think I want all those Blessings?'

I swallow hard. I have two answers. One restores my faith
in her humanity. The other destroys it.

I pick up the Fish pawn. 'You want to help the emperor
maintain the Bandage.'

'Fish Province has been stuck in the same cycle for years,
so it makes sense you would not understand progress.' She
spreads her hands over her skirt. 'Think about this – why
would I sacrifice Eudora if I wanted to work *with* her father?'

I cling to the Fish, rolling it in my palm.

In my heart, I knew this was the answer. Because then
everything falls into place. And the thing which has bothered
me finally makes sense. Apart from Eudora, the deaths were
never chaotic. They were ordered. Lower provinces, one by
one. A cull. Because if Cordelia carries out her plan, we won't
need our Blessings.

'You're going to move the Bandage.'

She claps, delighted that the dog has performed a trick.
'Excellent! Moving the Bandage so it sits below Tortoise
Province, where Concordia's arrowhead shape begins to
narrow, would reduce the size required by half. It will take an
enormous amount of power to pick it up from its position in
Ox Province and transport it to Tortoise, of course. By my
estimations, seven Blessings' worth, including my own,
added to the Primus Blessing.'

I wrap my fist around the fish until the ivory pierces my
skin. Grasshopper, Bunnerfly, Bear, Ermine, Ox, Fish and
half of Crow abandoned to the savage wastes. Without the
Bandage's protection, our homes and people will be easy
prey for all the horrors that lie beyond, especially the weakest
of us – the elderly and the children. I would also be a fool to
believe the Crabs would welcome us with open arms, if we

were thrust together so suddenly. We will slaughter each other, that is if the beasts do not tear us to shreds first. 'Millions will die.'

'Millions more will die if the Bandage breaks and *they* come rushing through. Progress rarely comes without sacrifice.'

She's cutting off the weak to save the strong. No, not even that. Cutting off the poor to save the rich.

'I'm not doing this because it's easy. I'm doing this because it's right. Because nobody else is willing to.' She clutches the table. 'If this empire keeps following a ridiculous fable it's going to be destroyed. I won't see my people slaughtered in the streets. I won't see what happened to Ly happen to anyone else.'

I focus on my breathing, try to keep it regular.

'I knew you wouldn't understand.' She rolls her eyes. 'Few people understand true progress. That's why we didn't tell the Elephant.'

And I suppose having free access to the Funnel didn't factor in this at all.

I moisten my lips. 'It's a remarkable plan.'

I don't disagree with her – Concordia *is* broken. I've known that since I saw two Crab bodies swinging in the snow. Since Ravi called me a miracle for simply not hating him for his parentage.

Concordia is broken. Just not in the way Cordelia believes.

'The new Concordia will be better,' she says with conviction. 'Everyone will be safer.'

Not my people. She doesn't even look conflicted. She's read that our provinces are wild and simple and hasn't considered us in the slightest, or the fact we provide their food. She doesn't know what she's throwing away. We are just pawns on a chessboard.

I place my fish down. 'Checkmate.'

She blinks. 'A pawn cannot move like that.'

I sit back in my chair. If Cordelia had expanded her mind beyond her own province, she would know that chess was born in Fish Province. She would know that baby Fish are taught how to play it by their grandparents, that well-worn sets are passed down over generations. She would know that pawns have so much potential Fish Province occasionally plays a version comprised entirely of them – Pawn Play.

'It's not a pawn any more,' I say. 'It reached the end of the board. It became a queen.'

'A pawn can't do that.'

'Yes, it can.'

She stares down at it, the white Fish smeared with my blood. 'I may have overlooked the pawn moves when I was learning.'

'A critical error.'

Her gaze holds mine, and for the briefest moment, her smile drops. 'Well played. You must be delighted.' She pushes away from the table, rising to her feet.

'One more question.'

She turns in the doorway. 'Yes?'

'What about Emperor Eugenios? You don't have the Primus Blessing, and you need it to move the Bandage.'

Before she can answer, the room lurches. I crash to the floor, chess pieces scattering around me. A terrible creak – like the dying wail of a legendary beast. Then all the lights go out.

Chapter Thirty-Five

Day Twelve – Feast of the Fish

Afternoon

I run my hand along the wall, navigating the darkness of the ship.

'Dumpling,' I call. 'Bring a light.'

But there is no poof of glitter. No 'Yes, Master Fish'. Just silence, then Cordelia's haunting tones, from somewhere in the darkness.

'That won't work.'

My throat closes around any response, so I follow Cordelia's footsteps to the deck.

Ravi, wearing Leofric's skin, stands frozen before the sails.

All the colour has been drained from them, like a rainbow bled of life. Where a gleaming white fish should be dashing across the linen, there's only dull grey fabric, hanging listlessly. The ship is eerily silent. It sits completely still in the water, as if an anchor has been dropped.

The *Dragon's Dawn* is powered by the emperor's Blessing, Which means only one thing.

'You killed the emperor,' I say.

'Not me. My parents. They know all about my plan and agreed to carry out that part of it.' Cordelia gestures forward. 'Isn't it beautiful?'

I follow her gaze.

The mountain pierces the sea like a shard of glass. It's surrounded by smaller shards, white against a grey sky. From this distance, the scene seems to me like waves crashing upon a shore, the tips frothing with sea foam.

Cordelia clasps her hands. 'My parents acted a little early. We'll have to row the rest of the way. The Bandage should remain for some time with help from the divinium, but not for long. We must reach the summit as soon as possible.'

That's why Eudora had to die, and fast. If she had been alive when the emperor was killed his Blessing would have passed to her. Cordelia needed the heir out of the way to ensure the Primus Blessing returned to the source.

'We need to move.' She dashes to the side of the ship, where a small rowing boat hangs from its davits.

I glance over the water. We're at least a mile out. And once we're on that mountain, getting Ravi alone will be impossible. And I have to discuss Cordelia's plan with him.

'I'll get some supplies,' I say, catching Ravi's gaze. 'Food and tools.'

'I'll go too,' Ravi grunts.

'No, Leo.' Cordelia tugs his sleeve. 'Stay with me.'

Ravi looks between us. I try to convey a silent need, feeling Cordelia's gaze upon me.

'I don't trust him alone. I'll keep an eye on the Fish.' Ravi grabs my arm and drags me into the cabins before Cordelia can protest.

'Ravi—' I start.

'Wait.' He leads me down the staircase, past the destroyed dining room, and finally releases me in the kitchen.

I rub my aching shoulder.

'Sorry.' He moves closer to me, but I flinch.

'Please change back. Leofric making that expression gives me the creeps.' *Also, I could really use a friendly face right now.*

'What if she—'

'Please.' The desperation must have leaked into my voice, as he obliges.

Leofric's clothes hang loosely around Ravi's slender body. He looks a little like that bundled-up boy I first met.

My chest flutters.

Dammit. He still sends all my senses haywire.

'Are you OK?' He touches my shoulder.

'She's planning to move the Bandage,' I say. 'She's going to sacrifice the southern provinces.'

His expression does not change.

He knew.

I step away. His hand falls heavily to his side.

'Why didn't you tell me?'

He glances aside. 'I thought it would be better if you heard it from Cordelia yourself.'

I sigh. 'Ravi, what she's proposing would cut your province in two.'

'I moved everyone north.'

Shinjiro mentioned that early into the journey. He asked me about earthquakes, said Crow Province had reported them in the south. That was a lie then.

'I just wanted to protect my people,' he says softly.

'You knew about the Blessings returning to the source too, I presume?'

He nods. 'That's what I used to blackmail Shinjiro.'

Of course. The monk would do anything to stop *that* getting out. Even hide the fact that someone was posing as his dead patient.

I throw up my hands. 'Her plan is madness.'

'True. But it's masquerading as pragmatic sense. Awful, but logical. She sold it to me.' He tugs at his sleeves. 'Sorry, Dee. I was a fool for letting her convince me.'

I push away the ache in my stomach. Focus on the real issue. 'We have to stop her. There's two of us – we could jump her, tie her up.'

'No, we can't.'

'Why not?'

His shoulders drop. 'She's the only one who knows the path up the mountain. She's the only one who has been there before.'

I tug at my hair. 'I couldn't give a flying shit about the mountain. She's going to tear Concordia in half. Millions will die. *Fuck the mountain.*'

'Dee.' He catches my arms. 'Please be calm.'

'How can I be calm?'

'Firstly – the Bandage *will* fall without someone sustaining it. Right now, nobody is. We're working against the clock.'

I freeze. 'True.'

'Secondly – those Blessings are at the mountain source, and if that power exists, someone is going to take it. So . . .' Something hungry prowls in his eyes, like Grasshopper when she sees sugar.

My legs tremble. 'You want to take it.'

'I want to do the best thing for all those people. The disenfranchised, the underestimated, the forgotten – they deserve a voice.' He swallows hard. 'I think it's what I was born to do. I will put the people's needs first – what I should have always been doing. I lost sight of it.' He spreads his hands. 'But now, I have a vision for this world I must bring to fruition.'

'What vision?' I ask.

His face hardens. 'One where your value is not determined by your place at a table. Where bodies are not hanged in snow-drenched squares to the cheers of mothers and children. Where a boy does not have to hide who he is, be ashamed of who he is for every day of his life, just because his mother dared fall in love with the wrong person.' His dark eyes hold me, that thread tugging. 'Will you help me?'

I stand still and silent in that cold room, locked in his gaze.

Everything he's said is true. Someone needs to take those Blessings. And there are only us five here – two of whom are playing dead.

Why shouldn't it be Ravi? The boy who sobbed over every death he did not prevent. The child of two worlds who I sailed with to the Bandage, who pressed his hand against that green wall, the immensity of it touching him in a way I could never comprehend.

Ravi understands more than anyone what the people of this world need. *All* the people of this world. He is both an outcast and a Blessed. A Crab and a Crow. He has lived both lives.

I trust his vision for this world.

'I'll help you, Ravi.'

He throws back his head, releasing a long breath. 'I knew I could rely on you.'

'So we need a plan.' I move away, rifling through the drawers. I grab a pot and a spoon. 'We'll accompany Cordelia to the source, but as soon as we see it, we'll need to act quick.'

Ravi waggles a cleaver suggestively.

'We're *not* killing her,' I say, with a smirk. 'Goddess knows enough blood has been spilt.'

Ravi nods, but attaches the cleaver to his belt anyway. 'For wood.'

'I'll subdue her. I reckon even I can take Cordelia. Then you grab the Blessings. Do you actually know how to do that?'

'No. But we'll work it out.'

I close the drawers. 'Not the most elegant plan. But why overcomplicate it?' *Also, I'll get great satisfaction from seeing her realize she's been outsmarted by a Fish.* 'She won't be expecting it – she trusts you, and underestimates me.'

'A dangerous mistake.' Ravi's fingertips linger atop my hand. 'It feels right.'

'What?'

'Us two together. Planning moves against them.' He smiles shyly, and heat rushes up my body. 'When I was with them, I always felt as though something was missing. This emptiness in my core. If you'd never . . . I'd be just like them.' His hand settles on my cheek. 'Thank you, for saving me a second time.'

'Just returning the favour.' I clasp my hand over his. 'Now come on. Cordelia likes learning, so let's teach this self-righteous scholar a thing or two.'

*

When we return to the rowing boat, Cordelia is waiting beside it. Thankfully, Tendai seems to have actually listened to my instructions and remained in her cabin with Grasshopper.

'Good idea.' Cordelia nods at the pot. 'The climb will take at least twelve hours. We will require sustenance.'

Ugh. 'Climb' sounds suspiciously like physical exercise.

'Let's get this in the water,' Ravi says in Leofric's gruff tones.

Cordelia holds out her hand to him. I snatch it, hauling her inside, to her obvious annoyance. Ravi follows, using the pulleys to lower us over the side of the vessel. We hit the water with a dull *plop*, ripples spreading around us.

Ravi takes the oars, putting those new muscles to work. Our tiny boat cuts through the ocean like a blade through flesh. The water is strangely still, as if the entire planet has been bled of its life force. I watch the disappearing shape of the ship. Drained of its colour, it looks like the stripped skeleton of some ancient beast, risen to the surface after a thousand years of underwater decay.

As we approach the mountain, a red shape spears through the blanket of fog. Twin pillars before a domed building, built into the rock. A looming statue of a dragon sits in front of it, fire burning in the chasm of its heart.

'That's the shrine,' I say, hushed. 'A monk mans it at all times.' *What a depressing existence.*

'Shinjiro took me there, and the monk led us to the source.' Cordelia points across the mountain. 'Take us to that little bay. We can ascend the mountain without them noticing.'

By the time we make it to shore, all of us are trembling. Cordelia isn't completely useless, as she's packed some woollen cloaks which we hastily wrap around our freezing bodies.

I tug the hood low and face the stark expanse of white rock. I grew up surrounded by cliffs, but this mountain is so sheer I can't comprehend how we're meant to climb it. One false step and we're dead, thrown to the jagged rocks below.

Cordelia steps forward, petticoats rustling in the breeze. She runs her hands along the walls. 'It's here somewhere.'

'I thought we were climbing?'

She giggles. 'You are a riot.' Her fingers stop. She places her palm flat against the mountain. 'Leo, push the rock here.'

Ravi moves stiffly, as if he's not used to the weight of this body. 'Here?'

'Yes. Just push.'

My stomach squirms. Why wouldn't she do it herself? 'Maybe we should—'

Ravi pushes. Nothing happens. He looks at Cordelia, but she stands still, staring at the wall.

Then there's a click from somewhere deep inside the mountain. The earth vibrates, shaking pebbles about my boots. An entire section of wall *moves*, slipping to the right, revealing a dark, twisting passageway.

I duck my head inside. The light is dim, but I see a vague outline. 'Is that a staircase?'

'Of course. Did you never wonder how twelve of us are supposed to climb a mountain in a day? Monks have been using this secret path for years.' Cordelia reaches up into the tunnel. 'If we were to hike, it would take a week. Plus, it is rather dangerous – the mountain is covered in snow. Aha!' She reveals a bamboo cylinder. 'A fire piston. There are torches inside. Could you light one, Leo?'

Ravi takes it with surprising confidence. I guess a boy who grew up in caves knows every way to start fires. He disappears inside the tunnel. A sharp *crack*. Then an amber glow illuminates the darkness.

Cordelia's breath escapes in wisps of white.

All her murders have led her here, to this final climb. I wonder if she thinks of her brother, and what he would say. She clutches the key at her neck. 'Let us end it,' she breathes, then enters the tunnel with purpose.

*

The path through the mountain is not designed for comfort. It's so narrow we have to walk single file – Ravi first, Cordelia, then me at the rear. I follow the bubble of orange light, running my hand along the walls. I slip three times on the slick steps, achingly aware there's nobody to catch me.

The only sound is the shuffle of our footsteps. I draw my cloak around my trembling form. It's impossible to tell the passage of time in this mountain tomb. It makes me think of Ravi, spending a childhood inside mountains, chasing spirits of the dead.

My legs are throbbing by the time light winds around the staircase. I drag my aching body up the final few steps.

After what I can only assume is hours of climbing, we emerge on to a small plateau, jutting out from the mountain. I glance over the side and almost have a repeat of my messy performance at the party. Stretching out below is an expanse of jagged rocks and sheer drops into the black sea. Cordelia wasn't wrong, trying to climb that would have been suicide. And I'm done with all that.

'Are we close?' I ask.

Cordelia removes her glasses; they've completely fogged up. 'No. We still have a way to climb.'

Ravi thrusts the torch forward. 'Which direction?'

Cordelia rolls her shoulders. 'I could use some rest.'

My body throbs a *yes please* in response.

'Shouldn't we push on?' Ravi asks. It's OK for him, he's got all those shiny new muscles.

'We should make a fire, warm up. Cook some food,' Cordelia says, putting her glasses back on.

'But—'

'Nobody is going to beat us there, Leo,' Cordelia says sharply. 'Sit down. We need fuel for the remainder of the journey.'

His grip around the torch tightens. 'I suppose a short break won't hurt.'

We use the wood from the torch to get a small campfire going. We huddle around it, on our tiny plateau, warming cold hands and cheeks. Once we're sufficiently toasty, I place the pot on the fire, and Cordelia makes use of some potatoes, onions and water she packed.

I cross my legs beneath me, studying her as she stirs the food. This skinny doll, so unyielding in her view of the world she's willing to sacrifice millions for it. Her face is set – chin high, eyes determined. But I know how faces can lie.

446

I also can't deny this connection I feel with her. Not only did we love the same man, but also, no matter how disturbing her plan, she wants to fix the world. To protect people. Ravi was right, there *is* a twisted logic to it.

And I know, deep down, she's fuelled by pain. She thinks she can fill a Lysander-shaped hole with all that power. But real healing doesn't come from power. It's the other way round. I didn't find my Blessing until I was ready to fight. To survive. To live.

I spent so many years believing a Blessing would give me worth. But Ravi was right – the miracle wasn't the Blessing. The miracle was the moment I chose to breathe.

If I can make Cordelia doubt her plan, maybe she'll abandon it. Maybe I can drag her back from the edge.

I clutch my knees. 'When you move the Bandage, how are you going to defend it? Ox Province will be gone.'

Cordelia stirs the bubbling mixture. 'Initially, Leo will place Tiger militia along the border, then over time each province will contribute members of their population.'

'Isn't the Tiger militia just a glorified police force? You think they'll be able to do it?'

Ravi stiffens. 'Don't question the efficiency of my troops, Fish.'

I resist punching him. He's way too good at being Leofric.

'The Bandage will be far smaller and so require fewer troops to defend it. Also there won't be any tears.' Cordelia fills several bowls. 'Would you like some?'

A lumpy grey gruel coats the bowl. It looks like someone's eaten it once already. 'I'm OK, actually.'

So long, life ambition to consume every food in Concordia.

'You should.' She thrusts the bowl forward. It smells like *nothing* that should ever be consumed. 'You'll need your strength for the final push.'

447

'Nah. I've got diarrhoea so . . .'

She recoils. 'That is vile.'

Diarrhoea is vile but killing millions makes you happy dance. Goddessdammit, Cordelia.

'Leo?' She holds out a bowl.

Ravi tugs his collar. 'I don't—'

'Come on,' she pouts. 'You always loved it when you visited Lysander.'

He forces a smile, then takes the bowl. 'Thank you.'

Tough break.

'What about all the food?' I ask. 'You won't have the lower provinces to transport the goods to you.'

Cordelia dips a spoon into her bowl of ghastly horrors. 'The Primus Blessing is *remarkable*, and because I'll have so much going spare, I'm going to terraform the land. I'll create areas perfect for farming and fishing.'

This motherfucker has thought of everything.

'What if people are angry? How can you be sure they'll support you?'

Cordelia twists her spoon. 'I do not believe that will be a problem.'

'Why not?'

'Because they'll be on the right side of the Bandage.' Her spoon clinks against the bowl. 'Nobody cried for the Crabs.'

My hand closes around a fistful of snow.

'Eat up, Leo!' She leans into him, smiling sweetly. 'You promised.'

Ravi spoons a little of the gruel. The concoction slops on to the spoon with a movement that isn't quite solid *or* liquid. He forces it into his mouth, fighting his own limbs.

'And?'

'Just as good as Lysander's,' he says.

Cordelia's hand wanders to the key about her neck.

'What do you think he would make of this?' I ask.

'He . . .' Her shoulders fall. 'I'm not . . .'

'I remember what he wrote in the book.'

'"Be open to all others,"' she repeats with reverence. Then her lips turn down. 'He *was* open to everyone. And they killed him for it. Those words aren't advice; they're a warning.'

I poke the fire, sending up a burst of orange embers. 'I didn't know Lysander well, but I don't think he would want anyone else blamed for his death.'

'No,' she says, her voice razor-edged. 'You didn't know him well.'

'He wanted to help people, especially the lower provinces.'

'And it led him to his death.'

Ravi moves behind Cordelia, silent eyes fixed imploringly upon me. *I know.* If she figures out I can't be trusted before we reach the source our plan is ruined. But I also want to believe in her, the same way Lysander did.

'The Crabs who killed your brother—'

'*Monsters.*'

'They weren't there to kill him. They were hungry, and scared.' I reach across the snow to her. 'If Lysander knew, I don't think he would hate those Crabs. I think he'd want to help them.'

Cordelia goes still, flames dancing in her eyes. 'Ly . . . he didn't . . .' A tear travels down her cheek.

'Cordelia.' I edge my hand closer. 'Lysander loved you more than anyone else. Think about what he would want for you.'

She faces me, eyes swimming. 'I have to bury him. Otherwise, I cannot do what must be done.'

Ravi coughs, then pounds his chest.

She places her bowl down, turning to him. 'Are you OK?'

'Apologies,' he croaks. 'I'm fine.'

'Good. When I lost Lysander, I felt completely alone. But then Leo came to me.' She smiles sweetly at him. 'I feared he would blame me for my brother's death, but I explained my theory regarding the Bandage, and he agreed that the lower provinces were to blame.'

She gave a devastated man someone to hate. No wonder he supported the whole horrific scheme.

Her eyes study Ravi. 'He'd tried to stop Lysander visiting them, but my brother was determined to *fix* Concordia. I saw myself in Leo, in his pain and grief. Finally, someone who understood what I was going through. So, I told him my plan, that *we* could fix Concordia, just as Lysander always dreamed of. But this time, do it right.' Her voice shakes. 'If someone took Leo from me, I'd have nobody left.'

Ravi places his bowl down. His forehead is gleaming with sweat. I glance into the pot, the grey sludge bubbling away. That unnatural scent washes over me. Certainly not onions or potatoes.

'Cordelia . . .' I begin. 'What's in that stew?'

'Do you know what I love most about Leo?'

Ravi clutches his chest, steadying himself against the ground.

'How committed to the plan he was. And I know it cost him more. It cost him *everything*. His life's purpose was to protect the empress. He betrayed his entire belief system. That's why it meant so much . . .' Her hand closes around the key at her neck. 'When he gave *me* the key to his collar.'

Oh shit.

I leap to my feet, accidentally tipping the pot and spilling its contents on to the fire. But Cordelia is faster. She seizes Ravi's cheek.

It happens in a flash. Leofric is stripped away. White skin turns brown. Blue eyes into obsidian.

Cordelia's mouth parts in perfect shock. 'Ravinder?' She looks between us – me, frozen in place, and Ravi struggling for breath in the snow.

At first, there is only shock. Because this girl who planned for everything, who foresaw every possibility, never imagined this reality. A reality in which the man she loved changed his mind. Where he chose a Fish over her.

Then the betrayal travels across her face. I know it intimately. The ache of losing this man, knowing his heart and sweet words are destined for another.

'Cordelia.' I hold out my hands.

She staggers to her feet, golden hair hanging limply. 'I knew you were lying the moment I saw "Leo" wasn't wearing his collar in the gallery. That's why I put the drug in the broth to incapacitate you. I knew I'd have to wait until your guards were down. Because it was two against one. I just assumed it was the Bear masquerading as Leo, not . . .' Pain flashes across her face. 'How did you do it?' She advances towards me. 'What did you offer Ravinder to get him on your side?'

I step back. 'I didn't offer him anything.'

'I took him in. I accepted him, even though he was only a Crow.' She steps closer, chest heaving.

I take another step back. Ravi has slumped over. I can't tell if he's breathing. What kind of drug did she use?

'Yet he betrayed me! He helped you. Why? It doesn't make any sense! You couldn't offer him anything I could not.' The wind whips at her hair, sticking it to her tear-drenched face. 'You are nothing.'

'I am not nothing,' I whisper.

She stops an inch away, cheeks flaring red, clothes stained with gruel. 'You will always be nothing.' She places her hands on my chest; then she pushes.

I stagger back. My foot jerks out behind me, searching for ground. But all it finds is empty space. And then I'm falling, falling, falling, into the great gaping nothing.

Chapter Thirty-Six

Day Twelve – Feast of the Fish

Night

Someone is screaming. A great crescendo of agony. It crests through the darkness, telling me to '*Get off your arse, Dee.*'

I open my eyes.

I'm not sure if the voices were real. Everything is blurred. I'm still falling. I blacked out and I'm still falling.

I move my arm and realize I'm not falling. I'm underwater. This is less of an issue than it would have been a day ago.

Thank you, Blessing.

Bubbles rise as I wave my bandaged hand. Definitely underwater.

It should be cold, but I'm encased within a bubble of warmth, like a blanket wrapped around me by a mother. Or a boy in a library.

It would be nice to stay here a while longer. In this floating paradise.

Then I remember the screams. I force my limbs to move, swimming for the surface.

As I break through the water, I expect to be greeted by jagged rocks, the sea stretching out endlessly around me. Instead, there are white cliffs, and a jutting plateau. I drag myself out of the water and roll on to my back, staring up at the starlit sky.

She pushed me off the fucking cliff. That's the last time I try to appeal to Cordelia's soul.

By some miracle I didn't fall to the bottom of the mountain. I must have crashed into the stream I just dragged myself out of.

The night is utterly silent, apart from the rushing water. I push myself to my knees and peer over the side. My arms go numb. There's a waterfall twenty feet away with a generous selection of sharp rocks to be impaled on. If I had woken later, I'd be dead.

I rise shakily to my feet, and then my world is pain.

I hit the snow. The screaming returns – horrific, choked noises. My throat throbs, which probably means *I'm* the one screaming. Something is spearing my left leg. Stripping skin from the bone. Burning it. When I gingerly move, the pain reawakens.

There's no way I can walk. Goddess knows how long I've been out, or how far I fell. I can't catch up with Cordelia now. Not like this.

I grasp handfuls of snow and release a guttural cry. It echoes across the mountain. It feels as though I'm the only person in the world.

But I'm not. Ravi is there. I picture his body, slumped in the snow. Ribbons of black hair splayed against white. Did I see him breathe, or not?

I can't remember.

He's up there with *her*. And he needs help. He needs me. If the positions were reversed, Ravi would climb this mountain without a second thought. If there's even a chance he's alive, I need to go to him.

I tug up my trouser and assess my leg. I can't see any wounds. I move it gently and feel bones *grating*. Broken for sure.

I may not have Tendai's experience mending injuries, but in Fish province we don't have hospitals, so fisherfolk have been 'making do' for generations. I've seen enough sailing injuries to know what I must do.

I flip myself to my front, wet curls of hair stuck to my forehead. I drag my aching body inch by agonizing inch towards a small bare tree. Every movement sends spasms of agony so sharp I have to pause and breathe and remind myself who I am.

You're Dee. And you're not nothing.

I reach the tree and grasp blindly for a branch. After five tries my hand closes around one. I put all my weight into breaking it off. It snaps and sends me hurtling back to the ground.

The pain flares.

You're Dee. And you're not nothing.

It's not a bad branch – thick enough to bear my weight. Maybe a little short. It'll do.

I press the stick against my leg.

Goddess, please accept this sacrifice.

I rip my beautiful fakinium trouser leg to shreds. The discs spill over the snow, like opals across a white neck. I use the strips to attach the branch to my injured leg.

I'm ready.

Using the tree for support, I haul myself up, sweat pouring down my brow. The splint stops my leg moving, so at least the pain has subsided slightly. Or I'm getting used to it.

I'm not far from the summit, but not particularly close either. I don't have the time to go back down and find the staircase again, which leaves me one option – I have to climb.

The cliff looks sheer at first glance, but there are plateaus dotted throughout. It's not impossible. Real fucking stupid, but not impossible.

I take a step, gritting my teeth against the pain.

You're Dee. And you're not nothing.

'I'm coming, Ravi,' I say into the wind. After all, this is not the first cliff I have climbed for him.

*

The climb is endless. I cling to the mountain with numb fingers, red and blistered from cold, dragging my broken body upwards, upwards, eternally upwards. My soaked clothes turn to ice in the wind. Water in my hair freezes to icicles. The pain is so all-consuming, I have to switch between which part I focus on – leg, hands, shoulders – or I'll lose my mind and cast myself into the sea to escape it.

I almost wish the climb was non-stop. The breaks the plateaus give me are a curse. Summoning the energy to move feels like starting the ascent from the bottom all over again. It reawakens the pain.

I tell myself lies – that I'm carrying bread and water to two Crab children in a cave. At one point, I forget it's a fantasy. Forget they're dead.

I drag my body over the next ledge. The remains of a fire and pot are strewn across the snow.

I lie on the ground, my body trembling with adrenaline, exhaustion and thrill.

I beat you. I fucking beat you, mountain.

But it's not over.

Pushing ice-encrusted hair from my eyes, I stagger to my good leg. Cordelia and Ravi are nowhere to be seen, but there's a thick path carved through the snow, as if something heavy was dragged.

Cordelia took him with her. She hauled Ravi up the mountain. Why would she do that? The girl's a stick. It would have taken her double the time, if not longer.

No time to ask why. Just thank the Goddess she gave you a trail to follow, Dee.

So I follow it.

I'm not sure how long I walk. Twenty minutes? An hour? The full moon lights my path the whole way. Maybe the piscero really did come from there, and it's blessing its child this night.

Or maybe it's just the moon.

The clearing at the summit is larger than I imagined. A circle of towering statues stare each other down – the twelve province animals recreated in grey stone. And in the centre, as if blooming from the ground, is a pillar of white light. I expected the source to be terrifying and beautiful, like a blade. Instead, it's gentle, like a fire in a hearth, welcoming sailors home after weeks at sea. It beckons like a mother's open arms. My skin tingles, and something deep within my core urges me to close the distance. To touch it.

Then I see him.

Ravi is tied to the crow statue – his injured left hand clamped in the same shackles Leofric put me in, the other end attached to the crow's leg. He's slumped forward, hair hanging over his face.

'Ravi!'

He raises his head. 'Dee,' he rasps.

A figure steps between us, her dress torn and covered in dirt. '*How?*' Cordelia gasps.

I laugh hoarsely. 'That's the thing about pissfish – they're impossible to kill.' Then my legs finally surrender, and I hit the snow.

I try to twist around. But my body won't respond. My limbs won't move. *I made the climb*, they say. *Now piss off.*

Cordelia stares at my slumped form, and then rushes to Ravi. She tilts his chin up, observing his half-open eyes. 'Good. You're awake.'

Ravi swings for her with his right hand, but she darts away. He strains against the shackles, inches short from grabbing her. 'I won't . . . let you . . .'

She sighs. 'I am afraid you do not have much choice in it, Ravinder.' She steps out of the circle and stops before me, turning my head with her foot. 'He climbed a mountain for you. Shall I kill him before or after I claim the Blessings?'

'Don't touch him!' Ravi screams, metal clinking against the stone.

I command my body to move. Jump up. Strangle her. But I can't even raise a hand. There's nothing left in me.

'I wish . . .' Cordelia's voice trembles. 'I wish you cared half as much for me as you do for this Fish.' Her foot slams down on my injured leg. My entire body spasms with pain.

Ravi screams. He fumbles at his side, then draws out the cleaver from the kitchen.

Yes. Throw it at her.

Instead, he slams it into the metal chains. *Chink. Chink. Chink.*

Cordelia returns to him. 'That will not work. It will just break the blade.' She crosses her arms. 'Do you know why I dragged you up here, Ravinder?'

He doesn't answer, just continues to hack at the chains. *Chink. Chink. Chink.* 'Because I wanted you to see me win. I wanted you to understand that a Fish and a Crow could never outsmart a Tortoise.' She raises her chin. 'Most of all, I need you to know you were wrong to put your faith in *him* over *me*.'

Chink. Chink. Chink.

Cordelia steps closer to the source. The white light floods her golden hair, and in that moment she looks every bit the Goddess from the legends. Beautiful and terrible.

I command my body to move. But all I manage is to drag one arm before me. One measly arm.

Cordelia holds out her hand. It hovers before the soft light.

I grip the snow. Drag myself an inch. It feels like a mile.

I'm not going to reach her. I don't have the energy. And it's so quiet. So suddenly silent in this place atop the world.

A thump. A movement too quick to understand – a streak of black and red against white snow.

Cordelia is yanked away from the source. She stumbles but does not fall, and standing behind her, holding her collar in his one remaining hand – Ravi.

He tugs her back. She staggers and crashes to the ground. His blood is everywhere. A ghastly crimson path from the Crow statue to his place in the snow, wrestling with Cordelia.

He cut off his hand. *He cut off his motherfucking hand.*

She's yanking his hair, biting him, snarling like a mad cat. He gasps heaving breaths. He's bigger and stronger than her, but she's not bleeding out. He has seconds before she flings him aside.

Finally, strength floods my limbs.

I half run, half drag what remains of myself over to them. I fall upon the tangle of limbs, pinning Cordelia's flailing wrists, forcing her face into the snow. She bucks like a horse, but there's two of us now. Ravi digs his knees into her shoulders as she shrieks.

'Go and take it!' I rock my head towards the source. 'I've got her.'

He settles his knees. 'No, Dee. *I've* got her.' Obsidian eyes meet mine, and in them I unearth the final secret Ravi has been keeping.

'No.' The word escapes my lips in a sob. 'No way. You're the one who's meant to take the power from the source. It's *yours.*'

Tears swim in his eyes. 'I've killed people. I've changed in ways that terrify me. I'm not that boy in the cave any more.' His hand rests upon mine, caked with blood. 'But you are. You're still him.'

Tears freeze on my cheeks. 'I can't—'

'You can,' he says through gritted teeth. 'Give me one reason it shouldn't be you.'

It's Ravi's. So obviously Ravi's – he's the child of two worlds . . . *who turned away from a genocide.* Who went on to a ship, knowing half the people aboard would be murdered, and let it happen. Who would be standing by Cordelia's side, silent and obedient, instead of holding her down, if not for me.

Me who loved him without question. A love so astonishing he called me a miracle.

Me who extended a hand to a child crying for their mother.

Me screaming alone in the midst of a jubilant crowd as two small bodies swung in the snow.

Somebody else might help them. Somebody else might care.

But they didn't then. I did. And I can't wait forever for someone else to fix things.

It has to be me.

Ravi's eyes are fixed upon me, the same way they were in

that cave on a cliff in a storm all those years ago. Utter adoration.

'Do you have a reason it shouldn't be you?'

I shake my head. No.

'Then it's you.' He smiles brilliantly. 'It has *always* been you.'

My hands slip away from Cordelia's. As I rise, Ravi takes my position, snow stained red around him.

I face that soft white light.

Cordelia screams, clawing at the earth. 'No! You're not strong enough!'

I drag my broken body a step at a time, transfixed by the light. As I draw close, it whispers in my mother tongue: *Vendu pær, parlskan.*

My mother said those words once, on a stormy night, when I was too young to understand why the house was shaking. She wrapped her arms around me, a bubble of protection against the fear and chaos.

Come closer, child.

I raise my hand to the glowing column.

'You're not strong enough!' Cordelia screeches. 'It'll destroy you, Fish.'

When I turn, I don't see her. All I see is Ravi. His smile hasn't shifted. His faith in me is unwavering, even as he bleeds out into the snow.

Sometimes all it takes is one person to make you believe you're worthy of something. Even all the power in the universe.

'Firstly – my name is Dee,' I say, turning back to the source. 'Secondly – *fuck you, Cordelia.*' Then I thrust my hand into the light.

My entire body is ablaze. Fire courses through my limbs. Then I don't have any limbs. I'm not a body. I'm a stream of light. The sun cresting over the horizon. A wave against the shore.

There is no battle between the magic and me. No struggle. It embraces me without question. It moulds itself around me, cracking open my ribs and filling my heart with warm white light. So when it pumps, the power rushes through my veins and into my organs and soon there is no 'it' and 'me'. There is only us.

In the distance, someone is screaming.

But someone else is laughing. Jubilant, victorious laughter, the joy of a man whose vision of the world has just slotted into existence.

Concordia stretches out before me like the tip of an arrow. Malleable. I could change it at will. It would only require me to think of it. To flick a finger.

That's right. I had fingers once. And others. A different set of fingers that held mine.

Ravi.

I fall. The wind whips at my form, sending soft hair billowing against my cheeks. I land at his side with all the force of a settling snowflake. I close his wounds, silence his pain.

Cordelia staggers to her feet and, for the briefest moment, our eyes meet. She is in pain too. But not from wounds my touch can heal. Even all this power has its limits. She turns and flees through the bloodstained snow. I do not follow.

Ravi rises. 'Get us out of here.'

I reach for him. What a remarkable thing – that two hands can fit so perfectly together. It is, I think, the most remarkable thing I've experienced today.

The mountain moves for me. The snow clears before me. I only have to think of it and already it's done.

I stop before we reach the bottom of the mountain. As I stagger, he catches me.

461

'It's a heavy burden,' he says.

The Bandage tugs at me like a hook within a fish's mouth. A demanding child. Give me more. More.

I'm breathless in his arms. Suddenly all too human, with aching limbs and a throbbing headache. 'Please tell me that looked cool.'

'The coolest.'

I feel Cordelia's heartbeat fluttering somewhere atop the mountain. Enraged. Robbed. But most of all – lonely. Because now it's over, and all she has left is her grief.

Ravi sits me down before a stream, running his hand over my face, checking for healed injuries. 'How does it feel?'

'Like I drank all night,' I croak. 'But the bar was only serving molten lava.'

He smirks, touching my hair. 'Suits you.'

'What does?' I crawl to the water's edge, examining my reflection.

Sweet jumping fishcakes.

My hair's not white any more. It's a blaze of colours – green, ice blue, grey, brown, red, pink, dark blue – all the colours Cordelia stole. I look like a motherfucking rainbow.

'You see.' Ravi's fingers brush my back. 'It was always meant to be you.'

I turn, clasping his hand. 'When did you decide that it was going to be me?'

'When I saw you in that costume.'

He knew for that long. He was planning this when I came to his door, asking for help. He knew I needed to solve the mystery alone. Because if I didn't believe in myself, I never would have taken the power. I never would have believed I could.

'The longer I spent with you, the more I was convinced I was right,' he says.

462

He may not be that boy in the cave any more, they may have made him into something cruel and ruthless, but Ravi has always believed in me. It's why he pushed me away five years ago, why he closed a door between us. Because he knew I was the only person capable of derailing his life.

He cups my cheek, looking at me like a child beholding the ocean for the first time – awe, and belief in the unimaginable. In a power you cannot understand or capture.

I will spend a lifetime, if that's what it takes, to nurture and protect all the wonderful parts of him. He became something brutal for me. I will never let that happen again.

I loved Ravi. Lost him. Then loved him again. I think that for my entire life I will be stuck in a cycle of adoring him.

I move closer, and the scent of smoke and lavender greets me.

'You smell like you,' I whisper.

'That's why I wore cologne when I was pretending to be "Wyatt".' He smiles. 'I knew you would recognize me from scent alone.'

'How?'

'Because whenever I smell the ocean, I think of you.'

I brush the hair from his face, map his features with my fingers – cheekbones, nose, lips. Every part more fascinating than the Blessing coursing through my veins.

'Did you appear to me?' I brush a finger across his jaw. 'In the library? I saw you. I thought I was dreaming.'

'I just wanted to touch you. With *my* hands.'

I lean into him, a breath away. 'Then touch me.'

His mouth is upon mine in a moment, ravenous lips forcing an opening. I moan into him, the same way I did in that greenhouse. And he smirks the same way too.

'Ravi.' I run my hands through his silken hair.

He tears at my clothes with that insatiable hunger. My

463

jacket slips from my shoulders, then my shirt. His hand is tugging down my trousers before I can take a breath.

I kiss his chin, neck, every glimpse of flesh my lips can reach. He lays me down in the snow and then tugs his shirt off, kissing me with mad abandon, as if the world would end if he didn't.

Fingertips run down my flesh, a featherlight touch upon my soft stomach. Then he pushes away. His hungry eyes devour my naked form, savouring every perfect inch of me as if I were crafted by the Goddess's own hands.

'You are the only worthwhile thing in my life,' he breathes. 'The *only thing*, Dee.'

I trace his collarbone with my thumb. I want to spend an eternity unpeeling the layers of this addictive boy, where every day with him is a discovery, an adventure.

He brings my hand to his lips. 'I can't wait to see what your world will look like.'

I wrap myself around him, pressing the heat of our bodies together. He reaches between my thighs, taking me in hand. My back arches into him, pleasure surging through my body like a thousand Blessings. And then I'm his. Utterly his. The final wall around my heart crumbles and his love fills the untouched space behind.

Epilogue

Feast of the Crab

The sun is a streak of brilliant gold the day I change the world.

It's like that because I designed it that way, of course. The last thing I need is a downpour to make everyone decide this is a terrible idea.

There are 120 people in this welcoming party. I wanted it smaller; the senate wanted thousands. A hundred and twenty was the compromise.

We stand in tight lines before the towering expanse of green that has been the pain in my backside for the past six months. Ever since I took the Blessing, the Bandage has been tugging at me, swiftly draining whatever I pour into it. I have a newfound respect for our murdered emperor, and all the others who came before. I have more power than them, and they kept this up for centuries.

I breathe out slowly, my heart hammering.

At my left, Ravi squeezes my arm, a luminous blue rose blooming in the darkness of his hair.

He wouldn't let me fix the hand he chopped off. *'It's a reminder of the things I allowed to happen. All those who died because of my inaction. I will not become that person again.'* I did replace my finger though.

At my right, Senator Janus stares dubiously at me, hoping

I will realize what a 'foolhardy fancy' this idea is, as he so kindly dubbed it when first put to the senate.

Not many were pleased when the *Dragon's Dawn* returned to the capital with most of the Blessed murdered, and a Fish at the helm with more power than anyone in Concordia's history. Despite me recounting what happened approximately five thousand times, I suspect a vocal minority still believes I'm the one who committed said murders. But all the remaining Blessed supported me unanimously. And since the emperor was murdered, the public quickly bought into the fallacy that the Goddess chose me, especially with my new hairdo. They will never know the truth – that *I* chose me.

Cordelia's still missing. I could find her easily, but I hold out hope she will come to me herself. I want her to work through her pain and then work *with* me. I won't begin my reign with the death of another Blessed, however much the people demand it.

But I *might* make her kiss my ring and say: *Oh infinitely wise All-Father. You were completely right. Also, I suck at chess.*

Ruling, it turns out, involves less handwaving and more bureaucracy than I had imagined. I wanted to do this immediately, but apparently big decisions need *plans* and *meetings*. So many meetings. That's where Ravi comes in. His acumen and forethought could defeat any senator. I suspect, if I was not standing between them, he and Janus would be throwing verbal blows this instant.

Ravi says I should get rid of the man. But he's as essential to me as Ravi. No ruler should fill their senate with people who only say 'yes'.

But I must admit, I didn't extend the same tolerance to my father when he came grovelling. He demanded I make him my second-in-command. Instead, Ravi created a special position just for him with so many bureaucratic obstacles between us, I could easily avoid him for the rest of his life.

As for my mother . . . we have a lot to work through. We will work through it. But I have other things I must fix first.

The first thing I did was decriminalize other languages. Concordia is already awash with an amalgamation of voices I've never heard before. It seems every province was dealing in dialects, old women hiding words in the back of their cupboards for when this day would come.

The ultimate goal is to grant independence to those provinces that want it, rather than me having to decide what's best for places I'm yet to set foot in. But as Janus says, 'There will be plenty of time for the rest of your absurdities later.'

For now, I must ensure this goes perfectly. It took fifty envoys to broker a peace with our 'enemies' beyond the Bandage. One of them came back minus an ear. Turns out the Crabs are not exactly *our* biggest fans either, and it took three months to convince them I wasn't going to immediately slaughter them all.

I've promised them land, free passage and protection. And I asked for nothing in return other than for them kindly not to kill us. After facing nothing but hate for a thousand years, I don't blame them for being suspicious.

They did confirm the whispers of the children in the cave – about how the Bandage seems to draw *things* to it. This was one of the few arguments I had to convince Janus and the others – that for whatever reason, wild beasts seem to be attracted to high concentrations of Blessings. The Bandage is a beacon for chaos.

Regardless, Ox troops have spent the last month clearing away as many creatures as they can. The last thing I need is a party-crashing dragon.

I'm going to change that too. No child is going to be forced into the army as long as I rule. It'll be a voluntary force. But . . . later. I have so much to do. Later.

'Dee!' Grasshopper slots herself between Janus and me, her

467

smile all teeth. I offered to fix her eye, but she refused. Apparently grievous injuries are badass in Grasshopper Province. 'Hurry up! Hurry!' Bancha nuzzles against her cheek.

We found the bunnerfly cowering inside Shinjiro's cabin on the return journey, and the pair bonded over a shared love of biscuits. The animal looks considerably *rounder* than when I last saw her.

'Ganymedes,' Tendai says, at Ravi's side. 'Are you completely sure about this?'

I swallow hard. 'No. Not really. But it's the right thing to do.'

'Of course. I have complete faith.' But she wheels her chair back a few feet.

'Not too late to change your mind, Majesty,' Janus mutters.

He may be right. It *is* foolhardy. Preposterous. Reckless. All those things. And I know though I stand with 119 people at my back, it's only really me who believes this will work.

Ravi's hand slips into mine. Our fingers lock. He doesn't need to utter a word. He just nods his head, and I know I'm not alone.

I lay my hand against the luminous green structure. It has a heartbeat. A pulse. That must be what Ravi felt all those years ago, when we paddled out into the ocean so he could look upon the wall that cut across his life.

I raise my head. 'Thanks for protecting us all this time. But would you kindly fuck off?'

And as I stand, palm pressed to the Bandage, feeling that immeasurable power stirring within me, all doubt vanishes. It will work. I'm sure of it. After all, I know the benefits of tearing down walls.

Acknowledgements

This book is the sum of all the books that came before it which now lie at rest in my book graveyard. Thank you, ill-fated stories, for your sacrifice. You walked (and died slow deaths) so Dee could run.

I must first thank my agent, Harry Illingworth, who is not only an unending source of guidance and knowledge about this bonkers industry, but has also been the constant calming voice of reason to my manic anxious energy. Thank you, too, for championing so many unique cross-genre books, it's agents like you who are pushing the boundaries of traditional publishing into exciting new places.

To everyone at Penguin Michael Joseph for not only taking a chance on this weird little cross-genre book, but for getting behind it fully with so much enthusiasm and vision. You have made my debut experience a joy and it is an honour to work with such talented, fearless individuals.

Special thanks to the ray of sunshine that is Rebecca Hilsdon, my editor, who gave me the confidence and space to tell this story the way I wished, but also the insight to reign me in when I made way too many terrible jokes during serious scenes. The readers, I am sure, thank you (but not as much as I do!). You are an absolute star, and I cannot thank you enough for all you've done in championing this book.

Also to Jorgie Bain for all her contagious unbridled passion for *Voyage of the Damned*. Witnessing your excitement as you shared your mood board for this book with me is a cherished memory I return to often when my own confidence dips.

To Sally Taylor who created the drop-dead gorgeous maps at the front of this book, and to Ellyish Studios who took my initial terrible sketches and gave Sally something far more helpful to work from. Thanks to Nina Elstad, who created the most beautiful cover a writer could ever dream of, and for everyone who indulged my magpie tendencies for *shiny* things.

Thanks to the sensitivity readers at Writing Diversely, for all your insightful comments. To all my beta readers, Eike Bentley, Allison Hubbard, Keshe Chow, Irene Wen, Bria Fournier and Raidah Shah Idil. I must also extend special thanks (and sheepish apologies) to Keshe, Eike and Allison who have talked me down from metaphorical ledges more often than I care to admit. Without you I would exist only as a puddle of anxieties.

Thanks to all the folks in the WMC and Iller's Killers discords, the wonderfully talented writers of 2024 Debuts slack, and to Cecile Lleweyn-Bowen and Melissa Oliver-Powell. Writing communities like these constantly motivate and inspire me, and it's been such an honour to witness so many of you rise and I simply can't wait to watch the rest of you follow. Special thanks too to A.Y. Chao, Vic James and Sunyi Dean for giving your precious time to advise this baby writer.

To Ellie Bibby, Lauren Smith, Faye Horsfield and Colzy Nye, my Salt Squad buddies. You are the best group of supportive friends anyone could ever want or need, even when you have no idea what I'm screaming about. You are the best cheerleaders, and I would be simply lost without you.

To all my family. I come from a working class background of builders and nurses who found themselves with a child who wanted to write about dragons and magic, and not only abided this, but encouraged it.

For my sister, Corinne, our slightly disturbing child's play of murder mystery has led me here. My dad who left Stephen King books unguarded around a 13-year-old, unwittingly encouraging me to become the monster I am today. And especially my mum, who sat for months upon months with a child who was behind in her reading, forcing her to sound out every single word until it stuck, who took her on weekly library trips where most of the books were consumed within hours, and has read every word she has written since. I can say, unequivocally, I would not be writing this without your enduring support.

And thank you, dear readers, for taking a chance on Dee's story. I have never been able to relate to the typical heroes, who kick ass and take names later, or don't have to psych themselves up for hours, lying in the fetal position before doing something scary. I believe the world has room for all kinds of heroes. Thank you for embracing mine.

Like Dee, I often struggle to believe in my own worth. In such an isolating field as writing, this can make it all the more difficult to forge forward against the waves of rejections nearly all writers inevitably face. For that, I thank every single person who has encouraged me over the years. However small or throwaway, your comments and nuggets of support have helped push me along this journey.

All of you are the Ravi to my Dee.

Finally, bookshelves can be a terrifying place for debut writers, especially those who are marginalized. Writers who are queer, trans, BIPOC, disabled, working class or otherwise marginalized fight tooth and nail for their stories to be told in a world that often seems increasingly unwelcoming to them. By buying, reading and sharing these books, you are sending the message that these people and their stories matter. That they deserve to be heard. Never underestimate the power you hold, readers.